THE RAVENSLEY TOUCH

THE
RAVENSLEY
TOUCH

CONSTANCE HEAVEN

COWARD, McCANN & GEOGHEGAN
NEW YORK

First American Edition 1982
Copyright © 1982 by Constance Heaven
All rights reserved. This book, or parts thereof, may not be reproduced in any form without permission in writing from the publisher.

Library of Congress Cataloging in Publication Data

Heaven, Constance.
  The Ravensley touch.

I. Title.
PR6058.E23R3   1982   823'.914   82-7247
ISBN 0-698-11109-5   AACR2

Printed in the United States of America

FOR
JUDITH AND EDWARD
with deep affection

Love, which allows no one who is loved to escape,
Gripped me so powerfully with such joy in him
That, as you see, it will never leave me more.

Dante, The Inferno

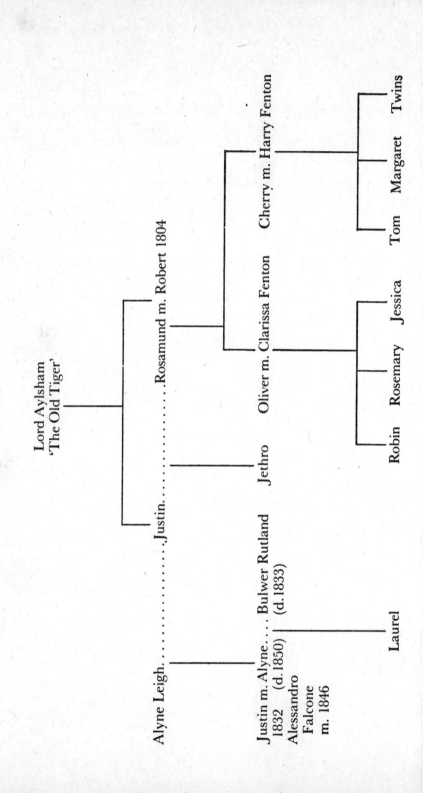

Part One

LAUREL

1

They met, those two whose lives were to become so stormily linked, on a spring day in 1852 without any knowledge of the dark past, the hate and passion and death from which they sprang. Her face haunted him from the first moment he saw her at the beginning of the carnival. Amid the shouting, screaming, wildly excited revellers surging down the mile-long Corso, she had seemed strangely aloof, holding a huge white dog by the collar and quietly grave amongst the whirling streamers, the showers of sugar plums and brightly-coloured confetti. Caught up in the press of the mob he had time to note a beauty of line, finely-modelled cheek-bones, widely-spaced eyes hinting at mystery. The crowd of laughing youngsters swept him inexorably forward, but the impression stayed with him against his will, elusive but demanding. He was Jethro Aylsham, aged twenty-eight, a rising young physician and surgeon, concerned solely with practical matters and not a man to indulge in fantasies about a young woman seen only once.

He would have preferred to ignore the days of the carnival and spend more time exploring the ancient city or watching some unusual experiments taking place in the hospital, but it was impossible with Rome given over to revelry. In any case it would have been churlish to deny Tom his fun when the boy had patiently followed him around the Anatomy School in Padua, which was the reason why he found himself wedged on to a balcony with a party of boys and girls in a splendid position to watch the procession of gigantic floats organized by the aristocratic Roman families creaking slowly down the Corso behind their teams of gaily caparisoned horses.

From windows and parapets, from rooftops of houses and *palazzos*, streamers and hangings of scarlet, green and blue, of white, gold and silver, fluttered madly in the brilliant spring sunshine. Beside them on the balcony were sacks of sugary sweetmeats and laundry baskets crammed with flowers to toss to any young girl who caught their fancy. Below them men, women, children and even babies in arms dressed in every conceivable kind of fancy costume, harlequins and pierrots, Turks and Arabs, nuns and cardinals, giants and punchinellos, jostled along the street, dodging in and out of the carriage wheels and diving perilously under the horses' hooves.

A large sticky sugar plum aimed with deadly accuracy from the opposite balcony hit Jethro in the eye. He wiped it off with an exclamation of disgust and Tom laughed at him.

"Don't take any notice of Jet," he said, his arm around the pretty girl beside him. "He'd rather be watching some poor devil having his leg sawn off any day in the week." He leaned over the parapet. "Gosh, look at that lot down there. That's really something."

Jethro hauled him back. "Take care, you idiot, do you want to break your neck!" Then he stopped, forgetting Tom, his interest captured.

The float below them was very impressive, mounted up like a miniature castle with turrets and battlements. There were capering devils with hideous masks and forked tails, brandishing pitchforks and squealing horribly, a tall lean figure in a long black robe and a great many others, but he had eyes only for the girl he had glimpsed once before, in a golden gown, a chaplet of white roses on hair the dark rich red of an autumn forest. A young man leaned over her, a brooding hunched figure in purple velvet. Dante's *Inferno*, of course, but what part was she playing? Acting on impulse he grabbed a handful of flowers from the basket and threw them down to her. They scattered over the golden dress and she caught at some, a nosegay the colour of blood. She looked up, their eyes met and she laughed, a low gurgling enchanting sound. A hint of recognition, dredged out of the past, shot through him and then was gone before he could capture it.

"She's a corker, isn't she?" said Tom admiringly. "I wonder if she's his daughter."

"Whose daughter?"

"Prince Alessandro Falcone. Proud as Lucifer, they say he is, but he keeps open house at his palazzo tonight, or so Luigi tells me. Shall we go?"

Jethro looked doubtful. "We have to make an early start tomorrow . . ."

"Oh bother that. Don't be such a grouch. It is the last day of the carnival after all."

4

Jethro smiled. Tom Fenton was seventeen, an irrepressible youngster determined to extract every ounce of enjoyment out of their Italian holiday before returning to the rigours of life at his university. "Very well, we'll go," he said, "just to please you."

"Don't put on those airs with me," retorted Tom affectionately. "I saw you eyeing the Signorina Falcone, old stick-in-the-mud that you are!"

"It's much too late to hire fancy dress, " objected Jethro.

"Never mind. Luigi says it doesn't matter and we can always wear masks." Tom was determined to sweep aside all objections.

The afternoon was by no means over. By five o'clock the Corso was miraculously cleared for the races. Barbary horses were led into the Piazza at the foot of the column brought by Augustus from Heliopolis, the obelisk that centuries ago must have looked down on the Roman games and chariot races in the Circus Maximus. At a given signal the horses were off flying riderless down the Corso from the Piazza del Popolo, shining ornaments on their backs and twisted into their plaited manes, heavy little balls stuck with spikes bouncing at their sides to goad them on, something which immediately sparked off a fierce argument between the tender-hearted English who thought it cruel and the more practical Italians. The horses plunged into the heavy carpets spread across the street to stop them, prizes were awarded amid thunderous applause and Jethro dragged Tom away before he and his fiery friend Luigi came to blows.

By the time the two young men had fought their way through the crowded streets to their hotel, they were hot, tired and very hungry since they had set out after an early breakfast and had eaten little during the day. Meals were always slow affairs in Italian inns, so it was nearly ten o'clock when washed, changed and carrying cloaks and masks they set out for the Palazzo Falcone. The streets were lively still with revellers, dancing and singing, cabs were hard to find and they walked to the Via Giulia. The palazzo when at last they reached it was a dark forbidding Gothic building, presenting a shuttered facade to the outside world. Torches flared in the gloomy courtyard where carriages were still arriving, disgorging guests in multi-coloured costumes, and the great hall was crammed to the doors and blazing with light from huge crystal chandeliers.

A strange place, thought Jethro, looking around him. Scenes

5

of classical mythology covered every inch of the walls, gods and goddesses, dragons and unicorns, goat-footed satyrs pursuing nymphs through groves of orange trees, all once brilliant with colour, but now sadly faded. The gilt cornices had lost their splendour and the crimson velvet of the chairs and sofas was worn and scuffed. Prince Alessandro might be a great aristocrat, but he was obviously short of ready cash.

Tom was immediately seized upon by a group of youngsters and swept into the dancing. Jethro, feeling out of place in his black evening dress, discovered an acquaintance he had picked up at the hospital and accompanied him to the lavish buffet table. He exchanged a stiff bow with his host. Prince Falcone was an imposing figure with the heavy handsome features of one of the Roman Emperors, Vespasian perhaps or Tiberius. The heat was intense and presently, after having played his part on the dance floor, Jethro escaped down a corridor leading off from the ballroom and cautiously opened a door at the far end. It was a small room panelled in gilded Spanish leather and set out with tables and chairs for cards. Thankfully he saw that it was empty. A lamp glowed on the table beside a tray of wine, but he decided he had drunk enough. He took out his cigar case and lighted a long black cheroot. There were books piled on a side table and he was idly glancing through them when the door opened behind him and he turned around.

It was the girl in the golden dress. She leaned back against the door panting, her eyes wide with shock. The chaplet of roses hung forlornly from one limp hand, the dark red hair fell in loose curls around her shoulders. The golden brocade gown had been roughly torn from one shoulder and there was a long bleeding scratch on the white skin. In her distress she had obviously not seen him. He waited a moment before taking a step towards her.

"Is anything wrong, Signorina?" he said quietly in Italian.

She started, one hand instinctively gathering together the torn dress. "No, no, nothing. I . . . I tripped and fell, that's all. I think I've hurt my ankle." She limped across to a chair.

He put down his cigar. "I'm a doctor. Perhaps I can help."

"It's not necessary . . ."

"Shall we see?" He knelt down in front of her. "Which foot is it?"

She hesitated and then stretched out the left. He took it in his hands, slipped off the gold sandal and gently prodded the slim ankle in its fine silk stocking. "Does that hurt?"

6

"A little."

He looked up. "I think the damage is only slight. A cold compress and it should be better in a few hours."

It did not explain the torn dress, the stark terror in her eyes, nor the fact that she had trembled violently at the touch of his fingers. Something worse than a mere tumble had caused her distress. He rose to his feet.

"All the same I think you have suffered a shock. I prescribe a little brandy."

He went to the table, poured a small quantity into a glass and brought it to her.

"Must I?"

"It will steady you."

She took the glass, sipped it and grimaced. "I don't like it. At the convent the nuns only gave it to us when we were sick."

"And how long ago was that?" he said a little teasingly.

"More than twelve months. I am not a child."

"Of course not."

She looked up at him with some curiosity. It was a good-looking face, a pale olive skin, thick dark hair that curled attractively around his ears and neck, cool grey eyes that watched her shrewdly though he smiled.

She said quickly, "I saw you at the carnival this afternoon. You were on a balcony with Luigi Manfredi and another young man. Are you English?"

"Yes. We greatly admired your float. It was a daring theme – Dante's *Inferno*."

She shrugged her shoulders. "It was Ugo's idea. He fancies himself in medieval costume."

She had switched to English with the faintest accent which only seemed to lend it enchantment.

"Of course I understand now. He was the Malatesta and you were Francesca da Rimini."

"Yes."

"Let me see . . . how does it go?" He groped for the words.

" 'Those two who are drifting hand in hand
    And seem to ride so light upon the wind.' "

Her eyes widened. They were deep violet, he noticed, with silky dark lashes. She said in surprise, "You know Dante?"

"In my student days."

"Do English doctors read poetry?"

"Why shouldn't they? It's not all pills and potions."

7

"Isn't it?" She laughed suddenly, the same delicious gurgle of laughter that had entranced him that afternoon, and then as quickly it died. "I must go. I shall be missed."

She got to her feet and he opened the door for her. She paused to hold out her hand.

"Thank you for your help."

"It was a pleasure. Mind now, rest that ankle."

"I will."

Gallantly he kissed the small cold hand. *"Arrivederci, Signorina."*

"Arrivederci."

She slid through the door and he stood looking after her for a moment. Francesca da Rimini married to the brutal hunchbacked Gianciotto had fallen desperately in love with his handsome brother Paolo. Discovered, the doomed lovers had been murdered by the jealous husband. He thought of the brooding face of the man in the float. He knew something of these old Roman families where the blood had run thin, become sterile and decadent. Was that the fate that lay in store for this lovely girl? Surely not. He was letting his imagination run away with him. Daughters were not forced into unhappy marriages in these modern days and cuckolded husbands did not murder their erring wives. He shut the door firmly behind him and went to search for Tom.

It was after midnight when they walked back to their lodging through the cool spring night. The carnival was over. It was Ash Wednesday, the start of Lent, the time for penance after the licence and the revelry. Already morning worshippers were on their way to early mass. In a few hours he and Tom would be setting out on the long journey to England and home. It was time to forget fantasies about mysterious girls with red-gold hair and think about his new appointment as assistant surgeon at St. Thomas's Hospital. It did not occur to him that life has a curious way of upsetting the most carefully laid plans.

Laurel did not return to the ballroom. Instead she climbed up the steep back staircase, making her way through the warren of the servants' quarters, until she reached her own room. It was lavishly furnished in the ornate style in keeping with the palazzo and sometimes she found it stiflingly oppressive. All the faded glory of a past age – the tapestry that covered one wall, the shrouding velvet curtains at the narrow window, the

8

elaborately-carved black oak headboard to the huge bed – but tonight it seemed a refuge rather than a prison and she went in thankfully and as an afterthought turned the key in the massive lock.

There was a fire burning in the grate for the nights could still be cold and the big white dog stretched in front of it thumped his tail as she stepped over him. The encounter with the English doctor had steadied her, but all the same the evening had been very unpleasant. Ugo had drunk too much as he so often did, although he had never been quite so pressing and she had been forced to teach him that he couldn't treat her as he did the maidservants, or the girls he picked up in the city. For all her convent upbringing Laurel was quite aware of how certain young men took their pleasures.

All the afternoon she had been forced to endure his attentions on the float, his hot breath on her cheek, his arm tightening painfully around her waist if she dared to smile at the young men who tossed her flowers. She had avoided him in the ball-room, but he had caught hold of her in the passage from the dining room to the hall and when she had pushed him away, he had been furious, "What's the matter with you? Why be such a prude? We shall be married in a few weeks."

"Who says so?"

"Father for one and Aunt Elena . . ."

"Well, I don't say so!" she exclaimed with such an angry vehemence that he promptly lost his temper.

"You'll do as you're told, you little nobody, or else you'll be sorry," he said viciously.

He had grabbed her to him and she had fought him then, twisting and turning like a wild cat, frightened of what he could do to her, tearing herself out of his hands and running anywhere simply to escape. He did not pursue her. It was not necessary. He was Prince Falcone's son and Alessandro was her guardian. She was caught like a helpless prisoner between the two.

The bed had been turned down and the fire made up, but there was no sign of Dina, her maid. She was probably off somewhere enjoying herself with one of the footmen, so Laurel did not ring for her. With some difficulty she unhooked the heavy golden gown and let it drop to the floor. Stepping out of it she looked dispassionately at herself in the long pier glass, the budding breasts pressing against the fine lace of her satin petticoat, the rounded hips, the long slender legs. She knew exactly what Ugo wanted and it was not the essential Laurel, or even her body – that would be merely added bonus. She was eighteen. In a few weeks she would come into possession of the money her English grandfather had settled on her with the promise of far more to come when he died. The fabulously wealthy old tea merchant worshipped his granddaughter and Prince Alessandro Falcone was urgently in need of ready funds. She knew that he had planned this marriage with his son ever since the death of her mother, but had not expected it to be so soon. The very thought of it turned her sick.

She took a towel from the washstand, dipped it in the water jug and bathed the long scratch left by Ugo's spitefully clutching fingers. She shuddered at the smarting touch. She thought of the English doctor's hands, firm but gentle on her bruised ankle. The pain had almost gone.

She pulled on her dressing-gown and went to pick up the silver-backed hairbrush. The scarlet nosegay he had tossed to her that afternoon was in a glass of water on the table. She touched it with one finger. Silly to keep it really. It was drooping already.

She had begun to brush her hair when someone tried the door handle and then imperiously knocked.

"Who is it?"

"It is I . . . Elena. Why have you locked the door?"

"I'm coming."

She hesitated, then put down the brush and went to turn the key. Elena Falcone burst into the room. She was the Prince's unmarried sister, a big handsome woman in her mid-forties, magnificently dressed in black and silver, and she was very angry. She turned to the girl as soon as the door was shut.

"What do you mean by running away from the ballroom and shutting yourself up in your room like this? Are you sick, or what is it?"

"I am tired. It has been a very long day and it is past midnight."

"That's no excuse. Alessandro is very annoyed with you. You know perfectly well that on the last day of the carnival it is the custom for the family to stand together bidding farewell to the guests. There were a great number of important people here tonight, people that matter."

10

"I am not one of the family."

Elena frowned. "Don't quibble. You very soon will be. Your place was by Ugo's side."

"So that everyone will believe us to be betrothed. That is why you forced me into that charade in the float, isn't it?" Laurel threw up her head defiantly. "You may as well know now as later. I am not going to marry Ugo."

"Now, now, my dear, don't be foolish." Elena observed the flushed face and the trembling hands. The girl was like a spirited young filly, she needed careful handling. You could not ride roughshod over her. She changed her tactics. Her voice softened a little. "You're tired and upset. You don't know what you are saying. Just think of the position you will have in Roman society as Ugo's wife. You should be grateful that Alessandro even considers such a marriage for his son. It will be a great match for you."

"A great match for the little nobody. Is that what you mean?" Laurel's eyes flashed scornfully. "I can live without it. I detest Ugo. He's a brute, a savage." She pulled aside her dressing-gown. "Look at what he did to me tonight because I would not let him rape me."

"My dear child, you shouldn't say such shocking things. I'm quite sure that Ugo would never commit such an outrage. You must have provoked him and he is hot-blooded like all the Falcone. Young men in love are sometimes apt to forget themselves."

"In love! Ugo doesn't know the meaning of the word," said Laurel bitterly. "It's my money he's in love with, my money to pay his gambling debts and prop up the crumbling fortunes of the Falcone."

"Don't you owe Alessandro something? Remember what he has done for you. Hasn't he treated you like a daughter all these years?"

"I owe him nothing. My grandfather has paid for everything. He has only kept me here to please himself."

"How can you say such a wicked thing! Alessandro is a great man."

"Oh I know he is a minister of state and he likes to think the Falcone go back to the middle ages, but he's a man too." Her lips trembled. She turned away her face. "When I came back from the convent after Mother died, he would have married me himself only the church would not have approved."

11

"I will not believe it. You are lying," exclaimed Elena.

"It's the truth," cried the girl passionately, "and you know it. That's why you want to marry me off, isn't it? You're afraid Alessandro might grow too fond of me and then where would you be? It would be back to your little apartment living on his charity . . ."

"You're out of your mind." With a swift movement Elena slapped the girl across the face. "You're hysterical. It's time you came to your senses and remembered who you are. Alessandro is your guardian."

"So is my grandfather . . ."

"He is in England, my dear, and an old man. Don't think you can run whining to him. Alessandro would never permit it." Elena moved towards the door. "I'll send Dina to you. You had better go to bed. I'll talk to you again in the morning."

"I don't want Dina. I don't want anyone," said Laurel childishly.

"Very well, please yourself, but tomorrow the notary is coming and we shall discuss the marriage settlements. The wedding will take place immediately after Easter."

"No," said Laurel desperately. "No, I won't marry him, I won't . . . I won't . . ."

"You had better control yourself unless you want the servants gossiping about you," said Elena coldly. "Goodnight and think over what I've told you." She gathered her dignity about her and sailed through the door.

When she had gone, Laurel threw herself on to the bed in a storm of angry tears. She was after all very young and very unhappy. But she did not weep for long. Presently she sat up. The big dog had come to her side, sensing something was wrong and pushing his nose against her hand. She bent to kiss the top of his head.

"It's all right, Carlo. I'm better now."

She went to sit on the hearthrug, her arm around the dog's neck, gazing into the glowing heat of the fire. It was time to think back, to take stock, to decide what she could do. She needed to. She was so desperately alone.

She was in such a strange position, part of the household and yet not truly belonging to the family. If only her grandfather had not returned to England, if only her mother had not died . . . useless speculations, thought Laurel despairingly. It was not that she had ever been really close to her mother. The ravishingly beautiful widow of an English army officer, she had always held her child at a distance, especially as Laurel grew up and she saw her daughter's beauty as a threat to herself. But she had always been practical. She would never have allowed Laurel to be exploited. The security of love that a child craves had come from her grandfather, a man who had fought his way up from poverty to a position of immense wealth, but still retained the sturdy commonsense, the honest doggedness that had won a grudging respect and a knighthood from Queen Victoria. He had spoiled her shamelessly.

Laurel had been born in Italy at a pink and white villa in Florence. Her mother had never spoken of her life in England, turning aside every question as if it were a sealed book she refused to open. The little Laurel knew came from her grandfather. He would speak to her sometimes of the father she had never known, tragically drowned in trying to rescue her mother from the terrible floods that had devastated the East of England in the year of 1833. Her mother already pregnant had only been saved by a miracle and afterwards he had brought her to Italy for the sake of her health.

Joshua Rutland had created a hero, handsome, gallant, endowed with every quality a child longs for in a dream father. Looking back now they seemed golden days of happiness. They had entertained a great deal. She remembered her beautiful mother always surrounded by men, but it was not until Prince Falcone came into their lives that everything suddenly changed. He was a great aristocrat and his capture a tremendous triumph, though her grandfather had been bitterly opposed to the match. Laurel remembered vividly the arguments that had raged and how one day he had drawn her close to him.

"Now listen to me," he had said in his gruff forthright way, "I'm not having this Italian jackanapes lining his threadbare pockets with my hard-earned cash. That's why it's going to be tied to you, my pet. Your mother will have the benefit of it while she lives, but afterwards it will be yours . . . every last penny of it. Do you understand?"

"Yes, Grandfather," she had replied dutifully, but the real significance of that statement had only come home to her this last year when the Prince had shown plainly what he intended to do with her. Ugo, his son by a former marriage, was seven years older than she was and she had loathed him from the very beginning. Insufferably arrogant, it had amused him to make

13

the leggy twelve-year-old girl look ridiculous in front of his elegant friends.

After the wedding her grandfather had gone back to England. She wrote to him constantly and sometimes a brief scrawl came back in the cramped hand he had learned long ago in the ragged school of his childhood. Her mother had achieved what she had always wanted, an assured position in the highest society and Laurel, uncomfortable reminder of the past, had been packed off to a convent in Lausanne. She hadn't minded it after the first month of homesickness. It was new and exciting. She had companions for the first time and there was Jane Ashe, a sensible well-educated Englishwoman who taught English and History, and who seemed incredibly wise to Laurel, though she was not much above thirty. They had taken to each other not least because they shared a passionate love of horses. Miss Ashe, like many Englishwomen, was a superb horsewoman and accompanied the girls on their daily rides. Laurel still wrote to her, long sprawling letters about everything that happened to her in the great rambling palazzo where she felt so much alone.

She remembered the day, eighteen months ago now, when she knew that her mother was dead, killed in a carriage accident crossing the Appennines. Alessandro had been thrown clear, but her mother had died. Jane Ashe had not said much. Instead she had taken her walking, climbing into the mountains, the snow-clad peaks and deep valleys bringing calm and strength, and later that night when Laurel lay sleepless, she had come to put her arms around the shivering girl, so that she should not feel alone when the healing tears came at last.

The fire had burned low and Laurel sat up with a jerk. Someone was coming down the corridor, stepping lightly, as if whoever it was did not wish to be heard. With sudden panic she remembered she had not locked the door after Elena left. She was on her feet and across the room at the same instant as the handle slowly moved. She turned the heavy key and it clicked into place. She waited trembling, almost afraid to breathe, certain that it was Ugo on the other side, angry and frustrated, seeking an opportunity to punish her for her rejection. It made up her mind for her. If she did not escape now she would be trapped, caught helplessly between Alessandro's ruthlessness and Ugo's dissolute sensuality. The palazzo was full of Falcone, uncles, aunts, cousins, every one of them bringing pressure to bear. She had seen it happen to other girls forced into loveless marriages and taking refuge in children and religion. Laurel was not like them. She had a good deal of her grandfather's stubbornness. She was not going to be smothered by ancient traditions, eaten alive by greedy parasites. She would go to her grandfather in England and Jane Ashe would be the one to help her. She had travelled between Rome and Lausanne half a dozen times. She knew the journey by heart. She had travel papers; there were public diligences, and her monthly allowance, a generous one, had just been forwarded to her by her grandfather's bankers. She scrambled to her feet with a rising excitement. It was now or never. If she waited her resolution might waver. Alessandro could send her to his country house at Frascati and shut her up there, a prisoner until she agreed to marry Ugo. He was quite capable of it.

She stood listening for a moment. Everything was very quiet. The household would be sleeping late after the exertions of the carnival. She glanced at the small gold clock on her bedside table. The hands pointed to half past two. If she dressed and left the house by four o'clock, taking a horse from the stables, she could be well away before her absence was discovered. She refused to think of the dangers she might have to overcome, a young woman travelling alone. Only a year ago a man had been publicly beheaded for robbing and murdering a Bavarian countess crossing the Campagna on pilgrimage to Rome, but it wouldn't happen to her, she told herself firmly, she knew how to take care.

She began to pack a small valise with a change of linen and a few other necessities. Then she took from her wardrobe her plainest riding habit. The dark blue velvet with its military style jacket fitted her slim figure to perfection, but she was not concerned with her appearance. She knotted her hair under a small tricorne hat and put her travelling permits and money safely away in an inner pocket.

When she was ready she paused for a second, then took a sheet of paper and wrote a short note saying that since it was Ash Wednesday she had gone to mass at the Convent of Our Lady of Sorrows and would stay on for a day of prayer and meditation. Laurel had not been brought up a Catholic, but at her convent school and in this household she had sometimes followed the services. She addressed the note to Elena and left it in a conspicuous place on her dressing table. With any luck it would delay them searching for her for a few hours.

15

Now came the difficult part. She hugged the dog, whispering loving words in his ear, then turned out the lamp, took her valise and tiptoed along the passage and down the servants' staircase. It was still very dark in the courtyard, the torches burned out, the cobblestones littered with dead flowers, confetti, streamers, all the forlorn debris of the carnival. She groped her way to the stables. In the ordinary way the grooms would have been already stirring, but they had eaten and drunk well the night before, so that no one stopped her when she cautiously opened the door of the Contessa's stall. The mare knew her and whinnied softly. As quietly as she could she led her out into the yard and saddled her. Then she took the bridle and moved towards the gate. It was the purest luck that the porter was not on duty. She was ready with her story of riding towards the Convent at Tivoli, but Pietro, high flown with cheap wine, had fallen from the top of the float during the procession and was now groaning over a broken leg in the city infirmary, so his post was deserted. With some difficulty Laurel lifted the heavy iron bar, swung open the gate and pulled the Contessa through into the street. She climbed on to her back and trotted briskly down the Via Giulia.

Men on their way to work stared at the unexpected sight of a well-dressed young woman riding out alone at such an unearthly hour, but were too sleepy to take much interest. By the time she reached the Via Flaminia and took the road out of the city, streaks of crimson were lightening the Eastern sky. The Campagna stretched before her, bare and desolate. She was hungry already, having eaten nothing the night before, and she wished she had thought of putting some chocolate in her pocket. But she was young and strong and accustomed to long days in the saddle. She had decided to make for Viterbo. Once there she could arrange for the Contessa to be sent back to the *palazzo* and then take the diligence to Arezzo on her way to Florence and Bologna. Absorbed in her dream of freedom she did not take much notice of the three soldiers who came up behind her and stared curiously as she drew to one side to let them go by.

2

A little later that same morning Jethro and Tom were wrangling amiably about the route they would take, deciding at last to ride as far as Viterbo so that they could visit the famous Orsini Palace, one of the sights no traveller should miss, and then go on to Lake Bracciano. They set out after an early breakfast, riding briskly through the cool morning and it was not until nearly noon that they overtook Laurel. They saw the arrow-slim figure in the dark blue velvet trotting ahead of them and wondered idly why such an elegantly-dressed young woman mounted on an excellent horse should be travelling alone on this country road, but that was nothing to the surprise Jethro felt when he caught up with her and realized who she was. He was aware of a curious feeling of inevitability, almost as if he had expected it to happen which was ridiculous. He brushed it aside, smiled politely and took off his hat.

"Good morning, Signorina. I had not expected to see you out and about so early after the carnival. May I ask where you are going?"

Tom had come up on her other side and Laurel glanced from him to Jethro in some dismay. It was something she had not anticipated and she was uncertain how to reply.

"I'm riding to Viterbo," she said at last rather lamely.

"Alone? Without an escort, not even your maid?" said Jethro incredulously. "Isn't that a little unusual?"

"I don't see why. I often ride alone."

"I say, do you?" exclaimed Tom. "Jolly plucky of you . . . I mean . . . well, not many young ladies I know would care to do so, not in country like this." He looked mischievously at his companion. "I didn't know that you and Jethro were so well acquainted."

"Hardly that. We met briefly last night. I was able to offer the Signorina Falcone some slight assistance," said Jethro curtly. "We had better introduce ourselves. I am Jethro Aylsham and this is Tom Fenton."

17

"Delighted." Tom gave her a little bow and a friendly grin.

"How is the damaged ankle?" went on Jethro.

"Much better, thank you."

"Does Prince Falcone know that you are making this trip?"

"Of course he does." Laurel was edging away from them, extremely anxious in case they should question her intentions. "The Prince is not my father, you know."

Jethro frowned. "But I understood . . ."

"My mother was his second wife."

"I see."

"She died over a year ago." Under his steady gaze Laurel began to flounder. "As a matter of fact I have an aunt in Viterbo," she improvised rapidly. "I'm on my way to visit her."

"Indeed."

Jethro was perfectly well aware that no aristocratic Italian girl would have been permitted to travel alone across the Campagna with, as far as he could see, no luggage but a small valise. She was obviously running away from something, but she was so young, hardly more than a child, and as tense and nervous as a restive pony. At a mere touch, he thought, she might bolt.

He said easily, "How fortunate. We are also going to Viterbo. We might as well travel together."

"I wouldn't like to take you out of your way."

"You won't be doing any such thing, I assure you." Tom opened his mouth to protest and received a crushing look. "You've no objection to our company, I hope."

"No, no, of course not."

They rode on side by side, Jethro keeping a conversation going with the help of Tom's lively comments to which the girl contributed little. He sensed something was wrong, but could not make up his mind what to do about it and, though it seemed extremely unlikely, there was just a chance that she actually was on her way to visit a relative. After about an hour they came into a straggling village and pulled up outside the inn. It was a post house of good repute where carriages often stopped to change horses and Jethro suggested they might take the opportunity of having a meal and a short rest. His experienced eye had noted the girl's exhaustion and Laurel, after a sleepless night and a long morning in the saddle, was glad to agree though she would have died rather than admit it.

They dismounted, the ostler took the horses and as they

18

entered the inn, three soldiers pushed their way roughly past them. From their ragged uniforms and unkempt appearance Jethro guessed them to be deserters from some band of peasant soldiers. A number of them still roamed the countryside after the abortive rebellion of a few years before. Unpaid and unemployed, they were a constant threat to decent citizens going about their peaceful lives. The innkeeper looked after them with disgust.

"Call themselves *soldati*!" he said and spat. "*Banditti*, more like. You need to keep a tight hold of your purse when such as they are about!" Then he changed his tune, ushering his new guests inside with much bowing. "This way, Signore, this way. What can I do for you?"

It was a clean, decently-run place providing good food and it was not until she tackled the ravioli with a rich sauce that Laurel realized how hungry she was. Jethro was relieved to see her eating with appetite and to note the faint colour creeping back into the pale cheeks when she sipped the wine he had ordered. He didn't want a fainting young woman on his hands in addition to everything else.

After the dishes had been removed and a tray of coffee placed on the table, he made up his mind. He sent Tom out to the stables to make sure the horses were being properly attended to and then sat back in his chair. He looked across at this girl with whom it seemed fate had entangled him, whether he wished it or not, and was struck again by the sheer beauty of line and colour in the lovely face. There was courage there and resolution too. He could think of no young girl of his acquaintance who would have set out on such a bold venture.

"My dear young lady," he began quietly, "tell me what it is that you are running away from."

She raised her head meeting his eyes defiantly, "Running away? I don't know what you mean."

"I think you do," he said with some impatience. "You don't really expect me to believe that you are making this long journey alone simply to visit an aunt."

Laurel hesitated. The English doctor had been kind the night before. In her loneliness she had felt an instinctive trust, but all the same he might feel it his duty to escort her back to Rome.

"Oh come now," he went on, stretching out his hand and putting it on hers. "Don't be afraid. I'm not an ogre. I've heard all kinds of stories in my time. I may even be able to help."

19

Perhaps it was rash, but she decided to take a chance. She said carefully, "It is true that I'm not staying in Viterbo. I'm going on . . . to Switzerland, to the convent where I was at school. It is in Lausanne."

"Lausanne!" repeated Jethro taken aback. "But you cannot possibly make that appalling journey alone."

"Why can't I?" she said stubbornly. "I have done it before many times."

"In the Prince's carriage and with suitable attendants no doubt. That's quite another thing. It's unthinkable that you should travel by public diligence."

"I am not an idiot," she said haughtily, "and I'm quite able to take care of myself, I assure you."

"May I ask why you are returning to the convent in this manner?"

"I don't see that it is any of your business, but if you must know, I have friends there who will help me to reach England. My grandfather lives in London. I intend to join him there."

"Surely Prince Falcone would not object to such a visit."

"Oh yes, he would," she said vehemently.

"For what reason?"

"He knows I would stay there and . . . and he has other plans for me."

"What plans?"

His questions pressed so hard on her defences that the tension suddenly broke into an outburst. "He wants me to marry his son Ugo . . ."

"Ugo? Was he the man who . . .?"

"He was with me in the float and afterwards he . . . I detest him, I loathe him. He is a brute, a beast . . ."

Jethro said gently, "My dear child, you're very young. There is plenty of time. No one can force you into doing anything against your will."

"Perhaps that may be so in England, but not in Rome," she said scornfully. "You don't know the Falcone, you don't know what they can do. They would all be against me, every single one of them. I don't intend to give them the opportunity."

"Supposing he catches up with you?"

"He won't," she said confidently. "They won't have realized that I've gone yet, not with the message I left . . . unless . . . unless you . . . but you won't, will you? Promise me that you'll not

20

prevent me from going on?" She was gazing at him with huge pleading eyes.

"I don't know," he said slowly. "I'm making no promises."

"That's unfair," she flashed at him. "You persuaded me to tell you and now . . ."

"Don't upset yourself." He smiled. "I shan't carry you back to Rome, bound and gagged."

"You like to joke, but to me it is very real, very important . . ."

"Of course it is. Let us decide when we reach Viterbo, shall we?"

"Do you mean that?"

"Indeed I do."

She eyed him doubtfully and then got to her feet. "In that case we ought to be leaving soon. Excuse me, I would like to . . . to wash and get myself ready."

He let her go uncomfortably aware that all he had done was to postpone a difficult decision. He had called the landlord and was settling the account when Tom burst into the room.

"She's gone," he said indignantly. "It's the damnedest thing! She fetched her horse out of the stable and has gone galloping up the road like a lunatic."

"What!" Jethro swung round. "She can't have done. You must be mistaken."

"I'm not. I saw her from the upstairs window. I called out, but she took no notice. Lord, what a madcap! What did you say to frighten her off like that?"

"Nothing." But it was obvious that the merest hint that he might take her back to Rome had been sufficient to send her running headlong into God knows what dangers. Damn the girl! It was really too much. He threw down some money.

"Keep the change. Come on, Tom. We must go after her. Are the horses ready?"

"Waiting outside. Heavens, what a lark!"

They threw themselves into the saddle and went riding hell for leather down the road, leaving the innkeeper to pick up his money shrugging his shoulders at the crazy antics indulged in by the English Milords. A lovers' tiff no doubt. He tossed a coin in the air and caught it again. The good God could send him as many such extravagant fools as he wished.

Laurel's reaction had been instinctive. She was not going to be turned back at this stage by a stuffy English prig with a

21

misguided sense of responsibility. Once out of his sight, she reasoned to herself, and he would probably be only too thankful to be rid of her. She urged the Contessa on relentlessly and the mare, rested and fed, kept up a good steady pace. They were passing through scrubland now with trees and shrubs and it was not until she had emerged from it that she came to where the roads divided. The signpost that should have indicated the direction was lying on its side, one arm snapped off, the other pointing cheerfully towards the sky. She had slowed the Contessa to a walk before she saw the man leaning against a tree watching her and called out to him.

"Can you help me? Which road to Viterbo?"

He strolled towards her. "The right fork, Signorina. That way." He pointed and then laid a dirty hand on her bridle. He was a big man with a great deal of coarse black hair and a buccaneering moustache. He grinned up at her. "That deserves a reward, isn't that so?" he said impudently.

Uncertainly she pulled out her purse from an inner pocket and immediately he gripped her wrist, twisting it so that the purse fell into his hand. He tossed it into the air.

"See, *amicos*," he shouted and laughed. "A good fat haul!"

Too late she saw the two other men who had emerged from the trees and were closing in on her. Really frighened now she slashed out with her whip. It caught one of the men across the face and he swore at her.

"*Basta*! A she-devil eh! We'll see about that."

He seized her leg, trying to drag her from the saddle. The Contessa neighed and reared up. The man fell back, but his companion grabbed at her ankle. The mare jerked and she lost the stirrup. In another moment she had been pulled to the ground. The big man seized her in his arms. She struggled to free herself and he slapped her face. They were all laughing by now, anticipating an enjoyable hour amusing themselves with this spirited young woman. One of them dragged her head back and clapped his mouth on hers; outraged, she kicked out hard and he tripped her up so that she fell to her knees. It was the shot that startled them into momentary stillness. Then the galloping horses brought the two young men into their midst. Jethro, smoking pistol in hand, was cursing them in a fluent Italian that took them by surprise. They were petty thieves, accustomed to easy victories over terrified victims. His air of authority scared them and they were not prepared to fight.

They edged away to their horses hidden in the trees pursued by Tom brandishing his own gun and backing it up with a splendid flow of English abuse.

Jethro helped Laurel to her feet. She was white and trembling. She had lost her hat and the rich red brown hair tumbled about her shoulders.

"I'm grateful," she muttered, trying to brush the dust from her skirts with a shaking hand.

"So you ought to be, bolting off like that," said Jethro crisply. "It wasn't very sensible, was it? In a few more minutes you might have been very sorry indeed."

She stared at him, resentment struggling with relief. "I thought . . . I thought you were going to stop me . . ."

"Well, you were wrong, weren't you? Are you hurt?"

"No . . ."

Tom came racing back laughing his head off. "That's put paid to those rascals," he said gaily. "They haven't even escaped with the loot," and he held out the purse.

"Thank you." She smiled dazzlingly at him. "I don't know what I would have done without you."

"Don't mention it. It was Jet's idea, not that I minded in the least, all in a day's work rescuing ladies in distress, you know," said Tom cheerfully. "What now, Jethro? On to Viterbo, or back to Rome?"

"On to Viterbo," said Jethro curtly. "It will be dark before we reach the city anyway. Do you feel strong enough to ride on?" he went on to Laurel.

"Of course I do," she replied indignantly.

"Very well."

He took her hand and lifted her into the saddle and they went on, the two young men riding one each side of her, just in case she took it into her head to bolt again. Tom chattered away gaily keeping Laurel amused in spite of herself, while Jethro was mostly silent, only sure of one thing, that whatever happened, he could not just abandon this girl and leave her to battle her way across Italy to Lausanne. Brought up in luxury, she obviously had no conception of the problems involved in hiring a carriage and driver, securing a place in a public vehicle, or of the horrors that could be encountered in posting inns on a thousand-mile journey. The whole exasperating incident was threatening to cause the most damnable trouble and delay.

He could not make up his mind as to the best course to follow and then the matter was settled for him the next morning in a way that he had never anticipated. Afterwards he could not imagine why he had acted as he did, except that he had always had a particular dislike of arrogant bullies, ever since the unhappy years at his public school.

There was not a great choice of inns in Viterbo and he decided on the quietest and most respectable and as a doctor advised Laurel to retire to bed early. She was too saddlesore and exhausted to argue with him. She had confided very little more about herself and for the moment Jethro did not press her.

"It's a dashed queer set-up," remarked Tom later that night in the privacy of the room he shared with Jethro. "What are we going to do about it, Jet? Go with her to Lausanne? Bit of a facer, isn't it?"

"It would be far more sensible to march her straight back to Rome."

"Oh to hell with that! That would be taking the easy way out." Tom plumped down on the bed to kick off his boots. "Much more fun to gallop across the Alps chased by a furious step-papa with a pistol in each hand."

"You have far too lurid an imagination. I've no intention of doing anything so wildly dramatic."

"Haven't you?" Tom gave him a quick upward look. "Come on, confess, you've taken rather a fancy to the little wench, haven't you, dear Uncle Jethro?"

"Shut up, you impudent dog. You mind what you say or else I will act the heavy uncle and you wouldn't like that one bit."

"It's no use putting on that face with me. I know too much about you. Hidden fires."

"Detestable brat!" and Jethro aimed a playful cuff at the boy which he quickly dodged, rolling back on the bed and laughing.

Tom was in actual fact his half-sister's son, but they were far more like brothers than uncle and nephew and Jethro was fond of the happy-go-lucky youngster. Despite his wiry look of health, the boy had a delicate chest. He had suffered a congestion of the lungs shortly before Christmas which had left him with a persistent cough and Cherry had begged her doctor brother to take Tom abroad with him into the warmth and sunshine of Italy. Tom loathed his weakness, refusing obstinately to give in to it, but though he was better, he was still far too thin. It was only March and Jethro didn't much care for risking the intense cold, to say nothing of snow and ice which they would surely meet

24

crossing into Switzerland, for the sake of a stubborn young woman of whom he knew so little. He had intended taking the coast road to Genoa and then the boat to Marseilles.

He slept badly and was up early tucking the blankets around Tom still curled up like a puppy with his nose buried in the pillow. He went down to the inn yard and was making enquiries about hiring a carriage to take them through to Genoa when a man mounted on a magnificent black horse came clattering through the gateway. Some sixth sense put him on his guard. He gave a quick look back at the inn. There was no sign of Laurel or Tom and the Contessa was happily munching oats in the far stable. The man did not dismount. Instead he beckoned imperiously and Jethro went to meet him. His doctor's eye noted the hunched figure, one shoulder slightly higher than the other, the high-bred face marred by dissipation, the narrowed eyes, the thin mouth that sneered. It was Ugo Falcone, the man who had sat beside Laurel in the float, the Malatesta to her Francesa. For no good reason Jethro took a violent dislike to him and made an instant decision.

In her stifling little bedroom Laurel was wide awake. She was still stiff and aching, the bed was hard and she was restless. The strong impetus that had driven her from the Palazzo Falcone had begun to fade. The unpleasant incident with the soldiers had haunted her dreams. She got up, splashed cold water on her face and tried to shake the nightmare away from her as she dressed. The sound of the horse's hooves on the cobbled yard sent her running to the window. Her heart missed a beat as she recognised Ugo. She had not expected him to catch up with her so quickly. She saw Jethro go to meet him and waited in an agony of frustration hidden behind the curtain. What was he saying to him? Ugo looked angry and she saw the English doctor stiffen, but after a moment he shrugged his shoulders and turned back to the stables. Ugo jerked his horse's head round and moved to the gateway. She waited until he had disappeared and then ran down the stairs, meeting Jethro as he came through the door.

"I saw him from the window," she said breathlessly. "What did he want? What did you tell him?"

"What do you think?" He took her arm drawing her out of the passage and into the dining room.

"How did he know about me?" she demanded.

25

"It seems he met up with those rascals of soldiers. They described us too closely."

"What did you say about me?" she demanded.

"I told him that as far as I knew or cared you were on your way to the convent in Switzerland."

"You told him that!" she exclaimed indignantly. "How could you? Where can I go? What can I do now?"

He looked at her frowning. "Didn't you say you had a grandfather in London?"

"Yes, I have. He lives in Arlington Street."

"It so happens that I live in London also."

She stared at him, her eyes wide. "You mean . . . that I can travel with you?"

"It seemed a good idea. While Ugo is pursing you to Bologna and Florence, we will take the coast road to Genoa. I've already arranged to hire a carriage."

Laurel was breathless with relief and excitement. "Oh it's the most wonderful thing. I never thought . . . I never dreamed . . . thank you a thousand times," and she flung her arms round Jethro's neck and kissed him. Instinctively his arms went round her, he felt her young body press against him, smelled the fragrance from the cloud of silky red hair, felt the warm touch of the fresh young lips, then Tom appeared in the doorway.

"Hey, what's going on? Aren't I included in this?"

Laurel pulled away, blushing a little. "I'm coming with you to England. Isn't it marvellous?"

"Marvellous indeed," commented Tom dryly. "What decided you, Jethro?"

"Let's say I didn't altogether care for Ugo Falcone's manners," said Jethro lightly. "I daresay I shall regret it. In the meantime we must breakfast quickly and be on the road as soon as we can just in case he smells a rat and comes back to hunt for it."

"You looked angry," said Laurel curiously. "What did Ugo say to you?"

"Nothing of importance," he replied shortly. He had no intention of repeating the Italian's sneer.

To protect Laurel he had acted a complete indifference towards her and saw contempt spring into Ugo's narrowed eyes. He had looked him up and down before he said slowly, "Didn't I see you at the ball with Luigi Manfredi and another, a young boy?"

"I was there."

26

"I thought so." He smiled unpleasantly. "Are all Englishmen cold fish like you, sawbones?"

He would willingly have struck the sly implication from the sneering lips, except that to have done so would have defeated his purpose.

He was fully aware of how rashly he was behaving. The girl was under age and Prince Falcone was a powerful man. If he found them, he would not scruple to charge him with abduction and, brought up before an Italian court, he would not have a leg to stand on. Trapped by an impulse of pity he had committed himself. He couldn't get out of it now. There were a dozen facts he had to know, but they would have to wait until later. The most important thing was to be on their way as soon as possible. He left Tom and Laurel sitting down to coffee and hot rolls while he made the necessary arrangements. By the time they had drunk the last cup, he had fixed the return of the horses to Rome and the carriage was at the door. Sweetened by a bribe, the stableman who was a romantic and suspected a lightning elopement, had been easily persuaded to give a false direction if Ugo should return and ask awkward questions.

Tom and Laurel came out of the inn laughing together like a couple of children setting out on a picnic. Jethro climbed on to the box and they were off, their driver another Italian romantic entering into the spirit of the adventure and galloping his horses at a terrifying breakneck speed along the winding country road.

Laurel was conscious of a wonderful sense of freedom. It was only now when she was liberated from it that she realized how oppressive she had found the Falcone Palazzo and the weight of the family pressure during the past year. She had loved her grandfather. He had been like a rock of security during her childhood and she never once dreamed that circumstances might have changed him. Her spirits bubbled up. By the time they stopped in the early afternoon to eat and rest the horses, she and Tom were on the best of terms.

They were half way through the picnic lunch which Jethro had had the foresight to bring from the inn when Tom burst his innocent bombshell.

"It's the oddest thing, Jet, but Laurel's grandfather is Sir Joshua Rutland. Isn't he the man Uncle Oliver had dealings with at one time? Didn't he own part of Ravensley?"

Oliver, Lord Aylsham, was Jethro's half-brother, older by a good sixteen years, and a highly respected member of the House of Lords. He had rescued the family estates from debt and mortgage and brought them to their present prosperity. Laurel saw Jethro's face change and his mouth tighten ominously.

She said defensively, "Grandfather is a dear good man. Do you know him?"

"We have met," he said curtly. "A very long time ago."

"My father was his son," she went on, her eyes shining. "Captain Bulwer Rutland. He was in the Guards. I never knew him. He was drowned before I was born."

"And your mother?"

"She nearly died in terrible floods in England. She was very sick. That's why my grandfather brought her to Italy."

"Where you were born?"

"Yes, in Florence. Grandfather lived with us until she married Prince Falcone. She was killed in a carriage accident eighteen months ago."

Jethro looked at the charming face in front of him with something like despair. Was it possible that she was innocent, that she knew nothing of the tragedy that had preceded her birth, the scandal that had precipitated that flight to Italy? Was she truly ignorant of what her mother had been, the woman with the strange witch-like beauty who had driven his own father into madness and death? How extraordinary that destiny should have led him to this girl of all others. The shock had been so unexpected that he could not deal with it immediately. He rose to his feet speaking more harshly than he intended.

"We ought not to delay. Pack up the food, Tom. We must drive on. There's no time to waste."

During the days that it took them to cover the long miles along the coast road, Jethro remained withdrawn and uncommunicative. He looked after them scrupulously, doing everything in his power to ensure Laurel's comfort, but she was hurt and sometimes bewildered by his cool manner. She thought that he regretted his decision and knew nothing of the dark forces within him that her revelation had aroused. There were times when their road took them near the sea where the pinewoods swept down almost to the shore and once they met the marble being brought down from the Carrara mountains and had to pull to one side to let the long shallow carts plod by drawn by yokes of cream-coloured oxen with spreading horns. They picnicked at midday by the roadside, falling into bed at night exhausted by the bone-shaking hours in the carriage, and

Laurel became more and more intrigued by the tall dark man whose baffling courtesy continued to hold her at a distance. Why? she wondered, why? and could find no answer.

Then on the last day of their tiring journey Tom developed a fever. All the morning the boy had been trying hard to make nothing of it, but he could eat very little and alternately shivered and sweated as they drove on relentlessly towards Genoa. Jethro would have preferred to stay in the city for a couple of days until his temperature dropped, but he did not dare to delay. The sooner they were out of Italy the better. On enquiry he discovered that the ship, a small coasting steamer, did not leave for Marseilles until the evening. He insisted on Tom remaining in bed and Laurel surprised him by coming into the room at midday carrying a cup of steaming liquid.

"It's a *tisane*," she explained, "the nuns taught us how to make it. It's a country remedy, but very good for fevers. I bought the herbs myself and persuaded the cook to let me prepare it in the kitchen."

Her thoughtfulness touched him. He took the cup and sniffed it doubtfully.

"You needn't be afraid," she said with dignity, "it won't poison him. I've tasted it myself. We were often dosed with it and it nearly always brought the fever down. Doctors don't always know everything."

"Perhaps not," said Jethro dryly. "Well, I don't suppose it will do him any harm."

"For goodness sake, don't fuss," said Tom impatiently. "If Laurel says it's good for me, then it probably is. I'll drink anything that will take away this damnable headache."

He swallowed it, grimacing at the bitterness, and if it did nothing else it certainly helped him to sleep more easily that afternoon. Laurel offered to stay with him, occasionally bathing his forehead with cool water, while Jethro negotiated for their passage to Marseilles.

They went aboard at nine o'clock. The small ship was crammed with cargo and a motley collection of passengers. Jethro had obtained tickets with the utmost difficulty and the help of a substantial bribe, but was only able to secure one cabin.

"I am sorry," he said looking anxiously from Tom to Laurel. "It's the best I can do."

"Then Tom must have it," she said decidedly. "He is already

a little better, but if he has to sit up all night he will be ill again. You need not worry about me. It's a beautiful night and quite warm. I shall enjoy remaining on deck."

They got Tom safely installed in the cabin and tucked up in the bunk despite his vigorous protests that he was perfectly well. Then Jethro took one look at the tiny saloon full of men, women, children, dogs and luggage and decided against it. It was stiflingly hot and unbearably noisy. He bribed one of the crew to bring a chair and set it up in a secluded corner of the deck. He wrapped rugs around Laurel and fetched her coffee.

"No food available, I am afraid, not until the morning."

"Never mind. This is all I want." She looked at him. "What will you do?"

He shrugged his shoulders. "Keep an eye on Tom. Have a word with the captain. Don't be anxious on my account, Miss Rutland."

Much later that night, having made sure that Tom was sleeping peacefully, Jethro was standing at the rail. The boat moved gently over the quiet waters of the Mediterranean. They were keeping fairly close to the shore and he could distinguish the dim outline of the coast and the occasional pinpoints of light twinkling in the scattered villages. The moon made a pathway of silver and the sky was dark velvet pierced with stars. A lantern hung in the rigging above his head shedding its light on Laurel as she lay back in the chair and his senses ached at the loveliness of her sleeping face. He knew now that without wishing it, with every instinct in active rebellion against it, he was in serious danger of falling fathoms deep in love with the daughter of the woman he had hated with all the painful intensity of a sensitive unhappy child, the beautiful strange creature who had ruthlessly pursued her own ambition, betraying his father, that bitter moody man whose wild passionate blood he had inherited, until his agony had ended in a lonely death on the marshes of Greatheart Fen. He knew now why Laurel's face had haunted him, every line, every turn and look, that indefinable grace that drew every eye, causing him delight and torment. How much of her mother's heartlessness lived in her? How could he ever bring himself to trust Alyne's child? His hands tightened on the rail. He must put her out of his mind, root her out of his heart. He would take her to her grandfather and that would be the end of it. He would have done his part.

30

Let Joshua Rutland deal with the problem child, bastard daughter of his wayward son and the woman he had seduced.

Her voice coming out of the night took him by surprise. Her hand on his burned like fire.

With her face hidden from him Laurel could ask the question that nagged at her. "Why do you dislike me so much, Dr Aylsham?"

"Why should I dislike you?"

"I don't know." She was looking straight out across the sea. "You were so kind at first, then suddenly I felt it . . . like a cold wind. You were angry with me. You still are."

"What nonsense," he said lightly. "You imagine what is not there. I have been worried about Tom. He is not strong and he is in my care."

"Oh no, it was before Tom fell sick. Is it because I'm causing you so much trouble?"

"No, you mustn't think that." She was very close to him. He could see her face, a pale blur in the faint light, the large eyes watching him. "Believe me, I would not have committed a dog into Ugo Falcone's care."

She laughed, the lovely enchanting ripple that was so completely hers. "That puts me very firmly in my place," she said ruefully. "But I am truly grateful. You don't know what it means. I feel light as air. It's like coming out of prison."

"Are you sure that your grandfather will be pleased to see you?"

"Oh yes," she said warmly. "I know he will. I shall take care of him. We shall be so happy together."

In some ways she was a child still. He hoped her confidence was justified. Joshua Rutland must be an old man now, well into his seventies. What would he do with a young girl standing on the threshold of life?

She said thoughtfully. "You know all about me. I wish you would tell me something about yourself."

"I think Tom talks quite enough for both of us."

"Only about himself and his family," she said seriously. "He does not say very much about you."

"What do you want to know?" he said indulgently.

"A great many things. What you do? Did you always want to be a doctor? What it was that brought you to Italy?"

"That might take all night to tell," he said smiling. "Briefly then. When I was about eleven, I had a dear friend, a boy

31

named Ben. He was always delicate and the first year I was away at school, he died. It was terrible. I asked myself why . . . why it should be he of all people? And I could find no answer."

"And then you wanted to be a doctor and find out?"

"I suppose so. It started me thinking about it at any rate. I worked for my medical degree in Edinburgh and Paris. After that I wanted to undertake surgery, so it was more years of study and practice. I have a friend who has been engaged in some experimental work in the Anatomy School at Padua and he invited me to join him there. It happens to be far easier to obtain dead bodies for dissection in Italy than in England. Does that disgust you?"

"Of course not. I understand. How can you find out how something works if you don't cut it up?"

"Very practical." Her sturdy commonsense pleased him. Slowly the tension had begun to relax. He surrendered to the magic of the night and went on talking about the subject that occupied so much of his thoughts and she listened intently, not always understanding, but eager to know and fascinated by a man who was quite different from anyone she had ever met in the secluded convent or in the narrow confines of the Falcone household.

He told her about his new appointment as assistant surgeon at St. Thomas's Hospital and she looked up at him with a little frown.

"I don't know how you can do it. The very thought of the knife terrifies me."

He smiled. "You have to remember always that the more skilful you become, the better for your patient, and it is easier now than it was. Have you ever heard of chloroform?"

"Is that a drug? I remember Miss Ashe – she was one of our teachers at Lausanne – telling us about an American doctor who used something called ether to send people to sleep when he operated."

"Chloroform is better than that," said Jethro. "It was discovered about twenty years ago now by chemists working in America and in Europe, but nobody knew what to do with it at first. Then a Scottish doctor, James Simpson, tried it on himself and his family. He held a chloroform party. They all inhaled it and in a very short time they were all flat on their faces."

"You don't mean . . . they were dead?" she asked horrified.

"Good heavens, no! They woke up none the worse and then

he realized how it could be used to conquer pain. Do you understand what that means? You can reduce the shock . . . you can amputate, for instance, far more quickly, and without the dread of agony patients stand a far greater chance of recovery. I have thought about its uses a great deal," he went on thoughtfully, "I even believe it could be employed in childbirth. Imagine what that could mean to a woman whose labour is prolonged for some reason. Think how many lives it might save." Then he stopped abruptly. "I'm sorry. I should not be speaking about such things to a young girl like you."

"I know exactly what you mean, Dr Aylsham. One of our maidservants died like that, and the baby too. Is that what you will be doing when you take up your new appointment?"

"I don't know yet," he said wryly. "The hardest job is to persuade hospitals, patients too for that matter, to accept anything new. I have argued about it with my colleagues. Some of the older doctors still refuse to use chloroform. Even the Church preaches against it. Pain is sent from God, so it must be borne as a necessary evil and if you die from the shock of it, then that also is the will of God."

"And you would fight that belief?"

"To my last breath."

The wind that comes just before the dawn swept across the open sea and he felt her shiver.

"I'm talking far too much and you are cold."

"Not really, but perhaps we could walk a little."

"Why not?"

He took her arm and they paced up and down the deck, wending their way through sleeping passengers, bales of wool, piled vegetables, crates of live chickens. A cock crowed suddenly and she started and then laughed.

"Messenger of the morning," he said, "I've been meaning to ask you. Why did they call you Laurel? It is charming but unusual surely."

"It's Laura really, but when I was very small, I used to get mixed up, speaking Italian to the servants and English to my mother and grandfather and for some reason I called myself Laurel. Grandfather liked it and so it stuck." She grimaced. "Elena, she is Prince Falcone's sister, always called me Laura."

Dawn found them standing in the prow of the ship watching the light begin to spread across the sky in a glory of pink and gold and purple.

"How long now?" she asked.

"We should dock by midday."

"Then what do we do?"

"Take the train to Lyons and Paris, then on to Calais. The packet to Dover and from there to London. If we're lucky and obtain good connections, you will be in Arlington Street in three or four days."

"Shall I see you again after that?" she said in a small voice.

"Of course. I shall call to make sure that all is well with you."

She raised her eyes to him. "Promise?"

"I promise . . . cross my heart," he said smiling.

"I'm hungry," she said suddenly and childishly. "Do you think there is any food yet?"

"We can go and find out."

As they turned away, the sun rose out of the sea in a sudden blaze of gold. Dazzled, they stumbled together over the coils of rope wound around a stanchion and he caught her in his arms. For a moment they were very close, everything else blotted out, and he kissed her. Her lips were warm and soft under his. Then it was over.

He said gently, "Are you hurt?"

"No, I'm all right," she said a little breathlessly. "Perhaps we had better go and see how Tom is."

"Perhaps we had. After that we'll look for some breakfast."

The young man was awake and sitting up, his fever gone and declaring himself starving. Laurel sat beside him teasing him a little while Jethro foraged for food and she seemed to Tom just the same as usual, but she was not. With that kiss she had given something of herself to Jethro, an unspoken bond existed now between them, silent and deep-rooted.

3

Five days later on a bitterly cold day in March Laurel alighted from a cab and mounted the steps of a tall house in Arlington Street, followed by Jethro. A sneaky wind whistling around corners had whipped colour into her face, but she shivered despite the warm cloak Jethro had insisted on buying for her when they had arrived in Paris.

"You're going to need it," he had said firmly. "England is not Italy, and London is decidedly not Rome. We can have snow even in April."

Scrupulously she had tried to pay him back from her dwindling store of money, but obstinately he had refused to take it.

She was young and resilient enough to have enjoyed the long train journeys and even the Channel crossing in the teeth of a spring gale had not daunted her. Tom, much to his chagrin, had succumbed to a miserable seasickness, but Laurel had stood beside Jethro rejoicing in the white-crested waves dashing themselves against the boat. But now, while Jethro rang the bell, she looked around her with apprehension. It was a fashionable street of handsome houses, each front door freshly painted and gleaming with brass. It was sedate, neat and elegant and totally unlike the rambling decaying splendour of the Palazzo Falcone. She was suddenly very frightened. It was more than five years since she had seen her grandfather. Supposing his affection had changed, supposing he no longer wanted her near him? Tom had been packed off home to Ravensley and she missed his cheerful chatter. She swallowed convulsively and Jethro smiled reassuringly down at her as he rang the bell again. The door was opened at last by a manservant in a trim livery.

He gave a discouraging answer to Jethro's enquiry. "I am sorry, sir, but Sir Joshua cannot receive anyone at present."

"I am afraid that I must insist. It is a matter of the very greatest importance."

35

The footman looked doubtful, impressed by the visitor's authoritative air.

"You had better come in, sir, and the young lady. I will enquire if Mrs Grafton will see you."

He showed them into what was obviously the dining room, richly if gloomily furnished in deep red mahogany. There was silver on the sideboard and an air of sombre magnificence and there they were forced to wait, Jethro with his back to the brightly burning fire, Laurel perched uncomfortably on the edge of a stiff, high-backed chair. They both turned as the door opened. The woman who came in seemed nondescript at first glance, neatly coiled grey hair under a black lace cap, grey face, grey silk morning gown, but her eyes were shrewd, missing nothing, and there was something uncompromising about the thin, tight-lipped mouth. A formidable woman and not to be lightly crossed, thought Jethro.

She scanned them both before she said abruptly, "I am Mrs Grafton, Sir Joshua's niece. What can I do for you?"

"My name is Aylsham and this is Miss Laura Rutland, Sir Joshua's granddaughter. She would naturally like to see her grandfather as soon as possible."

The eyes glinted frostily. "I am afraid that is quite out of the question."

"Indeed, and may I ask why?"

"My uncle was taken with a seizure just over a week ago. His condition is serious. He cannot see anyone."

Laurel sprang to her feet. "But I am not just anyone," she exclaimed impetuously. "I have come to stay with him and care for him."

"I cannot permit him to be troubled by importunate relatives at a time like this."

She was coldly hostile and Jethro intervened quickly seeing the light of battle leap into Laurel's eyes.

"You are mistaken, Madam. Miss Rutland is not asking for anything. She is the daughter of the late Captain Rutland and has made the long journey from Rome for the express purpose of meeting her grandfather again as she has every right to do."

Alice Grafton's mouth tightened. Her gaze travelled over Laurel taking in every detail of the travel-stained riding habit. "So this is Bulwer's girl," she said contemptuously. "Surely she and her mother have already traded sufficiently on my uncle's generosity. What more does she expect from him?"

The colour had flown up into Laurel's pale cheeks. She stared at the woman who stood there so implacably and then turned to Jethro. "I don't understand. Captain Rutland *was* my father. What does she mean?"

Jethro understood only too well, but this was not the time for explanations. "Don't concern yourself, my dear. I will deal with this." He turned back to Alice Grafton, his voice hardening. "I am a doctor, Madam, and I must insist on seeing Sir Joshua and judging for myself if he is fit to receive his granddaughter. If we were to leave and he were to find out how we had been turned away from his door, I think you might have cause to regret your action."

Alice Grafton hesitated. She was no fool and she had a hearty respect for her uncle's irascible and stubborn temper. She said unwillingly, "Very well. I will take you to him, but not the girl. She shall stay down here."

Laurel would have protested, but Jethro put his hand on her arm. "Don't distress yourself. Leave it to me. It will be all right, I promise you."

It was fairly obvious to him as he followed the rustling silk skirts up the stairs that Joshua Rutland was very sick and greedy relatives were already gathering around like vultures anxious to be in at the kill. How many more of them were likely to turn up and what might Laurel, so young and unprotected, suffer at their hands?

The bedroom was unbearably hot and smelled of drugs and sickness. His first instinct was to draw aside the heavy velvet curtains and bring some light and air into the room, but he had to restrain himself. The man in the bed was not his patient. Joshua Rutland was sitting almost upright supported by banked up pillows. His face sagged distressingly to one side and one hand and arm lay heavy and flaccid on the coverlet, but the eyes under the bristling grey eyebrows were bright and alert. Joshua Rutland may have been partly paralysed by a stroke, but his brain was still sharp and clear.

The young man moved at once to the bedside. "My name is Aylsham, Sir Joshua, Jethro Aylsham. I believe you once had dealings with my brother Oliver at Ravensley."

The heavy head with its thatch of grey hair nodded. "I remember . . . good fellow Oliver . . . had a pretty wife." His speech was slurred and a little disjointed, but perfectly intelligible.

"I've brought your granddaughter Laurel to see you."

37

"Laurel, eh? Lovely little thing," he murmured. The eyes went slowly around the room. "Brought her? Where is she?"

"She is downstairs," said his niece sourly.

"Then bring her up."

"It's not fitting. You are too sick."

"God damn it . . . do as I say . . ."

"With your permission I would like to have a word with you first," interrupted Jethro quickly.

The bright eyes in the twisted face watched him for a moment, then he waved a hand dismissingly. "Get out, Alice . . . leave us alone."

"You ought not to do it, Uncle. You remember what the doctor said . . . no worry, no excitement. You must not tire yourself."

"Stop yapping, woman," he said irritably. "Get out . . . I know what I can do and not do . . . better than any quack."

She went reluctantly, shutting the door after her, and the old man sank back against his pillows.

"Women," he muttered, "can't leave you alone. Never came near me for years . . . couldn't stand the sight of me . . . only turns up now when she thinks there might be pickings for her two brats . . . I'll see her damned first . . . and them too. Now what's all this about Laurel?"

As briefly as he could Jethro described what had happened and the sick man listened nodding his head from time to time.

"Never liked Falcone . . . all show and no substance . . . Alyne was dazzled by his title . . . thought he could give her what I couldn't . . . a place in society . . . can't trust Italians, all smiles to your face and a knife in your back when you least expect it."

He raised himself in the bed with a mighty effort. "Listen, Aylsham, you've got eyes in your head. You can see this is no place for a young girl. That damned niece of mine . . . like a dose of poison. She was the death of Grafton, poor devil . . . died to get away from her, I reckon." Sir Joshua gave the ghost of a chuckle, then choked, gasping for breath. He gestured to the table by the bed and Jethro held the glass of barley water to his lips.

"Gently now," he said, "don't exhaust yourself."

"I'm all right." He pushed Jethro's hand away. "In a month or two I'll have pulled out o' this . . . then I'll send the lot of 'em packing but till then . . ."

Jethro doubted if his sanguine hope of a rapid recovery was

38

justified, but he said nothing and after a minute or two the old man went on with renewed strength.

"I wouldn't trust Alice ... not an inch ... she'd lead Laurel a hell of a life with me out of action up here." He paused for a moment then turned his eyes to Jethro. "Tell you what ... your brother's wife Clarissa ... fine woman ... she was good to me in the old days ... didn't look down her nose on trade like some of 'em did . . . had more sense. Would she have Laurel at Ravensley? She has girls of her own, I believe ... only for a few weeks till I'm on my feet again ... no trouble about money ... she can call on my bankers."

"The money would not be important," said Jethro slowly.

"It's Laurel's mother ... that's the rub, isn't it? Old hates, old grudges, old jealousies, they hang on ... but it's a long time ago. Alyne is dead and the child knows nothing of it."

"Laurel won't want to leave you."

"Bring her up here. I'll make her understand."

Jethro was reluctant, but there was an appeal in the sick man's eyes that he found difficult to resist. He went down to fetch Laurel aware that Alice Grafton was watching every step he made.

He was right in one thing. Laurel refused point blank to go. She knelt beside her grandfather's bed, her fresh young cheek pressed against the inert lifeless hand on the coverlet.

"I want to stay and nurse you. I'm good at nursing, aren't I?" She looked appealingly at Jethro. "I helped to care for Tom when he was sick. I can care for you."

"No, my poppet." His good hand caressed the bright hair. "It's not that I wouldn't like it . . . but I don't want you to be shut up here ... not good for a young thing like you ... it would worry me. I shall get better all the sooner for thinking of you happy with boys and girls of your own age."

"But I shan't be happy. I shall hate them," she said vehemently.

"No, you won't, lovey ... try to understand ..." His tongue was thick, he was having trouble in getting the words out and Jethro could see that his small stock of strength was already exhausted. He raised Laurel to her feet.

"I think Sir Joshua is right. You'll like Clarissa, she is very kind and Ravensley is beautiful in the spring. The girls have horses and dogs ... they will welcome you," he said and hoped to God that he was right.

39

"I'm not a baby to be comforted with toys and sweetmeats," retorted Laurel fiercely, and it was only when she could see for herself how desperately weary her grandfather was that she gave in at last.

"You won't keep me away for long," she threatened. "I shall come and see you often."

She kissed him tenderly and let Jethro lead her from the room. Downstairs Alice Grafton grudgingly offered them refreshment which Jethro curtly refused.

As they came down the steps, a young man came bounding up them. He was a dashing figure in the uniform of the Hussars, cherry-coloured overalls, blue tunic and slung jacket heavily laced with gold. He had obviously just come off parade. A boy held his sleek black horse at the foot of the steps. He stood aside to let them pass, a fair-skinned face with a long narrow nose and full passionate mouth beneath a hair-line moustache. Insolent blue eyes took in every line of Laurel's slim figure, so that Jethro had a strong inclination to punch him on the nose. He gave a mock salute as Laurel, her head held high, sailed past him, one hand lightly on Jethro's arm. She looked back when they reached the pavement to see the soldier staring after her. He grinned and waved airily before turning into the house.

"Who do you suppose that is?" she said. "Is he that woman's son?"

"Probably," replied Jethro and thought that if indeed he were one of Alice Grafton's brats, then it was still another hoping to dip his fingers into his great uncle's fortune.

"In that case he would be my cousin, wouldn't he?" went on Laurel thoughtfully.

There was a sparkle in the eyes and a tiny smile around the young mouth. It gave Jethro a jolt carrying him back twenty years to another young woman who had ruthlessly thrust aside anyone or anything standing in the way of her own desires.

They took the midday train to Ely sitting silently opposite one another in the first class compartment, both of them occupied with their own thoughts. Far from shedding his responsibility, Jethro was now more deeply involved than ever and facing a difficult problem with his brother's wife. He felt guilty about presenting her with what for many reasons could only be an unwelcome guest, but what else could he have done? He had his bachelor apartment in the Albany and went from there to his consulting rooms and the hospital, but it was unthinkable that he should take Laurel to such a place. Scandal would have dubbed her his mistress in no time. Nor could she stay alone with him in an hotel with no maid and no luggage to speak of. The whole damnable situation was getting out of hand and his own confused feelings about the girl, the tenderness mingled with exasperation, only made matters worse. It would have been a relief to smoke, but that was impossible. He took a medical journal from his pocket and began to read an article on diseases of the joints by the famous Sir Benjamin Brodie, surgeon to Queen Victoria, who was reputed to earn a fabulous ten thousand a year, but he could not concentrate.

For her part Laurel leaned back in her seat studying the clear-cut features she had learned to know so well. Since the night on the boat they had drawn closer together, sharing the hazards of travel with a rare sense of companionship and laughter, but his moods were unpredictable. With a despairing certainty she thought that he was now her only friend and she was not at all sure that he even liked her. It seemed impossible to believe that it was less than a fortnight since she had fled from the Palazzo Falcone. She looked out of the window. The train was rattling through fields brilliantly green with spring grass. There were sheep with their lambs and slow-moving brown cows grouped around thatched farmhouses cosily sheltering in belts of trees just coming into bud. It had been raining earlier and a wet mist hung over the meadows, totally unlike the Italian landscape she knew so well.

Her grandfather's illness had come as a tremendous shock. She never remembered him ailing anything more serious than a winter cold. Now she faced the terrifying possibility that he might die. Then she would be alone indeed. Would Prince Falcone stretch out a powerful hand and pull her back to Rome and Ugo? Never, she vowed to herself, never, she would die first and she raised her head defiantly clenching her small fists.

Jethro looked up and smiled. "You're looking very fierce. What are you thinking about?"

"I was wondering about Grandfather. Please tell me. Is he really very sick?"

He had tried to avoid the question. Now he said carefully, "It is impossible to be sure. I have known men of his age to make a good recovery."

41

"While others die?"

"Sometimes . . . but Sir Joshua has a strong constitution and there is always hope."

"That's an easy way to get out of it."

"I'm afraid it is, but it is true," he said ruefully. "Doctors are not God. They cannot command life or death, but he has an exceptionally brave spirit and that counts for a great deal." He leaned forward and put a hand on her knee. "You're not frightened, are you?"

"I think I am – a little. I feel so alone."

"It will work out."

"Will it?"

"I am sure of it."

His strong fingers closed over her hand and she drew reassurance from him to help her face what had to come.

It was early evening when they reached Ely. The stationmaster knew Jethro well and they were soon installed in the cab that would carry them to Ravensley. It was a dark night and she could see nothing, was only conscious of a sense of space, of wide stretches of marsh and a wild blustering wind with scurries of rain. The carriage rocked over the rough road throwing her against Jethro. He put an arm around her waist steadying her. It seemed a long time before they turned in at tall gates and drew up in front of a huge house.

"Here we are at last."

Jethro helped her out and she looked about her while he paid the driver. Lamps burned on each side of the porch at the top of the steps. He pulled the bell handle and after a moment the door was opened by a young girl in a simple white dress, her long fair hair tied back with a satin ribbon.

"Jet!" she screamed. "Darling Jet, we didn't expect you," and she flung her arms around his neck and hugged him.

"Hold on, Jess," he said laughing. "Let me get my breath. Where's Barker?"

"I happened to be in the hall, so I opened the door for him."

They were inside by now and she was staring with frank curiosity at the girl beside Jethro.

"Are you Laurel? Cousin Tom was telling us about you this afternoon."

Before anyone could answer, two golden retrievers came bounding down the hall leaping up at the newcomers in a frenzy of greeting.

"Jessica!" exclaimed Jethro. "For heaven's sake, call off these confounded dogs of yours before Laurel is eaten alive."

"It's all right," she said breathlessly, "I like dogs."

"Sorry," said Jessica apologetically. "It's just that they're so pleased to see you," and with the girl tugging at the dogs' collars, Jethro exclaiming and Laurel laughing, the first ice was broken.

"Everyone is in the drawing room" announced Jessica when the dogs had at last quietened. "Papa has been reading to us." She put a friendly hand on Laurel's arm. "Come and meet them."

In spite of everything that was to happen afterwards, Laurel never forgot that first evening at Ravensley, the quietness, the feeling of love and security, the sense of home, something which she had never experienced. It was all there in that first sight of the family. Lord Aylsham was sitting by the wide stone hearth, the open book in his hands; another young girl, a year or so older than Jessica, was on a footstool beside him; his wife worked at her embroidery frame with a perky-nosed bright-eyed little mongrel at her feet, and a brown-haired young man lounged on the sofa idly tickling the ears of a large grey cat who opened one sleepy eye and then curled up again contentedly. For an instant of time they were held there like a picture, their eyes turned to her, and Clarissa, Lady Aylsham, knew instantly with an icy prickle that ran shiveringly up her spine that the young girl standing so shyly in the doorway brought trouble, trouble buried deep in the past that she had hoped never to meet again.

Then the picture broke up. Jessica said importantly, "Look who Jethro has brought with him. Sohrab and Rustum like her already."

"Jess, what a way to announce a visitor!" and her father put down his book and rose to his feet. "Jethro, my dear fellow, we had no idea you were coming."

"It was not my intention. They will be looking for me at the hospital, but . . . well, I'll tell you later, Oliver. This as you've guessed is Laurel Rutland. My brother Lord Aylsham."

She looked up at the tall, thin man, the kindly face, the thick fair hair turning grey, not a tremor betraying the shock he felt at seeing in her face the living likeness of the woman who had once caused him so much anguish.

"You are very welcome, my dear," he said gently. "I knew your mother. Have you come to stay with us?"

43

She glanced at Jethro doubtfully, "I don't know yet . . ."

"Well, never mind, time for that later. Now let me introduce you. Jessica you have already met, this is my elder daughter Rosemary and my son Robin."

The young man rose to a lanky height and gave her a little bow.

"And of course my wife."

By this time Clarissa had come to Laurel's side. She had been appalled at Tom's colourful account of their adventures that afternoon. What on earth had Jethro been thinking about bringing the girl out of Italy? There was certain to be trouble and Oliver would have to bear the brunt of it as he had done so often in the past. It was really too bad. Then abruptly compassion got the better of her. Why, this was no more than a child, wearied to death and badly in need of comfort and reassurance.

She said gently, "I know only too well how exhausted and grubby train journeys make you feel. I am sure you would like to wash. You come with me, my dear. We will find a room for you."

She led the way out into the hall and up the broad staircase, a manservant appearing and following them with the shabby valise.

The room to which Laurel was taken was pleasant, the curtains and hangings of cream linen sprigged with roses. The servant lighted the candles.

"Send Betsy to make up the fire and bring fresh linen and towels," ordered Clarissa and then turned back to Laurel. "We have dined already, but you must be hungry. Shall I have food brought up to you or would you rather come down again?"

"Lady Aylsham," she said hesitantly, "I hope you don't mind my coming like this. It has all happened so suddenly, so unexpectedly . . . I'd not expected Grandfather to be so ill . . ." Her voice broke and she turned away overwhelmed for the first time by a sudden rush of tears.

"Don't distress yourself, my dear. Jethro will tell us all about it. Rest for a little, then I'll send one of the girls to fetch you." She put a hand lightly on the girl's shoulder for a moment and then went out.

A young maid came with hot water in a brass can. She was a rosy-cheeked country girl who bobbed a curtsey and looked at Laurel curiously. She put the freshly laundered

44

sheets and towels on the bed and busied herself with lighting the fire.

It felt good to wash off the stain of travel, but depressing to have no change of clothes. There was still a clean white blouse in her valise, but it was hopelessly creased. She smoothed the crumpled lace and brushed out the rich red hair tying it loosely back. It made her look very young. Rosemary came to fetch her, a tall slender girl, very like her sister in appearance, but with a certain shy dignity of her own. When they entered the drawing room Lord Aylsham had begun to read again and they paused in the doorway listening to the deep pleasant voice.

"She left the web, she left the loom,
She made three paces thro' the room,
She saw the water-lily bloom
She saw the helmet and the plume,
She look'd down to Camelot.
Out flew the web and floated wide;
The mirror crack'd from side to side,
'The curse is come upon me,' cried
The Lady of Shalott."

Laurel shivered a little as if the words carried a warning. She would have moved to a chair at the back of the room but Robin stood up, heaved the indignant cat to the floor and motioned her to the sofa. Rosemary smiled and gave her a little push. She went to sit primly beside him.

Robin Aylsham was eighteen, only a few months older than Laurel. She stole a glance at him, noticing the pleasantly irregular features, a full rather sullen mouth, brown eyes that were looking at her with a frank appraisal.

He was a little bored, a little restless and at odds with his father who was insisting on his studying law at Cambridge. Jet had all the luck, he was thinking resentfully. He had wanted to go on this Italian trip instead of his cousin Tom. Lucky devils, both of them, travelling half across Europe with this gorgeous girl in the most unusual circumstances. He was damned sure he would have got a great deal more out of it than ever they did. He smiled suddenly and dazzlingly at her nodding carelessly towards his father.

"Dashed bore all this poetry, don't you think?" he whispered, "Especially Tennyson. It's my sisters who rave about him. Bet you don't read him in Italy."

"We don't need to. We have Dante," she murmured

45

mischievously and shook her head at him reprovingly. He grinned back at her with a disarming charm.

Then Lord Aylsham closed the book and conversation became general. Jethro must have told them about her because no one pestered her with questions, but made every effort to absorb her into their family circle and she was grateful for it. Food was brought for her and Jethro. She ate a little of it and sipped the wine. Afterwards, at their mother's prompting, the two girls escorted her to bed carrying her candle for her and making sure that she had everything she needed. Jethro had said goodnight to her holding her hand for an instant at the foot of the stairs.

"I shall be gone long before you are awake, Laurel, but I'll keep in touch with Sir Joshua. Any change and you shall have news of it at once."

She felt as if her one sheet-anchor had gone from her and she was embarked alone upon a wide and dangerous sea without guide or support.

The girls were friendly enough but they did not stay long. They said goodnight and went out. Left alone Laurel dropped wearily on the bed. Distress at her grandfather's serious illness together with extreme fatigue had made her abnormally sensitive. She knew very well that beneath the veneer of courtesy and good manners she was not really welcome in this household. She had been conscious of a coldness in Lady Aylsham's manner, a withdrawal, a tension in the atmosphere that Jethro had done his best to disperse by an amusing account of their journey. She wished passionately that he had not brought her to Ravensley and then left her to face it without him. And yet what could she have done, alone in a London of which she knew nothing? She felt an unexpected pang of homesickness for the palazzo in Rome, tears pricked at her eyes until resolutely she forced them back. It had happened and there was nothing she could do about it. She struggled to her feet and began to undress. She was already in her nightgown when she heard a faint scratching at the door. She listened for a moment, then thought it might be one of the dogs and went to open it. The candlelight fell on a shadowy figure, so old, so frail, so grey, he might have been a ghost. He stared at her from coalblack eyes smouldering in a dark-skinned face, then thrust out a long stick-like finger stabbing it at her and mumbling accusingly in a language she did not understand. For an instant she stared at

46

him unable to move, then she slammed the door and locked it. Shuffling steps went slowly, draggingly, down the passage and she waited until they had died completely before she relaxed, still shaking a little.

It's ridiculous, she told herself sternly, he's simply some old servant, some ancient retainer not responsible for his actions. She would ask the girls about him in the morning, but all the same she felt cold as if something evil had touched her with an icy hand, monstrous and frightening. It was a very long time before she slept.

4

Jane Ashe was sitting under the pink flowering trees in the Convent garden reading Laurel's bulky letter. It was cold but the sun had heat in it and she was well wrapped up. Only here could she escape the girls and find the solitude in which to read the dozen or so sheets scribbled in diary form. She frowned over the vivid description of her escape from the Palazzo Falcone and wondered about the young doctor whose name peppered these early pages. J. says this, J. says that, J. thinks that I ought to do so-and-so . . . the other young man, his companion, seemed to have made very much less impression. Her pupil had always had a tendency to rush headlong into things without a thought to the possible consequences. She hoped that it was not the case this time. She felt a certain relief when Ravensley came into the picture. The Aylshams appeared to be a county family of good standing. Surely the child would be safe among them until she could take her proper place in her grandfather's house. It was fairly obvious to Miss Ashe that Laurel with her disturbing beauty was as out of place in the quiet country home as a bird of paradise among a flight of doves but maybe it would not be for too long.

Later that day Miss Ashe took up her pen to reply, saying how she had made up her mind to give up her post at the Convent at the end of the year. She had no ties in England, her parents both being long dead, but all the same she was homesick for the sights and sounds of London. She would look forward to seeing Laurel again then and in the meantime was delighted to know that she was happy and that no evil result had followed her flight from Italy.

Laurel reading that letter in the quietness of her pretty room admitted its truth. She *was* happy, far more so than she had ever thought possible when she first came to Ravensley on that bleak March night. The coldness she had felt then, the very real doubt of her welcome had slowly faded. Robin and the two girls had accepted her unconditionally and if she were still aware of Lady

48

Aylsham's eyes on her with a searching, speculative look that puzzled her, Lord Aylsham was unfailingly kind. Hard to believe that was two months ago now. There had been trouble from Rome and it had only been settled by the powerful intervention of Lord Aylsham necessitating several visits to London and long sessions with her grandfather's lawyers. But now it was all over. She was free of them, she was her own mistress with a considerable income of her own. It was a heady experience for a girl of barely eighteen.

She put down the letter and looked in the mirror. The new riding habit in cherry-coloured velvet trimmed with black braid was very handsome. It had been fun to choose a completely new wardrobe with Clarissa's help and to the admiration and envy of Rosemary and Jessica. She would have bought wildly extravagant gifts for them if their mother had not restrained her, but she had had her own way in the selection of materials and colour. She had an inherent taste that prevented her choice from becoming too exotic, but nevertheless the gowns that hung in her wardrobe had a style and flair that were very much her own.

The only flaw in her happiness was that she had not seen Jethro since the day he had brought her to Ravensley. He had written twice to tell her that Sir Joshua was making slow progress, but nothing more. On the other hand she had learned a great deal about him. The girls had told her one day when they passed one of the portraits that hung along the wide landing. She had paused to look up at the young man with very black hair and lean arrogant face whose narrowed eyes under straight dark brows seemed to watch her contemptuously.

"It's queer," she said slowly, "but he reminds me of Jethro."

"It is like him in some moods," agreed Rosemary, "but then Great Uncle Justin was his father."

Laurel stared at her. "But I thought that Lord Aylsham was his brother."

"Half-brother. Papa does not like us to talk about it. It's the skeleton in our family cupboard."

"Whatever do you mean?" said Laurel vastly intrigued.

"Well, it was like this," said Rosemary rather reluctantly. "Great Grandfather had two sons, Justin and Robert, who was our grandfather, and they both fell in love with the same girl . . ."

"Justin was one of the wicked Aylshams. They crop up every

now and again even in respectable families like ours," went on Jessica airily, "and the funny part is they're always the ones who have black hair."

"Don't be silly," said Rosemary quickly.

"It's quite true, you know it is, and Justin did something really dreadful. It was all hushed up, of course, but two people died because of him and he had to leave England in a great hurry. He went to India and everyone thought that he had died out there, so the girl he wanted married his brother Robert, became our grandmother and had two children, Papa and Aunt Cherry, only Justin wasn't dead at all and our grandmother was still terribly in love with him, so one day she ran away to him in India and Jethro was *their* son," continued Jessica breathlessly, "that's why he is so much younger than Papa, more like our elder brother really."

Laurel, rather stunned by this revelation of family scandal, said thoughtfully, "So that makes Jethro . . ."

"A bastard," said Jessica brightly.

"Jess! What a word to use!" interrupted her sister reprovingly.

"It's true though. If he wasn't illegitimate, he'd be Lord Aylsham instead of Papa because Justin was the elder brother."

"Does he mind?"

"Heavens, no, but Mamma says that's why he works so hard. He has to prove himself as good as anyone else."

"He doesn't need to," said Laurel indignantly.

"Of course he doesn't. Jet's cleverer than any of us," went on Jessica, now thoroughly enjoying herself, "but you see, that wasn't all. Justin came back from India when his brother Robert died, pushed Papa out and claimed Ravensley for his own and after that . . ."

"I think that's quite enough," interrupted Rosemary firmly, giving her sister a quelling look. "I'm sure Laurel doesn't want to hear a lot of silly village talk. Papa would be angry if he knew."

"All right, if you say so. There isn't much more really," said Jessica rather lamely, "because he died out on the marshes when the floods came and then Papa became Lord Aylsham."

Laurel was sure that there was a great deal more that they had not told her, but it was all old history and did not really concern her. It was Jethro who mattered and what she had heard about him added to the vivid impression he had made upon her so that she thought about him constantly, and in the quiet content of the days at Ravensley she found herself often restless.

This morning she was riding with Lord Aylsham. She had got into the habit of accompanying him when he rode across the Fens to one or other of the outlying farms and he seemed to welcome her company. She adjusted the gay little hat with its curling ostrich feather and picked up her gloves and riding crop. As usual a shadowy figure crouched cross-legged in front of the portrait that had attracted her attention. She skirted carefully around him and ran down the stairs. She knew all about Ram Lall by now. He was an Indian whom Justin Aylsham had brought back with him from Calcutta and when his master was drowned, poor Ram had quietly gone off his head.

"He's not violent or anything," they told her, "he just doesn't seem to live in the present any more. Don't be frightened of him, he's quite harmless."

Just now and then when Laurel felt those black eyes fixed on her, she did not feel so sure that they were right, but mostly she dismissed him from her mind.

She arrived in the stableyard to find Seth Starling waiting for her. He was a stocky, well-built man in his early thirties. The Starlings had served Aylshams in some capacity or other for as long as anyone could remember and Seth had particular charge of the horses. He looked admiringly at Laurel's trim figure.

"Good morning, Miss. I'm afraid Gadabout is not himself today. A grass snake had curled up in his hay and it upset him. He kicked out and frightened the life out of one of the lads earlier on. He can be a tricky devil. You'd best take one of the others."

"But I like Gadabout. He has more spirit than any of them." She smiled suddenly, looking mischievous. "I know something that will cure him."

"Take care, Miss, don't try anything silly."

Seth would have prevented her, but she was too quick for him. She reached up taking hold of the horse's halter and, pulling him down to her, she whispered something into his ear in some queer gibberish. The horse tossed his head, a long shiver running along his satin coat, then he whinnied softly and nuzzled into the hand caressing him.

"By God, that were a fair miracle," breathed Seth staring at her.

Lord Aylsham who had just come through the gateway into the yard said sharply, "Where did you learn that?"

Laurel shrugged her shoulders. "I've always known it. It's only some funny old charm but it works."

"Oh aye, it works all right," muttered Seth under his breath, "but you're not one of us . . ."

"What are you mumbling about?" said Lord Aylsham crisply. "Is my horse ready? Come along, my dear, we must go."

He lifted Laurel into the saddle and turned to the big bay Seth held for him. Presently they were trotting side by side along the grassy bridlepath that took them across the park and out on to Greatheart Fen.

The fresh wind brought the sweet scents of the spring. All about them was green and lush, the meadowsweet that would soon be in bloom, the bog myrtle and the great beds of red-gold reeds. A flight of wild swans streamed across the sky with their honking cry and a solitary bittern with dagger-like beak and long greenish legs stalked amongst the sedge pausing occasionally to utter his queer haunting call. It was strange, thought Laurel, that she should feel such a deep affinity with this wild and desolate scene. It was as if the great stretches of marsh, the home of sparrow-hawks and curlews, of otters, weasels, hares and rabbits, were part of her and she had come home to them.

They had been riding in silence for a while before she said, "What did Seth mean when he said I was not one of them?"

"It was nothing of importance."

She gave him a swift sidelong glance. He was looking straight ahead, his face grave. "It was because of that old charm, wasn't it?" she persisted. "I only said it for fun. I learned it like a nursery rhyme. My mother taught it to me when I had my first pony. Do you know what it means?"

"I doubt if anyone does now, it goes back too many centuries," said Oliver Aylsham slowly. He glanced at the lovely girl beside him whose mother he had once loved so dearly and thought that with her passionate interest in this wild country, she might have been his own daughter. "The Fens have a magic of their own, Laurel," he went on, "an ancient lore that has come down by word of mouth and is never written

52

down. That charm is part of the old magic. Horses have been bred here from before the Romans came. There are fen dwellers living now who have an uncanny power over them. No one knows the secret of it except that among themselves they are known as 'Toadmen'. What they do or what rites they practise I don't know or want to know."

"Is Seth one of them?"

"Perhaps. I never asked. He is a wizard with horses and that is all I require from him."

Laurel frowned. "But why should my mother know of it?"

"Your mother was born and brought up here. She was a true child of the Fens. Did she never tell you about that part of her life?"

"No, never." It seemed strange to think that her mother with her pale beauty and sophisticated elegance had once been part of this savage countryside with its ancient traditions. "Perhaps that's why I love it," she said slowly. "The magic is part of me too."

In some odd way it thrilled her to feel she possessed some secret power, something different from others, and the man riding at her side sensed it too, a power to enslave men's hearts, and destroy them, as her mother had done and cared nothing. Then he told himself he was being foolish. This was an innocent and open-hearted child, no beguiling fen witch.

They were now in the heart of the Fens. Ahead of them the black shape of an old mill revolved its great bat-like sails churning out brown peat-stained waters in a yellowish flood. A punt came slowly down the stream, a tall fantastic figure guiding it with the long pole. He wore a leather jerkin, stained and worn, and water boots reaching to his thighs. The aquiline nose, high cheekbones and matted white hair might have belonged to one of his Viking ancestors. He ground the pole into the bank and brought the punt to a temporary standstill.

"Got a fine load of fish aboard, Mr Oliver. I'll leave it at the house for your lady."

"Many thanks, Moggy."

"Where's Master Robin? En't seen much of him this last month."

"He's working hard at his studies."

"Aye, but book-learnin' en't everything. You tell him the duck will be flyin' soon and I'll be waitin' for him."

"I'll tell him."

He looked hard at Laurel. "The little lady be *her* daughter, en't that so? You take good care of her, Mr Oliver . . . there be folks with long memories hereabouts." He dug in the pole and the punt shot up the stream.

With a faint shiver Laurel asked, "Who is that?"

"One of the old timers. 'Fen Tigers' they used to be called when I was a boy. He is one of the reasons why I've not had Greatheart drained like the other marshes. It's the last refuge of the old hunters. Moggy lives deep in the bogland with a shack that's flooded a foot deep in water every winter. I'd willingly give him a decent cottage on Ravensley land, but shut him up in it and he'd die in a week. He's racked with ague and crippled with rheumatism, all of them are on the marshes. Jethro despairs of them. He goes around dosing them with laudanum when he comes down here, but nothing would induce any one of them to change their way of life."

"You care for your people, don't you?" she said wonderingly. "Prince Falcone didn't. Some of the workers at the Frascati farm were housed worse than his pigs."

"I do it for purely selfish reasons," said Oliver lightly. "We have had our share of troubles, but treat your dependants decently and you get more work out of them."

"I don't believe you think like that at all," she said sturdily.

She had not been in England long enough to realize that the liberal atmosphere at Ravensley was the exception rather than the rule, but she did know that Cherry, Lord Aylsham's sister, had begun a village school. She had visited it once with Jessica. Twenty pairs of eyes had widened at the vision with rich red hair dressed dazzlingly in green and white striped taffeta who smiled so beguilingly at them.

Cherry Fenton was Tom's mother and she had the same good nature and easy acceptance of life as her son. She was not elegant and reserved like Clarissa, but warm-hearted and out-going, not caring too much whether her hair was tidy or her gowns fashionable. She lived at Copthorne only a short distance from Ravensley, so that the two families were constantly in and out of each other's houses. The rambling old manor which she had inherited from a great aunt was filled with dogs and kittens and children, all tumbling over one another, with Patty Starling vainly trying to keep the ten-year-old twins in order. Patty was Seth's elder sister and had been nurse to Ravensley children since Robin was a baby. Harry Fenton worked in the War Office

54

and only came home at weekends, a handsome, soldierly-looking man with a roving eye, but deeply fond of his eccentric slapdash wife. The odd one out was Margaret, Tom's sister, a strange secretive girl, who watched everyone and said little, quite different from her happy-go-lucky family.

When Laurel came in from her ride that afternoon, she met her in the hall and stopped for a moment. "Were you looking for Jessica?" she asked. "I saw her in the stables when I was unsaddling Gadabout."

Margaret stared at her. "I thought Robin was here."

"He's not coming home this weekend."

"How do you know?"

"He writes to me sometimes," said Laurel carelessly and was surprised by a flash of pure hatred in Margaret's eyes. It startled her. From the first she had been aware of the other girl's intense hostility and could find no reason for it. Margaret was small and plain, her one beauty the long silky dark hair she wore simply tied back with a ribbon. The sun caught it as she went through the door and it shone glossy as a crow's wing. Perhaps Margaret was one of the black Aylshams like wicked Great Uncle Justin, thought Laurel, then chided herself for being silly as she ran up the stairs.

In contrast to her daughter, Cherry had taken an instant liking to Laurel and said so very firmly to her sister-in-law when she came up to take tea with her one day at the beginning of June. The two ladies sat cosily together in Clarissa's little sitting room.

"I don't know what you are making such a fuss about, Clary," said Cherry in her forthright way. "Laurel is a very nice child, good-hearted too. She spent the whole afternoon telling the children about Rome because I asked her. They were enchanted. It was quite the best history lesson they had ever had."

"I don't doubt it. Laurel can charm a bird off a tree when she wants to," said Clarissa sharply, "just as her mother did. Robin is crazy about her already. Oh, he pretends to be indifferent but we have never seen so much of him as during the last few months. He finds every excuse to escape from Cambridge."

"He's just the age to lose his head over a pretty girl, that's all it is," said Cherry comfortably.

"I'm not so sure . . ."

55

"Clarissa, for heaven's sake! Just because Oliver was once madly in love with Alyne doesn't mean that Robin is going to feel the same about her daughter."

"I wish I didn't think so."

"In any case what does it matter? If all I hear is true, she is going to be rich when old Sir Joshua dies. She'd be a very good match for him."

Clarissa looked shocked. "How can you say such a thing? It's unthinkable and you know the reason why."

"I only know that there was once a great deal of scandal which has been dead and buried for years. Why revive it? It's over and done with."

"Not in places like this, believe me. Country people hang on to the past. And there's another thing. Oliver has been taking the girl about with him everywhere, far more than he ever took Rosemary or Jessica. That has been causing talk."

"What kind of talk? Clarissa, I do believe you're jealous, and of Oliver too, the most faithful husband in England. Now if it was Harry . . ."

"Cherry, what utter nonsense!"

"Is it? Harry may be your brother, but I sometimes wonder what he gets up to in London when I'm down here," and then she laughed. "Don't worry, Harry and I rub along together very well." She leaned forward and put a hand on Clarissa's knee. "Honestly, Clary, you're letting yourself become obsessed about Laurel and there's no need. It's not like you. Now I refuse to say another word on the subject. I want to know about Ravensley Boy. How is he shaping? Seth tells me you have him entered for the Derby. Isn't that flying rather high?"

The racehorse was owned jointly by Clarissa and Cherry, a very unusual hobby smiled upon by their indulgent husbands. They were both enthusiastic riders to hounds and had grown up with horses. The subject kept them earnestly discussing form and other absorbing topics for the next hour. Both families would be travelling up to London at the beginning of the following week, putting up at the house they owned jointly in St. James's Square and going down to Epsom for the races.

The Derby was one of the great sporting events of the season where all the world came together with the sole purpose of enjoying itself. From the open carriage which she shared with the other ladies, Laurel could see family barouches like their

56

own, together with rakish young men driving dashing four-in-hands, crowded brakes, pony traps, pearl-buttoned costers in donkey carts, to say nothing of gypsy caravans, all causing endless hold-ups at the turnpikes and waving madly to villagers watching from cottages or lining the route as they bowled along. On the course itself hungry-looking beggars, gypsy women in ragged finery with dirty bare-footed children, swarmed around the elegant carriages and coaches snatching at the scraps of food tossed carelessly from lavish picnic hampers. The cream of society mingled with workaday city clerks and rubbed shoulders with negroes, racing touts, hucksters selling cheap trinkets, boxers and hurdy-gurdy men, confidence tricksters and pickpockets, while behind them were painted booths and bookies' stands, shooting galleries and skittle alleys, with stall after stall laden with meat pies and jellied eels, gin and water and beer by the gallon.

Laurel had been deeply disappointed that Jethro had not joined the family at dinner the previous evening. It had been a merry party. They had all been there, only the twins left at home much to their fury. Laurel seated between Tom and Robin, was being instructed in English racing rules with much laughter. Margaret stared at them resentfully. Ever since she was a child tagging along behind the older boys and girls she had nursed a fierce consuming passion for her cousin Robin to which he had responded with a careless affection. Now for weeks he had scarcely even spoken to her. She dug her spoon into the ice pudding with a strong certainty that if it had been a knife, she would willingly have plunged it into Laurel. There was a lull in the laughter. She looked up. Robin was gazing at her rival with such a fatuous look of adoration on his face, she could have struck him. Anger boiled up inside her. She heard Laurel say plaintively, "But where *is* Jethro? I felt sure he would be here tonight," and a furious jealousy got the better of her.

She said loudly, "Aren't Robin and Tom enough for you? Must you have Jethro running at your beck and call as well?"

"Don't be silly," said her mother sharply.

"It's not silly. Why should she always have the best of everything? We were happy till she came, now it's all Laurel, Laurel, Laurel!"

"Margaret, remember your manners!"

But nothing now could stop her. "It's not I who am forgetting

57

them. You never wanted her here, Aunt Clarissa, so why don't you say so? Why couldn't she have stayed in Italy where she belongs? She has spoiled everything!"

She glared round at their shocked faces. None of them understood her or cared one jot about the feelings rioting inside her, but some day she would show them. A hard dry sob shook her. She pushed back her chair and ran from the room.

"I didn't mean . . ." began Laurel in the uneasy silence.

"Take no notice, my dear," said Lord Aylsham trying to restore calm. "The girl is over-excited. Margaret and Jessica are too young for this kind of trip. They should have stayed at home with the children."

"Oh Papa, that's not fair," exclaimed his younger daughter indignantly.

It was Rosemary who said placatingly, "Jethro did send a message. One of his patients took a bad turn. If he can get away, he'll join us on the course tomorrow."

They arrived at Epsom at about noon. Their luncheon had been laid out for them on a snowy cloth, game pie and cold chicken, lobster patties and sliced ham, with cakes and fruit. Laurel was sipping champagne from a long fluted glass when she first saw Jethro. For some foolish reason, she felt suddenly breathless, her throat closed up and her hand shook. She put down the glass. He was talking to a pleasant-looking woman dressed very simply in dove grey who held a small dark-haired boy by the hand. She thought he looked very handsome in the tightly fitting coat and tall silk hat, a pink flower in his buttonhole. She watched him bend down to the child talking and laughing with him. He took the woman's racecard and marked it before handing it back and there was something intimate in the looks exchanged between them, something beyond that of mere acquaintances that made Laurel's heart beat faster with a twinge of jealousy. Then he had raised his hat and come sauntering towards them.

The youngsters greeted him with shouts of welcome.

"Have you left your patients to die without you?" said Robin with mock gravity.

"What's more to the point, who were you cutting up last night?" asked Tom teasingly.

"Don't be disgusting," snapped Margaret.

Jethro took it in good part slipping an arm around Jessica's shoulders. "How's my best girl then, enjoying yourself?"

58

"Rather . . . and so is Laurel." She grinned up at him. "She'd never have forgiven you if you hadn't turned up."

"Is that so? I'm honoured," he replied lightly.

His eyes ran over the family group and rested on Laurel. She was dressed in sea-green muslin, layers and layers of it spread over the crinoline, the very latest fashion which did away with the bulky petticoats giving an air of lightness and grace. She had taken off her bonnet and the red hair was swept away from her small ears in a high cluster of curls. There could not have been a greater contrast between this elegant young woman and the tousled girl in the travel-stained riding habit with whom he had shared the Italian adventure and never had she looked more beautiful. It seemed to deepen the gulf that he had deliberately attempted to set between them. She swayed towards him and he took her hand and kissed it.

"You look very lovely today."

"Do you think so?"

The words meant nothing but just for a moment they seemed isolated into a world of their own. Then the others had joined them, telling him about Ravensley Boy. Presently they began to move down to the paddock, Jessica clinging to his left arm as he offered his right to Laurel.

Lord and Lady Aylsham were already there with Cherry and Harry Fenton, admiring the magnificent roan horse with his shining silken coat and discussing points with his trainer and jockey. Jethro was swept into the conversation and Laurel was alone for a few minutes. The sun was beating down and she put up the lace-trimmed parasol to shield her eyes from the glare. At the same moment a voice spoke behind her.

"Well, if it isn't my charming new cousin. Miss Laura Rutland, by all that's wonderful."

She swung round to see the young man she had last met on the steps of her grandfather's house. Even out of uniform he had the same rakish elegance and dash. He sketched a little bow.

"George Grafton, at your service. May I ask which of these splendid beasts has the honour of your choice?"

"Ravensley Boy of course."

"Naturally. I should have remembered. You are staying with the Aylshams, I understand. When are you coming to Arlington Street?"

"As soon as I am permitted to do so," she answered coolly.

"It's a bit of a teaser, isn't it? I'm afraid my Mamma does like

59

to rule the roost. She always has done. Poor Papa found that out and died of it."

She frowned at his bantering tone. "Do you live there, Mr Grafton?"

"Good God, no. I have my own quarters." He studied her for an instant. "I remember Uncle Bulwer," he said suddenly. "They used to call him the Bull in the regiment. Did you know that? A great one for the ladies by all accounts. Mamma disapproved so we didn't see much of him, but I remember him taking me on his knee once . . . I was about six, I suppose . . . I pulled his whiskers and he slapped me on the bottom and gave me half a sovereign."

She had an idea that he was making fun of her and yet the tiny picture of her father intrigued her. She said dryly, "How interesting. You must tell me all about it one day."

"I should be only too delighted." He looked towards Jethro. "Who is your tall friend?"

"Jethro Aylsham. He is a surgeon at St. Thomas's Hospital."

"Is he, by Jove, carves people up, does he? Well, it's one way of earning a living, I suppose."

"A very splendid way," she said, riled by the contempt in his voice.

He shrugged his shoulders. "If you say so."

They were interrupted by a vision dressed modishly if flamboyantly in crimson silk trimmed with knots of gold ribbon, a wide straw hat was tied over a profusion of black curls.

"George," she complained, "wherever have you been? We're waiting for you."

"I'm coming, m'dear." A hint of mischief lurked around the full lips. "First, let me present my cousin, Miss Laura Rutland . . . Miss Violet de Vere of the Princess Theatre."

"Pleased to meet you, I'm sure," bold eyes took in Laurel from head to foot before she put a hand possessively on his arm. "Oh do come on, George, for the Lord's sake, we're going to be late for the race."

He ignored her. "Doubtless we shall meet again, Miss Rutland, when dear Great Uncle Joshua snuffs it."

"Don't say that," she said quickly. "It's horrible."

"Always believe in facing up to facts myself," he said impudently and took her hand. Deliberately he peeled back the silk cuff of her glove and kissed the bare wrist. "*Arrivederci* . . . isn't that what they say in Italy?"

"They also say Goodbye and mean it," she said icily.

He laughed and allowed himself to be dragged away by the impatient Violet. Laurel stood looking after him, half attracted, half repelled, and very sure that it would not be the last she would see of him.

Ravensley Boy did not win but he came in third, quite sufficient to arouse interest and make his two lady owners the heroines of their party. Up in the race stand among fashionable sporting society Laurel was enjoying a small triumph of her own. Well-dressed young gentlemen of impeccable ancestry were besieging Lord Aylsham for introductions to the charming Miss Rutland. She had all the glamour of the unknown and slightly mysterious, her beauty and the faintest tinge of a foreign accent adding an intriguingly exotic touch. Jethro watched her from a distance noting that she did not fall into agonies of shyness as Rosemary did or blunder into girlish gaucheries like Jessica, but had a natural poise and self-possession. She was not for him, nor ever could be, for reasons that she did not yet know, but despite his resolution he could not tear his eyes away from her, nor prevent a violent stab of jealousy as he saw her smile and turn from one to the other with an unconscious grace. What havoc would she wreak when she learned how to use the power she had to arouse men's desires? He was not the only one observing her. Robin was also standing apart from the others. There was an anger, a frustration on the boy's face. He was too young to be tormented by such passion and Jethro put a friendly hand on his arm.

"Don't lose your heart to her, old boy. It won't do, you know."

Robin shook him off. "Damn you, don't preach at me."

"Have it your own way, but it's good advice, I assure you."

With a swift change of mood the boy smiled half apologetically. "Sorry, Jet, I'm acting the fool, aren't I? But I've never known anyone quite like her before."

"She'll ride over you without a thought if you're not careful," said Jethro roughly.

"Why should you say that? It's dashed unfair," flared Robin.

"Yes, maybe it is, but I mean it all the same."

Jethro looked at the boy's troubled face for a moment, then pressed his shoulder and walked away. He had a feeling that something had begun already and neither he nor anyone else could stop it. He only prayed that it would not end in tragedy.

*   *   *

61

It had been a thrilling day and Laurel had enjoyed every moment of it, though she was deeply disappointed that Jethro was not returning to St. James's Square with them.

"I've too much to do," he said when she demanded to know the reason why. "I shouldn't be here today except that I don't think Clarissa would have forgiven me if I'd missed seeing Ravensley Boy run in his first Derby. My time is not my own. I'm a worker, you know, not a gentleman of leisure."

He nodded and smiled to the lady in grey who was passing below them. She laughed and waved her racecard to him indicating that she had had a modest win.

"Are you going to spend the evening with *her*?" said Laurel and was immediately ashamed of the spasm of childish jealousy.

"Good heavens, no," he replied a little amused. "What on earth made you say that?"

"I don't know. I thought she looked like a friend of yours."

"She is a friend and a good one. I'm very fond of her," he said quietly. "If you really want to know what I'm doing tonight, I'm speaking at a fund raising event organized by a certain Dr Charles West."

"Oh," she was a little taken aback. "What are the funds intended for?"

"He has bought a house in Great Ormond Street, that's in an unfashionable part of London that you wouldn't know. He is planning to turn it into a hospital and dispensary for sick children, but he desperately needs money. Some of his rich patients have arranged this concert."

She was immediately captivated by the idea. "That's wonderful. Couldn't I do something like that?"

He smiled at her enthusiasm. "Perhaps one day when you've grown up a little. You should speak to Cherry about it. She has set up a mission in Stepney, that's a wretchedly poor part of the city. I go there once a week just to keep an eye on them. There's always risk of an epidemic." They were strolling towards the carriages and they passed George Grafton with his lady friend still clinging to his arm. He smiled and waved his hand to Laurel and she gave him a stiff little bow in return.

Jethro frowned. "I see that Lieutenant Grafton has lost no time in making himself known to you."

"We were right that day. He *is* my cousin."

"I should beware of him if I were you. He has quite a reputation."

"How do you know?"

"I took pains to find out."

"What is wrong with him?"

"Do I need to spell it out? Fast living, too much gambling . . ."

"And too many lady friends. I'm not stupid, Jethro. I do know about men. He introduced her to me."

"Damn his impudence! He had no right to do such a thing . . . a woman of that class!"

"I didn't mind so why should you?" She looked up at him sensing his disapproval and perversely irritated by it. "I want to go and see Grandfather before we go back to Ravensley."

He hesitated before he said, "I wouldn't advise it, not unless you want the door shut in your face."

"That's what he hinted at. Why, Jethro, why? I *am* his granddaughter. I have every right to see him."

"That's true enough, but there are other considerations." He paused a moment finding it difficult to explain. "Mrs Grafton, as you know, is the daughter of Sir Joshua's brother. Her elder son, Barton, is in charge of the family tea business. It is very extensive and very prosperous. They never approved of Captain Rutland's affection for your mother. Then again, you have grown up in Italy apart from them all. If you visit him now when he is so sick, then they might accuse you of exerting undue influence over him in his weakened state when the time comes . . ."

"When he dies, that's what you mean, isn't it?" she said bluntly. "They think he might leave me some of his money. I don't want any of it. He has been generous enough already, but I'm fond of him, I want to be with him."

Soon, he thought, she would have to know the truth about her birth, that dark tangle that still haunted him. He must speak to Clarissa about it. It would come better from her.

"Be patient, Laurel," he said gently. "I'm acquainted with his doctor and so I have seen him. It pleases him very much to know you happy and well cared for. Leave it like that for the time being."

"I suppose I must. It's good of you to take so much trouble for me."

"It does concern your future."

She looked up at him. "And that matters to you?"

"Of course it does. You should know that by now."

"I don't know it," she said impatiently. "You never come to Ravensley."

He smiled. "A doctor is not a free agent. I can't walk out on my patients however much I would like to do so."

"Couldn't you come sometimes?"

"Maybe." He took her hand and pressed it. "In the summer it is easier. Not so many people fall ill. And now you must go with the others. They're waiting for you."

And with that half promise she had to be content, but it left her restless and dissatisfied. The family stayed on in town for a few weeks, making a round of visits and taking her to see the Tower of London, Buckingham Palace and Westminster Abbey. They passed the Queen driving in an open carriage in Hyde Park with the Princess Royal in white muslin and one of the yellow-haired Princes in a sailor suit. She waved her hand graciously to Clarissa. Another day they caught a glimpse of the heir to the throne riding beside his father in Rotten Row.

"His name is Edward but they call him Bertie," said Jessica importantly. "Rosemary told me. She was presented at one of the Queen's garden parties. Next year it will be my turn."

But the Aylshams were essentially country people. They did not care for the summer heat and dust in the London streets, so at the end of July they went back to Ravensley.

5

It was fully light by now. The late October sun slanting across the fen dazzled her eyes, but the wind had a sharp bite to it. Laurel sitting in the middle of the boat pulled the thick cloak closely around her.

"Cold?" asked Robin.

"No, not really."

"Enjoying it?"

"Oh yes, tremendously."

She smiled up at him and Robin gave a mighty thrust to the pole showing off his lithe muscular strength and the punt shot forward.

"Hey, look out! You nearly had us in the bank that time. We'd look dashed silly stuck in the mud!" exclaimed Tom leaning over dangerously to fend off the thick clump of reeds and matted sedge. The dogs, dripping wet, sat bolt upright in the prow, their golden eyes alert for every stir of bird or animal.

Laurel had persuaded the boys to take her with them on one of their early morning expeditions out on the fen. It was not the first time that Robin had knocked at her door when it was barely light and she had crept down the stairs with him past the astonished servants, running across the dew-wet lawns to where Tom waited with the punt. It was not the shooting she enjoyed. In fact she always carefully averted her eyes from the dead birds tossed into the boat, hating to see the glazed eyes, the blood on the dulled plumage. It was the feeling of adventure, the sense of freedom, the strange enchantment that thrilled through her when the punt went gliding up the waterways where the bulrushes stood up stiff as pokers and autumn turned the reed beds to deep gold and purple red.

She sat up suddenly. Beyond the thin line of willows she could just see the outline of an old house set back from an overgrown garden.

"What place is that?" she asked curiously.

"It's Westley Manor." Robin exchanged a quick look with Tom. "It used to belong to your grandfather, still does, I suppose."

"Does anyone live there?"

"He let it for a time, now there is only a housekeeper."

"It could be beautiful," she said slowly.

"You'd need to spend a fortune on it first," said Tom flatly as the punt shot forward again.

The long summer days had passed peacefully at Ravensley with all the quiet country pleasures, garden parties, picnics, playing croquet when it was fine, needlework or reading on wet afternoons, visits to neighbours and being visited, a trip to Cambridge and the fun of a students' ball. Laurel had joined in all these simple events becoming more and more restless. She was not sure what she wanted, only that she seemed to be marking time. She needed a deeper interest, she longed to spread her wings and fly away, but where and in what direction she did not know.

They were late for breakfast and after the boat was moored, they ran hand in hand towards the house, Tom carrying the game bag slung over his shoulder and the dogs racing ahead of them. As they came to the stableyard they saw Rosemary talking to Seth Starling. There was nothing particularly unusual in that. She was a timid rider and her father had forbidden her to ride out alone, only there was something in the way they stood close together, something in the unguarded look on Rosemary's face that vaguely alarmed Laurel. In Prince Falcone's household there had been a deep unbridgeable gulf between servants and master. The more relaxed and casual atmosphere at Ravensley sometimes bewildered her.

She thought Robin had seen it too. He said, "Have you breakfasted already, Sis?"

"Not yet."

"Come on then, come and eat with us." He put an arm around his sister's shoulders and she went with him a little reluctantly.

Clarissa saw them come into the morning room together and frowned. She did not approve of Laurel's early morning expeditions, but the girl was not her daughter and she could hardly forbid anything so harmless without giving it too much importance.

"You're only just in time," she said getting up and putting

66

down her napkin. "Ring if you want fresh coffee. I'm just going up to Jessica."

"What's wrong with Jess?" enquired Tom inspecting the row of silver dishes on the sideboard.

"She has a sore throat," said Margaret, who had come up early from Copthorne with a message from her mother and stayed to breakfast.

"Poor old girl! She'll miss the hunt ball. That will make her hopping mad. Anyone want kidneys before I take the last two?"

"I don't know how you can bear to go out shooting with the boys," said Margaret as Laurel took the chair opposite her. "I think it's horrible."

"You don't say it's horrible when you eat roast duck," said her brother flippantly.

"That's different."

"Laurel is going to be a good shot one of these days," remarked Robin carelessly putting down his heaped plate and sitting beside her.

"You actually let *her* handle your precious gun!" Spite edged Margaret's voice.

"Why not? She got a snipe today . . . first attempt too."

"Beginner's luck, I suppose." Margaret got up pushing in her chair and stalking out of the room.

Robin looked after her frowning. "What on earth is the matter with her?"

"Touch of the old green-eyed monster," said Tom with his mouth full.

"What the devil do you mean by that?"

"Well, you never asked her to go duck shooting with you, did you, old boy?"

"She wouldn't have come if I had."

"Don't you believe it!"

Tom poured himself coffee and Laurel attacked her breakfast saying nothing. She was fully aware now that Margaret was bitterly jealous of Robin's interest in her. Well, that was not her fault. She liked him just as she liked Tom, but she did not particularly encourage him. Privately she thought Margaret acted stupidly. If she had wanted a man as badly as Margaret seemed to want Robin, then she would have fought for him tooth and nail. She shrugged her shoulders and went on eating.

After breakfast she went upstairs picking up the wet cloak she had dropped in the hall. It was the same mulberry coloured

67

velvet lined with fur that Jethro had bought for her in Paris. She held it for a moment against her face wondering when she would see him again. He had kept his promise and come down occasionally during the summer taking part in their country pleasures. On her way along the landing she paused in front of Great Uncle Justin's portrait. A ray of light from the window at the end lit the sardonic features to sudden malevolent life and she shivered remembering the day when Jethro had taken the boat and they had rowed far out into Greatheart Fen. It had been burningly hot, the air still and heavy with the overpowering scent of the meadowsweet. He rarely talked about himself, but as they glided under the shadow of one of the great black mills that still towered up like giants across the landscape, he had said abruptly, "That's where my father fell to his death."

"Was it an accident?"

"Not entirely. It was during the floods . . . there was a man hiding out on the marshes who had sworn to be revenged upon him . . ."

"Why?"

"I never knew exactly. It was something he had done many years before and at last it caught up with him. They fought up there on the catwalk and they drowned together locked in a strangling embrace."

She looked up at the gaunt sails hardly moving in the breathless air and shivered.

"It must have been terrible for you."

"In one way it was and in another it was a relief," he went on broodingly, "he was a hard man to love. He demanded instant obedience, whip in hand, and there was no mercy for anyone who crossed him. Later I knew he had done things no man could forgive."

She thought of the haunting face in the portrait that sometimes reminded her so vividly of the man facing her. "What kind of things?"

He did not answer directly. "There has always been a dark strain in the Aylshams. There's a legend that it began a thousand years ago when Torkil the Dane married a black-haired Iceni Princess and she made him suffer horribly for what he and his comrades had done to her people."

"Do you mean that they are mad?"

"Not mad, obsessed and utterly ruthless towards anyone who stands in their way."

68

"Are you like that?"

"Perhaps I'm halfway between the two." He smiled. "We've had enough of this gloomy talk. None of it need trouble a child like you."

"I'm not a child."

"No, of course you're not, you're a grown-up young lady," he said teasingly as the boat glided from shadow into sunlight. "I keep forgetting, don't I?"

He gave her the same casual affection he gave to Rosemary and Jessica and yet sometimes she surprised a look in his eyes and knew with an intuition older than her years that it was not at all the same, that something far stronger than casual affection lay between them, all the deeper for not being expressed.

She sighed at the memory and then went on along the landing and into Jessica's room. She found her sitting up in bed, looking very flushed. The large grey cat had curled itself up on the coverlet beside her.

"I would develop a cold," she croaked, "when it's my first hunt ball. Of all the beastly things to happen!"

"Never mind," said Laurel cheerfully. "Rosemary and I will tell you all about it."

"It's not the same as being there," she moaned. "You'd better not come too close or else you'll get a bad throat too."

"No, I won't. I never catch anything." She tickled the cat's ears and it yawned showing a wide pink mouth. "Will Jet be there?"

"Probably. He's never missed before. Oh go away," she wailed. "I can't even bear to talk about it."

The hunt was to meet at Sir Hugh Berkeley's house only five miles or so from Ravensley. The horses were sent over to Barkham the day before and the family set out early in the morning packed into the carriages. It was an exclusive gathering of friends and neighbours. Hugh Berkeley maintained his own pack of hounds and was a great sportsman. Everyone in the county knew that he had once been passionately in love with Tom's mother and when she turned him down in favour of Harry Fenton had remained a wealthy and extremely eligible bachelor. He was a very thin man with a look of frailty but it did not prevent him hunting all the winter. He greeted Laurel kindly. She looked around her eagerly. It was a splendid spectacle, the men in their 'hunting' pink, the magnificent horses circling around the courtyard in front of the manor house, the

69

hunt servants moving among them in neat green livery carrying trays of silver cups filled with hot spiced wine.

There were not a great many ladies and most of them were middle-aged. Laurel and Rosemary were the youngest there. It could be rough riding and Lord Aylsham had given Seth strict instructions to keep an eye on the young ladies when the field got away, not that he had much anxiety on Laurel's behalf, she had already proved herself a fearless rider. It was her first real hunt and everything about it excited her, the talk, the laughter, the smell of horses and leather harness, the cool whip of the breeze on her face. A great many eyes were turned to her conspicuous in her red and black riding habit. Gadabout was as excited as his young mistress, tossing his head, eager to be off and away. He fidgeted, dancing around in a circle until she bent down and whispered into his ear, bringing him under control.

"What is the magic you use?"

She looked up to see Jethro smiling down at her and it seemed then that her happiness was complete.

"No magic, only love," she murmured.

"Perhaps that is the greatest magic of all."

One of the servants offered her the silver stirrup cup. She took it and sipped, then held it up to Jethro.

"To a good day."

"To a very good day."

His eyes held hers as he took it and drank before handing it back to the servant and she knew with a queer inward thrill that this indeed was going to be a day like no other.

Then they were off streaming down the drive and out of the park gates. As she turned Gadabout she caught a glimpse of Margaret standing on the steps, the small pointed face staring after them. Her mother had thought her too young to ride with the others and as she watched Laurel's slim upright figure between Robin and Jethro, she dug her nails fiercely into the palms of her hands glad of the physical pain. When they had all gone, she called one of the dogs and went walking into the park woodland intent on a plan of her own.

It was a marvellous day. There had been a slight frost overnight. The trees were tipped with silver and the sun turned the spiders' webs into spangled networks of diamond spread across the hedgerows. It was glorious to feel Gadabout's lengthening stride, to gallop across the fields with the keen cut of a strong wind on her cheeks. The morning was filled with short bursts across open ground, checks at ditches and stiles and then on once more, the riders scattering and then coming together again. She knew that Robin and Jethro were competing with one another to keep pace with her and enjoyed the sensation of power it gave her.

It was much later when they came up to the high ragged brushwood that ran along beside a drainage ditch.

"Don't attempt it. Better take the gate," yelled Jethro.

Laurel shook her head. She had already seen and judged it. "Gadabout can do it easily," she called back over her shoulder.

Robin following close behind felt an instant of doubt. Most of the riders had turned to the gap jostling one another through the opened gate but he could not endure that Laurel should think less of him than of Jethro. Effortlessly Gadabout cleared the barrier and Jethro followed. Their laughter floated back to him as they galloped on and up the rising field. Robin swore under his breath and brought down the whip on the Baron's neck. The horse made a gallant effort but one leg trailed and was caught in the hidden strand of wire. Robin sailed over his head and fell heavily, fortunately rolling free of the threshing hooves. Seth bringing up the rear, one eye watching over Rosemary, saw what had happened and pulled up.

"Go on," he shouted, "I'll take care of Mr. Robin."

Rosemary wanted to stop but her excited horse ran away with her. It was a few minutes before she could bring him under control and come back. One or two other riders had stopped and were gathered about Robin.

Jethro and Laurel already far ahead had seen nothing of the accident. The hounds lost the scent and then found it again. Once Laurel caught a glimpse of the fox, a lithe red brown streak, tongue lolling, running swiftly and desperately. They found him sometime in the early afternoon after what everyone agreed had been a long and splendid chase. The hounds were going crazy, baying and circling around, the huntsman fighting them off until he could secure the brush. Sir Hugh took it from him, dipped a finger in the blood, marking Laurel's cheek with it before handing her the trophy. The savagery of the hounds, the rank smell of blood and fox were forgotten for the moment. She was flushed with excitement and triumph. Jethro leaned forward and fastened the brush to her tight-fitting jacket.

The sun was a great red ball sinking slowly behind the black frieze of trees on the skyline when she rode slowly back beside Jethro. Riders were scattered, tired now and walking their

71

sweat-darkened horses. It was strange, thought Laurel, all day they had scarcely spoken to one another and yet she was conscious of being closer to him than she had ever been. They were on the edge of a little copse only a few miles from Barkham when she felt Gadabout falter.

"I think he is limping," she said.

"Are you sure?"

"I can feel it. It's his left hind leg, I think." She pulled up and slid from the saddle. "Do you think he strained it when he jumped?"

"It could be a stone in the hoof. I'll take a look." Jethro dismounted. "Hold the bridles."

She waited anxiously as he lifted the foot and examined it. "That's all it is. A large stone lodged under the shoe. I think I can shift it." He brought out a pocket knife with a vicious steel probe. "You'd be surprised what I can do with this."

She soothed and petted the horse, whispering lovingly to him while Jethro patiently explored and dug. Then he straightened up. "There it is. A sharp flint. That's better, old boy, isn't it?" He patted the horse on the rump. The sun had almost gone by now and shadows began to lengthen among the trees. "It's growing cold," he went on. "We must get back or you'll be too tired to dance tonight."

He turned to lift her back again into the saddle. For months now he had tried to put her out of his mind and failed dismally. Despite all his resolution her face had come persistently between him and his work, tormenting and maddening. Without any warning it suddenly overwhelmed him. He crushed her against him, his mouth seeking hers and warming into an intensity that after the first shock enthralled her. He felt her response and yielded to it. Breathlessly time stood still but not for long. A furious anger directed against his own weakness surged through him. He drew back pushing aside the strands of silky hair and looking deep into her eyes.

"Jethro," she breathed and swayed towards him again, "Oh Jet darling!"

"Oh my God, don't say that . . . you must never say that."

Almost roughly he seized hold of her and lifted her into the saddle. Then he turned to his own horse, going before her through the little wood while she followed, bewildered by his manner and yet at the same time wonderfully, ecstatically happy.

When they reached Barkham most of the other house guests had already returned and were standing in the hall, drinking tea or brandy and water, talking over the day's run. Laurel ran up the stairs to the room she shared with the other girls where they could wash and change for the ball. When she opened the door, she saw that Lady Aylsham was there with Rosemary and Margaret. There was a silence as they turned to look at her and immediately she felt the tension.

"What is it? What has happened?"

"Robin was thrown," said Clarissa quietly. "Didn't you see it?"

"No . . ."

"Of course she didn't," interrupted Margaret. "She rode on. Robin could have killed himself for all she cared."

"That's not fair," said Rosemary hotly. "I was there. I saw what happened. Laurel and Jethro were a long way ahead. They couldn't have known."

"You always find excuses for her . . ."

"Be quiet, both of you," said Clarissa sharply.

"Is Robin badly hurt?" whispered Laurel.

"Not as much as we feared at first. He has a badly dislocated shoulder and some very painful bruises with a couple of cracked ribs."

"And the horse?"

"It broke its leg. It had to be destroyed."

"Oh, no, no . . ." Suddenly it seemed as if all the happiness of the day had been spoiled by a stupid unnecessary accident. The words spilled out of her. "Why did Robin take the jump? Why didn't he go round? Nearly everyone else did."

"Surely you know why," said Margaret pointedly.

Clarissa said, "The doctor has been here but Robin is still in great pain. I'd like Jethro to take a look at him. Did he come back with you?"

"Yes, he did."

"Good. I'll find him. Margaret, you had better come with me." She went out and the girl went with her passing Laurel without another look.

"I should have known. I should have stopped him." Laurel dropped wearily on to the bed.

"How could you?" said Rosemary reasonably. "Robin would have hated that and anyway Seth and I were there. He was wonderful. He knew exactly what to do."

"Why does Margaret hate me so much?"

"Don't take any notice," said Rosemary uncomfortably, putting a hand on Laurel's shoulder. "She saw Robin carried in and thought he'd been killed. She was dreadfully upset."

"Poor Robin."

"It was almost worse for the Baron. Seth had to shoot him. It was horrible."

Laurel began to unbutton her jacket. The plume of reddish brown fur tipped with black still hung from where Jethro had fastened it.

Rosemary looked at it enviously. "I see that Sir Hugh awarded you the brush."

"Yes." She touched it for a moment but all the elation and thrill seemed to have drained away.

Her depression lasted while she washed and dressed and when at last they were ready, she asked Rosemary to which room Robin had been taken and went along the passage to see him. She met Jethro coming out of the door.

"How is he?" she whispered.

"He'll survive."

"May I see him?"

"Don't stay too long. The doctor has given him a strong sedative."

Robin was propped up with pillows and looked very white and young, but he managed a smile as she came in.

"I made a complete ass of myself, didn't I?" he said ruefully. "And to make matters worse Father is furious with me because the horse had to be shot."

She came to the side of the bed. "Poor Robin, it was beastly for you."

"It was my own damned fault as Jethro pointed out just now."

"That was unkind of him. Anyone can make an error of judgment." She touched the bandages gently. "Is it very painful?"

"It was ghastly when they set my shoulder. It's not quite so bad now." He lifted his other hand and put it on hers. "You look so lovely. I'm cursing myself because all the other chaps will be dancing with you while I'm lying helpless up here."

"Never mind. There will be other balls." She saw that his eyes were already heavy with the drug. Impulsively she bent and gave him a light kiss on the forehead. "I'll be thinking of

74

you," she whispered and then was gone quickly before he could say anything of what was in his heart.

Jethro saw her come into the ballroom arm in arm with Rosemary. Her gown of ivory satin was very simple and she wore no jewels but her shapely head and shoulders rose proudly out of the foam of fine lace and there were white roses in the dark red hair. It reminded him of Rome and the first time he had seen her . . . Francesca da Rimini, the lovely and the doomed . . . and he damned himself to hell for falling head over heels in love with a chit of a girl who in all probability was as heartless as her worthless mother had been and who already had that silly young fool Robin dancing on the end of a string. If he had had any sense, he told himself, he would have gone at once after they came back from the hunt, ridden into Ely and taken the train back to the safe refuge of St. Thomas's Hospital. Most people thought him reserved, a proud cold man not given to talking about himself. They never suspected the depth of passion that burned within him, showing itself in the devotion to his work and his quixotic support of certain causes about which he felt strongly and tonight he was in a wild reckless mood. He threw caution to the winds for once and went forward to greet and claim her for his own.

The ball began quietly and turned into a gay rollicking affair. The Lancers, the Quadrille, sedate set dances made up of four couples, were abandoned for the Galop and Sir Roger de Coverley. Laurel danced them all in turn with Jethro, floating dreamily to the strains of a Strauss waltz, laughing through the intricacies of the Mazurka and whirling around, skirts flying, in the Polka.

To dance more than twice with the same partner was certain to arouse comment, but she never thought of it. She let her satin sandals be trampled upon by boisterous young men, always coming back to the sheer delight of Jethro's arms. They did not say a great deal to one another and yet every word seemed to hold a special significance. She did not notice Clarissa's frown or hear Oliver say curtly to his brother, "I hope to God you know what you are doing, Jet."

"What *am* I doing? Enjoying myself, that's all. It's only once a year."

"Don't break that child's heart."

"Who's talking of heartbreak?" he answered flippantly. "What nonsense you do talk, Oliver."

It was after two o'clock in the morning when they piled into the two carriages and were driven back to Ravensley, Jethro staying behind to keep a watchful eye on Robin before he returned to London.

He said goodnight taking Laurel's hands in his and kissing first one and then the other. All the evening she had waited for him to say "I love you", and was aware of a faint disappointment because he had not done so, but nothing could still the song in her heart.

It was a long time before she slept, still galloping across the fields with Gadabout, still dancing rapturously in Jethro's arms. She shivered with ecstasy remembering his kisses and thought how odd it was that she saw Robin so often and felt nothing, yet the merest touch of Jethro's hand awoke an instant response. She wondered daringly what it would be like to have him stretched beside her, those strong doctor's hands caressing her body, and then blushed, burying her face in the pillow half ashamed of her own thoughts and yet secretly rejoicing in them.

Some time in the dawn she imagined she heard her door open and then close again very gently. Heavy with sleep she sighed and could not be sure whether it was dream or reality. When she woke again it was broad daylight. She struggled up to look at the clock beside her bed. It was eleven already. No doubt everyone had been allowed to sleep late after the ball.

She climbed out of bed and went to draw the curtains. The fine weather had continued and a thin sunlight glinted on a lightly frosted world. She yawned as she turned to the dressing table and then stood still shocked at what she saw. Someone had put a dead bird in front of the mirror, a robin pinned through the breast with a steel skewer, one drop of blood had fallen and congealed on the white lace mat. Stupidly all she could think of was the old nursery rhyme –

"Who killed Cock Robin?"
" 'I,' " said the sparrow,
" 'With my bow and arrow,
I killed Cock Robin.' "

Then she pulled herself together. She remembered the opening and shutting of the door . . . someone must have put the bird there during the night, but who and why? A touch of malice, a jealous spite . . . Margaret, it had to be Margaret. She was suddenly bitterly angry. What had she ever done to deserve treatment like this? She splashed cold water into the wash

76

basin, bathing her face and then washing and dressing as quickly as possible. For some reason she could not bear to touch the bird. She took a clean handkerchief from her drawer, threw it over the robin, then picked it up and went out. On her way downstairs to the morning room, she had to pass what used to be the old schoolroom which had now been refurnished as a sitting room for the two girls. The door was half open. She caught the sound of her own name and paused.

"Laurel ought to be told."

"Told what?"

"You know as well as I do."

"I don't think we should." That was Rosemary, gentle, placating. "Mamma wouldn't like it. Besides we don't know the whole story."

"I do. They have tried to hush it up and tell us nothing, but I wormed it out of Patty Starling, all of it." Margaret's voice rose, shrilly triumphant. "After the way she behaved last night, Laurel ought to know."

She had listened long enough. She pushed the door further open.

"What ought I to know?"

Three pairs of eyes turned to look at her. Jessica still rather wan was in the armchair by the fire, Rosemary standing behind her. Margaret was in the middle of the room, one hand on the table. For a moment no one said anything, then Laurel came inside and shut the door behind her.

"Before you tell me what I ought to know, which one of you put this on my dressing table?"

She placed the handkerchief on the table and the dead bird rolled out of it almost touching Margaret's hand. She started back with an exclamation. Rosemary stared at it in horror, but Jessica got up and crossed to the table touching the robin curiously with one finger.

"I think it was probably Ram Lall."

"That poor old Indian . . . why should he do such a thing?"

"He adores Robin. Haven't you noticed? He follows him around sometimes just like one of the dogs," went on Jessica. "He might have thought . . ."

"That I wanted to harm him, but that's ridiculous," exclaimed Laurel.

"Well, he's not quite right in the head."

"But I've always been so fond of Robin."

77

"Have you? No one would have thought so last night from the way you and Jethro were carrying on," said Margaret.

"What did you expect me to do? Sit and cry over it all the evening. That's the last thing Robin would have wished."

"You're just like your mother. You don't care what happens to anybody so long as you get what *you* want."

"What do you know about my mother?"

"A very great deal . . . far more than you do."

"Margaret! Stop!" interrupted Rosemary.

"No, I won't stop. Why should I? She ought to know about herself, queening over all of us with her fine clothes and her airs and graces. You're a bastard, that's what you are . . . a bastard. Your mother was not married to Captain Rutland."

"She was, she was," whispered Laurel. "Grandfather told me. My father died before I was born, but I know all about him."

"Do you? Do you really know?" said Margaret. "He was a cad, a cheap vulgar bully . . . not even a gentleman."

"It's not true," said Laurel fiercely, but nothing now could stop Margaret. The words came tumbling out, low, vicious, filled with venom.

"Oh yes it is. Your mother was married to Justin Aylsham, to our great uncle, but that didn't prevent her from becoming Bulwer Rutland's mistress – and he wasn't her only lover – everyone around here knew about her and what she did – perhaps he wasn't your father at all, perhaps it was one of the servants, the footman or the stableman or a tinker out in the fields – "

"Stop it!" raged Laurel. "Stop it! I won't listen to your lies," and driven beyond herself she slapped Margaret hard across the face.

The girl did not attempt to retaliate. She stood there panting, the mark of Laurel's fingers scarlet across her pale cheek. In the momentary silence a log in the grate fell with a crash and a shower of sparks. Then Margaret went on in a curiously cool and controlled voice for so young a girl.

"Your mother was engaged to Uncle Oliver and she jilted him when Justin Aylsham came back from India and robbed him of his inheritance. She married Justin for his money and his title." She leaned forward whispering the words into Laurel's face with the hiss of a serpent. "Do you know what that meant? *In marrying him, she was married to her own father.*"

78

Laurel stared at her. "You're mad, you must be mad," she breathed. She looked desperately at Rosemary and Jessica. "Tell her she's mad. Why don't you tell her?" But the two girls did not move and Margaret drove on relentlessly.

"Oh no, I'm not mad. Ask Uncle Oliver if you don't believe me, ask Aunt Clarissa why she dislikes you so much. Justin Aylsham's crimes drove him into exile in India but the girl from Westley Manor, whose brother he had murdered and whose life he had ruined, drowned herself, only her baby didn't die . . . the baby who was plucked out of the fens and brought to Ravensley was your mother and his daughter."

Laurel could not move. Her mother, her beautiful mother, guilty of this monstrous thing – she said in a stifled voice, "Did she know?"

"Who can tell?" went on Margaret cruelly. "It was not until after her betrayal had driven him to madness and death that the scandal broke. Uncle Oliver tried to prevent it but everyone knew. They hurled stones at her when she came from church. That was why your grandfather took her away to Italy, that was why she could never come back to England, that's why you should never have come because you're part of her wickedness . . ."

Laurel felt a sickness rising in her throat. She could not speak. She saw it all now. Justin Aylsham, that bitter moody man who had gone away to India callously abandoning the girl he had seduced. He had stolen his brother's wife who had given him Jethro. Then when that brother died, he had come back to England failing to recognise his own daughter in the beautiful girl he so much desired. She shivered. Was it the strange perverse relationship that had driven her mother into Bulwer Rutland's arms? She knew it was true . . . things no man could forgive . . . that's what Jethro had once said of his father. Jessica looked white and shocked. Rosemary had turned away her face.

"So you see how it is, don't you?" continued Margaret with a silky nauseating sweetness. "Your mother's husband was also her father just as he was Jethro's father and that makes them brother and sister. It's funny really," and she began to laugh, a queer triumphant little giggle as if she found it exquisitely amusing. "Isn't it ridiculous? Jethro is your uncle, just as he is mine or Rosemary's or Robin's."

Laurel had a feeling of suffocation as if she were floundering in a bog and could not free herself from the foul clinging mud.

79

The blows had come so fast and so relentlessly that she had scarcely been able to take them in, but this last was so unbearable, so utterly unthinkable, that she could not face them any longer. She turned and ran out of the room, her mind in a turmoil, only certain that she must go away somewhere, anywhere so long as it was far from Ravensley.

She heard Rosemary call after her, but she took no heed. She brushed past Ram Lall and went down the stairs. She did not see him come stumbling after her. No one was in the hall when she crossed it. Out on the terrace Sohrab asleep on the flagstones opened one eye as she ran past. One of the gardeners straightened up to stare after her, then shrugged his shoulders and returned to his weeding. Laurel ran on making for the fens, the wide lovely fens that had been the refuge of haunted unhappy creatures since time began. There she could be alone. There she might be able to grasp the unbelievable and come to terms with it.

6

In the very centre of Greatheart Fen stood Spinney Mill, no longer used now that the steam engine had been installed churning out the waters so much more reliably than the fickle wind. The great black sails creaked as Laurel looked up at them and the sluggish stream below was covered with thick green scum. She had been running and walking for what seemed like hours, sometimes following the dry ridge paths, sometimes splashing heedlessly through shallow pools scarcely looking to right or left so that now she could not even remember how she had arrived there. Her kid boots were soaked through and the hem of her gown was clogged with mud. But however far you run, you cannot escape your thoughts and now she stood still, breathless and exhausted, and leaning her head back against the old timbered door of the mill, accepted the bitter truth.

The fantasy that had grown up around her childhood, the fragile framework of lies and truth built by her grandfather had collapsed like a house of cards. Her father was a scoundrel and her mother a whore . . . she was illegitimate, a bastard, that was bad enough but maybe she could somehow learn to live with it, only there was something worse, far worse, dripping like poisoned honey from Margaret's lips. She heard it over and over again . . . Jethro is your kin, your mother's young brother, your own uncle . . . and Margaret had laughed, mocking derisive laughter because Laurel had shown so plainly, so proudly, that she was in love with him. The words beat into her brain and with them came another word, a word with a fearful impact . . . incest . . . forbidden by Church and State. She had heard it once whispered in Italy, a shame to be hidden and never mentioned, and everything in her rose in rebellion against it. It wasn't true, it couldn't be true, she would ignore it, defy it. In that moment she grew from child to woman fighting for a love that had come unawares but taken possession of her. She hit her fist against the rough wall in angry revolt at the injustice of it because now she realized why Jethro had held back. It explained so many things, his withdrawal from her in Italy, the driven look on his face when he had kissed her yesterday afternoon, the bittersweet enchantment of the ball. Why had he not told her, why, why?

A gust of cold wind came sweeping across the marshes and the sails swayed and groaned above her head. There was a stealthy movement among the tall reeds and she suddenly had a queer sensation of being watched. She looked quickly around her but there was nothing, only one sparse tree darkly outlined against the sky and the whir of a bird flying low, a sparrowhawk perhaps hovering and then stooping swiftly to his prey. On an impulse she began to climb the steep steps inside the mill that led to the catwalk running around the outside. When she emerged through the gap at the top and stepped out on to the narrow ledge, the wind caught at her, blowing her hair into long strands that whipped stingingly across her face. She moved along it, clinging to the rail and staring over the flat empty lands towards the sea. Here and there skeins of mist drifted like white smoke in the frosty air. She felt very alone, all the happiness and serenity she had found at Ravensley smashed and broken. Why had Jethro brought her there? It had all been a lie. They had played their parts and hated her in their hearts, but she was still herself. They could not destroy the essential Laurel. Something strong and self-reliant rose up in her. She lifted her head proudly. She would go to London, go back to her sick grandfather, build her life around him. She would brave Alice Grafton and her sons. She had a right to be at Sir Joshua's side and would yield it to no one. She turned to go back and it was then that she saw Ram Lall, the white cotton garments he wore fluttering in the wind, the black eyes burning in the dark face, thin lips curled back in a snarl.

"He's mad," she thought, "and he hates me!" It was only then that she remembered what Jethro had told her. This was the place from which his father had fallen to his death hunted by a man who had nursed a long dream of revenge. Terror seized her. She was trapped and there was no way down. She could not push past him on the narrow catwalk. She trembled, not knowing what to do. He made a queer choking sound and she braced herself taking a step towards him, trying to speak quietly, soothingly, as she did to a nervous horse.

"What are you doing up here, Ram Lall? It's very cold and

it's dangerous. Don't you realize you might fall? Shall we go down together?"

He shook his head and took a step towards her, one hand outstretched. She backed away from him and they moved around the catwalk, step by slow step, the black eyes fixed on her like a snake paralysing its victim. They reached the gap into the mill where the remnants of the original door flapped in the wind. She made a movement to duck inside and he caught hold of her. The sticklike arms had a surprising power. She fought back, fear lending her strength. The hands crept up, she felt him clawing at her throat, he was going to strangle her and in desperation she pushed hard against him. On the narrow ledge the night's frost had melted into a slimy coating. His feet slipped. He fell backwards and with a rending groan the thin iron rail tore from its rusted bracket. The Indian gave a bird-like scream and went over, striking his head as he hurled down into the water. With a supreme effort she stopped herself from going over with him, clinging to the broken rail, shaking and sick with horror.

Moggy gliding up the stream in the punt saw the dark figure falling through the air, heard the splash as he hit the water, and for an instant believed he saw a ghost. Then the man crouched behind him in the boat shouted something and the mist cleared from his eyes.

"By the good Lord, there be a maid up there! D'ye see, Moggy?"

"Aye, I see right enough. You go after that poor devil, Nampy, I'll get the girl."

Moggy swung himself off the punt as it moved forward and began to clamber up the winding steps.

"I'm comin'," he called to her. "I'm comin'. Don't 'ee be afraid, Missy."

Laurel still clinging helplessly to the swaying rail saw the tall thin figure come through the gap and collapsed against him. The strong arms held her close, her face pressed against the sealskin jerkin, the rank smell of fish and sweat strangely comforting. He stroked her hair with one rough hand as he might have gentled a terrified dog.

"There, there, don't 'ee fret now. You're safe now, Missy, ye're all right."

"Ram Lall . . . he fell . . . he'll drown . . ." the words tumbled out incoherently.

"Nampy'll be lookin' after him. He'll have him out in no time. Now you come along o' me. Easy, does it. That's right."

He guided her down the steps still holding her firmly in case she stumbled and by the time they reached the bottom, Nampy had brought the punt around again. He shook his head and Moggy glanced at him. Something lay still in the bottom of the punt covered with a piece of old sacking.

Still shocked and shivering with cold and reaction, Laurel let Moggy help her into the boat. A brown mongrel dog came to inspect and pushed a tousled head against her hand. The two men muttered together with a glance at Laurel and then the punt glided forward again. In a few minutes it drew up beside a kind of island with a hut that was like nothing she had ever seen before. Thatched with dark brown reeds it seemed to be part of the bog and sedge from which it sprang.

Moggy bent over her lifting her to her feet. "You're near froze, Missy. I'll get something warm into you and then I'll tek you home." He put his arms around her and she stepped off the boat too numbed by what had happened to argue. He waved his hand to Nampy who nodded and the boat shot forward once again.

Laurel clutched at Moggy's arm. "The Indian . . . is he? Is he dead?"

"Aye, he is that."

"I didn't mean to push him . . ." she said pitifully. "It was horrible . . . I thought . . ." she put a hand to her bruised throat.

"It were an accident. He hit his head as he fell, see. Nampy'll tell 'em. Don't 'ee worry too much now."

Still dazed she let him take her inside the hut. It smelled mustily of smoke and food and animals. It was crowded with roughly fashioned furniture and hung with nets and fishing gear of every kind. Eel baskets were piled in one corner beside a sedge cutter and a stack of neatly cut peat. A tattered curtain half hid the bed and a goldfinch in a little cage of reeds twittered musically from the ceiling. Moggy pulled a stool towards the fire for her and then poked at the smouldering peat until it glowed. He pushed a blackened kettle deep into the red heart. A welcome warmth began to creep through her. He knelt down in front of her pulling off the sodden boots and chafing her frozen feet between his big hands. Then he draped an old blanket around her shoulders. Presently the kettle began to sing and he poured the water into the old brown pot. The mug of tea he

84

handed to her was a deep mahogany colour and thick with sugar but she drank it gratefully. A little colour came back into her face and gradually she stopped shivering.

"That's more like," said Moggy. "You sit there now and keep warm. Nampy'll be back with the boat in two shakes and then I'll tek you home before the mist comes up. They'll be worryin' where you be, I shouldn't wonder."

"Yes, I suppose so."

The warmth and the fatigue were making her drowsy. Here in this stuffy smoky hut she could forget what had happened and what still had to be faced. The dog lay close beside her and she could hear Moggy moving about outside. In some odd way it eased her loneliness. She was almost dozing when he came back into the hut.

"Nampy's back, Missy. I think we'd better go."

"Yes of course." Reluctantly she got to her feet. She looked up into the tanned weather-beaten face.

"Moggy, did *you* know my mother?"

"Aye, I did that. She were a queer one and no mistake."

"Am I like her?"

He looked at her consideringly. "Like and not like," he said gravely. "Folks is like animals, see. One fox looks like the next, one dog may be spittin' image of t'other, but they en't the same. They're different as chalk from cheese. You're yourself, you en't her. That's how I sees it."

Then Nampy appeared in the doorway and they went out to the punt. She climbed into it and both men took her back by ways known only to themselves and far quicker than the roundabout path she had followed that morning. They drew into the bank on the edge of the park and Moggy helped her out on to the grass.

"I'm all right now," she said. "You don't need to come to the house with me and thank you, Moggy."

" 'Tweren't nuthin.' " he mumbled.

"Yes, it was. Without you I could have died."

"Nay," he said, "not a lass like you. You've got the spirit, see. You mind me of Master Jethro when he were a bit of a lad. Weren't nuthin' much of him in them days, but he were brave as any Fen Tiger."

"Fen Tiger, I like that. Bless you, Moggy." Impulsively she stood on tiptoe and kissed his grizzled cheek and then ran across the grassy bank towards the house.

She had not realized how late it was, nor how much consternation her absence had caused. When noon came and she had not returned, Rosemary could not stand it any longer. She went to her mother and confessed everything. Margaret was sent home sulkily defiant under the lash of her Uncle Oliver's anger. Nampy arrived with the body of Ram Lall and a dramatic account of what happened at Spinney Mill just as Oliver and Seth were about to set out in search of Laurel.

"My God," exclaimed Oliver. "It was from Spinney that Justin fell to his death."

"Aye, t'were that very place," said Nampy nodding his head wisely. "For a minute t'were like seein' a ghost till we caught sight of the little maid."

"Thank heaven you were there. Now you get off to Moggy as quickly as you can and bring her back to us."

"Aye, my lord, you can trust me for that."

Clarissa watched the men carrying the old Indian into the house before she said, "We should have sent him away years ago."

"Poor Ram Lall seemed so harmless."

"He always hated Alyne as she hated him. The Devil's shadow, she used to call him. He blamed her for Justin's death and sometimes Laurel is extraordinarily like her mother. Her coming and Robin's accident must have turned his brain."

"Do you realize what it could have meant? Both of them drowned. I'll have that damned mill pulled down!"

"Jethro should never have brought her here. I knew that from the very beginning."

"Don't be hard on her, Clarissa. It's not the child's fault. What the devil got into Margaret to do such a thing?"

"I'm sorry that it happened so brutally, but Laurel had to know the truth."

"Be kind to her, Clary. She's young and easily hurt."

Lady Aylsham looked at her husband with exasperated affection. Years ago she had gone through agonies of pain and jealousy because of his love for Laurel's mother. It was old history now and yet she still felt a twinge because in some queer way the feeling still persisted in his obvious concern for Alyne's daughter. In her opinion Laurel was well able to look after herself, but all the same she was gentle with the girl when she trailed wearily into the hall. She had a fire lighted in her bedroom and insisted on helping her to strip off her damp

86

clothes and slip between the warmed blankets. She said nothing of what had driven her from the house thinking it best to let the shock pass and wait until Laurel spoke of it herself and the girl submitted, grateful to have still a little time alone and not have to face anyone else in the household. She thought she was hungry, but when Betsy brought food, staring at her curiously, she revolted against it and could only swallow a few mouthfuls. Clarissa, coming in to her again to find out if she had everything she wanted, saw the scarcely touched tray and put a hand on her forehead.

"Are you feeling feverish? Perhaps you have taken a chill?"

She moved restlessly away from her touch. "No, I am quite well. It's just that I can't help thinking of Ram Lall . . . it was my fault that he fell."

"You mustn't let it distress you too much. He should have been put away years ago, but Lord Aylsham thought it would be cruel. This was his home after all. Perhaps it is better as it is. I'm only thankful he did not do you serious harm."

"It was because of my mother, wasn't it?"

"Yes, I'm afraid it was. We should have realized it." Clarissa put a hand on her shoulder. "Try and sleep. It will help you."

"Lady Aylsham," Laurel stopped her as she moved towards the door. "Is it true . . . what Margaret told me?"

"Yes, it is quite true."

"I wish I had known."

"Jethro asked me to tell you, Laurel, and now I'm sorry I did not do so at once, but it is an ugly tangled story . . . it was not easy to find the right time."

"Did *you* hate my mother too?"

Clarissa looked down at the lovely troubled face and it was as if Alyne's detested ghost had come back to haunt her in the person of her daughter, but she was a compassionate woman and she avoided the question.

"If it makes you feel any better, my dear," she said slowly, "I believe that whatever your mother did, she loved Captain Rutland and he loved her."

Laurel's lips trembled. She looked away. "And the other thing . . .?"

"It was never proved that the child Justin had fathered was the girl he married," went on Clarissa steadily, "but everything pointed to it, everything . . . and when he knew, it drove him into a madness that ended in his death. It was a bad time for all of us

87

and especially for Jethro, but Justin was a bitter tormented man and he made your mother suffer for his own unhappiness."

"I understand. Thank you for telling me." She paused and then went on firmly, "Tomorrow I shall go away."

"Go away?" Clarissa was startled. "Where will you go?"

"To my grandfather. It's where I should have stayed in the first place. I should never have come here."

"But Jethro told us . . ."

"Never mind what Jethro said. He does not know everything."

Clarissa watched her for a moment. How deeply was she involved with him? Judging by the ball it could well be simply girlish infatuation for an attractive man who had shown her marked attention. She said quietly, "Rest now. We will talk about it in the morning. You'll feel differently then."

"I don't think I shall."

"We shall see. Would you like me to turn out the lamp?"

"No, leave it please."

"Very well."

When she had gone, closing the door behind her, Laurel lay, eyes wide open, sleep very far away, and thought about her mother, that beautiful woman who had always held her at a distance . . . a deeply unhappy woman, she realized that now. She had been like someone seeking a fulfilment, a peace which she had never found. Would it have been any different if Captain Rutland had not died? Laurel thought of Jethro and shivered. Was she to be haunted by the same fate? If what they had told her was true, then he was dead to her in a way that was worse than if he lay in his grave, only she was not going to believe it. What was it Moggy had said? "You're yourself. You en't her. That's how I see it." And he was right. She would not let anything defeat her. She loved Jethro and he loved her. Why should she let something that happened so long ago come between them? She could not give her mother the happiness that had eluded her, but she could fulfil it in her own life, and with that resolution there came a kind of peace. Clarissa, stealing in some time later, found her sprawled across the bed, sleeping like a child, one arm flung out, the red hair tumbled on the pillow. She watched her for a moment, moved in spite of herself, then pulled the coverlet over her and turned out the lamp.

7

The next morning Laurel clung to her resolution against strong opposition and it was Cherry's unexpected support that helped to clinch it for her. Margaret's mother had been extremely angry with her daughter, but all her life she had believed in facing facts squarely and honestly even if sometimes it led to trouble.

"What nonsense you do talk," she said sharply to her brother Oliver and her sister-in-law. "Laurel is not a silly schoolgirl. She has already seen a great deal more of the world than most girls of her age. It so happens that I'm going up to town myself. Harry writes that there has been an upset at the Stepney settlement. I want to deal with it myself."

"You and your wretched slum children," grumbled Oliver. "That place down there costs more in anxiety and money than it is worth quite apart from possible damage to your health. Last summer there was the cholera outbreak. God knows what it will be next time."

"If you and the other rich stuffed dummies who sit with you in the House of Lords passed a bill granting better housing, cleaner water supply and improved conditions for the poor and homeless, there wouldn't be any epidemics," retorted Cherry. "Jethro has said it over and over again. There was the business of the pump in that wretched district near the settlement. He told the Council the water was tainted by the sewers and was the cause of the sickness, but they wouldn't listen so he had it tied up and the deaths from cholera practically stopped. Even then they refused to believe him because it meant spending money on renewing the drains." She paused for breath before she went on more quietly, "However that's not the point at issue just now. Laurel can travel up with me and stay at the house in St. James's Square. It's only a stone's throw from Arlington Street."

"I don't like it," began Oliver, "after all I am responsible for her . . ."

"It's kind of you to say so, but it is not true," interrupted Laurel. "I'm responsible for myself."

"Bravely spoken," said Cherry encouragingly. "Now you go and pack your bag, my dear. I know my brother. He's obstinate, but he will accept the inevitable in the end."

So it was arranged. The carriage took them to the railway station at Ely and a bowing porter installed them in a first class carriage with their luggage. The rest of Laurel's clothes would be sent up by carrier.

Jessica had protested vigorously against Laurel's leaving them until her father reminded her tartly that they were not parting forever and that next spring the whole family would be going up to London for the season.

Rosemary said little but she came into Laurel's room to help her pack her valise which was all she was taking with her.

"I wish you were staying longer with us, but I do understand," she said folding stockings up carefully and putting them one by one into a linen bag. "Do you think you will see Jethro when you are in London?"

"Perhaps," Laurel was not willing to confide her intentions even to Rosemary.

"Seth asked me to tell you that Gadabout will miss you. He says he has never known anyone manage a horse or ride as well as you do."

"You're very fond of Seth, aren't you, Rosemary?"

"I've known him ever since I was a baby. He taught me to ride my first pony. It was very fat and called Snowball. Seth was sixteen and I was four. He seemed very grown up to me then."

Laurel took a gown from the wardrobe, folded it and laid it between sheets of tissue paper before she said quietly, "You're not in love with him, are you?"

"No, of course not. How can you say such a thing!" But a faint pink tinged Rosemary's cheeks and she turned quickly away.

"Because he *is* a servant, you know."

"He's not," she said indignantly, "at least not like that, not like Barker or Betsy. Starlings have lived at Ravensley for as long as Aylshams. Seth's eldest brother Jake was father's best friend. He worked hard to obtain better conditions for the farm labourers and he was murdered because of what he did. Seth is like him. He thinks for others." Her voice died away breathlessly as she saw the quizzical look on Laurel's face. "You think I'm being silly, don't you?"

"No, I don't, but I still can't believe that Lord Aylsham would welcome Seth as a son-in-law."

"Don't laugh at me," whispered Rosemary.

"I'm not laughing." Laurel leaned forward and kissed the other girl impulsively. "We'll go on being friends, won't we? I think I may need friends."

"Of course we will." Rosemary responded with a quick hug. "Perhaps later on I can visit you if Papa will permit it."

There was only a skeleton staff at the London house when the family was at Ravensley, but they were accustomed to Lord Aylsham coming up when he had to attend the House and Harry Fenton had the habit of dropping in occasionally, so it was not long after their arrival that Cherry and Laurel were sitting down together to a cosy supper.

Deliberately Cherry talked about the settlement she had begun many years before in the appalling slums of Stepney. "I lived in London after I was married because Harry was still with the regiment. He thought I was crazy and so did Oliver. We had a terrible fight over it but I won in the end. We started with a little school, not that we can teach them very much, but it does take some of the children off the streets. They are filthy of course, but it is surprising how quickly you get used to the dirt . . . and the smell. It's grown now and there's a kind of refuge for young girls and women who have nowhere to go. When the babies came, I had to put someone else in charge. Olivia Winter is very good and very hard-working, and quite a number of young people come down and help from time to time. Now and again we have little entertainments. I suppose you wouldn't like to come and sing some of your pretty Italian ballads?"

"I'd like that very much," said Laurel absently, only half her mind on what Cherry was saying.

The older woman leaned forward putting a hand on hers. "I know what is worrying you. Would you like me to come with you tomorrow and give that dragon Alice Grafton a piece of my mind?"

Laurel smiled. "I'm sure it would be very effective if you did, but this is something I must do for myself."

"Good for you, but remember you can always come back here if things become too unpleasant or you could go to Harry. He can be a tower of strength if necessary.

It was comforting to know that she did still have friends, but she said nothing at all of the worst problem gnawing at her.

The following morning Cherry went off early and Laurel asked the manservant to call her a cab. Where would she find Jethro? At St. Thomas's or at his rooms in the Albany? She had his address from a letter he had written to her in the summer. She had never penetrated into a hospital in her life and felt she might be very unwelcome in such a busy place.

"Where to, Miss?" asked the cab driver opening the door for her.

"The Albany," she said quickly before she could change her mind.

The man looked surprised. The Albany was a male preserve. He was not accustomed to carrying pretty young women there at ten o'clock in the morning. Now if it had been after dark . . . he scratched his head philosophically and whipped up his horses.

Laurel sat bolt upright on the hard leather seat. Would he think her shamelessly bold to call at his lodging alone and uninvited? And yet she had to see him, had to speak with him, hear him say that he did not believe in this old tangled story of murder and incest any more than she did. Once she knew that, she felt she could face anything. The cab clattered under the archway and drew up in the cobbled yard.

She got out and paid him, then looked around her uncertainly. A long gallery ran along the line of apartments each with its own front door. They were closed, yet she felt eyes on her as she walked briskly to the far end. There was a small plate with his name and under it a brass bell handle. She pulled it and waited. No one came so she rang it again a little more impatiently. The door was opened at last by a young man who looked as if he had just got out of bed. Brown hair stuck up in spikes all over his head. He was unshaven and a dressing gown had been pulled on untidily over shirt and trousers.

"What the dickens is going on?" he exclaimed and then stopped abruptly on seeing the fashionably dressed young woman standing in front of him. "I beg your pardon," he muttered. "I'd no idea . . . bit of a late night, you know."

"Doesn't Dr Aylsham live here?" asked Laurel crisply.

"Yes, he does . . . or rather he did . . ." He was suddenly conscious that this was no dolly-mop from the music hall or the ballet and that curious heads were poking out of doors and windows. "You'd better come in," he said hurriedly, "and I'll explain."

He ushered her through a narrow hall into an austere room furnished with dark red leather chairs and lined from floor to ceiling with weighty books. She turned to face him.

"Has Dr Aylsham gone to the hospital already?"

"No . . . look, would you mind telling me your name?"

"I'm Laura Rutland and I've been staying with his brother Lord Aylsham at Ravensley," she said with some impatience. "I must see him. It is important."

"I'm afraid you can't," he replied bluntly. "He's on his way to Vienna."

"Vienna?" she repeated blankly.

"Yes . . . do sit down, Miss Rutland. Perhaps I'd better explain. I'm Charles Townsend and my father Dr Townsend is medical officer at St. Thomas's. There's been talk of this Vienna trip for some time. It's a wonderful opportunity to work with Dr Semmelweiss who has been carrying out some remarkable experiments. Jethro was asked to go in the summer but he wouldn't say yes or no. Then yesterday morning he came back from some family affair he had to attend at Ravensley and said his mind was made up. He packed his bags and left at once in time to catch the night packet to Calais. I've been working with him in the hospital and he very kindly said I could use his apartment while he was away."

But Laurel was not listening any longer. She clutched the back of one of the chairs, feeling a little faint. So he had run away from her. Did he really believe that horrible tale? Did he really feel himself so closely related to her, or was she making a terrible mistake? Had he been simply amusing himself with her all the time and made his escape before it became serious?

The young man said gently, "I'm afraid it has been rather a shock. Can I offer you some refreshment? I'm afraid I haven't got myself settled in yet, but I could give you a glass of Jethro's Madeira."

"No, thank you."

"Would you like his address in Vienna? I could find it out for you."

"It's all right, thank you. I expect I shall be hearing from him." She moved to the door. "I mustn't take up any more of your time."

He came with her. "Shall I call a cab for you?"

"No, I think I prefer to walk. It isn't far. Good day, Dr Townsend."

He watched her go along the gallery. What the devil was Jethro up to running away from a lovely girl like that because that's what it looked like. Dashed funny business, he thought, might be worth investigating just for the hell of it. Rutland? Wasn't that the name of the rich old man who had been his father's patient for years? Odd if there should be any connection. He rubbed his chin reflectively. Pity he'd looked such a scarecrow. Still it might be fun to follow it up. He kicked the door shut and sighed. Time he was dressed and off to the usual daily grind at the hospital.

George Grafton stood in the front room in Arlington Street squinting through one of the Venetian blinds that his mother had insisted on being lowered as a mark of respect. In the late afternoon the gloom of the room with its dark walls and heavy furniture oppressed him. He had been summoned late the night before to attend the deathbed of his great uncle, not that the old boy had recognised him or known a thing about it. He had lain in a coma, breathing stertorously, and passed away quietly, almost without their noticing it, shortly before midnight. It was well known that Sir Joshua had plenty tucked away. He wondered how much he would cut up for and whether any of it was likely to come his way. He knew what Barton and his mother hoped. They had talked about nothing else all the morning. No one had yet seen his will but they were upstairs now going through drawers, making sure of what they could lay their hands on. He was not particularly squeamish and he needed money a great deal more than his brother did. Barton was a mean devil who lived like a penny-pinching clerk and would never lend so much as ten guineas without demanding interest, but something in George revolted against rifling through a dead man's possessions before he was decently laid in his grave.

The sound of a carriage drawing up outside sent him to the window again. He saw Laurel alight and the coachman stand by to close the door. It was a handsome equipage, must belong to Lord Aylsham. He grinned to himself. Barton and his mother would have an unpleasant shock. He had mentioned Laurel at breakfast when they were talking of funeral arrangements and had received an icy stare.

94

"The wretched young woman will be informed in due course," Alice Grafton had said coldly.

He watched Laurel mounting the steps. By Jove, she was a stunner all right in that tight purple jacket over spreading lilac skirts, a little cap of squirrel perched on the dark red hair matching the pretty fur muff. He heard the bell ring and the door being opened, then the manservant was showing her in.

"Miss Rutland, sir. Shall I inform Mrs Grafton?"

"It's all right, Franklin. You can leave it to me," he said easily. As the door closed, he smiled with all his considerable charm and held out his hand. "Good afternoon, cousin. Have you come for your share of the spoils?"

Laurel had seen the drawn blinds, had sensed the hushed atmosphere of the house and guessed the reason before she asked the question.

"I don't understand. Is it my grandfather?"

"I'm afraid so. The poor old boy snuffed it . . . last night actually."

"I didn't know . . ."

"It's been touch and go for the last month."

"Why wasn't I told?"

He shrugged his shoulders. "Mother may not have believed the end was so near," he said diplomatically.

"I wish I could believe that."

Laurel had received one shock that morning and had been forced to weather it. Nursing her sick grandfather had seemed to her then like a refuge where she could hide and recover her balance. Now even that was to be taken from her. She steadied herself against it.

"May I see him?"

That surprised him. "If you wish. I'll take you up myself."

The bedroom was heavy with the scent of the lilies that his mother had placed inappropriately he thought beside the bed. Laurel turned back the linen sheet. All lines of age and sickness had been erased from the heavy features and there seemed little resemblance between the waxen face on the pillow and the vigorous tough old man who had been the rock of her childhood. She bent down to kiss the icy cheek. When she turned to him, George saw with surprise that there were tears in her eyes.

She said. "Thank you. Perhaps I'd better go now."

In the hall they ran into Barton. There was not much likeness between the brothers. Barton in his early thirties was the elder by half a dozen years and looked his age. He closely resembled his mother, the same pale neat nondescript features but the eyes were as sharp as needles. Laurel felt them darting all over her, taking her in, summing her up.

George said, "I don't think you are acquainted with our cousin, Bart. This is Laurel, Uncle Bulwer's daughter."

The hand he held out was cold. There was no warmth or kindness in the limp grip.

"I'm afraid we meet on a sad occasion, Miss Rutland."

"I'm staying at Lord Aylsham's house in St. James's Square. Perhaps you will let me know about Grandfather's funeral."

"Of course. There will be an announcement in *The Times*." His voice was as colourless as his face.

George himself opened the door for her. He took her hand for a moment. "We shall meet again very soon."

"Yes."

She withdrew her hand and went down the steps to the waiting carriage.

He shut the door smiling to himself. "The nigger in the woodpile, eh Bart, old boy?" he said pleasantly to his brother. "What's the betting that she picks up most of Great Uncle Joshua's cash."

"If so, then I shall fight it," growled Barton.

"You won't win, you know. The old man employed sound lawyers."

"We'll see about that. You're a damned fool, George. Any pretty face can bowl you over," he said contemptuously. "You stand to lose as much as we do and don't think you can come crawling around Mother or me to settle your debts."

"You've always made that pretty plain," replied George airily. "There are other ways of winning a battle, ways far beyond anything you're aware of, dear brother." Barton snorted and George put a kindly hand on his shoulder. "Believe me, I know, I've tried 'em all. You'd better tell Mother I'm going back to the barracks. I still have to serve Queen and country, you know."

He picked up hat and cane and sauntered off whistling a little tune to himself as he strolled down to Piccadilly. There was something about Laurel that intrigued him. A young woman of spirit, he surmised, and he badly needed a new interest. He was bored to death with Violet, had been for weeks now. She had a one-track mind and dug a large hole in his pocket. It was time he moved on and here was metal more attractive. He had a fair conceit of his own charms and in any dealings with a young woman, felt sure of ultimate victory.

Laurel, fighting back tears in the carriage, never thought of him or Barton at all which was foolish of her. With all the violent despair of youth, she felt that life had betrayed her and nothing remained, no happiness, no purpose, but in that she was utterly wrong. The battle had only just begun and the first skirmish took place on the day of Sir Joshua's funeral.

It was a very grand affair indeed. Sir Joshua had been highly respected in the City and had a surprising number of acquaintances amongst the aristocracy to whom he had once done a financial favour. They either came themselves or sent their carriages. A long procession formed in Arlington Street and followed the hearse with its flowers and black plumes out into Piccadilly dislocating tradesmen's carts and the new horse-drawn omnibuses. There was a great deal of speculation amongst the mourners as to the identity of the slim young girl in elegant black velvet whose deep red hair could be glimpsed behind the gossamer thin veil. Beside her in the carriage sat Lord Aylsham, who had felt in duty bound to come up from Ravensley for the funeral. She looked very pale, he thought, but to his relief there were no tears.

He drew her arm through his. "Sir Joshua would have been amused at all this ceremony," he said. "He had an honest opinion of his own worth, but he loathed pomp and was not a man for show."

"I wish I had known he was so ill," she whispered. "I can't help remembering that at the last he had no one with him who really loved him."

He felt her tremble and patted her hand. "My dear, ultimately we must all die alone," he said gently.

A great many people came back to Arlington Street to drink Madeira and sherry wine and talk in hushed tones of the deceased, moving on to the state of the market, a threatened increase in taxation and the latest racing results, this last causing George to be frowned upon, it not being considered quite the thing on such a solemn occasion.

There was one unpleasant incident. A maidservant called in from the kitchen to help carry around the wine dropped a tray of glasses. Alice Grafton's overstretched nerves reacted in a storm

97

of anger that shocked the embarrassed guests. With quick sympathy Laurel knelt on the carpet beside the terrified weeping girl helping to gather the broken glass and wrapping her own handkerchief around the fumbling bleeding fingers.

"What's your name?" she whispered.

"Cindy, Miss," muttered the sobbing girl.

"Don't fret, Cindy. It will be all right. You'll see."

She raised the girl to her feet and saw the butler hustle her out of the room. Everyone began hurriedly talking again. By the afternoon most of them had left, bowing courteously to Laurel where she stood alone against the windows and apart from the family who had drawn together in silent hostility. A distinguished looking man with a neat grey beard and a quiet pleasant manner paused to speak with her.

"I am Dr Townsend, Miss Rutland. I thought you might care to know that Sir Joshua had been my patient for over thirty years except for the time he spent in Italy. He spoke of you frequently, but these last months have been very wearisome for him. Before the last stroke that took him off, he told me that except for leaving you alone, he would be glad to go." The lump in her throat prevented her from replying and he seemed to sense it. "Charles told me of your call at the Albany," he went on. "I understand that you are acquainted with Jethro Aylsham."

She found her voice. "Yes, I am. He was very kind to me in Italy when I was in great trouble."

"Was he indeed? A brilliant young man, Miss Rutland, one of our most skilful surgeons at St. Thomas's. He has a splendid future before him if he doesn't wreck it by too much plain speaking. Like all young men he is bursting with ideas, some of them too new and outlandish for old stagers like myself. Can't always trample on tradition, you know. It won't do." He smiled. "However if it wasn't so, I suppose we should still be in the dark ages and prescribing boiled nettles and fried mice to our patients."

She could not help smiling back at him and he said, "It is quite true, I assure you. The British pharmacopoeia used to include some very strange items." He gave a quick look around him and lowered his voice. "A word in your ear. I understand that Mrs. Grafton is insisting on the will being read immediately, so be prepared. I warn you there may be fireworks. Sir Joshua honoured me by asking if I would act as one of the trustees, but I daren't stay any longer now. It's quite extraordinary but the moment a doctor is off duty, his patients immediately take it into their heads to fall down in an apoplexy or indulge in a heart spasm. But remember if you should ever need any advice, which you probably won't, I'm always at your service."

He pressed her hand warmly and then followed the others out of the room.

Mr Jolly of Jolly, Black and Henderson, was nothing at all like his name. He was long, lean and cadaverous with scanty grey hair neatly brushed across a domed bald head. He took his place at the head of the table with Alice Grafton on his left. Barton sat on his right and next to him a pretty, fretful looking woman who was obviously his wife. There were other men and women whom Laurel didn't know and supposed to be distant relatives. George motioned her to an empty chair beside him, but she shook her head preferring to remain apart in the window seat. She looked at him dispassionately while they took their places. He had very bright blue eyes and thick light brown hair. He was handsome in a devil-may-care fashion, but his face had none of the brooding tenderness, none of the vivid play of expression that belonged to Jethro. She wondered where he was at this moment. He must have reached Austria by now. Viennese women were said to be the most beautiful and elegant in Europe. The lawyer began to read but she was not listening. Her head ached and she closed her eyes for a moment. Her thoughts went flying back to Rome and their first meeting, remembering little incidents and dwelling on those days of close companionship. It was less than a year ago although it felt much longer. She had been a child then, not realizing what was happening to her. How very different it would be now. Why, oh why did he have to go so far away from her when she needed him so badly? She came out of her abstraction suddenly and startlingly to hear her own name.

There was a silence and everyone around the table turned to look at her. She was aware that she had not heard one single word of what had been said. She met the lawyer's eyes. He nodded as if to make sure of her attention and then went on reading.

"To my granddaughter, Laura Rutland, all the residue of my estate together with the shares held by me in the Rutland Tea Importers . . ."

Then shockingly it happened. Alice Grafton seemed to take

leave of her senses. She was on her feet. "No," she was screaming, "no, it can't be! It's unjust! It's nothing but lies, all lies . . ."

"Mother, please . . ." said Barton.

George put a hand on her arm. "For heaven's sake, Mamma. Keep quiet. This isn't the time . . ."

But nothing could silence her. "I will not be quiet!" Her voice rose hysterically. "I will not permit you and Barton to be robbed of your inheritance by the bastard daughter of one of Bulwer's sluts . . ."

"Mrs Grafton, I beg of you," exclaimed the scandalized laywer. "It is all perfectly in order, I assure you."

"Of course you would say that. You've contrived it between you," she spat at him, "you and that girl working together on a defenceless old man, forcing him to sign a document he would never have agreed to if he had been in his right mind."

"Indeed, we have done nothing of the kind," said Mr Jolly with righteous indignation at the slur on his professional integrity. "The will was written over a year ago when Miss Rutland was not even in this country and the trustees as I have already stated are Dr Townsend of St. Thomas's Hospital and Lord Palmerston, at that time Foreign Secretary, and in any case a peer of the realm. Surely you would not question the good faith of these gentlemen."

"I don't believe you . . . I won't believe you . . . there are ways and means and she knows them all just as her wicked mother did."

By this time Barton had come to his mother's side, putting an arm around her shoulders. With George's help he led her from the room still violently protesting. There was a buzz of excited conversation. Then George came back. He said something quietly to Mr Jolly and strolled across to Laurel.

"Well, how does it feel to be an heiress?"

She stared at him. "What does it mean? I wasn't listening."

He raised his eyebrows not sure whether to believe this extraordinary show of innocence, then realizing by the look on her face that astonishingly it was true.

"It means something between nine and ten thousand a year, this house and another in the Fen country and a controlling interest in the tea business," he said dryly. "What will you do? Sack Barton and run it yourself?"

She looked puzzled. "But all that can't be mine."

100

"I assure you that it is. Oh, we have been given our slice of the cake but the icing, the cream and the trimmings are all yours."

"Oh my God!"

She was stunned. Her legs felt suddenly weak and she let herself drop on to the window seat again.

Then Barton came back. "Mrs Grafton is lying down. The housekeeper is with her," he said. "It's the strain. My mother has been nursing Sir Joshua night and day for many months now."

"Yes, of course, I understand," said Mr Jolly stiffly. "Shall I continue?"

"If you please."

George returned to his chair and the lawyer went on with his reading. There was not much more, only a few formalities before he folded up the document and placed it carefully in his leather bag. He came across to Laurel congratulating her and offering the services of his firm in any way she might require them. She thanked him, still not quite able to take it in. Then he went out of the room with George and Barton.

Nobody spoke to her. They drew closer together in a tight resentful group talking quietly among themselves and leaving her isolated, the outsider who had maddeningly won the race. She felt their dislike and it had a curious effect. It gave her a feeling of power. Perhaps this was what her dead mother had wanted so much and never achieved. Now her grandfather had handed it to her. She got to her feet feeling a little giddy, partly from a rising excitement, partly from sheer hunger. She had eaten nothing that morning. An untouched glass of wine stood on the small table beside her. She picked it up and drained the rich Madeira to the last drop. She looked challengingly round at them and they watched her as she moved to the door, going through the hall and down the steps, walking lightly and confidently as if she walked on air.

Late that night Nora Rutland sat up in the bed she shared with her husband in their trim newly built villa out at Bayswater. There was a frown on the face that had once been babyishly pretty and the small tight mouth was pursed in angry indignation.

"You ought to have seen her, Bart, looking down at us as if we were no more than the dirt under her feet! To think of all that money and that great house going to her of all people after the

101

work you have put into your great uncle's business! She'll have everything and our children can be beggars for all she'd care!"

"Don't talk rubbish, Nora," said Barton tartly. "I'm perfectly capable of supporting my family without help from anyone."

The whining voice went on and on, but he was not listening. He had received a substantial legacy but it wasn't what he had hoped, not by a long chalk, and it irked him unbearably that he would be taking orders from a chit of a girl who could sign away his very life blood to some waster of a husband. There must be something he could do. He thought of the fool of a serving girl whom he had himself recommended to his mother and Laurel's swift reaction. Trivial perhaps but illuminating. The germ of an idea began to take shape in his tortuous mind. There was no hurry. He could be patient and wait his opportunity. He turned his back on his wife, curled up his toes, and started to work out a plan.

At the same time George was supping at Romano's with Violet, drinking champagne and reflecting that what he would receive would just about cover his most pressing debts and pay for the ruby bracelet Violet was gloating over, not yet aware that it was intended as a farewell gift. All that lovely money infuriatingly beyond his reach . . . but was it? He also was mulling over a plan which unlike his brother he was prepared to find personally enjoyable.

In her room in St. James's Square, Laurel was writing to Jane Ashe asking if she would consider coming to stay with her at Arlington Street as friend and companion. She leaned back, nibbling the end of her pen. A knot of misery still tightened deep within her whenever she thought of Jethro but resolutely she tried to ignore it. A dazzling future stretched in front of her. She was setting out to conquer the fashionable world.

A fortnight later in Vienna Jethro read Charles Townsend's letter which gave a vivid account of Laurel's call at the Albany and ended with a jest.

"You'd better hurry home, old boy, before I beat you to it. Ten thousand a year is not to be sneezed at!"

He crumpled the sheet savagely and tossed it into the fire. If anything it only deepened the gulf between them. God damn his father and the havoc he had wrought with his destructive life!

He turned back to the notes he had been making. Dr Semmelweiss had been expounding a theory that puerperal fever which killed so many young mothers could be carried by contagion. Doctors and students moved from dissecting room to hospital ward and the patients died like flies. He had commanded them to scrub their hands with carbolic and miraculously the deaths were halved. If that was so, could it also be of value in operations where the surgeons merely turned back the cuffs of their old blood-stained frockcoats kept hanging in the operating theatre before they took up their instruments? Absolute cleanliness, hands and white coat washed in carbolic, might make all the difference between death and recovery. It was worth a trial if he could only persuade English hospitals to accept the necessity. One day it might even save Laurel's life. He thought of her in the agonies of bearing a child, fevered and sick like the poor wretches he had visited that afternoon in the lying-in wards, and his desire for her burned within him so strongly that he could sit still no longer. He slammed the books shut and got up, pulling on his caped overcoat and going out into the icy snow-laden streets. Wine, women and song were what this gay city possessed in abundance. To hell with Laurel and to hell with his work, tonight he was going to indulge himself in every pleasure Vienna had to offer.

Part Two

THE HEIRESS

8

The group of men, mostly sporting peers with their racing trainers, gathered around the stableyard on the corner of Covent Garden, turned as one man to stare as a charming little carriage painted in blue and yellow with a pair of finely matched bays drew up smartly and a fashionably dressed young woman tossed the reins to her companion, stepped down and walked towards them. In sheer astonishment they parted to let her through and one of them, a tall broad-shouldered man elegantly but casually dressed, raised his white beaver hat and went forward with outstretched hand.

"My dear Laurel, what on earth brings you here at this hour on a Sunday afternoon?"

"The same purpose as yourself, my lord. I am badly in need of a new riding horse and since I have no one to act for me, then I must choose for myself."

Henry Temple, Viscount Palmerston, might be rising seventy, but he still had an eye for a beautiful woman. He had not been nicknamed 'Lord Cupid' for nothing. He smiled down at the provokingly lovely face. He had consented to act as trustee somewhat grudgingly in return for much needed loans from his old acquaintance Sir Joshua Rutland and had accepted his responsibility with a shrug of impatience until a week or so after the funeral when reluctantly he had consented to meet Laurel. That was ten months ago and now it was very different. The elderly statesman and the young girl had become fast friends.

She said with a pretty show of deference, "Have you seen anything worthwhile? Will you advise me?"

"We'll take another look, shall we, m'dear?"

In the ordinary way he would have left this kind of thing to his racing trainer, but now he tucked her arm through his and led her into the yard where the horses were being brought out one by one for inspection before the sale on the following day.

"There was one," he said thoughtfully, "but he was a great

107

raking brute, far too powerful for a dainty little thing like yourself."

"You'd be surprised," said Laurel. "I like them difficult. It gives me something to conquer."

"Does it, by Gad! A veritable Diana, eh?" Lord Palmerston gestured to the man who followed them into the yard. "Ask the fellow to bring out the black stallion."

John Day who had trained his lordship's racehorses for many years looked doubtful, but knew better than to question an order from his autocratic patron.

The horse was a magnificent specimen with proudly arched neck and the slim narrow head of his Arab ancestry. But something had disturbed him. He dragged away from the boy holding the bridle, his eyes rolling. He reared up snorting angrily and the owner of the stables, a big brutal looking fellow, cracked his whip and gave him a sharp cut across the rump. The stallion plunged forward and Lord Palmerston took a hasty step backwards, but Laurel stubbornly stood her ground.

"That's no way to treat any animal and you ought to know it," she said sharply. "Give the bridle to me."

"He's vicious, lady, best not to come too near," said the man warningly.

She looked at him contemptuously. "He's nothing of the sort. He's terrified, that's all, and I'm not surprised if those are the methods you use."

She spoke softly and the horse whinnied and then stood still quivering. His ebony coat shone with sweat. The circle of men watched in breathless silence as she moved towards him and very gently blew into his nostrils. He snorted, tossing his head, and then immediately quietened. She went on talking quietly, some gibberish none of them could understand, and after a moment he stood peacefully while she fondled his velvet nose.

"My God, it's witchcraft, pure bloody witchcraft!" exclaimed the stableman, much inclined to be resentful.

"Magic it is, neither more nor less, and you mind your tongue, my man," said Lord Palmerston greatly relieved in spite of himself. "Where did you pick up that dangerous trick, young lady?"

"From the men of the Fens, my lord. I'm a 'Fen Tiger', didn't you know?" replied Laurel gaily. "I like him. I want to buy him."

"The sale is not until tomorrow," muttered the stableman looking at her sulkily.

"I'd not willingly let him remain another day in your hands," retorted Laurel.

"Leave it to me. My man can buy him for you," said the peer. "See to it, John, and have the account sent to me."

"Very good, my lord."

"I'll make you a present of him, my dear, but only if you promise not to break your neck."

"I can't accept it. It's too much," protested Laurel.

"Nonsense, of course you can. A gift from an old man at the end of his tether to youth and beauty just about to take the plunge."

"You'll never be old, my lord."

"You flatter me," said Lord Palmerston dryly. "I'm beginning to creak and I don't care for it. You'll take him, eh?" He slipped an arm round her waist and gave her a little squeeze. "Of course you will just to please me."

Laurel smiled up at him. "You are far too good to me."

"Better let John school him for you."

"I prefer to do that for myself. Will you send him to my stables? They are in Arlington Mews." She threw a brilliant smile around the group of admiring men. "Now perhaps I had better go, otherwise I shall only be in your way."

Lord Palmerston walked with her to the waiting carriage and touched his hat to Jane Ashe.

"What are we going to do with this young lady of yours?" he said jovially. "She leaves us all standing. We shall have her riding in the St. Leger before long."

"I wish I could," Laurel flashed at him as he gave her his hand to help her into the carriage.

He grinned. "I wager you'd have them all by the ears. Shall we see you at Emily's party on Saturday? It's the last before we go to Broadlands for the shooting."

"Of course. I wouldn't miss it for the world." She let her hand lie in his for an instant and then took the reins from Jane. He waved his hat to her as she drove away.

"When you have quite done flirting with Lord Palmerston!" murmured Jane Ashe ironically as they bowled along the Strand.

"What a vulgar word!" said Laurel lightly. "I never flirt. I just like him, that's all. He's a lot more amusing than men half his age and he enjoys it. Makes him feel young again." She

109

grinned at her companion. "Besides, you can't deny I'd never be where I am without him."

It was true enough. In the ten months since Laurel had inherited her grandfather's fortune, she had become the toast of fashionable London. Partly because she was an heiress and beautiful, partly because there was something exotic, something unusual and mysterious about her. There were intriguing tales told about her birth, about her childhood in Rome and high connections in Italy. But she would never have reached such a position in society, never been presented at one of the Queen's drawing rooms in the summer, if Lady Emily, yielding to the strong persuasion of her husband, had not taken her under her wing.

"I don't know that I approve all the same," said Jane austerely. "His reputation is not of the best. You should not have accepted such a valuable gift from him."

"Oh, rubbish! He would have been very hurt if I'd refused."

"People will talk."

"Let them. If his wife doesn't mind, why should we?" She gave Jane a mischievous look. "I'm not proposing to go to bed with him."

"Laurel, please! Do you have to talk so shamelessly?"

"Only to you, Jane dear, only to you, never to anyone else. Surely we can be frank with one another."

"I suppose so," sighed Miss Ashe resignedly. "But just now and again I wish you'd behave a little more like any other nice, quiet, properly brought up young lady."

"No, you don't," retorted Laurel giving a flick to the horses and rattling along Piccadilly at a pace that turned heads as they rocked by. "Think how dreary it would be if I did. You'd be bored to death if you didn't have me to scold."

And the worst of it was that she was perfectly right. Ever since that day in late December when Jane Ashe had arrived on the doorstep of Arlington Street with her trunk and hand luggage beside her, there had never been a dull moment and if asked, she would have been obliged to confess that she would not have it otherwise and found it far more to her taste than the five years spent quietly teaching in the Swiss convent.

The first time she saw Laurel she was struck by the change three years had made in her. The shy schoolgirl had become a woman. At nineteen she was surprisingly poised and self-confident, and it was not entirely the effect of the inheritance that had given her such a dramatic independence. By now Jane knew something about the illegitimacy and guessed at the disillusionment it had brought with it, though Laurel had taken pains to hide her feelings and told her little beyond the bare facts. Of Jethro and that other and more disturbing revelation she was careful to say nothing at all. During a busy, hard-working life Jane had learned a good deal about people and young girls in particular. She guessed that there was far more than Laurel had confided to her, some hurt that she concealed which accounted for the occasional moods of black depression that she sought to cure with a reckless whirl of pleasure. Wisely Jane did not question too closely, but she watched and she listened. In the meantime she acted as guide, chaperon and friend.

Laurel owed a great deal to her good taste, tact and discretion in the jungle warfare of high society. Jane Ashe might have had to earn her own living since she was eighteen, but she was a lady of unimpeachable ancestry. Her father, the fourth son of an impoverished baronet, had earned a precarious living as a country curate and then after the early death of his wife had gone as a missionary to China leaving his little daughter in the care of his eldest brother. Jane was the poor relation amongst a family of selfish boisterous children. Her father had died in a cholera epidemic when she was nearly eighteen and as soon as she could she escaped from the tender mercies of her Uncle James. She had little beauty, a fact her aunt had taken pains to point out often enough, but she possessed poise and intelligence and could always be relied upon to be useful, to take the vacant place at the dinner table, play the piano when the young people wished to dance, make a fourth at whist or allow herself to be beaten at cribbage by the tiresome elderly relative whom it was so vitally important to please. She was invited nearly everywhere with Laurel and the friendship between them grew and deepened.

With Jane's help Laurel had transformed her grandfather's house. Gone were all the ugly pieces of dark furniture, the chocolate paint, the sombre wall hangings. The drawing room when they entered it that afternoon was flooded with sunshine through the long windows lighting up the pretty Chinese wall-paper and the elegant gilded furniture. Alice Grafton had long retired to the house in Bath which she had only left to nurse her uncle and there she brooded, harbouring a grievance and writing

111

long nagging letters to Barton which he tore up angrily and showed to no one.

They were taking off bonnets and gloves when Franklin the butler knocked and came into the room. With him came a dog, a beautiful slim creature in cream and chestnut with a fine aristocratic head. Laurel bent to fondle him.

"Has Marik had his walk?"

"Yes, Madam, twice round the square," said Franklin who did not approve of this exotic creature. A Borzoi of all things! What was wrong with a good English spaniel?

"There is a person asking to speak with you, Miss Rutland. He called soon after you left the house," he went on. "I told him that Sunday was hardly the day on which to come seeking employment, but he insisted that you were already acquainted with him so I permitted him to wait downstairs in the kitchen. He says his name is Seth Starling."

"Seth!" exclaimed Laurel. "But he works for Lord Aylsham at Ravensley. What can he want with me?" She had a sudden recollection of Rosemary and the look on her face when they had spoken together months ago now and felt a touch of apprehension. "You'd better ask him to come up, Franklin, and then you can tell Cindy to bring tea."

"Cindy has gone out, Madam," said the butler disapprovingly, "she told me that you had given her permission to take the evening off."

"Did I? I don't remember."

"I fear Cindy has a follower," said Franklin austerely. "I've had occasion to speak to her more than once. She has the habit of running out of the house to meet with this young man. Cook has noticed it several times. It is not at all the proper thing in a lady's household."

"Perhaps she is in love," said Laurel, a little amused.

"If I may say so that is hardly sufficient excuse for such behaviour."

"No, maybe not. Leave it to me, Franklin. I'll have a word with her."

"Very good, Madam."

Jane waited till the door closed and then turned impatiently to Laurel. "I've said it before and I'll say it again. I wish you'd dismiss that girl. I don't like her. She's sly and she's deceitful."

"Oh Jane, you're exaggerating. The poor creature has been kicked from workhouse to orphanage, no home, nobody to say a

112

kind word to her. Is it any wonder that she is as she is? She's had to fight for everything she has ever had. How can I turn her out into the streets to fend for herself?"

"I've no doubt she'd find her feet soon enough," persisted Jane. "You know that Barton had her placed here, no doubt guessing only too rightly that you would keep on all your grandfather's servants. In my opinion she is a spy."

Laurel laughed. "A spy? Really, Jane, it's not like you to be fanciful. There's nothing hidden in this household. All the world knows about me. I've no dark secrets."

"That's beside the point. It worries me."

"Well, don't let it." Laurel put a hand lightly on Jane's arm. "You fret far too much about me."

"Well, if I didn't, who would?"

Then there was a knock at the door and Seth Starling came in and with him there seemed to come a breath of the wide open Fens which Laurel had only visited once since the day she had left. He was neatly dressed in his best cord breeches and brown coat and stood respectfully holding his hat in his hand.

"I understand you wished to speak with me, Seth."

"Yes, Miss Rutland. I hope you will forgive the liberty but Mr Robin told me that you had been dissatisfied with the man who cared for your horses and I wondered if you would consider me for the position."

"But you're employed at Ravensley. You've been there all your life," said Laurel doubtfully.

"A man can stay too long in one place," he said obstinately. "Sometimes he needs a change and looks to better himself."

"Does Lord Aylsham know about this?"

"I left his service a fortnight ago, but I think he will give me a reference if you should need one." He paused and then went on quickly. "If the vacancy is already filled, perhaps you or Miss Ashe would know of someone among your acquaintances who might be wanting a groom or a coachman."

He raised his head and Laurel saw the pain in the brown eyes and sensed the anxiety that lay hidden behind the quiet manner. Seth supported his widowed mother. He could not afford to be out of work.

"I'd be only too glad to have you looking after my horses," she said, impulsively making up her mind, "And I don't need any reference. There is a room above the stable that you can have and you can begin your duties tomorrow by going down to

113

the sale at Covent Garden and taking delivery of a horse from Lord Palmerston's trainer, John Day. He's a splendid black stallion who has been brutally ill-treated. He may need careful schooling. Can you do that for me?"

She saw his face light up. "It will be a pleasure, Miss Rutland."

"Very well. I will speak to Franklin about you. When you go back to the kitchen, please tell him to bring tea."

"Aye, I'll do that."

"Was that wise?" remarked Jane when he had gone. "To take him on so quickly and without reference."

"Oh there's no doubt about his character or his skill with horses. I'm only surprised that Lord Aylsham has let him go. I know how much he valued him."

"That's what I mean, my dear. There could have been trouble at Ravensley and it could involve you."

"I'm perfectly certain that Seth has never stolen anything or cheated his employer out of so much as a farthing," said Laurel lightly.

"I was not thinking of that kind of trouble. There could be other problems . . ."

"There could be of course. I did sometimes wonder . . ." and then she stopped, feeling that she could not betray Rosemary's pathetic secret even to Jane. If the feeling that had sprung between them was the cause of Seth leaving, then she would find out sooner or later and in the meantime she felt absolutely certain of his ability and trustworthiness.

"We shall have to wait and see, won't we?" she went on, yawning and stretching. "After tea I must change. George will be calling for me soon."

"Where are you going tonight?"

"Didn't I tell you?" said Laurel carelessly. "It's a little party at the Cremorne Gardens. A concert and supper, that's all."

Jane frowned. "The Cremorne Gardens are not what they were. You meet some very undesirable people there in the evening. I'm surprised that Captain Grafton should suggest it."

"Oh Jane, really, don't be such a wet blanket. One of his brother officers has his two sisters in town on a visit and they are anxious to see all the sights of London. The poor boy is quite worn out taking them everywhere. George thought to help him by making up this trip. We shall be a very respectable party, rather boring probably, though I understand that Grisi is singing."

114

Tea was wheeled in and it was while she was pouring it that Jane felt that she must say what was in her mind, no matter if it was welcome or not. She glanced around the room. It was filled with flowers from Laurel's many admirers, late roses, expensive lilies, baskets of country flowers. They arrived by messenger nearly every day, sometimes accompanied by more costly gifts, always scrupulously returned. She passed the cup to Laurel and began to sip her own tea. The girl was leaning back against the cushions of the sofa, her rich silk skirts spread around her. Although Jane knew that she rarely ailed anything, she thought she looked somehow young and fragile and very vulnerable. The eyes in the lovely face were enormous and the hand holding out a biscuit to the Borzoi lying at her feet was almost too thin. The dog raised a noble head, sniffed the shortbread delicately and accepted it with the princely air of conferring a favour. Laurel reached for another and broke it in half. Without father or brother or guardian she was so utterly defenceless, a prey to any man's greed, and as had happened once or twice before, Jane was overwhelmed with a weight of responsibility.

She said suddenly, "Laurel, may I say something?"

"Of course. You don't have to ask permission to speak."

"You may not like it."

"Oh dear," Laurel sat up. "Is this my day for a scolding? I know I shouldn't have accepted Marik from Prince Malinsky or my black stallion from Lord Pam, but what else have I done?" she asked humorously.

"I wish you wouldn't see so much of Captain Grafton."

Laurel's eyes widened. "Why ever not? What has George done? He is my cousin after all. Besides he can be very good company. He makes me laugh."

"He is also quite unscrupulous and has only one aim . . . to get his hands on your money."

Laurel was silent for a moment playing with the dog's ears, then she looked up. "I'm quite well aware of that, Jane. I've always known it. I'm not a baby, you know, and I learned a great deal about men from Ugo Falcone. It's what they are all after, isn't it, not me but Grandfather's money, but there's safety in numbers, don't you think?"

"There is one who doesn't, one who cares nothing about money."

Laurel gave her a quick glance. "Only one?"

"Only one that I can be sure of."

"And who is that?"

"Robin Aylsham."

"Oh Robin." Laurel sighed. "He's the faithful dog, isn't he? Boring, poor darling, but loyal."

"Don't make fun of him. That boy truly loves you."

"He thinks he does."

"Be kind to him."

"What more can I do?" she said impatiently. "I let him stable his horse here. I ride with him in the park occasionally. He's always welcome to dine when I'm giving a party. I keep on reminding him that he is supposed to be studying law at the Temple. Is it my fault that I don't love him?" She got up so quickly that she disturbed the big dog. He looked indignant and stalked away to the hearthrug. "I think that's enough scolding for one day, don't you? I promise I'll remember all you have said and I promise I'll behave myself tonight. Will that do?" She dropped a kiss on the top of Jane's head. "Now I must go and dress."

Jane caught at her hand. "Take care."

"What are you afraid of?" she said flippantly. "That George will whip me off to Gretna Green and marry me out of hand?"

"It has happened."

"Only to fools."

She thought about George as she changed her gown. Jane was right. She had seen a great deal of him all this year. As her cousin he was in a privileged position. He came and went in the house almost like a brother and sometimes provided useful protection against the importunities of other young men, but she was under no illusions about him. He might be amusing and possess charming manners but he was also ruthlessly ambitious, in some ways even more so than Barton. The commission in the Hussars purchased for him by Sir Joshua and the ability which had won him his rapid promotion to Captain and the favour of Lord Cardigan, his Commander-in-Chief, had given him the entry into the highest circles and he was determined to stay there. Barton for all his business acumen had no style. He was barely tolerated in fashionable society. Sometimes she had thought he was riled by his younger brother's social success.

She glanced in the mirror. Against the pale ivory lace of her gown, her hair shone richly auburn. She fastened a cluster of late tea roses in her bosom and picked up a shawl of Persian silk.

116

She was humming a little tune as she went down the stairs to where George waited with the carriage.

The Cremorne Gardens in Chelsea had once been a riverside farm, but during the last few years had been transformed into delightful pleasure grounds. Kate and Lucy, Lieutenant Dent's twin sisters, who were only sixteen, were entranced with everything they saw, the green lawns, the flower beds still blazing with colour, the fountains falling with a sparkling shower into stone pools where goldfish darted, the pretty little temples discreetly tucked away in shady groves, the splendid ballroom with its magnificent gas chandeliers where Laurel sat through Grisi singing madrigals followed by a flute fantasia with George yawning his head off beside her.

The girls giggled irritatingly all through supper. It was all unutterably boring so that afterwards when they strolled in the gardens, the twins clinging to their brother's arms and chattering nineteen to the dozen, Laurel caught George's eye and they quietly allowed the others to draw ahead of them.

It was a beautiful evening, still and warm. The coloured lanterns strung along the trees were reflected in the dark water of the river and added to the enchantment, but there were a great number of other couples walking on the main path and quite suddenly a party of young men came tearing by chasing a couple of gaudily dressed young women in and out of the shrubbery with a good deal of shrieking and laughter. It made Laurel think that Jane had been right after all, while George gave one disgusted look at them, drew her arm though his and took one of the other paths leading into a more secluded part of the grounds.

"Heavens, what a frightful evening!" he complained. "Why is it that one's good deeds always turn out to be so abominably dull. I'm afraid I'm not cut out for nursery frolics."

"Don't be so unkind. Kate and Lucy are only three years younger than I am."

He smiled down at her. "I refuse to believe that you were ever such a wide-eyed innocent or so appallingly naive. Some fairy godmother endowed you with magic from your cradle. Was your mother a witch?"

"So they say," she said lightly. "A Fen witch."

They went on strolling together, not saying very much, and after a time she noticed that there were far fewer people about in this quiet corner of the gardens and that it was already growing

117

dark. For some minutes George had been oddly silent and she glanced up at him.

"It's later than I thought and Jane will be growing anxious. I think perhaps it's time you took me home."

"To hell with Jane!" he said explosively. "She's not your keeper, is she? I don't often have you all to myself. I want to talk to you."

"What about?"

"Can't you guess?"

She raised her eyebrows quizzically. "Oh dear, not another proposal surely?"

"Why do you always choose to laugh at me?" he said discontentedly. "I'm serious, Laurel."

"I've no doubt you are," she said impatiently. "The answer is still no."

They had come to a secluded little arbour with a stone bench and he drew her to sit beside him. The lantern hanging in the willow arching above the seat cast grotesque shadows across the handsome face giving a devilish twist to the straight nose and mobile mouth.

"Why, Laurel, why? We're two of a kind. We've had a great deal of fun together all this summer. We understand one another. We laugh at the same things. Why not make it permanent?"

"I'll tell you why if you wish. There are a great many reasons." She counted them off on her fingers. "One, I don't love you. Two, you don't love me . . ."

"Oh love!" he snorted.

"Yes, love," she went on quietly. "I happen to believe in it. Three, all you really want is Grandfather's money. Four, I don't mind giving you a loan to help pay your debts, but that's as far as I'm prepared to go, five . . ."

"Do you have to be so brutally frank? This isn't a business proposition."

"Isn't it? I thought we made a bargain at the beginning that we should be completely honest with one another."

"It was different then."

"How different?"

She looked at him curiously. He was frowning. His usual light-hearted air of ironic amusement seemed to have deserted him for the moment.

"You think I'm like Barton, don't you?"

"What has Barton to do with it?"

118

But she knew exactly what he meant. Barton had left her in no doubt of his hostility whenever they met.

Suddenly George turned to her. "There is someone else, isn't there?"

"Maybe," she said tantalisingly. "What of it?"

"Who is it?"

"I'm not telling you."

"Don't tease me, you little devil," he said dangerously. "I want to know. Is it that baby-faced boy Robin Aylsham or is it that Russian who is always mooning after you?"

"It's not Robin, nor Prince Malinsky, nor Lord Palmerston, nor in fact anyone you know . . ."

"Damn you, who then?" He seized her by the shoulders shaking her.

"Don't be foolish, George. There is no one. I was only funning."

But he didn't relax his grip. "Is it that sawbones? That surgeon fellow I saw you with once?"

She laughed a little unsteadily. "Don't be ridiculous. Jethro is in Vienna. It's a year since I've seen him."

"Then what is wrong with me? Answer me that." He stared down at her. "You know I could make you love me very easily."

"I doubt it," she said tauntingly.

He kissed her then violently and searchingly and she remained passive in his arms neither responding nor fighting against it. Reluctantly he released her.

"You don't care, do you, you simply don't care at all."

"On the contrary I've grown quite fond of you, George," she said trying to sound calm though her hands shook as she unfastened the crushed roses at her breast and let the petals fall through her fingers to the ground.

"Fond, for God's sake!" he repeated derisively. "Fond! What good is that? You lead a man on, you let him think . . ."

"What do I let him think, George?" she said coldly.

"You know well enough."

She had never seen him in quite this strange mood. Always before she had been mistress of the situation, but tonight she was aware of something disturbing about him. She was trembling a little though she would not let him see it. She realized that perhaps Jane was right and she had been playing with fire. It would be easy for him to compromise her so that she would be forced to marry him in order to avoid scandal. Somehow she must escape but the very last thing she wanted to do was to attract attention by running away from him. Then he surprised her by abruptly getting to his feet.

"We'd better find the others before I forget myself," he said curtly. "Come," he stretched out his hand to her.

They walked up the path side by side saying nothing to find Kate and Lucy with their brother anxiously hunting for them.

"What the devil happened to you?" exclaimed Lieutenant Dent. "We looked everywhere."

"We lost ourselves," explained George briefly.

The carriage dropped the others at their lodging and drove on to Arlington Street. George alighted and gave her his hand to help her down. She saw his eyes glitter under the light of the lamp.

He still held her hand. "You won't believe me but I do love you, Laurel," he said quietly.

"Don't say what you don't mean. There's no need," she replied quickly. "And it doesn't impress me in the very least."

"The odd thing is that I do mean it. I wish to hell I didn't!" he gripped her hand hard for a second longer then said goodnight and got back into the carriage. She watched it drive away before she went up the steps.

Franklin was waiting up for her. "Cindy is still out, Madam. I thought I ought to let you know."

"Very well," she said wearily. "I'll speak to her in the morning."

She felt tired and considerably shaken by what had happened. When she was undressed she stood for a little while at the window thinking over what George had said. He was right in a way. Maybe she had not been fair to him. She leaned her forehead against the cold window pane. Oh God, where was Jethro? Why did his face come between her and every other man? She had tried to put him out of her mind, had deliberately allowed herself to be courted by others and felt nothing at all as if they were no more than shadows and had no power to break through the icy armour of her indifference.

She sighed and was about to draw the curtains when she saw the pair who came walking together out of the darkness. One was Cindy, she was sure of that, the other was a tall young man who had something vaguely familiar about him though she could not see his face. The girl flitted down the area steps and after a moment the man moved away walking with a slight but

120

noticeable limp and it was then that she remembered. It was the day she had visited the offices of her grandfather's warehouse to talk to Barton about a matter that had arisen. The clerk who had shown her into the private room had had a limp. She had asked him about it and he told her he had been knocked down by a cab in a busy city street. She remembered his bitter, discontented look. What was he doing with Cindy? No doubt it had a perfectly simple explanation, but all the same it gave her a queer jolt.

9

The next morning Laurel woke late. When Cindy knocked and brought in her tea, she lay still for a moment, all that had happened the night before flooding slowly back into her mind. The girl had gone to the window pulling back the curtains. Except that she had filled out a little with the months of good food, she was not much different from the skinny big-eyed waif who had first attracted Laurel's pity on the day the will had been read. She came back to the bed.

"Shall I pour the tea for you, Miss?"

"No, thank you. Give me my shawl."

Cindy brought the white fleecy wrap, put it around her mistress's shoulders and then moved to the door.

"Don't go," said Laurel quickly. "I want to speak to you."

The girl stopped and then came back, standing humbly with downcast eyes.

If there was one time when Laurel regretted her youth and inexperience, it was in dealing with servants. In Italy, except for her personal maid, she had scarcely known the men and women who swarmed in the kitchen quarters of the Palazzo Falcone, but here in England a lady was expected to deal with her staff. She could have left it to Jane, of course, but she had always felt a responsibility for this bastard child of an unknown father dragged up in an orphanage and knowing neither love nor kindness in all her sixteen years. Perhaps at the back of her mind lay the uncomfortable thought – there but for the grace of God go I – but all the same there were matters that had to be cleared up. She braced herself.

"Who was the young man with you last evening, Cindy?" she asked a little tentatively.

The girl looked startled. "I . . . I dunno what you mean."

"Don't lie," said Laurel coldly. "I saw you both myself. It was late . . . after eleven o'clock. I thought that Mr Franklin preferred all the servants to be in by ten."

"I know but it weren't my fault. It were Jack. He took me to the country, see, and we missed the last omnibus. We had to walk."

122

For some reason it did not have the ring of truth and Laurel frowned. "And this Jack works in Mr Barton Rutland's office? Is that right?"

"Yes," admitted the girl reluctantly. "Jack Webb's his name. He's a clerk there."

"How did you meet him?"

"When I was workin' in the packin' factory. He used to come in there sometimes with Mr Barton's orders."

"Packing factory?"

"Yes, it's the tea, Miss. We had to put it into them fancy tins and then seal it."

"I thought you told me that you came straight from the orphanage as a maid to this house," interrupted Laurel.

"So I did . . . well, almost . . . I weren't tellin' no lie, not really. I were only at the packin' factory for a few weeks, then Mr Barton sent me here 'cos his mother couldn't find no one to suit and he told me not to say a word about it so I didn't."

"Did he indeed. Why?"

"I dunno why. How should I? Gentlemen like him don't let on to the likes of me." Quite suddenly the girl fell to her knees. "Don't send me away, please don't send me away. I ain't done nothing wrong, I swear I haven't . . . and I bin so happy here . . ." she began to sob wildly.

Laurel was uncertain whether it was truth or lies. She had an uneasy feeling that something lay behind it and yet couldn't imagine what game Barton was playing.

"For heaven's sake, get up," she said at last a little impatiently. "It's ridiculous to cry like that. Nobody is going to send you away if you behave yourself. Are you going to marry this young man?"

The girl stumbled to her feet snuffling into a rag of a handkerchief. "He ain't asked me yet," she said sullenly.

"Well, dry your eyes and get back to your work. And don't take time off in future without Mr Franklin's permission. Do you understand?"

"Yes, Miss."

"Very well. You can go."

She wondered about it for a few minutes while she drank her tea and then dismissed it from her mind. It seemed heartless to dismiss the girl for so small a fault as running after a young man. Laurel's life was too full and too enjoyable to waste time speculating over servants' peccadilloes. Later that day she went

123

down to the mews to see the black stallion that Seth had brought back from the Market. He looked just as splendid as he had done the day before.

"What do you think of him?" she asked running her hand along the arched neck.

"He's got fine breeding, good bones and plenty of stamina, but, he's nervous as a kitten, shies at almost anything," said Seth. "In my opinion some fool has tried to break his spirit and very nearly succeeded."

"Has it turned him vicious?"

"Not yet, but I wouldn't like to see a lady ride him, not even you, Miss, not before I've tried him out thoroughly."

"All right, do that and let me know when you think he is ready. I've given him a name already – Lucifer, don't you think it suits him?"

Seth smiled. "He's certainly got a dash of the devil in him, I'll say that, Miss."

"A devil we must tame."

"I'll do my best."

All the same it was a full month before Seth considered Lucifer sufficiently schooled for riding in Hyde Park and even then he watched Laurel settling herself in the saddle with some misgiving.

"I think you should permit me to come with you, Miss," he said, "just in case you have any trouble."

"Don't be absurd, Seth. I'm quite capable of managing a horse, even one like this, aren't I, my handsome?" and she patted the glossy neck.

Privately Jane was of the same opinion as Seth, but she knew Laurel and kept silent. Opposition would only make her more determined. She often accompanied her on her morning rides, but this particular day she was suffering from a slight chill and thought it better to stay at home.

The fashionable hour for displaying yourself and your horse was between eleven o'clock and noon, but Laurel with her usual disregard of what everyone else took for granted always chose to ride at seven o'clock in the morning, compelling all those young men who yearned to distinguish themselves in her eyes to drag groaning from their beds if they were not to be outdone by their fellows. And so it was there that Jethro, taking brisk early morning exercise with his friend Charles Townsend, saw her for the first time for what was almost a year.

124

It was a fine day in October. The trees had just begun to change colour and a thin uncertain sunshine turned the leaves gold and cinnamon and crimson. The two young men had pulled up after a hard gallop and were taking a breather by the rail exchanging a few words with an acquaintance when Charles suddenly clapped his hand on Jethro's shoulder.

"By Jove, just look at her riding that great brute as easily as if he were a rocking horse in the nursery!"

"Who do you mean?" said Jethro idly, turning his head to follow his friend's gaze.

In her dark red riding habit Laurel was a striking figure on the jet black horse. He felt curiously breathless as he watched her talking animatedly with the men riding beside her. George Grafton was a splendid sight in full rig of cherry coloured overalls and blue Hussar jacket laced with gold since he was taking guard duty at the palace later that morning and on her other side rode a tall fair man in a black and silver foreign uniform. The white and chestnut dog loped along at their heels.

"That's Dmitri Malinsky, he's with the Russian Embassy," murmured Charles. "He gave her the dog, lovely creature, isn't it? Oh, she's a high flyer all right. They say even old Pam is head over heels and Gods knows how many others."

"And all of them her lovers, I presume," remarked Jethro sardonically.

Charles glanced at him uncertainly. "Not a bit of it. Oh, they'd like to be, that's for sure, but she's not to be pinned down. She keeps them at a tantalising distance when it pleases her. 'Queen and huntress, chaste and fair,' that's how that new young artist Millais painted her, spear in hand on a great white horse. It was the sensation of the summer exhibition."

"She must be really something to have inspired you to poetry."

"Oh Lord, I'm not in the running, never have been, but she invites me to dine now and then. She's father's patient, you know, not mine, not that she is ever sick."

Afterwards Jethro did not know what it was that impelled him to act as he did. It was utterly senseless and he was deeply ashamed, but he could not stop himself. He deliberately rode forward across their path raising his hat with a flourish. Laurel recognised him at once and the unexpectedness of it took her breath away. It distracted her from the close control she had been holding over the restive horse so that Lucifer, bored in any case with the slow ambling pace, shook his fine head gaily and

125

bolted forward. It happened so quickly that it left them standing. Laurel fighting to keep herself steady lost the stirrup and her balance at the same time and the next moment slipped sideways and fell from the saddle. She hit the ground hard, was dragged for a few yards and then lay very still while Lucifer, frightened now, galloped on. The men spurred after her, but Jethro outdistanced them. He flung himself from his horse and knelt beside her, an icy chill of fear running through him. George and the Russian were close behind. They dismounted, crowding around her.

"Is it serious?"

"Is she hurt?"

Jethro looked up at them. "Better leave her to me. I am a doctor."

Laurel had opened her eyes. Still stunned she stared unbelievingly at Jethro and then tried to sit up.

"Don't move . . . lie still," he said pressing her back.

"My horse," she murmured. "What has happened to my horse?"

"He's not harmed."

In fact Charles with admirable presence of mind had gone after the stallion and brought him back, subdued now, his head hanging guiltily, sweating and trembling.

Jethro's hands were moving gently but expertly over her. "Are you in pain?"

"I'm all right," she said faintly. "Help me up."

By now quite a crowd had gathered and watched as with Jethro's arm around her, Laurel struggled to her feet. She was very white and gasped once as she straightened herself, but she was also determined.

"Where's Lucifer? Help me back into the saddle."

There was a chorus of protest.

"You must not risk such a thing. The horse is dangerous," exclaimed Malinsky.

"I wouldn't advise it," said Jethro more quietly.

"I'll call a cab and take you home at once," was George's practical suggestion.

She looked from one to the other. "You're very kind, but I'd never forgive myself if I gave in. I'll not conquer my black devil if I let him believe he has won." She managed a faint smile. "I'm riding him back to his stable."

There was a steeliness about her, a courage that refused to be beaten, and it moved Jethro unutterably.

126

He said, "If you must, then I'll ride with you."

George and the Russian would have prevented him if they could, but Laurel herself effectively stopped their objections.

"Thank you, Jethro. I would be grateful."

She leaned against him as with infinite care he lifted her into the saddle. He saw her mouth shut tight on an exclamation of pain but resolutely she took the reins he put into her hands. Then he looked round at the others.

"Don't be anxious, gentlemen. I think perhaps she is right. Miss Rutland and I are old friends and I am acquainted with her doctor. I'll make sure that she has every attention. Charles, have you my horse there?"

He swung himself into the saddle saying quietly to the young man, "Send a message to your father, will you? I'll wait until he comes."

Then watched by curious spectators always avid for any kind of drama, he moved close to Laurel and they rode together out of the park.

She was staring straight ahead. "It was very silly of me but it was because of you . . . I never thought . . . it was the shock . . ."

"I'm sorry." His hand closed over hers for an instant. "I should not have acted so foolishly."

"How long have you been back from Vienna?"

"Only a week. Don't talk. We shall soon be there."

The road was busy and she was having difficulty in keeping her restive horse steady. He guessed that every jolt was causing her pain, but she hung on bravely till they reached the mews. Jethro was surprised to see Seth hurrying to meet them, but he put that on one side for the moment. Laurel slid half fainting into Jethro's arms and he carried her into the house past the gaping servants. In the hall Jane Ashe came to meet him, her voice sharp with anxiety.

"I was afraid of something like this. How bad is she?"

"I'm not sure yet. Where shall I take her?"

"I'll show you."

Jane led the way and he followed her upstairs to the room where he had once spoken to Sir Joshua. The four poster bed was the same but everything else had been transformed, pale satin-striped walls, silk hangings, elegant furniture, silver and glass on the lace hung dressing table, a faint elusive perfume in the air, everything of rare beauty like the girl he placed on the bed with such lingering gentleness.

"I hope it is not too serious and I've sent for Dr Townsend who, I understand, attends Miss Rutland, but I'd like to make sure myself before he comes."

"I really don't think I can allow that," began Jane frowning at this impertinent stranger.

"Don't be stupid," he said abruptly. "I'm a doctor . . . Jethro Aylsham. You must know my brother Oliver, Lord Aylsham."

"Yes, yes . . . I do . . ."

"Well then," he said impatiently, "help me to undress her. I fear the fall may have cracked some ribs."

Faced with this tall authoritative young man with the smouldering grey eyes, there was nothing Jane could do but obey. Together they unbuttoned Laurel's jacket and peeled it off. She loosened the white stock and with impatient fingers he unhooked the blouse and the filmy under-garment with its fine lace trimming.

Dreamily Laurel was conscious of Jethro's cool strong hands moving over her body with a steady firm pressure and instead of feeling shocked or embarrassed was aware of a sensuous sweetness that thrilled through her and that she only half understood. Then suddenly the probing fingers touched a sensitive place and she opened her eyes wide.

"That hurt," she said indignantly.

"I thought it might. Take a deep breath. I shall probably hurt you again. I must explore a little further."

For a moment the pain was sharp, then he drew back. "I was right. You've cracked a couple of ribs. When Townsend comes he will strap them up for you. They will be painful for a week or so. You must take great care."

"My head hurts too," she complained childishly.

"Let me see." He bent over her, parting the silky hair with searching fingers. "Yes, there's quite a bruise, some blood too. You must have fallen against a sharp stone." He looked across at Jane. "If you'll fetch some warm water. I will bathe it and take another look."

"Very well." She looked anxiously at Laurel. "Will you be all right if I leave you?"

"Yes, of course."

Jane went out of the room and Jethro moved away to the window. Outside a landau drawn by two horses clip-clopped slowly down the street and a dark-skinned man, Indian probably, with a tray of spices went up and down the area steps

128

peddling his rhubarb, nutmeg, cinnamon and ginger. Jethro stared at them unseeingly. He was a doctor accustomed to examining women's bodies clinically as cases to be diagnosed and treated as might be necessary, but this was different. It had taken all his self-control to stop his hands trembling as he explored that beautiful body which still tormented his dreams. What the hell was he going to do about it, he thought distractedly? He had believed himself cured, armoured against temptation and here he was shaking like some boy infatuated for the first time.

A cool voice from the bed broke in on him. "Did you enjoy your stay in Vienna?"

He turned round. "Enjoy is not really the word. I learned a great deal."

"Which you intend to put into practice at St. Thomas's?"

"I'm not going back to St. Thomas's. I'm going to Bart's."

"Is it true that all Viennese women are very beautiful?"

"Quite true."

"Did you fall in love with them?"

"With all of them, but as they had either just given birth or were lying on the operating table waiting for my knife, love didn't really enter into it."

She laughed, a pretty rippling sound ending in a painful gasp. "Ouch, that hurt."

"It will, I'm afraid, for quite a while."

Then Jane came back with a bowl of water and cotton wool. He carefully wiped away the blood. "It's not serious, just a bad bruise, but it may give you a headache. I would advise some days in bed and taking things very quietly for at least a fortnight." He turned to Jane. "I'd like to wait until Dr Townsend comes."

"Yes, of course, Dr Aylsham," she said. "If you care to go down to the dining room, I'll tell the servants to bring you some coffee."

"Thank you." He took Laurel's hand in both his. "Your own doctor will be looking after you, but take care of yourself and don't ride that stallion again, at least not for the time being."

"I won't . . ."

"Good." He turned away and she stopped him.

"Jethro . . ."

"Yes," he smiled indulgently. "What is it?"

129

"You're not going to desert me, are you?"

"Of course not."

"I shall see you again?"

He paused, then lifted her hand and kissed it lightly before he went out of the room.

Laurel was unusually reticent after he had gone and she looked so small and white and was obviously suffering such a painful reaction from the fall that Jane did not question, but simply busied herself with undressing her as gently as possible and slipping the silk nightgown over her head. Presently when she had made her as comfortable as she could and sent for some tea since Laurel refused all food, she went downstairs to the dining room.

Jethro was standing in front of the fire, a cup of coffee in his hand. He turned as she came in. He saw a slender woman with light brown hair drawn smoothly back from a broad forehead. No real beauty, perhaps, except for the large hazel eyes regarding him shrewdly, but a sensible face that combined charm and firmness. He felt a sudden relief that Laurel had made such a wise choice of companion.

"What a number of changes you have made in this room," he said smiling. "I remember it being dark as a tomb."

"That was Laurel. We worked on it together. Perhaps I had better introduce myself. I am Jane Ashe."

"The lady in Lausanne whom Laurel was so determined to reach when I met her in Italy."

"Yes. I was teaching in the convent there and you of course are the gentleman who was so instrumental in bringing her to England."

"Yes. We meet at last. I heard a great deal about you one way and another," said Jethro.

"And I about you, Dr Aylsham."

"Without meeting we appear to have become well acquainted." He smiled. "Are you on a visit, Miss Ashe?"

"No. I've given up my post at the convent. I'm here permanently, or perhaps I should say until Laurel marries."

"And will that be soon?" It was quite absurd how much he hung upon her answer.

"Who knows? She has a string of admirers, but I would be hard put to it to place my finger on the lucky man."

"I see."

She thought he looked relieved. Then Dr Townsend's carriage

drew up outside and he came bustling in. Jethro went to greet him and she took the two doctors upstairs.

While they examined Laurel and conferred together, she studied Jethro with interest and decided that she liked his looks. So this was the young man whose name had come up so frequently in those first scrambling letters from Laurel and then was never mentioned again. She wondered why. He was not so obviously handsome as George Grafton, but the lean face with the straight dark brows, clear grey eyes and generous mouth had its own distinction and charm. Not an easy man, she thought, too fine-drawn, too sensitive. There were already faint lines about the eyes and mouth. She could not help noticing how he took the bandages from the older doctor's hands, his fingers deft and skilful, almost as if he could not endure anyone but himself to touch Laurel.

When it was all done, he piled up the pillows behind her. "There, that was not too bad, was it?"

"No," she murmured. Their eyes locked together for an instant then he abruptly moved away.

"You're very fortunate, young lady, that it wasn't a great deal worse," said Dr Townsend warmly. "You must take care of her, Miss Ashe, she takes too many risks and she's far too thin. You should feed her up."

"I'm not going to become a tub of lard to please anyone," protested Laurel from her pillows.

"Not a tub of lard, my dear, but just a little more flesh on those pretty bones wouldn't come amiss. After all that is what the gentlemen admire, isn't that so, Jethro?"

"I wouldn't know," he said shortly.

"Oh come, my boy, Vienna wasn't all work, I'm sure." Dr Townsend was being deliberately jovial. He turned back to Jane. "Light food today and not too much of it and rest, plenty of rest. I've left a draught. Let her take some now and again this evening. I'll look in again tomorrow morning."

"Very well, doctor."

"Don't come down. We can find our own way out. Goodbye, my dear. We'll soon have you on your feet again." He took Jethro's arm. "Can you spare me an hour? I've had an interesting case that I'd like to discuss with you."

Their voices died away as they descended the stairs. Jane turned to the windows, adjusting the curtains so as to shield Laurel from the morning light. Then she came back to the bed.

131

"Is it very painful?" she asked sympathetically.

"Painful enough." Laurel moved restlessly. "It was such a stupid thing to do. I've never fallen from a horse before."

"I thought all along that he was too powerful for you."

"Oh, for heaven's sake, don't keep saying 'I told you so'," snapped Laurel with unusual petulance. "It's so boring."

"I'm sorry." Jane smiled and began to tidy the bed. "So that was Jethro Aylsham," she said lightly. "I found it interesting to meet him at last. He's even more fascinating than your description of him in Italy."

"Do you mind? I don't want to talk about him . . . or about anything just now."

"I understand. You're shaken and I'm not surprised." Jane measured a dose of the medicine the doctor had left into a glass and held it out to her. "If you take this, it will help you to rest more easily."

Silently Laurel swallowed the draught and grimaced. Jane took the glass from her and put a hand gently on her forehead. "I'll leave you for a little and come back later."

"Bless you. What would I do without you?"

"Manage very well, I expect. Now try and sleep. You'll feel a great deal better if you do."

When she had gone, Laurel lay still against the pillows, her bruises beginning to stiffen, her head aching and unable to take more than short shallow breaths without acute pain, but worse, far worse than the physical discomfort, was the shattering knowledge that nothing had changed. To see Jethro, to know him close to her, feel the touch of his hands, had been enough to awaken the emotions which she liked to believe she had conquered. If this was love, then it was agony. And he . . . what did he feel? She had to know . . . she must know. He was not going to walk out of her life again without saying a word. Oh God, why did this have to happen to her? She shut her eyes against it and slowly, very slowly, felt the opiate begin to deaden the pain and dull the conflict in her mind.

Downstairs in the drawing room Jane stood at the window absently caressing the head of the big dog and finding it oddly significant that Laurel, who always talked freely and amusingly about the young men who circled around her and pursued her with proposals, honourable and dishonourable, should be so absolutely silent about Jethro Aylsham.

132

10

A week later Laurel was out of bed, but still under strict doctor's orders to take things very easily. She was lying on the sofa in the drawing room, Marik the Borzoi as usual close beside her, when unexpectedly Rosemary was shown in. She stood just inside the door looking shy but very pretty in a dark blue gown and a little cape edged with squirrel.

"Papa had to come up to London rather suddenly. There's been a crisis in the House over Russia invading Turkey," she said rather breathlessly.

"Heavens, that doesn't concern us surely?"

"Papa says it does and England might have to declare war on the Tsar."

"Poor Dmitri Malinsky. That means he will have to leave London and go to St. Petersburg and he does so love it here," said Laurel with no real belief that anything so outlandish as a war could possibly disturb the luxurious life of the capital. "It will blow over, I expect, like most crises."

"Yes, I suppose so," agreed Rosemary, dismissing it airily as of no consequence. "Anyway, I asked if I could come with him and he agreed. Robin dined with us last night and he told me about your accident. I'm so sorry. Are you feeling better?"

"Very much better. Almost as good as new and bored to extinction with lying here and doing nothing." She stretched out a hand. "Dear Rosemary, it's lovely to see you after all this time. Let's have some tea and a nice long gossip."

"Yes please." She came across to Laurel.

"Do you mind ringing the bell?"

"Of course not. Is Miss Ashe here?"

"Jane has gone out for the afternoon."

"Good. I know it's silly of me, but I'm always a little frightened of her. She reminds me of a governess Jess and I once had."

"Afraid of Jane? Oh Rosemary, she is the kindest person."

"I'm sure she is . . . it's just me, I suppose. Anyway I'd much rather have you to myself."

Until tea came, they talked about family matters, how Jessica, who had been presented at the same royal drawing room as Laurel that summer, already had a string of beaux at her beck and call though she was only seventeen.

"She takes it all in her stride, not like me," confessed Rosemary. "I never really enjoyed all those parties and balls. I was scared to death I'd make some dreadful *faux pas* most of the time. Aunt Cherry has sent Margaret down to the settlement. She says everyone should spend a few weeks there from time to time for the good of their soul and to give them a more balanced view of society."

"Oh, dear, that sounds very formidable. I've been down there once or twice, but not for lofty reasons like that. In a way I quite enjoyed it, especially the school."

"Oh Laurel, did you? I went with Mamma once." She wrinkled her nose fastidiously. "It smelled horrid and they were all so dirty."

"Well, they can't help that. You ought to see the hovels they live in," said Laurel practically. "Jethro's friend, Dr West, has set up a dispensary for sick children in Great Ormond Street. One of the girls at the settlement goes there once a week. She told me that some of the children from the poorest homes are sewn into a shift at the beginning of the cold weather and it is not taken off again until the following spring. One of the first things they have to do is to cut them out of it and then bath them."

"Oh, how disgusting. I don't know how they can."

Laurel shrugged her shoulders. "It's just a job. If you take it on, then you must do it."

"Would you?"

"I don't know. If I had to, I suppose I could."

It was not until they were drinking their tea that the real reason for Rosemary's visit emerged. She was looking down at the cup in her hand and trying to sound casual.

"I hear that Seth Starling is working for you now."

"Yes, that's right. He came asking if I would take him on," said Laurel carefully, "and I was only too glad to do so. The man I had inherited from Grandfather was not at all satisfactory."

"Did he tell you why he had left Ravensley?"

"Not really, only that he felt he needed a change."

"It wasn't that at all. It was because of me."

"Because of you? What on earth do you mean?"

134

"Oh, it was all so stupid." Rosemary put down her cup. "We'd come in from riding one morning. He helped me to dismount and somehow I got the reins all caught up. He had to disentangle them . . . and we were very close . . . and then he kissed me . . ." She paused, faint colour running up into her pale face.

"Well, that doesn't sound very serious," said Laurel lightly.

"Perhaps it wouldn't have been but Papa happened to see us. He didn't fly into a rage on the spot. You know that is not his way. But the next thing I knew, Seth had left. He didn't even wait to be dismissed."

"How do you know?"

"Papa told me himself. You see I was so distressed about it that I went to him. I told him that it was all my fault . . . that I *wanted* Seth to kiss me . . ."

"You actually told your father that?"

"Yes, I did," said Rosemary defiantly. "Why shouldn't I when it is true. I love him and he loves me."

"And what did Lord Aylsham say to that?"

"He was very kind, but he told me that it was quite impossible and I was being cruel to Seth to let him think it ever could be anything else. He was so reasonable and understanding that it made it ten times worse. I'd far rather he'd been angry . . ."

"Because then you could have been angry too. Oh I know exactly how you felt," said Laurel, "but he's right, you know. It *is* unfair to Seth and he did the wisest thing to leave Ravensley."

"Without seeing me, without saying a single word," exclaimed poor Rosemary. "It's easy for you to say that. Everyone adores you. You don't know what it is like . . . how wretched it makes you feel, how humiliated."

"It happens to all of us at some time," said Laurel sombrely.

"Not to you, never to you."

"Yes, even to me, and it hurts terribly, but there's nothing you can do about it."

Rosemary stared at her for an instant struck by the ring of truth in Laurel's voice, then she went back to her own troubles. "Could I . . . do you think I could speak with Seth?"

"No," said Laurel decisively. "No, it wouldn't be right. Your father would be very angry with me if I permitted such a thing."

"What does it matter if he is? Oh Laurel, how can you be so unkind?"

"I'm not being unkind, believe me. I'm very sympathetic,

135

but it wouldn't be any use, Rosemary. It would only make it even more difficult afterwards. Can't you see that?"

"No, I can't. It's very little to ask."

"Listen to me. I'm right, I know I am, but if you want to write him a little note just to say goodbye, then I'll see that he gets it, but nothing more. If I'd known all this, then I wouldn't have taken him on."

"Oh don't dismiss him, Laurel, not because of me. It wouldn't be fair."

"I don't want to," said Laurel ruefully. "He's too useful. I couldn't manage Lucifer without him."

"May I write the note now?" asked Rosemary eagerly.

"Yes, but make it short and I don't want to know what is in it."

"All right, bless you."

Rosemary dropped a kiss on Laurel's cheek and hurried across to the small bureau. It was while she was bent over her letter that they had another visitor. Charles Townsend came in carrying a huge basket of country flowers.

"Jethro asked me to bring them. Lady Aylsham sent them up from Ravensley and he did intend to come himself, but was kept at the hospital."

He seizes on any excuse not to come near me, thought Laurel unhappily. She bent over the flowers. Clusters of late roses were buried amongst sprays of autumn foliage. The tangy scent of the ferns carried her nostalgically back to the Fens that she had scarcely visited since that dreadful day almost a year ago now. She had a curious longing to go back there.

Rosemary had folded her letter and brought it to her. She took it from her hand.

"I don't think you have met Dr Charles Townsend," she said. "He used to work with Jethro at St. Thomas's hospital. Charles, this is Rosemary, Lord Aylsham's daughter."

"Delighted to meet you."

The young man bowed over her hand. A remarkably pretty girl, he thought, but she looked as if she had been crying and he wondered why.

"I ought to go," said Rosemary.

"I too," added Charles. "No rest for a doctor. I only called to bring the flowers."

"Perhaps you'd escort Miss Aylsham to St. James's Square," suggested Laurel. "It's not far."

136

"With pleasure."

"I wouldn't dream of troubling you," said Rosemary quickly.

"No trouble, I assure you. It's on my way."

"Tell her about the work you have been doing with Dr West at the children's dispensary," said Laurel. "She will be interested."

Rosemary bent to kiss her. "I'll come again if I may before I go back to Ravensley."

"Yes, do."

Laurel watched them leave, Charles taking Rosemary's arm solicitously. He was a personable young man. Perhaps he might help to distract her a little from thinking about Seth. She looked at the note on the table. She was not at all sure that she ought to pass it on, but she had promised and that was that.

A fortnight or so later Jethro was washing his hands in the small room adjacent to the operating theatre at St. Bartholomew's Hospital. It had been a long and exhausting day and unlike some of his colleagues he was scrupulously careful to make sure his instruments and everything connected with his work that day had been scrubbed in boiling water and powerful carbolic. It should have been general practice, but it was not always observed and he was well aware that his assistants and the students who thronged the theatre to watch him operate and who were only too anxious to be off duty, regarded him as quite infuriatingly fussy, but more and more he was becoming convinced of the necessity of absolute cleanliness in checking infection. He was feeling depressed because one of his patients that morning had died under the chloroform. It should have been quite a routine operation and he had seen the unspoken accusation in the eyes of the wretched man's wife. She was condemning him for the use of the anaesthetic and yet he knew he had been right. An undetected heart weakness had been the cause of death. It could have happened at any time and yet obscurely he felt himself at fault. He knew perfectly well that no doctor can allow himself to become personally involved with his patients and yet sometimes he felt an enormous anger because progress was so slow, prejudice was so hard to overcome and people died simply because medical science was still groping helplessly in the dark.

He had not gone back to Arlington Street only because he could not entirely trust himself, but he had still made sure that he was kept informed of Laurel's condition; so much so that Dr Townsend had begun to lose patience with him.

"My dear fellow, it's quite a simple case and the young woman is mending fast. If you don't believe me, call and see for yourself." He smiled. "You'll not be alone. Half the gilded youth of London are camping out on her doorstep and as far as I know, have not been granted a look-in. Little minx, she knows how to keep them all on tenterhooks."

She did indeed. In the month he had been back from Vienna he seemed to hear tales about her everywhere, some of them admiring, some envious, some purely scandalous. Oh she knew very well how to keep men dangling. She was not her mother's daughter for nothing. He had known that long ago when they had come back from Italy and now the child had grown into a woman, beautiful and dangerous. There was Robin breaking his heart over her and now this business with Rosemary – what the hell did she think she was doing? Townsend was right. He should call on her, make her realize how recklessly she was playing with the lives of others. He dried his hands, shrugged himself into his coat and took a cab back to the Albany. Robin was waiting for him in the sitting room and he knew at once by the boy's hangdog look that he was in trouble. He sighed impatiently.

"Now what is it?"

"Can you spare a few minutes, Jet?"

"You'll have to be quick. I'm due at one of Lady Emily's routs at Carlton Gardens and I'm late already."

"I thought you didn't care for these affairs."

"I don't as it happens, but it doesn't do one any good to turn down every invitation. Is it important?"

"It is rather."

"All right. Come and talk to me while I change."

In the bedroom he stripped off coat and shirt while Robin stood by the dressing table fiddling with the toilet articles. He put an encouraging hand on his shoulder. "Come on, boy, out with it. It's not Rosemary again, is it? She's not run off with Seth, I hope."

"No, nothing like that. The fact is that during the summer I got involved with a sporting set," began Robin awkwardly.

"George Grafton and his cronies, I suppose."

"Well, yes, you know how it is – they plunge pretty heavily..."

"And now you want a loan, is that it?"

138

"Not exactly. You see you were still in Vienna and I didn't want to ask Papa, so I went to a money lender."

"You young idiot! And now he's pressing you, I suppose."

"It's worse in a way. Somehow Laurel found out and she's paid it, the whole debt."

Jethro stopped in the act of putting studs in his shirt to stare at him. "She's what?"

"I know. I feel terrible about it. I mean I can't let her do a thing like that – it's so . . . so dishonourable . . ."

The anger against Laurel that had been simmering inside Jethro suddenly exploded. "What the devil is she up to?"

"I *must* pay her back," went on Robin wretchedly, "and I don't know how I can do it without going to Father . . ."

"No, don't do that. Leave it to me. I've a very sizeable bone to pick with Miss Rutland."

"She meant it kindly . . ."

"Oh yes, I'm sure she did," said Jethro grimly. "How much?"

"Five thousand."

"Good God, you must have been out of your senses. Don't worry. I'll see she gets it."

"Are you sure?"

"Quite sure. Fortunately Vienna proved quite profitable." He took one final look in the mirror and then turned to Robin. "Forget her, boy, put her out of your mind. It's the only way."

"I know damn well I don't stand a chance, but I can't help going on hoping."

Jethro looked at him for an instant. He understood only too well how the boy felt. Then he picked up hat, cloak and gloves. "I must go."

Robin held him back for a moment. "I can't tell you how grateful I am."

"Nonsense, nothing to be grateful for. Come on. Can I drop you anywhere?"

"No, I think I'll walk a little."

They went out of the Albany together.

Lord Palmerston had been kept in town by the increasing trouble abroad. Turkey maddened by Russian invasion had declare war on the Tsar and the first onslaught had been exceptionally bloody. There was a strong wave of political feeling against Nicholas and his ruthless policy of expansion. The Russian bear must be taught a lesson. The Cabinet was wavering and the Prime Minister had been accused of cowardice because he was still unwilling to commit the nation to war. No particular thought of what the future held in store for him entered Jethro's mind when he came into the drawing room, whose wide windows looked out on the green lawns of St. James's Park. He was captured immediately by Lady Emily with whom he was something of a favourite. She still had remnants of the great beauty that had captivated old Pam forty years ago. They had been lovers long before her husband died and despite his eye for any pretty woman, they were wonderfully happy. She slipped an arm through Jethro's in her usual cosy way.

"The very person I wanted to see. Now come along. I would like you to meet someone with whom I'm sure you will have a great deal in common. She doesn't often attend our parties now. She thinks we're too frivolous, but I intend to prove her wrong."

He smiled and followed her across the room to find himself facing a tall young woman in her early thirties, very slight and willowy, with rich brown hair and delicate colouring. Her black silk dress trimmed with fine lace had an expensive simplicity.

"Florence, my dear, I want you to meet Jethro Aylsham," said Lady Emily. "He is one of the very cleverest of our young surgeons. Pam swears by him, says he would never allow himself to be cut up by anyone else. He has just come back from Vienna and is bursting with all kinds of novel notions, just the kind of thing you would find most interesting. Jethro, may I present Miss Nightingale? She is struggling with the Institute for the care of sick gentlewomen and is a neighbour of yours in Harley Street. She is performing absolute wonders as matron and nurse and wearing herself to the bone, though I suspect she enjoys every minute of it."

She patted him on the arm, gave them both a beaming smile and left them together. Jethro took the slim cool hand in his.

"I have been wanting to meet you for a very long time, Miss Nightingale. It is the most courageous task you have set yourself."

A pair of fine grey eyes sparkled at him merrily. "Isn't that just like Lady Emily? She goes on and on praising me for all the wrong reasons. I'm very far from acting as matron or even nurse. Head cook and bottle washer is nearer the mark at number one. You'd never believe the chaos left behind by the committee who ran it before me – dirty linen, ragged blankets,

140

filthy kitchens with not a pan fit to use, no drugs in the medicine cupboard, not a mattress unsoiled, not even a bed pan! The very first thing we needed were buckets of boiling water, chloride of lime and scrubbing brushes!"

Laurel, who had arrived late and had been immediately surrounded by some of the younger set, saw the two of them talking together. She had heard of Florence Nightingale and her quite desperate struggle with her reluctant family to take up nursing. Nurses for the most part were recruited from the very lowest rank of society. No gently born young lady had ever dreamed of such a revolutionary idea and Laurel had thought of her with faint scorn as an eccentric, prim, unattractive kind of person. Now she knew she had been quite wrong. The grave face alight with interest had its own beauty. She heard their laughter as they exchanged hospital gossip and was quite unreasonably jealous.

Florence was saying, "It's quite absurd the problems I still have to face. A woman is at a great disadvantage. She is regarded as little more than an idiot who can be tricked and deceived at every turn. Only the other day the chemist sent me spirits of nitre in a bottle marked ether if you please. Thank goodness I smelt it before giving it to a patient or I might have been faced with an unpleasant inquest. Then one of the builders set up a flue for a gas fire so carelessly that it collapsed and if I'd not been there to catch it in my arms, it could have killed someone. As it was we were nearly suffocated by escaping gas and in dire fear of an explosion."

"I sympathise," said Jethro, recognising at once the steely determination that lay behind the amusing account of her difficulties. "If I can help at any time, please call upon me."

"Don't be too rash, Dr Aylsham. I might take you at your word. You could find yourself operating on a choked boiler instead of a diseased abdomen. I'm quite ruthless, you know. Sidney Herbert tells me I'm like a boa constrictor and no one who is of use to me escapes being swallowed up. Who is that lovely girl talking to him over there?"

He followed the direction of her eyes. Laurel was standing hand in hand with Dmitri Malinsky and in deep conversation with Sidney Herbert who was Secretary of War.

"I'm surprised to see that boy from the embassy here," went on Florence. "Anyone Russian is being shunned just now, quite unfairly I'm sure. Even poor Sidney has been looked at askance because his mother, the Countess of Pembroke, was once Katerina Vorontsov. You know there's a great deal of character in that young woman's face. She might be of use to me some day."

Jethro smiled. "Oh no, surely not. I can't see Laurel becoming one of your nurses."

"Is that her name? How pretty." She regarded him earnestly. "I'm right, you know. There's quality there and I've become something of an expert in detecting it. It's not the 'do-gooders' I want, Dr Aylsham. I have plenty of them on my committee and they are a constant source of trouble. They float around the wards with sweet words carrying bowls of broth and egg custard, but ask them to wash a floor or clean up after an operation and they either come over faint or discover immediately that they are due somewhere else."

"I wish you would come and supervise my nurses at Bart's," said Jethro feelingly. "I order a patient a light diet of beef tea and arrowroot and find it congealing into a disgusting mess by his bedside because the poor devil is too weak to lift a spoon to his mouth and it's no one's job to feed him."

"I know exactly what you mean," sighed Florence. "It's not your surgical skill that's at fault, but the nursing afterwards and with the best will in the world one cannot do everything oneself. Tell me about Vienna, Dr Aylsham. I've heard something of the remarkable work being done in the hospitals there."

Their mutual interest kept them absorbed in one another for most of the evening and it was not until much later that Laurel suddenly found herself face to face with Jethro. There had been some music and a song or two, then the big room was cleared so that the young people could dance and Lord Palmerston with Laurel on his arm captured Jethro just as he was about to make his escape.

"Oh no, you don't run off like that, young man," he said jovially. "Here's a young lady pining to dance and my stiff bones won't stand up to it. Wish to God they did. I can manage a quadrille or two with the best, but not these modern jigs. You give her a whirl and I'll beat a retreat, eh? I'm not a gambling man but I'll try a flutter or two in the card room." He pinched Laurel's cheek. "Go on, enjoy yourself, my girl. It doesn't last, you know. 'Youth's a stuff will not endure.' Who the devil said that?"

"Shakespeare, I believe," said Jethro.

"Did he, by Jove? Fancy me remembering it. Long time since my schooldays." He grinned at them both and ambled off.

Laurel looked up at Jethro from under her lashes. "I'm afraid that is more or less a royal command if you can bear to drag yourself away from Miss Nightingale."

"Miss Nightingale has gone already," he said austerely.

"Has she? What a pity. You looked so happy together." She paused and then said quietly, "Why did you never come and see me again after my fall?"

"Many reasons. I followed your progress very closely however. Are you sure you're strong enough for one of old Pam's jigs?"

"Quite strong enough."

"Good. Then shall we take the floor?"

The music had broken into a lively polka and Jethro slid an arm around the slender waist and led her into the dance. Soon they were spinning around as gaily as the other twenty couples, but she was not quite as strong as she had believed. By the end she was breathless with a painful stitch in her side and furious with herself because she was obliged to cling helplessly to his arm. He guided her to a chair and sat beside her.

"Now take a deep breath and don't talk," he advised.

"I'm quite well," she gasped.

He stopped a passing servant and asked for a glass of water. "Sip it slowly," he commanded, "and don't be foolish. It's been too much for you. You're exhausted and I'm going to take you home."

"I'm perfectly all right," she protested.

"No, you're not. Anyway I want to talk to you and I can't do that here."

"You're being very masterful. Supposing I refuse to go?"

"You'd be very silly if you did."

She sipped the water uncertain whether to be pleased at the way he had taken command or whether to resent it.

"You're looking better already." He took the glass from her. "I think we should leave now. Come."

He offered her his hand, but at that moment George Grafton crossed the floor towards them.

"Malinsky told me you were here, Laurel," he said, ignoring Jethro. "May I have the honour of dancing with you?"

"I'm not dancing any more this evening, George. I'm rather tired."

"If that is so, then may I take you home?"

"I have already claimed that privilege," interrupted Jethro curtly. "Miss Rutland is in my charge."

George frowned. "Indeed and since when?"

"Is that important? It so happens that I have known her a good deal longer than you have, Captain Grafton."

"And what does that mean?"

"Take it how you please," was the cool reply.

They were facing one another, mutual dislike crackling between them. There was a taut angry look on Jethro's face and George's eyes glittered. He looked handsome and dangerous and suddenly Laurel lost her temper.

"I'm not a parcel to be bandied about between you," she said. "I can decide for myself."

They both turned to look at her.

"Choose then," said George abruptly.

She hesitated, glancing from one to the other. "I would prefer to take neither of you," she said sweetly, "but for tonight Jethro has been acting as my physician so maybe I should do as he says. I'm sorry, George."

Jethro took her arm and they moved away together while George stared after them, the baffled look on his face turning to a black anger.

Malinsky who had seen what had happened said a little maliciously, "What is wrong? Has she left you standing?"

"Damn you, don't laugh." George glanced irritably around the room. "Confoundedly slow affair, this, I'm going," and he made his way towards the door.

It was Laurel's carriage which took them back to Arlington Street. When they stopped, she looked at the silent man beside her.

"Seth can drive you to the Albany if you wish."

"I did say I wanted to talk to you. May I come in?"

"Isn't it rather late?"

"Not much after eleven."

She shrugged her shoulders. "Very well."

He followed her up the steps and into the house. Cindy was standing at the bottom of the stairs. She looked curiously at the tall dark man she had only seen once before when he had carried her mistress into the house on the day of her accident.

144

Laurel said impatiently, "I won't require you tonight, Cindy. Has Miss Ashe gone to bed?"

"Yes, Miss. Some time ago. She had a headache."

"Very well. You had better get to bed too. Goodnight."

She went quickly into the dining room. For a whole year she had longed for an opportunity to talk with Jethro alone, but now it had come she felt apprehensive. One of the lamps had been lit filling the room with a soft mellow light and the fire still burned on the hearth. She crossed to it with a little shiver and stretched out her hands to the warmth. Then she dropped her cloak on to one of the chairs and turned to face him.

"Well, now you're here, what is it you wish to say to me?"

"How can you be so utterly irresponsible as to encourage this ridiculous affair between Rosemary and Seth Starling?"

The unexpected attack took her by surprise. "But I haven't done any such thing."

"Do you deny that you passed on correspondence between them?"

"I do deny it," she exclaimed stung to indignation. "When Rosemary came to see me, I impressed on her how impossible it was." Then she faltered. "The note she wrote was only to say goodbye. She was distressed because Seth had left Ravensley without seeing her."

"In that note she begged him to meet her secretly."

"Oh no! You don't mean . . ."

"Luckily there's no harm done. Seth, it seems, has more good sense than you have. He convinced her of the folly of it."

"How do you know all this?"

"Robin found out. He and his sister have always been close. He was worried about it for her sake and he told me instead of his father. Rosemary is very unhappy."

"I'm sorry about that, but I can't see that I'm to blame."

"Can't you? Can't you understand that simply by employing him you're causing trouble?"

"He came to me asking for work," she said defensively. "He is a good man with horses and I was in need of someone reliable."

"You never thought of Rosemary."

"You're being very unfair."

"I don't think so. And it's not only Rosemary. There's Robin too. All he dreams about is you. Don't you realize that? He used to be fond of Margaret, now he simply ignores her. He is

145

beggaring himself to keep up with the rich young fools who swarm around you and what do you do? Keep him dangling, smile at him occasionally like throwing a bone to a dog and then humiliate him by paying his debts. How do you think he felt when he found out?"

"I wanted to help him," she said in a stifled voice.

"Has the possession of your grandfather's wealth made you utterly insensitive to how others may feel? The Aylshams don't need your charity. I'll send you a cheque tomorrow."

"As you please." She turned away from him.

"It amuses you to have them all on a string, doesn't it?" he went on relentlessly. "That dissolute bounder George Grafton, popinjay Malinsky, that old roué Lord Pam, even Sidney Herbert, married and respectable, and tonight he couldn't keep his eyes off you. What are you playing at? I thought better of you. I believed you had it in you to be something rare – you have beauty, a fortune, everything a young woman could wish for and you waste yourself."

"I'm sorry that I'm not dedicated to good works like your Miss Nightingale," she exclaimed, anger flaring.

"That was cheap, a vulgar jibe. You should be ashamed." Then he stopped, remembering suddenly what Florence had said, 'There's character there and quality . . .' and he knew that he was lashing out at her, that he was being deliberately unjust because the very sight of her standing there maddened him.

The glow from the fire brought out golden autumn tints in the silky hair, her head was drooping, eyes downcast, long dark lashes on camellia pale cheeks . . . he wanted to seize her in his arms and kiss and kiss . . . he closed his eyes against the swift surge of desire and saw in her place the fatal beauty of the woman who had bewitched his father into a passion that had madness in it, an unlawful passion for his own daughter, and knew that the same wild passion burned in him held back by that bond of blood, that damnable relationship that he couldn't escape or forget.

She raised her head and met his eyes. "Have you quite finished?" she said quietly. "Because I also have something to say. Why did you run away from me after the hunt ball last year?"

He took a deep breath. "I'm not aware that I ran away from anything. I had an important engagement to fulfil in Vienna and I was forced to leave England earlier than I had anticipated."

"Don't lie, Jethro. Charles told me how undecided you had been about it. You ran away because you hadn't the courage to tell me the truth."

He walked away from her to the table. "I'm sorry," he said in a muffled voice. "I didn't know how to tell you."

"So you left me to find out for myself . . . in the worst possible way."

"I didn't mean it to be like that. I thought Clarissa would make it easier for you."

"And so she did . . . afterwards," she went on steadily. "Oh she was very kind. She explained that in marrying my mother, Justin Aylsham, your father, had married his own daughter. Is it true? Is it really true?"

"Everyone believed it."

"But you . . . did *you* believe it? There was no absolute proof."

"What need was there of proof?" he said, the words bursting out of him savagely. "What need of proof when everyone believed it? It was talked of everywhere, even at school, thrown into my face over and over again – the bastard brat whose stepmother was no better than a whore and whose father had died hideously because of the terrible thing he had done. Can you imagine what that was like? Have you any idea how long it took to live it down, how long it took to forget?"

He had always been so self-controlled that now his violence frightened her. She longed to go to him, put her arms around him, comfort him, love him, and perhaps if she had done, there might have been healing in it, but he was not a hurt child any longer, but a man older and more experienced than she was.

"It's a long time ago," she whispered helplessly, "and it was never certain. Is it so important?"

He turned a tormented face towards her. "Of course it is important. Can't you understand? Uncle and niece – what a fine scandal that would be! How they would enjoy digging up the old slander!" And then he paused pulling himself together with a mighty effort, aware that the greatest service he could do for her and for himself was to crush ruthlessly the powerful bond that had sprung up between them, unbidden and unsought. He said more quietly, "It is particularly important to me because I feel a responsibility for you. I brought you here from Italy. I owe it to your grandfather to see that you are happy and make the best of your life."

It was not what she had hoped for and the formal words hit

147

her like a douche of cold water. She said shakily, "But I thought
... I was sure ..."

"If by any chance," he went on in the same cool level tone, "I
accidentally gave you the impression of any warmer feelings,
then I blame myself severely. We were all a little foolish and
lighhearted that day of the hunt, weren't we?"

She stared at him for a moment, unbearably hurt and bewildered, and then a glimmering of the truth struck her. She
said slowly, "I don't believe you."

"You must believe me."

"No, I can't, I won't. If that were so, then you would be a
different person, someone who plays heartlessly with the
affections of others not caring whether he hurts or destroys."

"That was what my father did and I am his son," he said
sombrely.

"But you are not like him. I know it," she said passionately,
"You are yourself. The past is over and done with."

"I wish it were. My God, how I wish it were!"

They were standing at opposite sides of the room yet the
feeling between them was so strong they might have been in
each other's arms. Then she broke. The unbearable tension
snapped. She had no strength left to go on fighting.

"Please go, Jethro," she whispered. "Please go. I can't bear
any more."

It took all his strength not to cross the room, snatch her into
his arms, hold her close to his heart, tell her nothing mattered
but their love for one another, but instead he turned without a
word and went out of the room, out of the house.

Cindy, watching from the landing above, saw him go and
heard the hall clock strike midnight. Now she had something to
tell Jack Webb that he could pass on to Barton Grafton, something that would please him and might win an extra kiss or two.
He had been angry with her lately because there had been so
little to report. She hugged it to herself. Then, as she saw her
mistress come out of the dining room and begin to climb the
stairs with slow dragging steps, she escaped quickly to the room
in the attics she shared with Biddy the housemaid.

11

It was pure chance that took Laurel to the bonnet shop in a small court just off fashionable Bond Street. Jane taking an early morning stroll had discovered it, was impressed and proposed a visit. Laurel had told her nothing about the night Jethro had brought her home and she only heard of it in a roundabout way from the servants. That something had happened between them, she was certain. Not that Laurel showed any signs of distress. On the contrary she seemed in tearing spirits and when questioned, had shrugged her shoulders carelessly. "Jethro doesn't approve of the way I live," she said flippantly. But Jane who knew her well by now was not deceived by the brittle gaiety and the fact that she accepted every invitation that turned up, going racing with George, to the opera with Prince Malinsky who had a passion for music and flirting shamelessly with Robin. She guessed rightly that all this restlessness was Laurel's attempt to escape from some private unhappiness.

It was a few weeks later on a grey November morning that they called at St. James's Square, found Rosemary still in town with Lord Aylsham and invited her to accompany them on a bonnet-hunting expedition.

The shop had a charming bow window with the name "Lydia" prettily picked out in gold. It displayed one enchanting confection in palest pink trimmed with roses, tulle and ribbon. The owner of the shop saw the three ladies alight from the carriage and hurried to the door to meet them. She was an attractive woman in her mid-thirties quietly but stylishly dressed in grey poplin trimmed with black braid. After one startled glance Laurel recognised her as the lady she had once seen with Jethro on Epsom racecourse. The shop was small but Lydia Chester's designs certainly had flair. Rosemary who had been miserably determined to show complete indifference to everything was reluctantly won over by pale blue velvet and white daisies,

149

while even Jane succumbed to a dashing evening creation in black lace sewn with pearls and surmounted by a coquettish bow.

Laurel trying on and discarding one model after another said suddenly, "Are you by any chance acquainted with Jethro Aylsham?"

In the mirror she saw Lydia Chester frown before she said evenly, "If you are referring to the doctor, then I have met him professionally."

"I believe I saw you with him once at the races."

"Quite probably. I sometimes attend Ascot and the Derby." She smiled. "I find it useful to compare my own creations with others in the royal boxes."

"I see." Laurel stood up. "I'll take those three," she said choosing at random among the hats she had tried on. "What about you, Rosemary?"

"There are two I rather like," she said shyly, "but I can't decide between them."

"Take both of them as a present from me."

"Oh, it's too much. I can't let you buy them for me."

"Nonsense, of course you can. You too, Jane. Now don't argue, either of you, it's all decided. Will you pack them please, Mrs Chester? We'll take them with us and you can send the account to Arlington Street."

It was while the hats were being swathed in tissue paper and placed in the blue and white striped boxes that a small boy came running down the stairs at the back of the shop and burst through the bead curtain.

"Edwin, you know you're not allowed down here when I have customers," said his mother frowning.

The pretty dark-haired child stood his ground. "It's Uncle Jethro, Mamma, I saw him walking down the road. Do you think he's coming to see us?"

"You've probably made a mistake. Now go upstairs at once, there's a good boy. I'm so sorry, ladies. My maid who usually looks after my son has had to go out on an errand."

The boxes were ready by now. They picked them up and came through the shop doorway just as Jethro reached it. He looked surprised, then raised his hat politely.

"Good morning, Laurel . . . Rosemary . . . Miss Ashe." He glanced smilingly at their parcels. "You look as if you've been buying up the entire stock."

"Surely you are not indulging yourself in a new bonnet," said Laurel.

"No. My visit is purely professional."

"Really. Is Mrs Chester ill then?"

"Her little boy was my patient some time ago. I like to look in now and again to check his progress. Forgive me, ladies." He bowed and went into the shop.

"How extraordinary meeting Jet like that here," remarked Rosemary stepping up into the carriage. "I thought that child looked rather frail."

"Jet has been away for a year," objected Laurel settling herself beside her.

"There are some conditions that require to be checked even after a year or eighteen months," said Jane equably, taking the seat opposite.

It was perfectly plausible, so wasn't it ridiculous to feel so jealous? Even if Lydia Chester was his mistress, even if the child was his, what was it to do with her? He had made it plain enough that there could never be anything between them, hadn't he, and yet she could not accept it. She could not root him out of her heart, try as she would, and she rebelled against his decision angrily and uselessly.

The days went by and relations between England and Russia steadily worsened. Everyone was saying that if old Pam had been at the Foreign Office, then the fleet would have been in the Black Sea by now and the Tsar and his Russkies sent packing.

But amongst the fashionable pleasure-loving set war still seemed very far off and it was certainly not in Laurel's mind one foggy morning when Seth drove her down to spend the day at the Stepney settlement. Smarting under the lash of Jethro's criticism she had found time amid myriad engagements to spend an occasional morning or afternoon there, carefully choosing a day when she knew he was not holding his weekly clinic.

It was on that same morning that George Grafton took a cab to his brother's office in the city of London. It was a handsomely furnished suite of rooms in a tall old-fashioned building in Fenchurch Street. The ground floor was occupied by the shop whose expensive plate glass windows proclaimed Rutland's Fine Teas in splendidily scrolled black and gold. In Sir Joshua's

151

day the firm had been purely wholesale. The shop and the small packing factory had been Barton's idea and he was justly proud of its success. Rutland's Darjeeling, Lapsang, Suchong and even green Russian teas were rapidly becoming a household word. With some of the money so unjustly given to Laurel he could have expanded, opened more shops in some of the major cities, Liverpool perhaps and Bristol. It had rankled every time he thought of it until it had become an obsession. He brooded over it, savouring the time when he would right the wrong that had been done to him and his mother's letters arriving week after week acted as a goad urging him to action. Slowly but surely he was working towards his aim.

He looked up when George came in. "Well, stranger," he said sourly, "to what do I owe the honour of your visit?"

"Sarcastic, aren't we? Oh come on, Barton," said George easily. "Did you bite on a lemon this morning? Can't I pay a little brotherly call on you?"

"How much?" asked Barton sardonically.

"You've got no finesse," sighed George perching himself jauntily on the desk. "If you must be so crude, then what about five hundred? That's not too bad now, is it?"

"It's bad enough. What is it this time . . . horses or the gaming tables?" Barton reached for his cheque book. "What's happened to your famous charm? Six months and Laurel will be eating out of my hand – isn't that what you boasted?"

"So she does . . . so she does . . . now and then." George got up crossing moodily to the window and watching a huge brewer's dray with two magnificent shire horses calmly plodding down the narrow street. "The trouble is," he went on slowly, "the bird takes wing before I can close my hand and all is to do again."

Barton stared at the straight back struck by an unusual note of gravity in his brother's voice. He said casually, "It may interest you to know that I've made some intriguing discoveries about our little cousin."

"What kind of discoveries?"

"Oh this and that. It would appear that even the respectable Aylshams have an ugly skeleton or two in their cupboard."

George swung round. "What the devil do you mean? What have you been poking into with your dirty little spies?"

"Spies?"

"Yes, spies," said George firmly. "I know why you planted

152

that damned slut in Laurel's household so you needn't try to deny it."

"I don't intend to. What's wrong, George? You didn't think like this a year ago. Have you become her champion all of a sudden, her knight in shining armour?"

"No, of course not. I don't pretend to be any better than the next man, but I draw the line at some things and smearing a young girl's reputation is one of them. I won't have Laurel blackmailed, do you hear?"

"Who is talking of blackmail?" Barton leaned across the desk. "Don't be a fool, George. I know what I'm doing and I don't suppose you'll be slow in taking your share of what pickings may come out of it."

George studied him for a moment. "You're a cunning bastard, Bart. What have you got up your sleeve? What are you plotting?"

"Never you mind. Perhaps you don't know that she came down here a short time ago insisting on going over the factory. She had the impudence to criticize my methods, talking a lot of damned radical nonsense about hours of work, payment of wages, amenities for workers, making them feel they are hard done by – I tell you I had the devil's own job with them afterwards. I may have to teach her a lesson one of these days."

"What kind of a lesson?" said George curiously.

"Well, who knows?" Barton was smiling but it didn't hide the suppressed anger.

"You'd better take care. I'll not have her harmed."

"Don't worry. I know what I'm doing. Here's your cheque. Usual rate of interest."

"Bloodsucker! Thank you for nothing." George took it and put it in his pocket. "You may be rid of me sooner than you think if this war with Russia breaks out."

"Is it certain?" Barton's eyes glinted with sudden interest.

"Why? Are you hoping to purvey tea to the great British army and make a damned good profit by filling up the chests with dust?"

"George, that's an outrageous thing to say. Rutland's has a name for honest dealing."

"Oh, to hell with it. Can't I make a joke? As for the war your guess is as good as mine."

Barton sat back and looked at his brother musingly. "Why not use it as a lever, George? Women always become emotional when their hero goes into battle."

153

"The trouble is I'm not Laurel's hero," said George bitterly.

He sketched a salute and went out and down the stairs, a little surprised at his own fierce reaction to Barton's deviousness. He had never worried very much about it before. Now it disturbed him. What the hell was he planning in that tortuous mind of his? Damn Laurel! She had a devilish way of getting under a fellow's skin!

Seth Starling had driven his mistress to the Stepney settlement several times, but he still disapproved of it. He was immensely grateful to Laurel. Anyone else might have dismissed him after finding out the real reason for his leaving Ravensley. It seemed to him sometimes that he had loved the shy gentle Rosemary since she was a tiny child and he had known at the very moment he had kissed her that it was utterly impossible. He cursed himself for a damned fool, but he still found the loss painful and guessed from the extra tasks Laurel gave him that she sympathised and wanted to help him fill his days. In his opinion a lady like her shouldn't be soiling her hands with the idle layabouts to be found in these parts.

After threading his way through the narrow congested streets of the city he emerged into Aldgate and was immediately surrounded by a motley collection of higgledy piggledy market stalls. A raucous vulgar crowd milled in and out, arguing, bargaining and blaspheming. A maze of alleys with tumbledown houses, their windows patched with rags and blackened paper led off on each side of the road. Beyond the market ragged children and squabbling women wallowed in muddy gutters and hunted through piles of filthy garbage, fighting off the mangy dogs and lean fierce cats. Live worse'n pigs, most of 'em, thought Seth with the countryman's contempt for city slums. The thin fog clinging greasily to broken roofs and squalid courts gave it an eerie atmosphere while every now and then the low moan of a ship's siren came hollowly from the river. He cracked his whip threateningly as a tribe of half grown boys ran alongside the horses. One of them shouted something obscene and hurled a stone that only just missed cracking the carriage window.

The settlement was housed in a huge gaunt building of ugly yellowish brick stained now with soot, but despite the look of squalor it had become a source of warmth, comfort, food and loving care to numbers of homeless children, derelicts from the

154

water front and hopeless starving waifs who had once been rosy-cheeked country girls come to London with high hopes that had been drowned in despair and destitution.

A swarm of dirty youngsters, some of them hardly more than babies, surrounded the carriage as soon as it drew up. Seth swore under his breath as he climbed down from the box and opened the door. They gaped at the vision that stepped out in a dark green velvet mantle edged with silver fox. One or two of them crept forward reaching out grimy hands as if by touch a dream would become reality. Seth would have thrust them back but Laurel stopped him.

"Leave them and bring the hamper," she said crisply.

He followed her with an anxious backward glance at the carriage. He'd skin the little devils alive if they harmed his beloved horses.

In the dingy hall she said, "You'd better come back for me at about five o'clock, Seth."

The hamper was filled with sweets, chocolate, cake and toys all wrapped in bright paper to be distributed among the children in the school. When Laurel had first come to the settlement, Olivia Winter who ran it for Cherry Fenton had said a little disapprovingly, "It's good plain food they really need, you know. Milk and bread, sound nourishment," and Laurel had smiled at her.

"I know what you mean and that you think me pretty useless, but it is fun sometimes, isn't it, to have jam on the bread? I'm not awfully good at the useful things, but I *can* supply the jam."

Afterwards when Olivia saw her with the smaller children, telling them stories or singing to them and noticed that she did not push them away when they fingered her gown or tried to climb on to her knee, her austere heart warmed to the girl. Maybe it was good occasionally to bring a touch of glamour into drab lives.

She exclaimed with pleasure at the box of bright parcels. "May I keep some of them for Christmas? We've been promised a tree from Covent Garden. I told the children that when it's decorated, it will be just like the one for the Queen and Prince Albert at Buckingham Palace."

"What can I do to help today?" asked Laurel practically, untying the strings of her bonnet and taking off the fur-trimmed mantle.

155

"Well, Miss Rutland, I hardly like to ask you, but do you think that you could assist Dr Aylsham? It's an unusual day for his clinic but he's pressed for time and some of our usual helpers are away. This wretched fog has caused a lot of coughs and colds and Miss Margaret, Mrs Fenton's daughter, has her hands full with the older children's lessons."

"I'll do my best," said Laurel doubtfully, "but I'm not experienced in medical things."

"None of us are but we learn as we go along," replied Olivia cheerfully.

The surgery, if it could be dignified by that name, was a big bare room smelling strongly of some powerful disinfectant, the floor still damp from the scrubbing that Jethro insisted upon and the walls roughly whitewashed. When she went in she saw him at the far end unpacking his bag, his back turned to her.

"Is that you, Margaret?" he said. "How many have we on our list today?"

"It's not Margaret."

"Then who . . .?" He turned around and saw her. "Good God, what on earth are you doing here?"

"I'm acting as your asistant."

He frowned. "Oh for heaven's sake, this isn't a game, you know. You'll spoil your pretty dress."

"Olivia has provided me with an apron." She put it on, tied the strings behind her and began to roll up her sleeves in a business like fashion.

He watched her for a moment. "You'd better tie something over your hair," he said grimly. "Most of these children are verminous."

She looked startled for a second and he pulled a silk scarf from his greatcoat pocket tossing it across to her.

"Use that."

She tied it round her head pushing the curls out of sight while he took off his coat and turned back his cuffs.

"Do you often come here?" he asked.

"Not all that often."

"Slumming, is that it? Putting in a day now and then to soothe your conscience."

"Not at all. I come because I happen to enjoy it," she said coolly, ignoring his sarcasm. "Shall I tell them you are ready?"

"Yes please. We'd better get started."

156

The first patient was a baby with an unpleasant case of ringworm followed by a boy with a running ulcer on his leg. It took a good deal of courage on Laurel's part to watch and assist as Jethro probed and cleansed and bandaged.

"That was the result of a kick from his father's hob-nailed boot when he was blind drunk," he explained briefly when the boy had limped from the room. "Are you all right? You're not going to faint on me, are you?"

"Of course I'm not," she said curtly.

The morning wore on. She handed scissors, unrolled bandages, mopped up blood, helped to cleanse dirt encrusted sores, trying hard to ignore the smell of sickness and stale unwashed humanity which threatened to overpower the strong carbolic.

They paused only briefly to share a cup of watery coffee and a humble bread and cheese sandwich with Olivia Winter and then went back to work. In different ways the day was a revelation to both of them. Laurel was impressed not so much with his skill, she had expected that, but with his gentleness, his patience with ignorant mothers stubbornly refusing to change age-old customs and his ability to win the smallest child's trust when he was forced to hurt them. He got through an enormous amount of work and yet never seeemed to be brusque or hurried. Jethro in his turn was touched by the unflinching way she carried out the most unpleasant tasks and though she was ignorant, often handing him the wrong instrument or the wrong dressing, she was quick to learn.

The last case was the worst of all. It was a young woman cheaply but gaudily dressed in a red skirt and unsuitably flimsy blouse. She had a grubby shawl over her head and pulled half across her face. When she pushed it back, Laurel caught her breath with shock. The skin of one cheek and part of her neck was hideously lacerated and suppurating.

"My God, this is the result of a burn," exclaimed Jethro. "How did you come by it?"

"He did it," the woman said unemotionally, "with the flat iron. Took it red hot from the stove."

"You must have been in agony. Didn't you have it treated?"

"Wouldn't let me. Said he weren't wastin' no silver on any bloody doctor."

"Is he your husband?" Jethro was cutting away tissue with infinite care.

157

The young woman winced but bore the pain stoically. "He's the feller I live with. He were wild, see, 'cos I didn't hand over all I earned out on the streets that night. I had a right to keep a shillin' for meself, hadn't I?"

"Every right," he said abstractedly bent over his delicate task.

Laurel shut her eyes for an instant against the horribly disfigured flesh; the yellow pus, the fearful stench was almost more than she could bear.

"Tweezers," said Jethro without looking up.

She fumbled blindly and handed him something.

"Tweezers," he said impatiently and got them for himself. "Do think what you're doing. Now the gauze."

She groped for it and then stood rigid, her head swimming. "I won't faint," she told herself, "I won't . . . I won't . . ."

Jethro was working slowly and carefully. It seemed to take a very long time but somehow, stirred by pity, she managed to remain on her feet and do all that was required of her. Dimly she saw the young woman leave, then without realizing quite how it came about, she found herself sitting in a chair and a glass was being put in her hand.

"Drink that," commanded Jethro.

It was cold and bitter. She opened her eyes.

"Better now?"

"Yes. How stupid of me. I'm so ashamed."

"Don't be. You've done very well." His hand brushed against her cheek. "Astonishingly well."

She managed a smile. "And you didn't think I could."

"Did I show it?" he said contritely. "I take it all back. Now drink that up and wash your hands. We've done for today."

She felt enormously proud of his praise. "May I help you again?"

"By all means," he smiled, "if you really want to after today." He had turned to take his greatcoat from the nail in the wall. "I have to hurry. The fog is thickening and I must get back to Bart's, so I am afraid I can't see you home. Will you be all right?"

"Seth is coming back for me."

"Goodnight then, my dear . . . and thank you."

For the first time they had worked together as friends on equal terms. Maybe that was enough, thought Laurel wistfully. For the rest of November and all December she went each week

to the settlement and although it could be gruelling and sometimes almost more than she could stomach, she faced it resolutely
and found a simple happiness in working beside him that she
would never have believed possible.

The young woman whose face had been so badly burned and
whose name Laurel had discovered was Liz healed very slowly.
The skin was puckered and raw looking. When she came in the
week before Christmas she stared into the fly-spotted mirror on
the wall.

"It's never goin' to look no better, is it?" she asked.

Jethro was gentle with her. "The scars will fade in time."

"Not so as you'd notice. I know. I've seen some of 'em. I
won't be comin' no more."

"You should, Liz. The skin is still very tender."

"My feller's walked out on me. I've had to get meself a new
job. It's up West, see. I ain't got nothin' to give but I'd like to
say thank you."

"There's no need," said Jethro.

It had been an exceptionally cold day and Laurel had brought
with her the Persian silk shawl. It lay across a chair, rich
jewel-like colours glowing in the drab room. Almost uncon-
sciously Liz's hand stroked it as she turned to go. Impulsively
Laurel picked it up and put it around her shoulders.

"A Christmas present for the new job," she said.

"For me?" For an instant Liz stared incredulously, then with
a sudden grace she flung it around her head and went jauntily
out of the room.

"You've given her back a little of her self-confidence," said
Jethro. "Poor creature, she needs it."

"I didn't think . . . I just felt sorry for her."

That was a day when Jethro had to leave early and Laurel
was putting on her bonnet when Margaret came out of the
schoolroom and stood watching her. They had only met briefly
since that terrible day at Ravensley, but Laurel could feel it still,
a burning hate, a destructive jealousy, all the more powerful
because it had no outlet. Margaret knew that Robin cared
nothing for her and yet perversely blamed Laurel for his indifference. She was only seventeen but looked older, her hair
brushed back into a plain knot, her dark woollen dress closely
buttoned to the throat. Why does she do it? thought Laurel
impatiently. There is no merit in making yourself look unattractive.

159

Margaret said suddenly, "That's a very fancy bonnet. Did it come from the shop near Bond Street?"

"Yes, it did."

"I thought so. Rosemary showed me the two you bought for her. You know who Lydia Chester is, don't you?"

"I know she is an excellent milliner," said Laurel coolly.

"Oh stuff! That's not what I mean. She's Jethro's mistress, has been for years."

She had dismissed it from her mind and here it was again with all the venom of Margaret's malice. "Why should you say that?"

"I thought everyone knew. The boy is his too. That's why he makes such a fuss over the child."

Laurel turned to face her. "Why are you telling me all this?"

"I thought you ought to know."

"Well, you're quite wrong. I like Jethro. I think he's a fine doctor and I wish him well, but his private life is no concern of mine and let me tell you something else. If you want Robin, or anyone else for that matter, to take an interest in you, then stop attacking me and buy yourself some pretty clothes. Why don't you? Your hair is so lovely. I'll help you if you like."

Margaret bit her lip. "No, thank you. I don't run after men. I leave that to you."

Rebuffed, Laurel shrugged her shoulders. "If that's how you feel, then don't blame me if you are left behind in the race."

Seth was waiting for her and she was trembling when she climbed into the carriage. She thought she cared nothing for Margaret's spite but she did. In her malicious way she had contrived to shatter the simple happiness of the last few weeks. She wished she could forget Lydia Chester, but she couldn't. The thought of Jethro finding love and peace in another woman's arms was unbearably painful.

12

It was shortly before Christmas that Laurel made up her mind to go to Westley Manor. She had visited the house that had come to her with her grandfather's inheritance only once when the Fens and all that had happened to her there were still raw in her memory. Now quite suddenly the gaieties and pleasures of London had become flat and without purpose, while the vast lonely peace of the marshes drew her irresistibly.

Jane protested strongly. "It's December, Laurel, the place will be cold as a tomb. Horribly damp too, I shouldn't wonder. It's not been lived in properly for years and years."

"There are the caretakers. They've been keeping it in good condition. We'll light huge fires. We'll take the horses and some of the servants. It will be something new, something different. I'm bored with London, sick to death of seeing the same faces day after day. I need a change and the Fens can be quite wonderfully beautiful. You've never seen them as I have, Jane."

"And I don't know as I want to, not in the middle of winter. Great open spaces with a biting wind." She shivered dramatically. "If you must go down there, can't we find a comfortable hotel somewhere?"

"There aren't any, only inns for the fishing, and you wouldn't like them. Rosemary says her father would make us welcome at Ravensley, but I'm not so sure about Lady Aylsham and anyway I would much rather be independent. Oh come on, Jane, where's your spirit of adventure?"

"I lost it a long time ago. I'm at an age when I like my comforts."

But of course when it came down to it, Laurel had her way. Vast quantities of baggage which included extra bedding, thick quilts, blankets and several hampers of delicacies from Fortnum and Mason, were packed up and despatched down to Westley under Seth's direction, while Laurel and Jane followed on the next day.

161

Despite gloomy predictions the house, though shabby, was bone dry and it was tremendous fun opening up the neglected rooms, lighting enormous fires and exclaiming over the fine old pieces of furniture, pictures and ornaments. The housekeeper trailed after them from place to place, whipping off dust sheets and opening shutters. Servants were set to work cleaning and polishing and they were still more or less in the midst of it when one morning an unexpected party rode over from Ravensley. Rosemary and Jessica had brought Robin and Tom and with them came a reluctant Margaret. The weather had turned crisp and cold. A light frost glinted on trees and bushes under a weak sun and as yet there was no snow and very little wind.

"In a few days we shall be skating," said Tom. "The ice is pretty thick already. I tested it this morning. Have you ever tried it, Laurel?"

"Not yet."

"I'll teach you or Robin will. He is our expert."

They laid out a huge picnic in the big living room with the tapestry covered walls and vast fireplace. Afterwards they wandered together over the house making all kinds of discoveries and at Laurel's instigation they carried down a quantity of broken furniture and household debris from the attics and piled it outside on the flagstones. Then they heaped on twigs and logs from the garden and lit a bonfire. They roasted chestnuts on a shovel, burning their fingers as they peeled and ate them and capered about the blaze like children laughing at each other's soot smudged faces.

It was there that Margaret came with a small faded picture of a young girl's face drawn in crayon and hardly discernible beneath layers of dust and grime.

"Look," she said. "I've just found this. It's your grandmother – Alyne Leigh who was Justin Aylsham's mistress. Is she like your mother? She's buried here, you know, but not in the churchyard. It had to be in the field outside because she drowned herself. It's old family history, isn't it? You ought to keep the picture and show it to your dear Uncle Jethro."

Laurel gazed at the shadowy face lit by the dancing light of the fire. Was this the girl who had given a daughter to Jethro's father and so created the relationship that kept them apart? The pointed features were like and unlike. With a swift movement she hurled it into the heart of the blaze. The flames caught the wooden frame and devoured the haunting face.

162

Margaret was staring at her. "You shouldn't have done that."

"I've killed it," said Laurel. "I've killed the past."

Robin said curiously, "What were you burning just then?"

"Nothing of importance. Only an old picture."

"Rosemary and Jessica are toasting muffins. Come and help them." He slipped an arm around Laurel's waist leaving Margaret to trail after them.

The muffins were burnt and tasted of woodsmoke, but they loaded them with honey and ate them hungrily with mugs of steaming tea. Tom who had some skill with a penny whistle started up a jig and they danced around the fire while a fiery sun slowly sank in the west and the leafless trees stood out black and spectral against a blood red sky.

"If we were witches," said Jessica breathlessly, "we would dance widdershins."

"What's widdershins?" asked Tom.

"Anti-clockwise, silly, and then we'd wish."

"All right, let's do it." Tom grabbed Laurel's hand. "Come on, everyone."

"No," she said quickly, pulling away. "No. Wishes made like that are unlucky. They come true in some horrible way that you don't expect."

"It's only fun," protested Tom. "It's not for real."

"My wish would be for real," said Robin, his eyes on Laurel.

"I know," announced Jessica gaily. "Let's all promise to meet here again this time next year and find out if any of our wishes have come true. Shall we, Laurel?"

The sun had suddenly vanished and the sky began to turn the colour of lead. A sneaking wind whipped across the neglected garden and she shivered.

"I never look further than one day ahead," she said. "It's too frightening. It's growing cold. We'd better go in."

"If Moggy were here he'd say he smelled snow in the wind," said Robin. "I think we ought to ride back, girls, before it's completely dark. Father would like you and Miss Ashe to come to us on New Year's Eve. You will, won't you, Laurel?"

"Maybe. If the snow doesn't come and Jane and I are not imprisoned by it," she answered lightly.

It was morbid, she knew, but remembering what Margaret had said, she went the next morning to the church. It was a small dark place for the congregation was sparse and very poor.

163

She searched the field outside, parting the frosted grass, but found neither grave nor headstone and went back to the manor chiding herself for her folly.

The crisp frosty weather held and so Laurel and Jane rode over to Ravensley on the morning of New Year's Eve carrying a portmanteau with a change of dress. Jethro arrived in time for supper bringing the first snow and Charles Townsend with him. Jessica laughed at the white mantle on hats and caped coats as the young men shook it off in the porch.

"It's not really heavy yet. The horses got through quite easily from Ely," said Jethro, "but it's thickening up. I hope you don't mind an extra guest, Clarissa. Charles and I have been working like Trojans all over Christmas. This icy weather has resulted in a series of falls with broken arms, legs, wrists, ankles and I don't know what else. Half London seems to be hobbling about on crutches."

There were no outside guests, only the family, and after supper Lady Aylsham, looking at them as they gathered around the fire, was reminded of the spring evening of Laurel's first arrival. It was strange, she reflected, how the child had become a woman, had learned to stand alone winning society to her feet and yet it had not spoiled her. To her surprise there was a simplicity and a charm that she warmed to in spite of herself and yet the uneasiness she had felt then, had not vanished completely. Laurel was sitting quietly, the exotic Borzoi close beside her. She fondled him half listening to Robin though her eyes never strayed far from Jethro. Clarissa had noticed the flash of joy between them when Jethro had come in, instantly controlled. She was also deeply conscious of Robin's look of adoration and worried by Margaret's still watchfulness that had something unnatural about it. The only thing that cheered her was Tom's irrepressible good humour and the lively interest on Rosemary's face as she listened to Charles Townsend. It was good to see her looking happier after that foolish business with Seth Starling.

Jethro and Oliver were deep in the latest war news. "You know of course that Lord Pam has sent in his resignation as Home Secretary," Lord Aylsham was saying. "Ostensibly because he doesn't agree with the new proposal for electoral reform, which by the way is long overdue, but everyone knows it is just as much his strong disapproval of the government's attitude to Russia. The Prime Minister is being pushed into war by public opinion."

"God help the troops if we do send them in," remarked Jethro. "I happened to meet MacGregor of the army medical corps. He tells me that the whole outfit is in the doldrums, has been ever since Waterloo. Their methods and equipment are like something out of the dark ages. It should have been updated years ago. The French are much in advance of us, to say nothing of the Russians."

"I've never known Britain to move a step unless her back is to the wall," said his brother dryly.

"That's not much consolation to the poor devils who are going to die for sheer lack of medical care."

Later in the evening Jane was persuaded to take her place at the piano. Rosemary sang a favourite ballad and Tom who prided himself on his comic turns gave them one of the more respectable of the music hall songs he had picked up. In no time he had persuaded them into singing with him and they were trolling out the chorus when there was some kind of a commotion in the hall outside. Barker came in and spoke to Lord Aylsham who went out with him. In a minute or two he was back looking concerned. They stopped singing and turned to him.

"It's Nampy," he explained. "Moggy has met with an accident. Nampy thinks he's broken a leg and he is in great pain."

"Is he at the cottage?" asked Clarissa.

"No, some little distance away, Nampy says. He's covered him with blankets but he's too heavy for him to lift. How the poor devil has got here through the snow, I don't know, but he desperately needs help."

"I'll go back with him," said Jethro at once.

Charles joined him. "I'll come with you. You're going to need assistance both with carrying him and setting the leg."

"Good man. What's the snow like, Oliver?"

"Not too thick yet, but it's still coming down. Do you need me?"

"No. Charles and I can manage with Nampy."

"You'd better take horses for part of the way. Then you may have to walk."

"We'll do it. Nampy will guide us. Come on, Charles, we'd better put together what we're going to need."

They hurried into the hall. What it was that decided Laurel she was not sure. She only knew that in her hour of greatest misery, the old Fenman had been there giving her strength and courage to face it. Without him she could easily have died and now she wanted to repay her debt. While the two doctors were collecting what was necessary, she slipped upstairs. She stripped off her silk gown and pulled on her riding dress and stout boots. She tied a scarf over her head and buttoned up her jacket. Then she ran down the stairs.

The two young men in boots and greatcoats were with Nampy at the door when she joined them.

"I'm coming with you."

"No," exclaimed Jethro. "No, Laurel, don't be foolish. There's nothing you can do."

"Yes, there is. You and Charles will have your hands full. I can heat water, prepare hot drinks . . ."

"Laurel, please. Oliver, you must prevent her coming with us."

Lord Aylsham put a hand on her shoulder, but she shook him off. "I'm sorry but you can't stop me. I'll saddle my horse myself and follow after them. It's not the first time I've helped you, Jethro."

"This is different."

"No, it's not," she said stubbornly.

"We can't waste time in argument. Come if you must," he said in exasperation and so she had her way.

The horses were brought round, the sturdiest and most sure-footed in the Ravensley stables and they set out. The snow was falling more heavily now and made it difficult to see ahead. Nampy led the way, the light from the lantern hung from his saddlebow bobbing and flickering like one of the Jack O'Lanterns which haunted the marshes and were said to lure travellers to their doom. They dared not travel too fast since every now and then the horses slithered dangerously as their hooves struck through the soft snow to the ice beneath.

The Fenmen were usually as nimble-footed as mountain goats, but it seemed that Moggy had gone out to visit some of his snares hoping for a rabbit or hare and had slipped on the ice falling awkwardly with his leg twisted beneath him. The old man's brittle bone had snapped like a matchstick. They found him lying under a roughly contrived shelter of branches, the blankets Nampy had put around him already covered with snow. He was quite conscious and managed a weak grin as Jethro bent over him in the shadowy light of the lantern.

"It's a fair wicked old night to bring you out, Mr Jethro," he whispered, "but I willna say I en't glad to see you."

"What were you after, you old devil, poaching on Lord Aylsham's land?" said Jethro jokingly as he slid his hands beneath the blankets to assess the damage. "Never you mind. We'll soon have you fixed up right as ninepence. Come on now. Let's get him shifted as quickly as we can."

They made an improvised litter out of the blankets, Jethro and Charles carrying him between them the half mile or so to the hut while Nampy and Laurel followed with the horses. It was not a great distance, but it took the best part of an hour with frequent rests to ease the pain. They took him into the cottage while Laurel helped Nampy to put the horses into the rough thatched shelter among the stacks of peat and winter fuel. They brushed the snow from their coats and covered them with old sacks which was the best they could do before they went back to the hut.

It was stiflingly hot inside from the banked fire of peat and the overpowering reek of smoke, food and animals reminded Laurel vividly of the day Moggy had brought her there from Spinney Mill.

Jethro and Charles were already at work stripping off the old man's moleskin breeches and examining the injured leg. The oil lamp did little to dispel the gloom and Jethro looked up.

"Is there any more light?"

Silently Nampy hunted around bringing out a box full of half burned candles and Laurel helped him stick them on a board lighting them from the fire. The flickering flames cast huge shadows on walls and ceiling. The mongrel dog had flattened himself to the earth floor as close as he could to the bed. Laurel busied herself putting the kettle into the heart of the fire and then trying to bring a little order into the confusion on the hearth. She found an iron pot filled with a thick soup. It smelled pleasantly of chicken and rabbit so she stirred it and put it on to heat, while Nampy knelt by the side of the truckle bed with an agonized look on his wizened face. He was a little gnome-like man, a round woollen hat pulled over his head down to his ears and wearing a queer assortment of garments one on top of the other.

Jethro said quietly, "It's a straight break, but I must stretch

167

it if it is to be properly set and it's going to be painful. I've some chloroform in my bag. Give him a whiff of it on a pad, Charles."

But Moggy had heard him. He tried to raise his head shaking it vigorously. "Nay, I dinna want that there stuff. I en't a dog to be put to sleep. I've never been afeard of a bit o' pain and I en't goin' to start now. That other thing . . . it en't natural."

"It will make it easier, Moggy, both for you and for me."

"Nay, it won't then. I en't dead yet, not by a long chalk, and I'm no babby to cry out at it. Give me one of them there bits of wood, Nampy."

So with Moggy biting on a piece of black bog oak that he had been whittling into shape in his spare time, Jethro set the splints, straightened the broken bone and bound it tightly into position. When it was all done, he took his own handkerchief and gently wiped the sweat from the old man's face.

"Sorry if I had to hurt you, but you're a brave man, Moggy."

"How long," he gasped, "how long afore I'm on me feet again?"

"Can't say exactly and you'll be lame at first, I'm afraid, but you'll be out on the Fens with that punt of yours by spring, I promise you that. Now let's make you more comfortable."

They unfolded the extra blankets they had brought from Ravensley and wrapped the old man warmly in them.

"I've made some tea and I've heated the broth," said Laurel. "Shall I give him some of it?"

"Good girl," said Jethro approvingly. "Just a few spoonfuls while I prepare something to ease the pain and help him sleep."

Laurel filled a little bowl and knelt beside the bed so that Moggy noticed her for the first time.

"I never thought to see you here, Missy," he muttered wonderingly. "It's a fair long time, en't it?"

"Yes, it is, but you saved my life that day, Moggy, so I had to come to help you."

With Nampy's assistance she raised him a little and began to feed him with spoonfuls of the broth.

"Nay," he protested feebly, " 'tain't for the likes of you to be doin' that. I en't a babby."

"You drink it up and don't argue," she said sternly and even in the midst of his pain he managed to give the ghost of a chuckle.

"Never had a beautiful young lady feedin' me before. You'll

have old Nampy breakin' his leg if this is what comes of it," and he obediently swallowed it to the last drop.

It was near midnight by the time Jethro had mixed the laudanum and given Nampy some brief instructions and they gathered around the hearth sipping mugs of milkless tea that had an odd smoky flavour and discussed what best to do. Nampy who had been out to look at the horses returned to say that it had stopped snowing but a wind had sprung up and was blowing it into deep drifts. The little man looked from one to the other.

"It's nearer Westley, we are, than Ravensley," he said, "and 'twould be easy for me to put you on your way there. 'Tain't hardly right for the lady to stay here with no place for her to rest."

"I don't mind," said Laurel quickly.

Jethro frowned. "No, he's right, but I'm not sure . . ."

"I have it," interrupted Charles. "I'll stay here with Moggy, while you take Laurel to Westley. Then you can come back in the morning, Jethro. According to how our patient is, we can then decide whether it would be best to take him to Ravensley where he can be properly cared for."

They argued a little about it, but in the end it seemed the most sensible thing to do. The opiate had begun to take effect and Moggy was already drowsy. They wrapped themselves up and went out into the black freezing night.

Nampy by some unerring instinct guided them by paths known only to himself across the fens and frozen waterways until they came in sight of a derelict inn called the Black Dog, the sign flapping dismally in the sharp wind. He pointed ahead to where they could see the gates into the park. Then he bobbed his head awkwardly to them both and turned back.

The servants had long since retired to bed. A sleepy house-keeper came down to unbar the door staring in astonishment at her mistress and the tall dark man with her. Behind her on the staircase Cindy peered curiously over the balustrade.

"It's all right, Mrs Birch, you can all go back to bed," said Laurel. "I can manage. There's been an accident to one of the fenmen and I've been helping Dr Aylsham."

"I'd better attend to the fires, Miss. They've been banked up for the night in the living room and the kitchen."

"You go in, Laurel," said Jethro. "I'll look after the horses. Make sure that you take off those wet clothes."

Her riding skirt was soaked to the knees and she shivered as she followed the housekeeper into the hall while Jethro led the horses round to the stables. He unsaddled them, roughly rubbed them down and found some oats for their feed. When a little later he came into the house, the fire was blazing merrily in the big living room and Laurel had stripped off her riding clothes and was wrapped in a warm velvet dressing-gown.

He discarded his heavy caped coat and kicked off his boots. Then he knelt down on the hearthrug spreading his icecold hands to the comforting heat.

"I've sent them back to bed," she said, "I thought we could look after ourselves. Are you hungry? I am."

The glow from the fire lit rich red lights in the hair tumbled about her shoulders. She looked very lovely and very young, he thought, and smiled indulgently.

"I'm starving. What can you offer?"

"Shall we forage in the larder?"

They went hand in hand rather like two guilty children raiding forbidden territory. The kitchen stove was still burning. Laurel gave it a vigorous poking and put on a kettle. Together they explored the shelves of the pantry bringing out cold chicken, part of a pork pie, some bread and a hunk of cheese. They carried it through to the living room and when the kettle boiled, they made coffee.

"I may not be very expert at it," confessed Laurel, "but at least it will take away the taste of Moggy's tea. What *does* he put in it?"

"A veritable witch's brew, I suspect," said Jethro. "The Fenmen use all kinds of plants and herbs to ward off the aches and pains caused by the marsh mists. Boiling hot onion water flavoured with nutmeg is one of their favourites. I remember it from my childhood. Moggy used to take me with him and show me how to catch eels," he went on as they spread the food on a low table in front of the fire, "great big chaps, they were, thick as my arm. I was terrified of them but would have died rather than let him see it. Afterwards we used to come back to the hut and eat what he called 'sparrer pudden' a glorious mixture of thick suet crust and all kinds of meat and game, just the thing for a hungry youngster who was wet and cold and had been out since dawn."

He pulled up the huge old sofa, so large it might have served as a bed. The feeling of companionship that had grown from the days they had worked together at the settlement was still strong

170

between them. They ate the food hungrily and she fetched brandy for him to drink with his coffee. He offered the glass to her but she shook her head.

"I still don't like it. Do you remember when you made me drink it at the Palazzo Falcone?"

He smiled. "Francesca da Rimini, the golden girl – Ugo Falcone must be biting his nails in fury at what he lost in you."

"Perhaps. It's not all fun, you know. I thought it would be at first, all that money to play with."

"Not disillusioned already surely?"

"No . . . but sometimes I wonder if Barton and George have a better right to it than I have."

"Nonsense. Your grandfather intended it for you and that's the end of it."

"Is it? I wonder." She glanced at him leaning back against the sofa, glass in hand. He looked tired but relaxed, the tension gone from his face. She leaned forward staring into the fire. "Jethro, we are friends now, aren't we?"

"Yes. We are friends."

"Why didn't you tell me about Lydia Chester?"

"Tell you what?"

"Well, if she is . . ." then she floundered. "I mean . . . if her little boy is . . ."

He put his glass down and sat up. "What is all this? Who has been talking to you?"

"It was Margaret. She told me about you . . . and her."

"Oh she did, did she? Damn Margaret! That young woman seems to enjoy creating mischief. I suppose she told you that Lydia is my mistress and Edwin my son?"

"Isn't it true?"

"No, by God, it's not!" he said violently. "I like her. She's an intelligent woman and I spend an occasional evening with her and that's all."

"Are you sure that is really all?"

"Quite sure for more reasons than one. People can think what they damn well please!" He got up to put another log on the fire and then looked down at her with a wry smile. "If you really want to know I don't talk about her because she has a right to her own secrets. She has bravely lived down the past, so why should I spread it abroad?"

"You can trust me with it."

He studied her for a moment and then went on quietly. "It

171

happened about five years ago. I had only just taken up my first hospital appointment and shared a consulting room in Harley Street. She came there one day and was turned away. It was purely by chance that I found her on the area steps. She was clinging to the railings, half fainting and desperately ill. I learned afterwards that her lover had abandoned her when he knew she was with child and in a mood of despair she had gone to a back street abortionist. What he had done to her was unforgivable. I managed to get her into the hospital and risked being accused of performing the botched operation myself. I had a hell of a job persuading the director of my innocence. Thank God they believed me or my career would have come to an abrupt end there and then."

She was sitting up watching him in the glow from the fire. "What happened?"

"We saved her and the baby, though it was touch and go for weeks, and the child suffered some malformation as a result of it. That is the reason I've watched his condition ever since. In time I hope that he will be able to lead a normal healthy life."

"Did you set her up in the shop?"

"I lent her some money which she scrupulously pays me back a little at a time, but its her own courage and ability that have made a success of it."

"She must be very grateful to you."

"Oh, gratitude!" he said a little contemptuously. "I only did what any doctor would have done in the circumstances."

Not every doctor would have been willing to risk his future for a betrayed woman, she thought, and was ashamed of her ready acceptance of Margaret's malice. It was foolish, but the knowledge that he was not Lydia Chester's lover gave her an intense happiness.

He yawned and stretched. "It's a queer way of welcoming in the New Year, isn't it? But maybe it's better than getting drunk." He smiled down at her. He had taken off his coat and looked young and boyish in shirt and breeches, his dark hair tousled. "It's very late and you ought to be in bed. I can rest down here for a few hours, then somehow I must find my way back across the marshes. It won't be so difficult in daylight. I can't leave Charles to cope alone. Besides I'd like to be sure there's no fever. Moggy is not so young. The cold and the shock could bring on a congestion of the lungs."

"I don't want to move," she said dreamily. "It will be cold

172

upstairs and it's warm and cosy in here. I'd like to curl up like a cat and sleep on the hearthrug."

He laughed. "Come along, my tawny kitten, time for bed."

He reached down to her taking both her hands to pull her to her feet and abruptly the lazy feeling of content, the brittle sense of comradeship was shattered. They had been lulled into it by circumstances and quite suddenly it was torn apart. The desire between them was like an electric current that instantly flared into life, so powerful, so intense, that they reeled under it, clinging helplessly to one another. He kissed her, gently at first, and then more and more deeply. Breathlessly he tore himself away, but it had gone too far. She was swaying towards him, eyes enormous in her white face. In her there was no inhibition, no holding back. She had none of his grim memories, the sadistic father, the witch woman who had haunted his boyhood. At that moment he was only the man she loved. She had killed the past on the day she had hurled the picture into the bonfire. She reached up to him, her hands touching his face, her mouth seeking his, and he was lost. She was in his arms. He felt her melt against him and everything was forgotten except that they were born for each other. Ever since that first meeting in Rome, the fire had been there. Now it flamed up and consumed them utterly.

When she woke the room was still dark with only a faint rosy glow from the banked up fire. She lay with closed eyes for a moment remembering everything, his tenderness and strength, the pain mingled with sweetness and joy, the fierce soaring ecstasy of their coming together before exhaustion claimed them both. With a sigh of pure happiness she stretched out a hand and found him gone from beside her. She sat up then looking wildly around her and saw him outlined against the grey early morning light from the window. He had pulled back the curtain and was already fully dressed with boots and great-coat. He turned when she spoke his name and came back to the sofa.

"Jethro, are you going to leave me?"

"I must."

"Why?" She knew by his face that the past was not over after all, it was not forgotten and the barrier still lay between them. She rebelled strongly against it. "Why, why, Jethro? We love each other. Isn't that enough? What does it matter that by

173

some twist of fate my mother may have been your sister? We never knew it. We met as strangers. We met and we loved. Why should we let it trouble us?"

"We can't escape it. Oh God, how I wish we could!" he said desperately. "But it is there, it will haunt us, destroying everything, poisoning our love."

"I don't believe it — I won't believe it."

"You must. Trust me, I know." He knelt beside the sofa cupping her face between his two hands. "I can't forgive myself for last night."

"I wanted it as much as you."

"I should have been stronger and I failed. I should have foreseen the danger and avoided it."

"No," she said passionately, "no, no. I'm glad. I know now that you love me. Nothing can take that away, nothing." She leaned forward, touching him, stroking his face. "Oh Jethro, don't go, please don't go. Stay for a little longer. What will it matter?"

For a moment he was tempted. He felt the stir within him, his body still craved for hers, but it was more than that, much more. Ever since he came back from Vienna, it seemed he had grown closer and closer to her without being aware of it. He had been fighting a losing battle and there was not a thing about her, not the smallest look or gesture that he did not know and love. With a tremendous effort he shut his eyes against her pleading and stumbled to his feet. He took both her hands, kissed each palm, closed her fingers tight over them and then went quickly from the room.

She scrambled off the sofa, clutching the dressing-gown around her and ran to the window. Outside the snow stretched pure and untouched. It lay piled on the ragged hedge and hung in soft clusters along the dark leafless boughs of the trees. Presently she saw him bring out one of the horses followed by Seth. They spoke for a moment, then he swung himself into the saddle and rode down towards the gates. He did not look back and she didn't know how she was going to bear it. It had been bad enough before but now they had stepped across a boundary and it would be worse, far worse. Something within her raged against it and yet she knew it was part of the man he was, the man she loved. He would never take anything lightly.

She had turned back into the room when Mrs Birch came in looking surprised and a little agitated.

"I was worried about you, Madam. Cindy went to your room and the bed had not been slept in."

"No, it was so cold, I stayed down here by the fire."

The housekeeper's eyes roved around the room. "Has the gentleman gone already?"

"Yes. Dr Aylsham had to return to his patient as soon as possible."

"Shall I serve breakfast, Madam?"

"Bring me some coffee and toast to my room, that's all I shall want. Then ask Seth to come in. I think he had better try to get through to Ravensley and bring back Miss Ashe."

"Very good, Madam."

Laurel went wearily up the stairs to find Cindy waiting for her on the landing and was too occupied with her own thoughts to notice the girl's sly look at her. It did not once occur to her what implication might be drawn or how the servants might gossip.

13

The snow began again at noon and continued all that day and through to the next with a vicious wind that blew across the marshes from the sea in a fierce bitter gale. The drifts were twelve to fifteen feet high in places. It was impossible for Seth to reach Ravensley so for the time being, and much to her frustration, Laurel was imprisoned in Westley Manor. It was over a fortnight before the siege was lifted, a passage was cut through the drifts and one morning Robin and Tom accompanied by a determined Jane Ashe arrived flushed and laughing from the perilous journey on skates and snow shoes. They reported that Moggy was making excellent progress and already demanding crutches, while Jethro and Charles had gone back to London.

By February in the unpredictable way of English weather a thaw had set in. Laurel and Jane returned to Arlington Street to find London and indeed the whole country in the throes of war fever. It was forty years since the long revolutionary conflict that had ended at Waterloo and apart from those who could purchase commissions in crack regiments, the professional soldier had become the most despised and neglected member of the community, the scum of the earth, a needless drain on the national economy. Now suddenly the scorned redcoats had become heroes, the gallant defenders of their country's honour. Wildly cheering crowds swarmed around the troops marching from their quarters to embark at Leith or Liverpool or Woolwich – Hussars splendid in blue, their jackets looped with gold, Dragoons in scarlet, black plumes waving from brass helmets, outsize Guardsmen in outsize bearskins, each man a volunteer and trained as near perfection as the drill sergeant could bring him. At the end of February Laurel and Jane taking a turn in St. James's Park saw the Scots Guard marching down the Mall, banners flying, while the Queen and her family watched from the balcony of Buckingham Palace and the band played the plaintive lament of "Oh where, oh where has my highland laddie gone?" The crowd threw flowers, while wives and

176

sweethearts ran alongside the marching men hoping for a last glimpse of their loved ones.

The Tsar had recalled his embassies from London and Paris and Louis Napoleon, the newly created Emperor of France, had already committed himself to war on behalf of the Turks when Prince Malinsky came to say goodbye.

"It will grieve me to fight against my many friends," said the tall melancholy Russian sadly.

"Maybe it will all blow over," Laurel was determinedly cheerful. "After all England is not at war yet."

"It will come and in the meantime I must rejoin my regiment."

"Where will you be sent?"

"Sebastopol probably." He smiled. "You will never have heard of it, but it is a great naval base on the Black Sea. It breaks my heart that I shall never see you again."

"Yes, you will. It will be all over in a few weeks and then you will come back to us again."

"No, I feel it here," and he touched his heart. "I wish it were true, but I fear not. You will think of me sometimes when you caress Marik?"

"Of course I will."

She stretched out her hand and he took it in both his pressing it warmly before he kissed it and took his leave.

It seemed that spring that every party she attended was a farewell to someone leaving for the war.

"It will be our turn next," said George riding beside her in the park one morning. "Cardigan who has never fought a battle in his life already sees himself as another Wellington. There's been quite a flurry of marriages among the officers as well as the men." He looked across at her half smiling. "What about it, Laurel? Why not marry me and take part in the adventure?"

Something wild and untamed in her responded to his challenge. She knew already among her acquaintances that many young brides were determined to accompany their husbands, but she was not yet prepared to take such a decisive step. She had scarcely seen Jethro since they had parted on that January morning, although the bond between them still held firm and he was never far from her thoughts.

"Constantinople is a fine city by all accounts and the ambassador keeps damned nearly royal court," went on George lightly. "There'll be no lack of fashionable society."

"Are you trying to tempt me? Prince Malinsky told me he would be sent to Sebastopol."

"More than likely," said George more soberly. "It's in the Crimea and it is there that the war will probably be fought out."

At the end of March the Prime Minister driven by his cabinet and by the pressure of public opinion reluctantly yielded and war with Russia was formally declared. A few days later Marik the Borzoi disappeared. The loss of one pet dog in the midst of preparations for war, the movement of troops and Mr Gladstone's shocking proposal to increase income tax from seven pence to one and twopence in the pound might seem a very small affair, but Laurel was deeply distressed. It happened one evening. Cindy who had taken him for a walk returned in floods of tears with a long tale of woe about a foreign gentleman who had stopped her in the park to enquire the way. Her attention was distracted and when at last he had gone and she looked for the dog, he had disappeared. She had called and called, searching everywhere until it was dark, and had come back to Arlington Street in a state of despair.

The police, when informed, shrugged their shoulders philosophically. The stealing of dogs with demand for a ransom was common practice, the constable told Laurel, especially when the owners were known to be wealthy.

"In most instances the animals are returned safe and sound," he went on, "after the money has been handed over, usually through a third party, though of course if the dog is valuable..." he shook his head doubtfully, "a Borzoi you say he was, that'll be some foreign breed no doubt. A robber could get a good price for a dog of that kind."

"I'll pay anything ... anything at all to get him back," said Laurel frantically.

"I'd advise you not to put that about too freely especially among your servants, Miss, it's asking for trouble," said the policeman warningly. "Don't you worry now. Best thing is to wait and see. When the information is passed to you, then you let us know and we'll see what can be done."

The demand came early the next evening as she stepped out of her carriage, pushed into her hand by a ragged urchin who bolted up the road before Seth could lay hands on him.

She took the note into the house with her and unfolded the sheet of grey-looking paper. The message printed in clumsy capitals said simply, "If you want the dog back, then come to the corner of Princess Street at ten o'clock tonight and bring the rhino with you, fifty pounds in gold. Keep the Peelers off or you'll get him back with his pretty throat slit."

She stared at it unable to make up her mind. It was an enormous sum for the return of a dog. She could expect anything from five to ten pounds, the policeman had told her. There was something odd about the whole affair. Cindy had protested almost too much when she was questioned and the note though printed badly on grubby paper was not ill spelled. It looked very much like an attempt to copy the methods of a common dog stealer by someone unaccustomed to it. If Jane had been there with her practical mind, Laurel might never have behaved so foolishly, but Miss Ashe was reluctantly spending the night with some distant cousins who had suddenly arrived in London and moved by thoughts of the young Russian who had given her the dog and had now gone to fight in a dangerous war, Laurel made a rash decision.

She knew that Princess Street was somewhere near Leicester Square, not an area in which any young woman ought to venture after dark, but, she argued to herself, all she had to do was to alight from a cab, hand over the money to whoever was waiting there and Marik would be returned. She looked for something inconspicuous to wear and decided on a long dark hooded cloak that she had bought for travelling and never worn. She put the gold into a small embroidered purse and slipped out of the house walking quickly up to Piccadilly. She stopped a cruising hansom looking for a fare and saw the driver grin knowingly as she gave the direction. It was not the first time he had picked up one of the nobs discreetly muffled up to avoid recognition. Leicester Square was notorious for what were called houses of accommodation, where rooms could be hired and lovers could meet with no husband or prying relative any the wiser. When he pulled up and she got out, she surprised him by putting a guinea into his hand and telling him to wait.

"Better not take too long about it, Miss," he said slyly, "it's a parky night to keep the old mare standin'."

It was very dark, the street lit only by a faint light from the gas lamp on the corner. She looked about her shivering a little. People seemed to be everywhere moving in and out of the shadows and she saw women lurking in doorways sheltering from the biting March wind while they waited for customers. She took one or two uncertain steps forward and a man slid

179

silently up beside her and took her arm. She shook herself free.

"I have the money. Where is my dog?"

"Not here. Come." He took her arm again.

"No."

Frightened now, she would have pulled away and run back to the cab, but it was too late. Another man, taller and heavier, had appeared at her other side. She tried to call out, but a hand was clapped over her mouth. She was hurried along between them down a long dark passage to a door at the far end. It was opened at once and then shut after them. In the darkness the first man said quickly, "Now give me the money."

"Not until I know whether my dog is still alive."

"Damn you!" He swore under his breath.

The other man said nothing, only gripped her arm tighter and pushed her forward. She stumbled and then was hustled between them up a flight of stairs and into a room at the top. The sudden change from dark to light dazzled her and it was a moment before she could take in what she saw.

It was a large room softly lit by a great chandelier and handsomely if gaudily furnished with shabby gilt chairs and sofas upholstered in red damask. The walls panelled with long mirrors in ornate moulding reflected about a dozen girls. Bare-shouldered and painted they lounged on settees or sat primly by small tables loaded with bottles and tall glasses. There were men too, sprawled at their ease, long legs stretched out, tall hats tipped over their eyes. The air was thick with the smoke from their cigars mingled with a curiously sweet musky smell.

At the far end in a high-backed carved chair rather like a throne sat the fattest woman Laurel had ever seen. She had a pale blotched face and squatted there like some gigantic toad tightly encased in brown satin, brooches and necklaces glittering on the shelf of her bosom, combs studded with diamonds in the high pompadour of dyed red hair. Two eyes brilliant as jet stared unblinkingly at Laurel.

Bewilderment was followed by sickening realization. She was aware of the purpose of this place and wanted to run, but something stubborn in her made her stand her ground. She was not leaving without the dog. She gave a quick glance behind her. The two men who had brought her there still stood at the door. One of them she could have sworn was the young clerk whom she had once seen with Cindy. She conquered her fear

180

with a tremendous effort of will, took a deep breath and threw up her head proudly.

"I don't know why I have been brought here, but I have the money you ask. Now where is my dog?"

For an instant there was silence. They had all turned to stare at her, the girls with an avid curiosity, the men with a studied insolence. Then the fat woman began to laugh. The huge body quivered and shook with a silent amusement horrible to watch.

"Dog? D'you hear that, girls? She wants her dog." Her voice was husky, thick, deep as a man's. "Lord bless us, what a jest to be sure. Come closer, my dear. Let's take a look at you."

Laurel did not move and the fat woman lifted a lazy hand. Two of the girls rose to their feet, grabbed hold of Laurel and pushed her forward. She resisted them at first, then proud and disdainful, refused to fight. She stood silent and upright while they stripped the cloak from her. Underneath she still wore the gown in which she had been visiting that afternoon. The tawny velvet set off the rich lustre of her hair. She shuddered as curious fingers handled the necklet with its gold locket and the slender pearl drops in her ears. One of the men got up from the table where he was sitting and came towards her. He was tall and broad-shouldered with a coarsely handsome face. He walked around her grinning, looking her up and down, the hard eyes stripping the garments from her. She would have done anything to remain indifferent, but knew the bold gaze had brought the colour up into her cheeks. He took the cigar from his mouth.

"Pretty as a peach," he said lazily, "and ripe for plucking. How much do you want for her, Kate?"

The fat woman chuckled hoarsely. "You keep your hands off her, my lord. She's not one of your prize fillies."

"Reserved goods, is she?"

"Maybe."

"Damned pity. I'd have given a good deal for such a prime piece."

Laurel shivered at the mockery in his voice. She thought she recognised him as a sporting peer whom she had once seen on the racecourse and only prayed that he had not remembered her. A fierce anger surged up in her at the humiliation. She took a step forward.

"What is it you want from me?"

"All in good time, my lady," said the fat woman, "all in good time. Take her upstairs."

"No. I'm not going."

She turned to run, but again the fat woman lifted a hand and the big man stepped forward from his place at the door. With an adroit movement he twisted her arm so that the purse fell to the ground. It was picked up at once and tossed into the fat woman's brown satin lap. Laurel fought then to free herself, but the big man took no more notice than if she had been a small child. He picked up the cloak, wrapped it around her and carried her bodily from the room still struggling violently. They went up another flight of stairs and along a corridor. Then he opened a door, thrust her inside and slammed it shut. She heard the key click in the lock.

The room was pitch dark. She took a step forward and stumbled over something that she realized was a chair. Very slowly as her eyes grew accustomed to the dark a faint square window took shape and she crossed to it, but it was firmly shut and bolted and would not yield however hard she wrenched at it. She looked around her, very close to breaking point. It was a small room with a bed, a dressing table and a washstand with a basin and pitcher of water. One of the rooms no doubt to which the girls brought their men. The air smelled stale and reeked of some cheap perfume. She felt sick and disgusted and at the same time very frightened. If it had been simply a plot concocted between Cindy and her lover to extort money from her, then surely the young man would have taken the gold and returned Marik to her. Why this horrible charade of bringing her to what was obviously a brothel? There had to be some deeper purpose, but what it was she could not imagine and she paced up and down the room enraged at her own folly in allowing herself to be caught. How they must be laughing at her, the innocent, walking so easily into their trap.

How long she had been there she had no idea when she suddenly heard the lock click, the door opened a crack and a tray was pushed inside. She leaped forward and grabbed the handle. The door flew back and for a second she was staring into the face of a young woman wearing an ugly mob cap pulled down tightly over her hair and a starched apron over a cotton gown. Then the door was slammed shut again by some unseen hand and she was left with a startling certainty that somewhere she had seen that face before.

There was food on the tray, although she could not touch any of it. She sipped a little of the coffee, but it had a queer bitter

182

taste and she dare not drink more in case it was drugged. Time passed hideously slowly. She heard movement, the sound of voices, muffled laughter, once a scream quickly silenced, doors that opened and shut, all the traffic of sex going on around her, closing in on her, until she could have cried out and it took all her self-control not to start hammering wildly at the door.

Once there was the sound of a scuffle outside on the landing. She stood breathlessly as a heavy fist pounded on the door so that it creaked and shook. A thick drunken voice shouted, "God damn it, what the hell is going on? If it's a free-for-all, why shouldn't I take my turn?"

Laurel backed away to the window terrified that the door would burst open and the pack would be on her. Then the thick wheezy voice of the fat woman was raised in command, there was a heavy thud and shuffling footsteps as if someone was being dragged along the passage, then silence again. She sank down on the edge of the bed shaking all over. She had not been touched and yet she felt degraded, soiled, unbearably humiliated.

Towards dawn the house quietened and Laurel, lying on the bed, the cloak closely wrapped around her so that no part of the sheets or bed covering touched her, fell into a light doze from which she woke with a jerk. It was already faintly light and her room must have looked out on to the street because she heard the clip clop of horses and then a carriage pull up. She was off the bed at once but from the window she could not see much, only that a man got out and walked quickly towards the side alley that led to the discreetly hidden door.

Wearily Laurel poured some water into the basin and splashed it on to her face. There was a towel, but she had the greatest repugnance to touching anything in the room and she wiped her face with her handkerchief. Surely by now her absence must have been noticed and the police informed. She tried to still the rising panic. The tray of food was still untouched and she felt weak and exhausted. The sound of footsteps in the corridor brought her round facing the door. It opened and a man came in. He shut it behind him and stood looking at her. Unbelievably it was Barton.

At first she thought that in some fantastic way he had discovered her abduction and had come to her rescue. Then she saw him smile and the grateful words died on her lips.

"Good morning, Laurel," he said, his voice smooth as cream. "I trust you passed a comfortable night."

She knew then without any shadow of doubt that it was Barton who had engineered it, Barton who had been the cause of her being brought to this horrible place.

She stared at him. "It was you, wasn't it? You who bribed Cindy to steal Marik, you who had me imprisoned here. But why, why?"

His eyes examined her from head to foot so that she was acutely conscious of her tumbled hair and dishevelled dress. Then he said calmly, "Shall we sit down?"

He moved further into the room. Her legs seemed suddenly to give way and she sank down on a corner of the bed. He took the only chair and pulled it round to face her. His look of smug self-assurance maddened her. She wanted to scream abuse at him, but knew she must not. It would be a sign of weakness. She dug her nails into the palms of her hands and tried to outface him.

"Well," she said, "you still haven't answered my question."

"I wanted to teach you a lesson. I thought it was about time you found out how the other half of the world lives."

"I don't believe you," she said contemptuously. "You never cared anything about how others live. I knew that when I visited the factory."

"Ah yes, the factory. You tried to teach me my business, didn't you? Now I'm going to teach you yours." He got up, his calm broken, his face suddenly ugly though his voice was still tightly controlled. "No bastard child of a beggarly slut is going to tell me what to do or rob me of what I earned by years of honest, decent work. You're not leaving here until you've given me back what should have been mine by right."

"And what does George have to say about it?"

"Oh, George!" he made a scornful gesture. "George has suddenly discovered he has principles. The fool believes he is in love with you. You know that, don't you? and it amuses you, but he'll come around afterwards looking for his share, you can be sure of that."

She was trembling but she defied him. "I'm not afraid of your threats. You can't keep me here. They'll be looking for me by now. I told the police where I was going."

"Oh no, you didn't, my dear, don't try and lie to me. They would have been here by now if that were so. The people here know me and they will do exactly what I say. One word from me

184

and you could disappear. Young women do, you know, even rich young women when they become tiresome. Only you're going to be sensible, aren't you? I don't want everything, you know, only the shares you hold in Rutland Tea Importers, that fine house in Arlington Street and the income you enjoy spending so lavishly. You'll still not be quite penniless."

The outrageousness of the demand took her breath away. "You are mad . . . you must be mad if you believe I shall give up what is mine. If Grandfather had wanted you to have it, then he would have left it to you. Once I was sorry for you but not any longer. It's mine and I'm not parting with it. I'd throw it into the sea before you had one penny piece of it."

And suddenly without any warning Barton lost his temper. He seized her by the shoulders dragging her to her feet, his face close to hers, his breath hot on her cheek.

"Now you listen to me. I know something about you, my fine lady, and it makes a very pretty tale. The Aylshams are not God Almighty. I know all about Justin Aylsham who had to flee the country before he was indicted for murder and who came back to marry his own bastard daughter. I know all about his son. What would Jethro Aylsham's patients think of their handsome young surgeon if they found out that he was sleeping with his own niece? Don't try to deny it. I know how he comes to your house in London and down at Westley. No profession more easily blasted by scandal than that of a doctor and I'll do it, I swear to God I'll see you and him brought down and hounded out of society if you don't give me what should have been mine, do you understand, *mine*, but for a sick old man's whim."

He spat the words at her and then carried beyond himself struck her across the face so hard that she fell back on to the bed, one hand to her bruised cheek, shocked at the savagery of his attack. He stared at her for a moment, then turned away to the window. He took a handkerchief from his pocket, fastidiously dabbing at his mouth before he faced her again.

"Well, what do you say?"

"You couldn't do it," she whispered, "you wouldn't dare. Nobody would believe you."

"Oh yes, they would. There is nothing society enjoys more than a juicy scandal. You've not reached where you are without making enemies. The envious will take pleasure in pulling you off your little pedestal, my dear Laurel. There won't be a place left to hide when I have done with the pair of you."

185

She knotted her hands together tortured by the thought of Jethro, angry with herself because she had not sent Cindy away, not shown more discretion, had been so easily fooled.

He had regained his self-control. He stood there, a small man but implacably sure of himself. "It's very easy," he said, "I've had papers prepared. You only have to sign your name."

Her proud spirit hated being forced to yield, but how could she let him destroy Jethro and the work which she had often felt he valued more than her, more than his life. She said dully, "If I sign these papers, what guarantee have I that you will not still ruin me?"

"You will have my word."

"The word of a scoundrel and a liar," she said with contempt.

He shrugged his shoulders. "Take it or leave it. You have a choice, but must accept the consequences." He glanced around the bare room. "I'll have them bring pen and ink. It will be done in a moment and then you will be free to go."

"And my dog?"

"The dog is safe enough," he said carelessly. "It has served its turn."

He was maddeningly triumphant and she felt sick and angry that he should have won his victory so easily, but there was nothing she could do about it. It was not the money so much – in some ways it had become a burden – it was the realization that she had put Jethro and herself so completely in his power.

He went to the door and opened it and it was at that very instant that the uproar began. There were shouts and screams, the sound of a scuffle, the opening and shutting of doors. The police, she thought with rising hope, it must be the police.

In the passage half-clad girls, sleepy-eyed and irritable, peered out of doors asking what the commotion was. There was a rush of feet on the stairs, a powerful voice rising above the clamour, "Out of my way, you damned rogues and let me through!" and the next moment Jethro appeared at the end of the corridor.

The relief was so enormous that she pushed Barton aside and ran to meet him. He caught her up in his arms.

"Thank God I've found you. You're not harmed?"

"No. Oh Jethro!" She clung to him speechless and for an instant he held her very close.

Barton, his exit blocked by Seth with the men and girls who had come crowding into the passage, had retreated back into the room and Jethro followed him. The light from the window

186

fell on Laurel's face and he saw the mark of the savage blow. In ungovernable fury he seized him by the shoulder.

"You rat!" he exclaimed. "You double-crossing dirty-minded rat!" and his fist shot out. Barton staggered back, one hand to his bruised mouth, and Jethro hit him again so that he collapsed helplessly to his knees. It was the first time that Laurel had seen Jethro lose self-control so completely and some primitive instinct within her rejoiced at it until the black look on his face as he towered above Barton frightened her. She grabbed his arm.

"Don't," she whispered, "don't. Leave him. He's not worth it."

For a moment he did not seem to hear her, then he steadied himself. "You're right," he said with disgust. "Even a rat behaves with more decency. Shut the door, Laurel, shut out that rabble. We'll settle this between us here and now."

Outside she saw the staring faces craning over each other's shoulders greedily watching the drama taking place before their eyes. The fat woman had pushed her way to the front, a hideous purple dressing gown clutched around her, a lace cap awry on top of the red hair. Laurel slammed the door on them and stood with her back against it.

"What was he trying to do? Blackmail you?" said Jethro. She nodded and he turned back to Barton. "Get up off the floor, you snivelling bastard. What have you to say for yourself?"

Barton had by now recovered part of his self-assurance. He rose to his feet slowly, a handkerchief pressed against his bleeding mouth.

"I'll make you suffer for this, both of you," he muttered thickly, "by God I will. You'll not get another patient, never see the inside of a hospital by the time I've done with you. Every door in London will be closed against you and that slut of yours." His eyes narrowed. "Incest is an ugly word, but the Aylshams appear to favour it – father and daughter, uncle and niece."

"It's true, Jethro," murmured Laurel faintly. "He knows about us and he'll do what he says. He means it. He will ruin you unless I give him what he asks."

"Money, that's what he wants, isn't it? Money, and when he's forced it out of you, he'll go on asking, month by month, year by year, until he has bled you white." He stretched out an arm, pulling Barton towards him, one hand on his throat, jerking up his head. "Now listen to me. If you harm her in any

187

way at all, I'll kill you, do you understand? I'm a doctor – I know a dozen ways to kill."

"A murderer, is that it?" snarled Barton, "a murderer like your father."

For a few seconds it seemed to hang in the balance and Laurel held her breath, then Jethro released him. "Don't be afraid," he said contemptuously, "I wouldn't soil my hands with your dirty neck. There's a better way to silence you. I have discovered something about you, Mr Barton Grafton, that your rival colleagues in the City would dearly like to know, something that will destroy once and for all any hope of the knighthood you've been angling for."

With her eyes fixed on his face Laurel said breathlessly, "What do you mean?"

"He knows what I mean, don't you Barton? You own this house and one or two more like it. The profits from gambling and sex are very considerable, aren't they? But they still weren't enough. Is that why you wanted Laurel's inheritance? To increase your investment in vice and misery?"

Barton said hoarsely, "You have no proof."

"I can find proof. I am not without friends or influence. You thought no one knew, not even your brother, but some of the poor creatures you've exploited are ready enough to talk. You injure Laurel again or breathe one damaging word about her and I'll make very sure that the whole world knows about you. You can consider yourself lucky I didn't bring the police with me, but I would prefer no scandal to touch her."

For a long moment they stared at one another, but Barton was the first to break. He turned his back on them.

"Damn you both to hell," he muttered. "Get out of here. Leave me alone."

"Willingly." Jethro put his arm around Laurel. "Come along, my dear, the sooner we're free of this vile place the better."

He flung open the door. The fat woman with some of the men and girls were still crowded in the passage. She opened her mouth to protest, but Jethro silenced her with a gesture.

"You'd better settle the matter with your employer in there," he said bitingly, "and consider yourself fortunate that I don't have you arrested for abduction, the whole pack of you."

He thrust his way through them and down the stairs taking Laurel with him and closely followed by Seth.

In the hall she stopped suddenly. "My dog!" she exclaimed. "Where's my dog? I'm not going without Marik."

For the first time Jethro laughed, the tension breaking. "Oh my God, I'd clean forgotten the dog. Seth, make sure you get him from them. He'll be tied up somewhere."

He had a cab waiting outside and bundled her into it. She clung to him, overwhelming relief and gratitude giving way to curiosity.

"Jethro, how did you know where I was? Who told you?"

"It was the luckiest chance. I tremble when I think how easily it could have gone wrong. Didn't you recognize the serving girl who brought you supper last night?"

"It was so dark. I thought I knew her face, but I wasn't sure."

"It was Liz. You remember that poor creature at the settlement whose face had been so badly burned. Her beauty had been her only asset. After she was healed, there was nothing left and she drifted from house to house doing the meanest of work until she landed up at Kate's establishment in Leicester Square. She'd already heard something of the plan to bring you there. There'd been talk about it in the kitchens, a fine joke for them to giggle over, but until she saw you, she had no idea who the intended victim was. Somewhere inside her there's a spark of generosity. She was much too frightened to go to the police and she had no idea of where I lived, so she walked all the way to Stepney, roused Olivia Winter and asked where I could be found. She managed to get a lift on a tradesman's cart back to the Albany where she arrived in the early hours of this morning, pouring out the whole story. I went first to Arlington Street to make sure you had not returned, found the servants off their heads with anxiety, collected Seth and you know the rest."

"Oh Jethro, poor Liz!" She felt guilty because she had done so little for the girl who had remembered the careless gift of a shawl and risked everything she had to help her. "What can I do to show my gratitude? She can never go back to that house. Barton would find some terrible way to punish her."

"She's safe enough at the moment."

"She could come to Arlington Street," she said impulsively.

"Oh no, Laurel. She's a good-hearted girl, but in a house like yours she'd be a fish out of water. The other servants would not tolerate her and they'd show their resentment. I'll speak to Olivia Winter. She'll find something for her."

Franklin was in the hall when they arrived, the other servants hovering behind him.

"When you went out and didn't return, Madam, we didn't know what to think or what to do for the best," said the butler gravely concerned. "I was on the point of going to the police when Dr Aylsham arrived."

"Well, it is all over now," said Jethro, "and fortunately Miss Rutland is none the worse, but she has had a very unpleasant experience and I'd be grateful if you would stop the servants gossiping about it as far as possible."

"I will indeed, sir. It's a terrible thing to have happened."

"Seth will be bringing the dog back. I think you had better make sure that he is bathed as soon as he returns."

"Very good, sir. Would Madam like breakfast?"

"Presently?" said Laurel wearily. "I will ring when I want it."

In the dining room she dropped the cloak from her shoulders and pushed back the disordered hair. "I need a bath even more than Marik," she said ruefully. "I feel unclean all over after that place. I want to strip off every garment and have them all burned. It's a good thing Jane is not here. She would give me such a scolding."

"And quite rightly. You deserve it," said Jethro abruptly. "Wasn't it very foolish to go running after a lost dog? Why didn't you take the note at once to the police?"

"They swore they would cut his throat if I did," she said simply. "I couldn't bear the thought of that. It was too horrible. It never occurred to me that Barton might have a hand in it."

"He's a cunning devil," said Jethro slowly, "with a queer twisted mind. He must have longed for a chance to humiliate you and worked out this scheme to frighten you into giving in to his demands."

"And he would have succeeded. I would have given him everything he wanted if it had not been for you."

"That's what worries me."

"How did you find out about him?" she asked curiously.

"Liz told me a great deal. Servants in places of that kind know more than their employers think but he is right, I have no proof. I hope I've frightened him into silence but don't trust him, Laurel, or that brother of his."

"George had nothing to do with this."

"How can you be sure?"

190

"I don't know . . . and yet I am sure. George would never do a vile thing like that. He may be all kinds of things, but he's honest."

"You're fond of him, aren't you?"

"Yes, I am . . . in a way."

"Fond enough to marry him?"

"Jethro, how can you say that?"

"It might be a solution."

"A solution to what?"

He studied her for a moment as if making up his mind what to say. "It troubles me very much to think of you so alone with no one to protect you."

"I can look after myself."

"You've just proved to me that that is exactly what you can't do," he said with a faint smile.

"I can always come to you."

"I shall not be here."

"What do you mean?" she said in quick alarm. "Where are you going?"

"I've been intending to tell you. I've volunteered for the Army Medical Corps. They are desperately in need of surgeons, especially younger men with experience of modern methods. In a month or so I expect to be on my way to Constantinople."

It hit her hard. Her heart felt like stone in her breast. "But you can't go, not now, not after . . . Jethro, it's not fair. To know that you are here in London, not far away, to be able to see you even if it is only at the settlement helping you with the clinic, that is something at least, but if you go away – into danger – into war – I can't bear it, I can't . . ."

He turned to face her, the grey eyes sombre and full of pain. "It's because of that, Laurel. It's impossible to go on as I am – fighting a hopeless battle to keep myself away from you. It's got to end. At least out there I shall be doing something useful – in a war there is no time think . . ."

"You're running away," she cried out in bitter accusation, "just as you did before."

"Can't you understand?" he said desperately, "And after what happened last night, it's even more important. You know as well as I do how people talk, how rumours can spread. With me out of England, they will die soon enough."

But she wouldn't listen to reason. "You don't care about me – you think only of yourself."

191

"That isn't true . . ."

"It is, it is," she said passionately. "Have you forgotten what happened on New Year's Eve? Supposing I were pregnant. What would you do then? Give me an abortion?"

"Laurel, don't say such things." Then he turned to her quickly. "My God, it's not true, is it? You're not with child?"

"No, you needn't worry, but I wish I were, if you knew how much I wish I were! Then you would have to take me away. We could go abroad to some place where no one knows or cares about us. Can't we do that? Please please, Jethro. I love you – I want to be with you – can't you ever believe that?"

"Oh yes, I believe you. That's what makes it so much worse."

The air seemed to quiver between them and in another moment the flame of their threatened love might have overwhelmed them if there had not been the sound of raised voices in the hall and if Jane Ashe had not come hurrying into the room.

"I've just seen Seth with Marik and he had some shocking story of your going to rescue the dog and being abducted . . ." Then she looked from one to the other, seeing their faces, sensing the strain. "Is there anything wrong?"

"No, nothing at all," said Jethro with an effort. "I was just on the point of leaving. I'm glad you are here, Miss Ashe. Laurel has had a most trying experience and she is very shaken."

"Oh my dear, then it *is* true and all the time I was with those wretchedly boring cousins of mine and did not know a thing about it." Jane moved protectively towards her but Laurel evaded her, speaking directly across to Jethro.

"Must you really go?" she said.

He knew what she meant and answered the deeper question. "Yes, I must. There is no way out and I am already committed."

"What do you think, Jane?" she went on in a high, brittle voice. "Jethro has volunteered to act as surgeon in this beastly war. He has given up all his friends, all his valuable work at the hospital, everything. Don't you think it is a stupid waste?"

"No, I don't," said Jane warmly. "I think it is a wonderful thing to do and it must have needed great courage to make such a decision."

"Sometimes there comes a moment when there is no choice," said Jethro quietly, "and this seemed right for me. I'll see you again before I leave, Laurel."

"Oh you needn't take the trouble," she said still in the same light, brittle tone. "I have plans of my own. I'll probably be busy and so will you. We might as well say goodbye now."

"Very well. If that is what you wish." He hesitated and then came across to her taking her hand and kissing it. "Goodbye, my dear. Remember what I told you." He bowed to Jane. "Take care of her, Miss Ashe."

"I will indeed. Goodbye, Dr Aylsham, and God speed. We shall be thinking of you." As soon as the door closed behind him, she turned back to Laurel. "My dear child, you look shattered and your poor face – what have you done to it? What happened last night and what has Dr Aylsham to do with it?"

"Please, Jane, not now. It was my own stupid fault," said Laurel wearily. "I'll tell you all about it later, but at the moment I feel filthy. All I want is a bath."

"If you're sure . . ." Jane looked at her anxiously. "I'll have the maids take up hot water at once."

"It's all right. I'll tell them myself."

It would have been a great relief to throw herself into Jane's arms, pour out the whole tangled story, not only of last night, but of the torment of her love for Jethro, except the habit of silence was too strong. All her life she had been alone, keeping her troubles to herself, fighting her own battles. It had begun as a child when she had turned to her mother for comfort and found none. Even at school with girls of her own age, she had felt herself different from the others with their easy family relationships. She crossed to the door and then paused.

"One thing I wish you would do for me, Jane. I want you to dismiss Cindy. Give her a month's wages, but tell her she is to go at once. I don't want to see her again."

"I can't say I'm sorry," said Jane in some surprise. "I never liked the girl as I've mentioned often enough, but what reason shall I give?"

"She'll know the reason. I was sorry for her and she lied to me. She was in a wicked plot to steal Marik and . . . if it had not been for Jethro, I don't know what might have happened . . ." She caught her breath in a half sob and went quickly out of the room before she broke down or Jane could stop her.

Later that morning, bathed and clean, every stitch she had worn the night before put on one side to be disposed of, she was sitting at her dressing table brushing her damp hair when a door slammed violently downstairs. She put down the brush and went to the window. Outside a wild wind blew gusts of rain

193

along the pavements and rocked the newly budding branches of the plane trees lining the street. She saw Cindy come up the area steps struggling with the strapped basket that held all her few possessions. There was something forlorn about the small figure in the shabby black coat and jaunty flower-trimmed hat that Laurel recognised as one she had tossed aside a month or so before. She almost opened the window to call her back and then told herself it was foolish to show weakness. Cindy had deceived her and would probably do so again and yet she felt guilty because she had so much and the girl so little and perhaps all she had done had been for her lover's sake. Perhaps Cindy felt for Jack Webb as she herself felt for Jethro.

She leaned her forehead against the cold glass with a feeling of despairing anger. He was going away into something unimaginable, into a war from which he might never return. Perhaps that was what he hoped. After the night they had spent together in January she had cherished a dream, but now it had ended. He would never change. She felt angry and rejected and utterly wretched. If he had truly loved her, surely he would have swept aside the past, taken her into his arms and defied the laws of God and society. She looked around the room with a wave of distaste for its luxurious prettiness. All the money in the world could not give her the man she loved. She must find some other use for it.

She had never been one to give in tamely and wait for life to come to her. If he did not want her, then other men did, and if ugly rumours circulated as a result of last night's escapade, then the best way to defeat them was by putting a bold front on it and behaving as if nothing had happened. In an angry, reckless mood she threw off her morning gown and began to dress, taking particular care and astonishing Jane by sweeping down the stairs and ordering the carriage. No one was going to be able to say that Laurel Rutland was afraid to show her face in the usual morning fashion parade in Hyde Park.

Part Three

THE CRIMEA

14

It was several days before any hint of what had happened reached George Grafton's ears. The Hussars had already embarked from Plymouth docks for Constantinople. Lord Cardigan was not sailing with his men but would travel more comfortably via Paris and George, who was rather a favourite of his, had been detained for special duties with his Commander-in-Chief. He saw his detachment on board the troopship with their horses and then returned to London to find some very queer tales about Laurel going the rounds. In one of them it seemed she had been kidnapped by unscrupulous rascals, a huge ransom had been demanded but she had escaped in the nick of time and was apparently none the worse. Another far more damaging was being gloated over in the officers' mess and in Club smoking rooms and it was there that George heard it first from the lips of Lord Lowhurst, a sporting gentleman of his acquaintance whom he did not much care for. As George came in he saw the tall heavily built figure straddling the hearthrug, a cigar in one hand, a glass of brandy in the other, holding forth to a bunch of admiring cronies.

"Never came up against anything so damned peculiar in me life," he was saying. "There she stood, lovely as an angel, ripe for plucking and not a hope in hell of getting anywhere near. The queerest set-up that I ever encountered. I'd have given a good deal to know who the lucky man was but Kate wasn't talking. There was a devil of a commotion later on so I heard. Missed that," he went on regretfully, "and Kate's mum as an oyster with some reason. Let the police get a smell of it and her doors could be shut for good and all. But damn my eyes, I saw the girl myself the very next morning, bold as brass, driving that pair of bays of hers in the park as though she'd never seen the inside of a whorehouse in all her sweet life. There's pluck for you. I took off my hat to her, a thoroughbred filly if ever I saw one."

There was a greedy relish on every face, a pleasure in the

197

destroying of innocence, that turned George sick with anger. He said icily, "May I ask, my lord, the name of the lady concerned?"

"Why not? It's no secret. Who else but the lovely Laurel, 'Queen and Huntress,' fair still but, alas, not quite so chaste."

A guffaw of laughter ran around the circle of men and George frowned. He took a step forward.

"You'll take that back, my lord."

"Take what back?" said Lord Lowhurst lazily.

"That damnable aspersion on a lady's honour. I'd have you know that Miss Rutland is my cousin and a lady whom I happen to hold in high regard."

Lord Lowhurst's eyes narrowed. "I'm taking nothing back," he said insolently. "A lady, even one whom you favour, is hardly likely to emerge from Kate's establishment with honour intact."

"Nevertheless, whatever the circumstances, you'll take it back or answer to me for it."

"I've no intention of being called a liar by any man," replied the peer haughtily, "least of all by the jumped-up son of a tradesman who has bought his way into decent society."

That touched George on the raw. He was of a height with Lowhurst and he flicked his hand deliberately across the other's swarthy cheek. "You can send your seconds to me as soon as you please, my lord. I'll meet you at any time or place you care to appoint," he said grimly and strode out of the room.

He knew perfectly well that duelling was strictly forbidden and in the case of a soldier, technically at least on active service, it was an extremely serious offence that could earn a term of imprisonment. He did not care. He was still determined to go through with it. The details had already been settled – Wimbledon Common at six o'clock on the following morning – when Lord Cardigan got wind of it and sent for him.

His lordship's fiery temperament had led him into similar scrapes with consequences from which only his rank had saved him but all the same he looked at his young officer with considerable displeasure.

"In case you've forgotten it," he said freezingly, "we are at war with Russia. Lowhurst's a deuced fine shot and I'm not going to have one of my best officers killed out of hand at a time like this."

"I'm considered a fair shot myself," said George stiffly, "and I would beg you to remember, my lord, that the affair concerns a lady's honour."

"Hm-m," grunted Cardigan, not very much impressed, "May I ask who the lady is?"

"I would prefer not to say except that I hope one day to make her my wife."

"Do you indeed? Are you engaged?"

"Not yet."

"Well, you'd better make haste and settle it, my dear fellow. We'll be off soon and God alone knows what the outcome will be. However, honour or not, I absolutely forbid this duel. Your life belongs to your country and is not to be thrown away for a triviality. If you must come to blows, then settle it with Lowhurst when you come back."

"And in the meantime I'm to let him brand me coward in every Club in London," said George bitterly.

"If anyone has the impudence to call one of my officers a coward, then he'll have me to deal with," said Lord Cardigan dangerously. "I don't like Lowhurst, I never did, a pestilential fellow, but I swear to God if either of you persists in this business, Grafton, I'll have you both arrested and that's a promise."

In the face of Lord Cardigan's absolute command there was nothing George could do but obey but it went much against the grain and he unwillingly sent a brief note of explanation to his opponent, his chagrin at having to withdraw a little comforted by his Commander's unqualified support. Lowhurst opening his mouth too loudly at a Club dinner about young gentlemen who spoke out boldly and then beat a hasty retreat at the last moment received a fierce glare from ice-cold blue eyes and the comment that it did not become gentlemen who skulked in England in the midst of a bloody war to question the courage of a serving soldier.

It was not till later that same day that George connected Barton with this wretched affair. He had known something of his brother's unsavoury dealings with gambling houses and worse but had preferred to shut his eyes to it. Now thinking over what he had heard, the curious tale of a maidservant and a lost dog suddenly struck a chord reminding him of a conversation he had had with him back in November. Immediately he took a cab to Fenchurch Street only to be told that Barton had gone to Bath with his family ostensibly to visit his mother though to George it looked suspiciously like flight from some hopeless blunder. He shook some small part of the truth out of Jack

Webb and returned to his lodging filled with disgust and convinced that his brother's heavy-handed action had only succeeded in killing any hopes he himself had cherished.

His own furious reaction surprised him. For twenty-six years he had lived easily and blithely with his own particular brand of style and cynicism, neither better nor worse than any other young man of fashion, and suddenly discovered to his dismay that he possessed deeper feelings than he had ever imagined and did not quite know how to deal with them. The thought that Barton's crassness might have destroyed Laurel's affection for him distressed him quite inordinately. He had not realized how she had wound herself into his heart and faced with the certainty of having to leave England very soon with no knowledge of how long the war would last or whether he would ever return, he was profoundly unhappy. For once he was at a loss, unable to make up his mind whether to call on her and declare his own innocence of any plotting against her, except that it went against his pride to make excuses, and it was while he was still irresolute that he met her by accident early one morning when she was cantering Lucifer in the park. She saw him first and slowed down to let him come up beside her. It was only a few days since a hint of the affair with Lord Lowhurst had come to her ears and she spoke of it with her usual directness.

"I've been hoping to see you, George. I want to thank you for defending me so gallantly."

"I would have done more to prove it," he said ruefully. "I was looking forward to facing that foul-mouthed brute pistol in hand but a soldier has no choice. Cardigan put a veto on it."

"I'm glad," she said impulsively putting a gloved hand on his. "I know you're a splendid shot but it could have gone wrong and I would never have forgiven myself if anything had happened to you."

"I'd do a great deal more for you, Laurel. You do realize that, don't you?"

She smiled at him. "Of course I do."

"I still don't know all the truth of it," he went on awkwardly, "except that I believe Barton was responsible and it has made me feel deeply ashamed."

"Don't be," she said impetuously. "It's over now and I don't want ever to speak about it again, but it was not your doing. I was always sure of that."

"I'm grateful for your trust in me."

It was barely a week since it had all happened and Jethro had walked out of her life seemingly for ever. She was still deeply disturbed, angry and very unhappy. She glanced at the young man riding beside her. George had changed, she thought, during the past year. He had become graver, more concerned for others, more reliable, and she felt a warm rush of liking for him and the ready way he had championed her, willing to risk his life to protect her reputation.

She said, "I hear that the regiment has sailed already."

"That's quite true. I went down to Plymouth to see them embarked. Lord Cardigan doesn't leave until early May and I'm going with him as one of his aides."

She was staring straight in front of her, hearing Jethro say, 'You're fond of him, aren't you? Fond enough to marry him?' Well, why not? It was true that she liked him better than any of the other young men who had dangled their offers in front of her. She could never love anyone as she loved Jethro but there was such a thing as affection and she and George had much in common. They shared the recklessness she had inherited from her long dead soldier father, a quick response to a challenge, a sense of fun. If she married him, she could go with him to the Crimea as so many other young wives were preparing to do. Fanny Duberly who was married to the regimental paymaster in George's own company had sailed already with her husband. Excitement quickened within her. That would prove to Jethro that she also could make a difficult decision and meet a problem with courage. But it was not easy to come out with it boldly. Maybe George no longer wanted her. They rode on in silence for a little.

She was not the only one to feel at a loss for words. George too was finding it hard to say what was in his heart. His brother's action had inhibited him. He approached it in a roundabout way.

"Cardigan wanted to know the name of the lady concerned."

"Did you tell him?"

"Certainly not. All I did mention was that it was a lady whom I hoped one day to make my wife."

"And what did he say to that?"

"That I'd better make haste as there wasn't much time left if I intended to enjoy a honeymoon in Paris."

"Didn't you say a few minutes ago that Lord Cardigan was leaving London in May?"

"Yes, I did."

"That's a month away," went on Laurel steadily. "Time enough for a special licence surely."

He turned to look at her unable to believe his ears. "Laurel, do you mean . . . ?"

"Do you still want to make the lady your wife?"

"You know I do, now more than ever, but I didn't dare to hope. Laurel, please don't make a joke. I don't think I can laugh at it, not now."

"I'm not laughing."

"You mean it's true . . . you'll marry me?"

"If you still wish it."

"Oh my dear!" He stretched out a hand and she took it. "Are you sure? Is it a promise?"

"It's a promise."

He wanted to throw up his hat like a schoolboy and shout his joy aloud but that was hardly suitable in Hyde Park with riders in front and behind him. Instead he said exuberantly, "I'll race you to the end of the ride."

She smiled at him. "Done."

She touched her whip to Lucifer and the horse was off at once. They galloped together and ended neck and neck, breathless and laughing. He leaned towards her from the saddle and their lips met briefly.

"We're matched in more ways than one," he said gaily. "It's the most wonderful thing. Oh my darling, my love, I still can't believe it. There are a thousand things to be done and I don't know where to start. Tell me to whom I must go for permission to marry you?"

"I suppose officially Lord Pam and Dr Townsend will have to be told. They are trustees under Grandfather's will but I'm my own mistress. No one can tell me what I must do or not do. George, can we keep it just between ourselves for a little while? I don't want any fuss to be made, not yet."

"Anything, dearest, anything you wish so long as you don't change your mind."

"I won't do that, I promise you."

Now that it was done, Laurel didn't know if she had been wise or foolish, only that it was an immense relief to have made a decision and given herself a strong purpose. She could devote herself to making George happy and she would be going with

202

him into this most tremendous adventure. She shut her mind obstinately against what the future might hold for them. There was a great deal to be done during the next month not least to gather together a suitable wardrobe. Turkey was said to be scorchingly hot in summer and bitterly cold in winter and God alone knew what the conditions would be like out there. Everyone was sure that the war would be all over in a matter of months but you never could tell and it was as well to be prepared, but just for a few days she said nothing to anyone, half afraid of what she had done on impulse and wanting to be sure in herself before she faced her world.

At her urgent request George did not call at Arlington Street but contented himself with meeting her as often as he could at their morning canters in the park. But every day he sent her flowers and he went about his duties so blithely that his soldier servant remarked on it.

"You mark my words, his nibs is up to something," he said to one of his cronies over their morning draught of ale.

"New bit of skirt do you think?"

"Wouldn't put it past him though he's bin livin' mum as a monk for months now." He tapped his nose significantly. "Somethin' more serious, I shouldn't wonder."

"Like a weddin' eh? He's caught the infection. Half the regiment is down with it. Marry in haste, repent at leisure," said his mate sententiously.

"Not the Captain. If he makes up his mind to somethin', then he sees it through."

There was however one duty that George knew he could not ignore. He had had little contact with his mother during the past year. Barton had always been her favourite but he still felt he ought to inform her of his intended marriage personally. So he took himself down to Bath one morning and when he was shown into her sitting room, was irritated to find his brother there. He was still angry with him for the shameful way he had treated Laurel but he would not quarrel with him in front of his mother.

"So you've condescended to come down to us at last, George," she said in her tart way when he bent to kiss her cheek. "It's taken you long enough."

"I'm sorry, Mamma, but you must understand that with the regiment preparing for war, I've had my hands full during the last few months."

"And to what do we owe the honour of this visit?"

He had intended to bring it out more tactfully but with Barton sitting there grinning like an ape, he was finding it difficult to keep his temper. "I could have written but prefer to tell you myself. I'm going to be married."

She sat up abruptly. "Married?"

"Yes and very soon. Laurel has promised to become my wife."

Her reaction astonished him. Despite the hostility she had always shown, he had expected her to be gratified. After all she had never ceased to feel a bitter resentment at Laurel's inheritance of Sir Joshua's great fortune.

She had risen to her feet, her face white and pinched. "You fool, George, you great fool!" she hissed at him. "Can't you see what she is doing to you?"

"No, I can't," he said coolly. "On the contrary, I consider myself fortunate when she could have had the pick of a dozen men. We are to be married in May and she will accompany me when I leave for Turkey."

"So that's the reason she accepted you," sneered Barton. A cold fury possessed him that his careless happy-go-lucky young brother should have won the coveted prize when his own devious plotting had failed so lamentably. "She's making use of you, my dear fellow. I suppose you realize that."

George stiffened. "I haven't the faintest idea what you're talking about."

"She's trapped you," said his mother venomously, "just as your poor Uncle Bulwer was trapped and she'll destroy you as her slut of a mother destroyed him."

"Oh for God's sake," exclaimed George, anger overcoming his good manners. "Can't you forget the damned past for once? It's dead and buried. Why go on brooding over it? I love Laurel and she has consented to marry me, that's more than enough. I will let you know the date of the wedding as soon as it is settled. Come or stay away as you damn well please!"

He turned to the door ignoring his mother's outstretched hand, the sudden pleading in her voice. "George, don't go. Stay and listen to what Barton has to tell you about her."

"There's nothing he can tell me about Laurel that I don't know already. She has forgiven what he did to her which is more than I can do. I've told you and that's the end of it. I've no intention of listening while you abuse my future wife," and he

204

went out of the room slamming the door, angry with them but more disturbed than he cared to admit. What did they know about Laurel? What could Barton understand of the happiness that surged up inside him when he knew he had won her?

But all the same his mother's poisonous tongue had sown a tiny doubt that lingered in his mind and when he reached London he knew he had to see her. He took a cab to Arlington Street.

Laurel was alone in the drawing room when Franklin showed him in. She looked up in surprise and rose to greet him.

"George, I didn't expect you."

"I've been to visit my mother."

"Oh dear," she smiled a little wryly. "I'm afaid she doesn't like me."

"Never mind her." For a moment he stood, his eyes devouring her, then he crossed swiftly and took her in his arms holding her hard against him, his voice muffled in her hair.

"It's all right, isn't it? You are really going to marry me."

"Of course. What a foolish question."

"I had a sudden feeling you might have changed your mind." He held her away looking into her face. "You won't, will you?"

"Silly boy." She touched his cheek gently. "Of course I won't. If I make a promise, I keep it."

Then Jane came in and after a little he took his leave, reassured and thrusting the memory of his mother's spite behind him. Why should he let her malice or Barton's envy disturb his peace of mind?

One day at the end of that week when Laurel and Jane were spending a quiet afternoon at home, Rosemary was shown in. The gentle shy girl was so glowing with happiness that both ladies remarked on it and she clapped her hands together looking dismayed and radiant at the same time.

"Oh dear, is it so obvious? But I did want you to be the first to know. I'm engaged. Isn't it wonderful?"

"Wonderful," repeated Laurel smiling at her. "It's Charles, of course."

"How *did* you guess?"

"Darling Rosemary, no one could have failed to notice something was in the wind. I'm so happy for you."

"And it's all your doing. It was you who introduced him to me," and Rosemary threw her arms around Laurel and kissed

205

her. "Of course we can't be married for years and years because Charles is so poor. Papa and Mamma would far rather I married someone grand and rich but luckily they both liked him when he came down to Ravensley at the New Year and his great uncle does happen to be Sir Giles Townsend of Thorney Manor, a horrible old man so Charles says, but it does make him quite respectable."

"It all sounds splendid," said Jane. "And do you think you will enjoy being a doctor's wife?"

"Oh yes. I hope I shall be able to help him in some way. You see Charles is going to specialize in treatment for mothers and babies. It was Jethro really who first gave him the idea and it might mean him going abroad for a time like Jet did, perhaps even as far as Vienna. If he does, then we shall be married and I shall go with him whatever Papa says even if we have to live in a garret!"

Breathlessly she talked on and on quite taken out of her usual quiet self and Laurel thought how easily she had forgotten Seth and that first puppy love that had been so painful last summer and wished passionately that she too could put aside the past so joyfully.

Tea had been brought in and while Jane poured, Rosemary looked around at them apologetically.

"How selfish I am. I've done nothing but talk about myself and quite forgotten the most important thing. Jethro is leaving England next week. He has been talking to Papa about it. He intends going to France first. He wants to find out more about their medical missions. They have a much better system than ours, he says, organized by Sisters of Mercy. Charles and I with Robin and Tom are going to see him off at Dover. Will you come with us, Laurel, you too, Miss Ashe? We could make up a party."

"I'd like to do that very much," said Jane promptly. "What do you say, Laurel?"

"I'm not sure if I can," she replied. "I'm going to be very busy next week. You see, I'm going to be married myself."

They both gaped at her in sheer astonishment.

"Married? But you've not said one word about it," exclaimed Rosemary. "You're not even engaged."

"We only made up our minds a few days ago and there's hardly time for an engagement because he has to leave the country early in May."

206

"Is it George Grafton?" asked Jane quietly.

"Yes, it is."

"Captain Grafton?" repeated Rosemary. "But he's your cousin, isn't he?"

"Second cousin actually and does that prevent him from becoming my husband?" said Laurel with a ghost of a smile. "Don't stare at me like that, both of you. I'm perfectly serious. George has been asking me to marry him for a year now and at last I've said yes. That's all there is to it."

"I'm delighted," said Rosemary loyally, "and I wish you every happiness. Only won't it be very painful to be married and then immediately be forced to part?"

"We don't intend to be parted. I'm going with him."

"Oh no," exclaimed Jane quite appalled. "You can't do that, Laurel."

"Why can't I? Mrs Duberly has gone already and a great many other wives as you know quite well. George says I may take Lucifer and one other of my horses and I hope very much that Seth will come with us to look after them."

"If you insist on doing something so exceedingly rash, then I shall come with you," said Jane decisively.

"Not on our honeymoon," said Laurel humorously. "I don't think George would care for that."

"I can follow on afterwards."

"No. It's kind of you to suggest it but it's utterly impossible. George as one of Lord Cardigan's staff will be travelling part of the way with him. It is going to be difficult enough to persuade him to accept me as George's wife. I think he'd be taken with an apoplexy at the mere hint of another lady being attached to his party. I intend to keep everything as simple as possible and even dispense with the services of a maid."

"I think it is the bravest thing I've ever heard," said Rosemary enthusiastically. "It almost makes me wish that Charles had volunteered for the medical service like Jet, then I could have gone with you."

"Someone must be left behind to look after the babies in England," said Laurel with a smile.

It was not until Rosemary had gone that Jane turned upon her.

"I never heard anything so preposterous in my life. You cannot marry George Grafton."

"Why not?"

"You know perfectly well why not. It's even more impossible now after what his brother did to you. Oh I know you've not told me the half of what happened on that night but I'm quite sure that Barton was at the bottom of it. I simply don't know how Captain Grafton has had the effrontery to propose to you again in the circumstances."

"As a matter of fact he didn't. I more or less proposed to him."

"Why, Laurel? In God's name, why?"

"I'm very fond of him," she said obstinately, "and I've grown weary of always saying no."

"Fond! Don't be ridiculous and don't turn it into a joke. Is it because of those idiotic stories that have been going about because if so, then you can forget them. They will die soon enough."

"They have nothing to do with it."

Jane stared at her for a moment, then she said shrewdly, "There's something behind this, isn't there? Is it because of Jethro Aylsham?"

"No, of course not," but Laurel had turned away from her busying herself with putting the cups together on the silver tray.

"Laurel, don't lie. I'm not a fool, you know, and I've seen you together. If ever I saw a man in love, then it was Dr Aylsham, hard though he tried to conceal it. I've said nothing because I didn't want to interfere but now I must. What has happened between you?"

"Nothing."

"Is it you?" persisted Jane. "Is it because of something you have against him?"

"No, no, you're wrong. It's not my fault," said Laurel turning on her passionately. "I love him, I'd go anywhere with him, do anything he asked me to do. It's Jethro who keeps us apart, not I."

"But why? I cannot believe that he does not care."

"Oh he cares – he cares very much." Now the floodgates had opened at last, it was as if she could not stop the words pouring out. "It began in Rome the very first time we met – I can't explain it but it has been there always – but then we didn't know who we were or how closely the past had entangled us . . . Oh Jane, if you knew how wretched I've been, how miserable I am now. Why did this have to happen to me, why – why?" She dropped on to the sofa, one hand beating futilely at the cushions.

Jane sat beside her. "Tell me about it, dearest. Don't go on bottling it up inside you. It's easier to share trouble with someone else."

"I've wanted to, Jane – I've felt so alone – only it did not seem fair to burden you with it. You see it goes back, a long way back to before I was born. I told you about my mother and Jethro's father and about her love affair with Captain Rutland who was my father, but what I didn't tell you was that in marrying her, Justin Aylsham married his own bastard daughter."

"Oh no," exclaimed Jane. "Surely that cannot be true."

"Oh he didn't know about it till afterwards and it was never absolutely proved but then when he died horribly out on the marshes, it all came out, there was a terrible scandal and that was why my grandfather took my mother to Italy."

"But if it was never proved . . ."

"What does proof matter when Jethro believes it? You see, Jane, he lived through it as a boy, even at school he was tormented by it, the slights, the insults, a step-mother who was no better than a whore and a father tainted by murder and incest. To him it is very real, it haunts him and he can't escape from it, the fact that my mother was his half sister and that we are uncle and niece. I thought I would die when Margaret first told me."

"It was Margaret, was it?" said Jane thoughtfully.

"She hates me bacause of Robin but it was all true and I had to know and I made up my mind there and then that I would ignore it. It was all so long ago and I thought I could make him forget about it too." She paused and then went on bravely. "You remember when Moggy broke his leg on New Year's Eve and we went to help him and afterwards Jethro and I went back to Westley . . .?"

"Were you lovers?" asked Jane gently.

"Yes. Oh I know it was all wrong but we didn't plan it, it just happened and it seemed wonderful and right and I was so happy because that night I knew he loved me just as much as I love him, but now," she paused unhappily, "now I believe he hates himself and me too because of it."

"That I'll never believe."

Laurel was sitting up dry-eyed, staring in front of her. "He is leaving me, isn't he? Going away as far as he can and not caring what happens to me."

"He is going because he loves you too much," said Jane quietly.

"I wish I thought that was true."

"And you are marrying George Grafton simply because it gives you the opportunity to go where Jethro is."

It was putting into words something she would not acknowledge even to herself and she denied it emphatically. "No, no, it's not so. That was not in my mind at all."

"Wasn't it? I believe it was and you mustn't do it, Laurel. It's not fair to George or to yourself."

"I've promised and I'm not breaking my promise. At least I can make one man happy."

"But can you? Do you think he won't realize, that he won't know?"

"I've not deceived him. I've never said I loved him."

"He'll deceive himself. Men always do, and when he finds out that he is hopelessly wrong, he will make you suffer for it."

"It's no use, Jane. I've made up my mind and I'm not changing it."

Nothing that Jane could say shook her resolution and she steadily maintained her purpose even when Lord Palmerston and Dr Townsend both frowned at it and talked about her being far too young at twenty to make such a rash decision while Mr Jolly of Jolly, Black and Henderson shook his head doubtfully and muttered about the special provisions set out in Sir Joshua's will guarding against this very situation.

"Do whatever you think best," she said to the lawyer. "Tie the money up in marriage settlements if that is what my grandfather wished. Captain Grafton will raise no objections."

And strangely enough it was perfectly true. George who had once seen marriage to Laurel as fulfilling all his ambitions, now no longer appeared to care about the financial side of it. He had won her when all hope seemed lost and in the few weeks before the wedding thought himself the happiest man on earth.

They were married quietly at St. George's, Hanover Square, at the beginning of May, an unlucky month for a wedding muttered some of those watching them come down the aisle, George looking so radiantly handsome in his magnificent uniform that every young woman was green with envy. Jane seeing them together at the small reception given for them by Lord Palmerston at Carlton Gardens thought she had never seen Laurel appear lovelier in her shimmering satin wedding gown or behave more unlike her real self. She was quicksilver gay, laughing at nothing, brittle nerves stretched almost to breaking point. It was after her bridesmaids had taken her away to change into travelling dress that Jane caught sight of Robin. The boy looked white and distraught and moved by pity she crossed to him.

"Why has she done it?" he said abruptly after she had greeted him. "Why, Miss Ashe? She can't possibly be in love with him."

"Why can't she?"

"All he has ever wanted is her money and she knew that. She told me about it once. It amused her and she laughed at him."

"That may have been true at one time but people change," said Jane thoughtfully. "Now I think that Captain Grafton is genuinely in love."

"I can't believe it," said Robin flatly. "It is all this war fever and Laurel has let herself be carried away by it. It is such a wicked waste. I wouldn't have minded so much if it had been Jet . . ."

"Don't be absurd, Robin. That was never possible, was it?" Margaret had come up beside them. She had been asked to act as bridesmaid with Rosemary and Jessica and had refused. Now the pale pointed face framed by the glossy black hair looked smug and pleased like a small dangerous cat that has been feeding on cream. "That was killed right at the start and a good thing too. Can you imagine Laurel married to a dedicated doctor?"

"Yes, I can," retorted Jane loyally. "She was a great help to him at the settlement clinic."

"So *she* said, I suppose. I heard differently. Anyway there's one good thing. Now she is going away, we can all breathe more freely."

"What a beastly thing to say," exclaimed Robin. "Laurel is one of those people who make you feel happier just by being in the same room with you, just by being alive."

"Well, now she can amuse herself by making her husband and his fellow officers happy out in Constantinople or wherever it is they are going," said Margaret spitefully.

"Why not? That's better than making people miserable as you like to do," retorted Robin cruelly. "Why don't you admit that you're jealous?"

211

"Jealous, I? Of Laurel," she laughed shrilly. "That's ridiculous."

"Is it? For my part I wish to God that I was going out there with her."

"Don't be absurd. How could you? You're not a soldier."

"I could always volunteer."

"You couldn't. Uncle Oliver would never allow it." In sudden alarm she had grabbed him by the arm.

"I'm old enough to make my own decisions," he said impatiently and pulled his arm away from her. "Oh for God's sake, leave me alone, Margaret."

On the evening of the following day Laurel and George were dining together in the Hotel Europa in Paris. They had a few days to themselves before they must join Lord Cardigan's party and travel down to Marseilles where they would embark on the *Asian Star* which would carry them to Turkey. Seth with George's manservant had already gone ahead with the horses and a greater part of the baggage. The journey from London had been particularly frustrating. Their cabin on the night packet from Dover had been so small and stifling and smelled so disgusting that Laurel with a throbbing headache and taut with nerves had taken one look at it and insisted on spending the night on deck. George not altogether unfamiliar with women's fancies had been both kind and understanding. They had drowsed through the train journey from Boulogne to Paris. Alone in their first class compartment Laurel had accepted his kisses and fallen asleep with her head on his shoulder.

But now it was different. They had been merry over their meal, waiters vying with attentions to the handsome honeymoon couple, but she was very aware of the fact that he was no longer simply the amusing companion obedient to her slightest whim as he had been all during the last year. He was her husband and she was his wife. The responsibilities she had undertaken so lightly suddenly weighed heavily upon her. She had married one man when body and spirit she belonged to another. She shivered a little and he noticed it and was immediately solicitous.

"You've not taken a chill from the boat last night?"

"No. I'm perfectly well. A little tired, that's all."

"We'll go to bed early. Would you like cognac with your coffee?"

"Yes, I think I would."

212

Perhaps it would steady her as it had done in Rome when Jethro had prescribed it for her. How long ago that seemed, part of another life and George was not Ugo Falcone. She must put that thought right out of her mind at once.

Later when they went upstairs to their lavishly furnished suite, she tried to still the rising panic. Only essentials had been unpacked and hung up. She had been severely practical in the clothes she had chosen to take to Turkey but for these few days in Paris she had bought extravagantly.

When George came in from the dressing room she was brushing her hair. It shone red gold in the shaded lamplight. The thin silk and lace of her nightgown clung to the slender figure and he caught his breath still astonished at his unbelievable luck in capturing this elusive wisp of a girl whom he had wanted for so long. He came up behind her slipping his arms around her, his hands cupping her breasts. The faint perfume of her hair intoxicated him as he brushed it aside with his lips and kissed her neck. He plucked the brush from her hand and turned her round to face him.

"I still can't believe we're really married," he muttered thickly before his mouth closed down on hers. She fought the instant recoil and leaned against him. "Darling, darling!" he was murmuring, his mouth on her throat, on her breasts, his hands moving over her before he lifted her in his arms and carried her to the bed.

She woke very early and for an instant could not think what she was doing in this strange bed. Then memory flooded back and she sat up abruptly looking around the empty room. She knew an instant of panic before George came in from the balcony and pulled the door closed behind him.

"What is it?" she said quickly. "Is anything wrong?"

"No. It was hot in here. I needed air."

"Is that all? What time is it?"

"Just after six."

"Much too early for breakfast. Hadn't you better come back to bed?"

He crossed the room and stood looking down at her, his hands in the pockets of his dressing-gown.

"Are you sure that you want me there?"

"Of course. What a strange thing to say."

George was not inexperienced with women but he was not a

213

brute. He had never in his life made love to a girl who was unwilling. He knew the difference between passive obedience and a kindling passion and his disappointment at Laurel's reaction was acute and mingled with a certain resentment.

"You don't really care for me at all, do you?"

"That's a silly question. I married you, didn't I?"

"Yes. And I'm beginning to wonder why. Who is it you really love, Laurel?"

She chose to treat the question lightly. "Oh George, don't be tiresome. I might as well begin asking you about the women you have been fond of. What's past is done with. We are starting a new life together."

"Are we when on our first night you turn away from me?"

"I'm sorry," she said quickly and repentantly. "You must be patient with me . . ."

But he went on steadily. "Patient, I suppose, even when you murmur a name in your sleep that is certainly not mine. Who is it, Laurel, who?"

She turned her head away. "There is no one."

He put a hand on her shoulder swinging her back to face him. "Damn you, don't hide from me. I'm not to be fooled. Married, is he? Or perhaps he just doesn't care enough," he went on, his voice edged with bitterness. "What was it that made you agree to marry me so suddenly? Are you pregnant?"

"No" she said angrily and vehemently. "How dare you say such a thing to me? I'm not a cheat."

He stared at her, one part of him wanting to seize hold of her, hurt her, make violent love to her, and knowing that if he did, it might very well kill what little affection she had for him.

She said in a low voice, "I told you that I was fond of you and I am, George, very fond . . ."

"Oh Christ, what does that mean? I believed, I hoped . . ."

She remembered then what Jane had said and realized the folly of what she had done. She had not meant this to happen and did not know how to mend it. She scrambled up on to her knees and put her arms around his neck.

"I'll make it up to you, George, I swear I will. We've plenty of money, we can have fun . . ."

"Money!" he said violently. "You think that's all I want. I'm not Barton. To hell with your damned money!"

"Don't be angry with me, George, please don't be angry."

He looked down at the lovely face raised to his, tears in the

214

violet eyes and trembling on the dark lashes, and cursed himself for a trusting fool caught in a trap of his own making. Then abruptly he pulled himself free from her and walked away.

"I'll order breakfast," he said. "We had better get dressed. We've only a couple of days before Cardigan and his mob are here, we might as well make the most of them."

15

A fortnight later Laurel was standing beside George on the deck of the *Asian Star* as it glided slowly up the Bosphorus. It was very warm and only the gentlest of breezes stirred the silk shawl around her shoulders. The harsh realities of war were still far away. At their embarkation at Marseilles they might have been going on a picnic, so many baskets of fruit, cases of wine and bouquets of flowers had been handed up the sides of the ship. The excitable French had given them a great send-off. Now through the faint mist of the May evening Constantinople on the opposite bank was a city of enchantment, a paradise of gaily painted houses, white domes and fretted minarets massed with brilliantly coloured flowers and creepers that seemed to rise from the sea against a background of tall dark cypresses. It was an illusion that was to vanish on closer acquaintance but that was to come. For a few fragile moments the magic remained and Laurel felt a stir of excitement as George's hand closed over hers.

"Well, there it is," he said, "we're here for better or worse."

After that first night together there had been a truce between them and as soon as they had joined Lord Cardigan and his staff, he was so demanding of George's time that there had been little opportunity for intimacy. Cardigan was a strange man, thought Laurel, nearly sixty but still handsome with his slim figure and long legs, an exacting, narrow-minded martinet with his men, but rakishly gallant with women. It both amused and irritated George to see how easily she had charmed him, playing the battered piano in the ship's saloon after dinner and singing sentimental Italian ballads that had the old man twirling his moustache and giving her killing glances.

"Don't trust him too far," he said frowning at her one night in the privacy of their cabin. "He has a shocking reputation."

"For what? Ravishing village maidens? Don't be silly, George. We want him to be on our side, don't we? It could be useful."

"I don't need my wife to forward my career," he said touchily.

"I was not thinking of you so much but of myself," said Laurel ruefully.

She had already realized that cavalry wives even of officers were barely tolerated in the army and she had no intention of being separated from George and left behind with tiresome grumbling women in some frowsty hotel or bug-ridden apartment in Constantinople.

George well aware that he was the envy of every man on board with a wife who combined beauty and fortune, still felt himself cheated though once on the voyage they had drawn very close. As a cavalryman he was accustomed to the problems of transporting horses by sea but to Laurel it came as a shocking revelation. As soon as the *Asian Star* sailed from Marseilles and they were settled into their cabin, she had made her way down to the hold where Lucifer and the bay were tethered. In the semi-darkness she could just make out the rows of stalls where the horses stood facing each other secured by headropes and slings. A blast of stifling heat polluted by fumes of ammonia and the sharp smell of vinegar nearly drove her backwards but she went on resolutely until she found Seth with Lucifer and Brownie. Every lurch of the ship sent them stumbling forward pitching them against their mangers and she visited them every day soothing and petting them. It was not until the storm broke that the full horror was revealed.

As the ship sailed through the Greek Islands and into the Aegean, the full blast of the wind caught them. It was one evening when she had retired early and she was hurled across the cabin, baggage, boxes and toilet articles falling all around her. She picked herself up, her first thought going immediately to the horses. She was not yet undressed and she pulled a cloak around her groping her way down to the stalls, losing her footing and scrambling up again, clinging on to the ropes, lashed by gales of rain. In the darkness of the hold it was like a scene out of hell. The horses plunged and reared in terror. Their frantic screams and the shouts of the men trying to calm them were deafening. Some of them had fallen dragging others down with them. Seth was pouring buckets of vinegar water over the nostrils of the terrified Lucifer.

"You shouldn't be down here, Madam," he shouted to her. "It's far too dangerous. Go back before you are hurt."

"No. I'm here to help," she shouted back.

217

Lucifer sensed that she was close by and neighed wildly. She fought her way towards him speaking quietly and soothingly, using her own particular magic. The grooms stared in amazement at the small figure soaked to the waist moving about among the great plunging scared beasts seemingly without fear and avoiding their flailing hooves by a miracle. It was there in the midst of the pandemonium that George anxiously searching the ship found her at last clinging to Lucifer's mane and whispering loving words into his ear. She refused pointblank to leave when he would have taken her away and so he stayed beside her finding a queer comradeship and happiness in doing what they could to ease the sufferings of the wretched animals they both loved.

They disembarked at a wooden jetty at Scutari on the Asiatic side of the Bosphorus. The ground was broken and uneven, littered with discarded rubbish and dotted with ragged tents and awnings of rough sacking where the wives of the troopers had attempted to find shelter for themselves. There were little fires burning here and there with cooking pots, children stood staring, babies were crying and mangy starved dogs rummaged amongst the food scraps.

Shocked and distressed Laurel said, "Isn't there anywhere better for the women? Why is no proper lodging arranged for them?"

George shrugged his shoulders. "The regiment gives them transport if they wish to follow their men. After that they must look out for themselves."

"But it's inhuman."

"It's army regulations."

Some little distance away a magnificent three-storied building with tall towers at either end glimmered palely through the twilight.

"What is that place? Couldn't they go there?"

"Originally it was one of the Sultan's palaces, now it is to serve as a barracks," said George curtly, occupied with overseeing the collection of their baggage, arranging transport for the horses with Seth and his batman and hiring a caique from the noisy gesticulating ferrymen all clamouring for his custom. They climbed into the slender curved boat and though the cushions were dirty and the boatman's scarlet shirt and full breeches were soiled, there was something romantic about his merry black eyes and the gold rings in his ears, and he grinned

218

admiringly at Laurel as they sailed across the shining water to the ancient city.

There was a severe shortage of wheeled transport but George somehow contrived to find a ramshackle carriage and took her to the Hotel d'Angleterre where already a number of English ladies were installed. It had the same tawdry splendour as the city. Their bedroom was handsomely furnished in gilt and red plush but Laurel woke in the night to hear rats scuffling and squeaking through their baggage, the sheets were spotted with bedbugs and with the coming of the dawn a little army of cockroaches scuttled for shelter into cracks and crevices.

George was obliged to go off very early to attend to his duties leaving his wife to breakfast with the other army wives. After listening to them complaining of the heat, the food, the hard beds, the flies, the fleas, the impudence of Turkish servants, the disagreeable smells and the sheer impossibility of obtaining a smoothing iron to restore crushed gowns, Laurel made two resolutions, never to grumble at anything however unpleasant and to go with George on campaign no matter where it was or how hot and dusty the journey rather than be left behind in this dispiriting company. Later that morning dressed in her coolest gown of lavender muslin with a wide shady hat and the protection of a white parasol, she ventured out to explore Constantinople and found to her dismay that the faery city of the night before was indeed an illusion. The painted houses were in grievous need of repair, narrow reeking alleys were pitted with gaping holes and littered with piles of filth and the bloated corpses of rats, dogs, cats and in one instance a donkey. It was hot, crowded and unbearably noisy while passing Turks gazed curiously at the slender Englishwoman in her cool muslins so different from their plump veiled women in their heavy dark draperies. But for those who persevered it was not all squalor and there were shops displaying fine eastern silks, fascinating jewellery and curios of all kinds. She did not dare to venture into the dark bazaar but the market was piled with pyramids of delicious fruit and massed with flowers. George returning late, exhausted and sweating in his heavy uniform, found their shuttered room fragrant with the scent of roses and his wife, already dressed for the reception at the Embassy, pinning a cluster of crimson rosebuds to the bosom of her gown of white silk organza, the flounced skirts over the wide crinoline caught up with knots of silver ribbon.

219

"Will I do?" she asked turning to him and dropping a little curtsey.

"By God, you will. The Ambassador's wife and daughters will be ready to scratch out your eyes," he said smiling at her.

"Good. I want you to be proud of me."

"So you do care for me a little," and he reached out a hand and drew her to him.

"Just a very little," she said teasingly, "but not just now. You must wash and change or we shall be late and Lord Cardigan who has a mania for punctuality will have one of his tantrums."

Lord Stratford de Redcliffe, Ambassador to the court of the Sultan, was wealthy and lived in considerable state. His magnificent palace was surrounded by terraced gardens luxuriant with myrtles, azaleas and all kinds of fragrant shrubs. Roses spilled from gigantic pots with trailing creepers as they went up the stairs. Invitations to the reception in honour of Lord Cardigan and Lord Lucan, brothers-in-law and, gossip said with truth, deadly enemies, were eagerly sought. Those not fortunate enough to receive a card had looked very sourly at Laurel when George handed her into the sedan chair, an ancient form of conveyance but something of a commonplace in a city where carriages were still few and far between.

Heads were turned when she entered the ballroom on George's arm, the small queenly head glowing a rich auburn under the magnificent chandelier as she curtseyed to her host. The elderly Lord Raglan, Commander-in-Chief of the British Expeditionary Army, who had lost an arm fighting under Wellington at Waterloo, welcomed her with kindness and within a few minutes the officers on his staff headed by Cardigan himself were besieging her to dance with them. She glanced prettily at George for permission and he gave it reluctantly pleased that other men should desire his wife but sharply aware of a pang of jealousy that he had never before experienced. If only he could be sure of her!

Ever since their marriage Laurel had tried loyally to put Jethro out of her mind and yet from the moment they had landed in Turkey she had found herself scanning each face even in the crowded streets of the market that morning and now, though she would never have admitted it even to herself, her eyes were searching among the guests for the tall figure, the proud dark head. When she did meet him, it was purely by accident. She had gone to pin up a flounce ripped by her

220

partner's spur in a lively mazurka and on her way back down the long white corridor hung with garlands of ivy and scarlet creeper, something about the man ahead of her seemed familiar. He paused at a door, she caught up with him, he stood back to let her pass him and it was Jethro. He was wearing the plain dark blue undress uniform of an officer in the Medical Corps and for an instant she was too breathless to speak. Then she saw the utter astonishment on his face give way to a frown.

"Laurel, what on earth are you doing here?"

"I am with my husband."

"Husband?" He caught his breath. "I don't understand..."

"Didn't you know? I thought Rosemary would be sure to have told you. George Grafton and I were married at the beginning of May."

"Why, in God's name, why?"

"You suggested it yourself – don't you remember?"

"George Grafton of all people! You can't care for him. It's not possible." He was filled with an illogical anger.

"I'm very fond of him," she said quietly.

"And he, I presume, has brought you out here with him. He has no right to do such a thing, no right at all."

"On the contrary he has every right," she said coolly. "He is my husband and naturally I wish to go with him wherever he is sent."

He had opened the door by now and they had moved into the small antechamber off the ballroom.

"You've no notion of what is going to happen out here," he said angrily. "Do you imagine war is all like this – receptions and balls and picnics? It is not – it is filth and blood and disease and death."

"I understand," she said steadily. "You need not spell it out. I'm not alone. There are many other women here."

"Sensation-seekers, pretty fools, who think they are going to watch their toy soldiers march to war like a children's game," he went on savagely. "A grand reception at the ambassador's palace followed by a little battle, something to add excitement to a picnic."

"I don't understand why you are so angry about it. After all you are here at the palace yourself."

"Not for pleasure, I assure you. I'm here for one purpose only and that is to try and batter some sense into the ambassador's staff about the barracks at Scutari."

221

"I saw it as we landed," she said in surprise. "What is wrong with it? It looked a wonderful place."

"Wonderful indeed!" he said sarcastically. "A Sultan's palace that is also a cess-pit. I've been investigating it with some of my colleagues. Do you realize that it has not been cleaned for years? The floors are inches deep with filth and decaying refuse, the walls ooze damp, dead animals, rats and vermin are mingled with indescribable litter, the sewers beneath have been choked for a century spreading poisonous effluvia throughout every part of the building. The stench is beyond description and this is to be our principal hospital for the disabled and the wounded. Within those walls a healthy man would scarcely survive a week, a sick man a matter of hours."

Horrified she said in a whisper, "Can't it be cleansed?"

"It would need an army to do the work properly and no one here or anywhere else in this shambles of an organization considers it of sufficient importance to merit a second thought. They will wait until the dead pile up and they're digging plague pits for the corpses before they will make a single move to obtain the necessary authority." In his anger he had temporarily forgotten her but now he stopped seeing the shock on her face. "I'm sorry, Laurel. I shouldn't be saying all this to you but for a week now I've been hammering at doors that refuse to open. No one listens, no one cares."

She did not understand fully but was vividly aware of his frustration and instinctively she stretched out her hand to him.

"There must be some way . . ."

"If there is, then God help me to find it before it is too late," he said sombrely. He took her hand drawing her close to him. "But now it's you I must think about. Don't stay out here, Laurel. Go home to England."

"No."

"You must," he went on urgently. "It's ridiculous. Of what use can you be out here?"

"I don't know yet, but I shall find out."

"I can't bear the thought of you here and what you may have to go through. Please, Laurel, listen to me . . ."

They were dangerously close. She wanted to draw away from him and couldn't. The magic was still there, still potent between them. His hand was on her wrist setting her blood on fire. She swayed towards him and it was at that moment that the door opened and George came in with a couple of his brother officers.

222

He saw how close they were though Jethro released her wrist at once. He walked across to them, his voice carefully controlled.

"Laurel, do I know this gentleman?"

"I think you met some time ago," she said a little unsteadily. "This is Jethro Aylsham. He is with the Medical Corps."

George's eyes ran up and down the plain uniform. "Ah yes, I remember. A surgeon, I believe. Well, sir, you are likely to be busy as soon as the troops go into action." He turned to Laurel. "Come, my dear, I've been looking for you everywhere. Lord Raglan is just leaving." He took her arm to lead her away but Jethro stopped him.

"Captain Grafton, I've been trying to persuade your wife to return to England. A seat of war in a country such as this is hardly the place for so young a lady."

"Indeed. When I require your advice, Dr Aylsham, I will ask for it."

"You've only just arrived here," he persisted. "You've no idea how bad the conditions are, conditions that will certainly become far worse."

"I don't scare easily," replied George icily, "and I think I'm the best judge of my wife's actions. Come, Laurel."

He pulled her arm through his and led her out of the room while Jethro looked after them despairingly. He had absolutely no right to be jealous and yet he was fully aware that part of his natural desire to save Laurel from the dangers he could foresee, the hardships, the risk of sickness, was also a passionate desire to know her parted from the man she had chosen as her husband.

George was silent as they drove back to their hotel and was in a strange restless mood while they prepared for bed exchanging trivial gossip about the evening. It was stiflingly hot with the heavy stillness that precedes a storm. Laurel was glad to strip off ballgown and petticoats and slip into the cool lawn of her nightdress. George pulled on his dressing-gown, poured himself a glass of brandy and then left it untasted. He crossed to the windows thrusting them wide open to the black starless night. There was a low distant rumble of thunder.

"Is it raining yet?" she asked.

"No, not yet. It will be cooler when it does. We've had our orders," he went on abruptly. "The army is to move up to Varna. It's a small port in Bulgaria on the Black Sea – about a hundred and thirty miles from here."

"When do you go?"

"The day after tomorrow. We shall travel by sea. Horses and baggage will be moved on to the transports tomorrow."

"Then I shall go with you."

George turned round. "It may not be possible. Lord Lucan is in command of both wings of the cavalry and he is putting a ban on all officers' wives."

"Then I shall go to Lord Cardigan," she said confidently. "He loathes his brother-in-law especially now that he is officially under his command. Anything he can do to annoy him, he will, even in a small matter like this. He'll listen to me, you'll see, and even if he doesn't, I shall still come. Nothing will stop me even if I have to hire ponies and ride the hundred and thirty miles!"

George smiled reluctantly at her vehemence before he said quietly, "All the same, I've been thinking. Perhaps it would be better if you went home to England."

She looked across at him startled. "Whatever makes you say that now?"

"I hadn't realized how hard the conditions out here were likely to be."

"That's no reason. Do you think I've made this long journey only to turn tail at the first hint of discomfort and bolt home? They'd all laugh their heads off at me." Then she paused, watching his face. "Is all this because of what Jethro said tonight?"

"Maybe." Then abruptly the tight control he had been keeping over himself broke. "That damned doctor fellow is in love with you, isn't he?"

"No . . ."

"Don't lie to me, Laurel. I'm not blind. I saw you there together. Is he the reason you married me? Were you looking for an excuse to come out here so that you could be with him?"

"No, you're wrong," but she had turned away from him and in a couple of strides he had reached her side and swung her to face him.

"Am I wrong? Am I? Answer me, Laurel."

Lightning suddenly flashed through the room followed by a growl of thunder. Anger flooded up in him. He gripped her shoulders, his fingers digging painfully through the flimsy nightgown.

"You were lovers, weren't you?"

224

She tried to pull away from him. "Let me go. You're hurting me."

"Damn you, answer me. I want the truth!" and driven quite beyond himself he struck her across the face.

Outraged her hand flew up to her bruised cheek and she fell back on to the bed. The storm was increasing in strength now. Lightning lit his face followed by a clap of thunder that seemed to shake the whole building. She stared up at him defiantly, her eyes blazing.

"Yes, we were lovers, once only, but I love him, do you hear, I love him, love him . . ."

"You dare to say that to me . . ."

"You wanted the truth so now you know and can make what you like of it."

"Oh my God!"

He stood looking down at her, tormented by doubt and jealousy, appalled at what he had done, half wishing he had left well alone. At last he said in a strangled voice, "If that is so, then why marry me and not him?"

"There are reasons . . ."

"What reasons?"

"I'm not telling you. They belong to him . . . not to anyone else."

"I have a right to be told."

"No."

Anger welled up in him again. "And what the hell do we do now?"

She pulled herself upright, lifting her head proudly. "We go on as before. I'm your wife, George, and I'm going with you to Varna or wherever else you are sent. I'm sharing your life, the good things and the bad whether you like it or not."

"Do you mean that?"

"I mean it."

He stared at her for a moment while outside the storm raged, lightning and thunder all about them and the rain lashing into the room through the open window until it seemed to become part of the stir in his blood and the fury of love and jealousy that consumed him. He threw off his dressing-gown and seized her in his arms. She cried out but he did not heed it. That night he made violent love to her as if he sought to drive out of her mind the thought of any other man but himself and she let him have his will following where he led but when at last he lay exhausted

225

and she was still and quiet in the crook of his arm, he knew with a feeling close to despair that though she had given herself to him freely, the essential Laurel still escaped him.

In late August the sun blazed down on Meni-Bazaar, a high dry almost treeless plateau to which the army had been moved in a vain attempt to escape the cholera that was ravaging Varna. Lord Cardigan who always knew exactly how to look after his own comfort had had his tent pitched in the middle of the one small oasis of trees with a spring of cool water. His two marquees with his cooks, grooms and valets took up most of the available shade. Seth had been forced to set up George's green canvas tent on slightly higher ground and had contrived a latticework of boughs and branches to provide some kind of shelter from the broiling sun.

It was here that Laurel sat one afternoon, the flaps of the tent pinned back to allow the passage of what air there was. She was opening a food parcel sent by Jane which had at last found its way through to them. Carefully packed by Fortnum and Mason it held tea, coffee, cocoa, chocolate, sugar, cheese and biscuits and even though the potted ham and pheasant had gone rancid in the heat of the journey, the rest provided a welcome addition to their sparse and monotonous diet of salt pork, scrawny tough chicken and barley bread hard as a rock. There were letters too, a brief loving note from Jane with the parcel, a fat packet from Rosemary and a small package. She trembled when she saw the handwriting and put it on one side, opening the others first. She wondered as she settled down to enjoy them if those at home had any notion of what the last three months had been like.

Her trust in Lord Cardigan's support had been justified. Enraged at having to knuckle under to his brother-in-law's arbitrary commands, he took a childish pleasure in overriding his objection and Laurel embarked on the transport to smiles from his brother officers and cheers from the men. Very few wives had braved the hardships of campaigning with their husbands and though George said nothing, she thought he was glad that she was one of them. She still remembered vividly the first night at Varna in the pretty white house he had found for them and the horror when darkness fell – a sound like a pitter-patter of rain and the candle hastily relit revealing vast armies of vermin on the move, streaming from between the floorboards, swarming up the bed and across the sheets, dropping from walls and ceiling. Nothing kept them away except the light so they slept that night, as Laurel said giggling, like royal corpses lying in state surrounded by candle flame. Next day George sent Seth to purchase tents and camping equipment and it was astonishing how quickly they had adapted to the rough and ready life. The worst problem was trying to care for the horses. The only practical shelter from the heat was a specially dug pit where they could be tethered with wet bandages over their eyes and a covering of rags to protect them from the tormenting flies. It distressed her when she woke in the night and heard the kicking and screaming from the horse lines. Brownie died and she wept bitterly over him, but Lucifer survived and she rode him around the camp morning and evening when it was cooler. To the men, bored and dispirited in this hot and dusty place, she had become something of a mascot, a bearer of good luck. They would come to greet her, shyly offering little gifts, a ripe peach, a few hard apples, an armful of roses plucked from a Turkish garden.

It had been a desperately hard struggle for the first few weeks and she thought sometimes that she would never have got through them if it had not been for Polly Cobb. Polly was a cheerful Cockney from the East End of London married to Private Cobb, a big clumsy young man very nearly inarticulate but he could turn his hand to anything practical and shared Seth's devotion to the horses. Polly was small, wiry, indomitable and talked enough for both of them. She was determined that her man should be better sheltered and better fed than any other trooper in the regiment and nothing daunted her. The day she saw Laurel struggling helplessly with an army of large red ants that marched regularly through the tents devouring everything that stood in its path was the start of an enduring friendship.

"Boilin' water, ma'am, that's what you want, boilin' water and plenty of it. Don't stop 'em for ever but it does the trick for a day or two and that's worth something. Here, you let me do it for you. I'm a dab hand at it, got to be things bein' as they are. 'Im in there," she went on nodding to Lord Cardigan's camp, "he wouldn't care if his men were eaten alive!"

After tackling the ants she looked around her at the chaos Laurel was valiantly trying to keep under control. "Say the word and I'll come in reg'lar and give you a hand, washin' and such as you want done. My Fred, he thinks the world of the

227

Cap'n and you too, ma'am. 'Fancy,' he sez to me only the other night, 'fancy a pretty little lady like that comin' out 'ere and not a peep out of 'er, not like some as I could mention.'"

Money she always refused to accept but tidbits from the food parcels, some tea and cocoa and half a bottle of George's carefully hoarded wine were received gratefully. When the grim spectre of the cholera stalked through the camp and deaths became so frequent that military funerals were forbidden and the victims buried secretly by night, she accepted it stoically helping those who couldn't help themselves and it was then that Laurel remembered what Jethro had told her once when they had been working together at the settlement.

"If only I could teach these poor devils the value of cleanliness," he had said. "It may not cure but it helps to check infection and another thing, if only they would boil all water and never eat anything unwashed or uncooked. Why it should be, I don't yet know for certain, but what I do know is that it prevents the disease spreading."

So she followed his simple rules scrupulously and impressed on Polly to do the same. At first it had been terrifying. A man could be strong and healthy in the morning and dead by nightfall and she never saw George leave her without a twinge of anxiety, but gradually she learned to live with it. It was either that or give way to nerves and run home and that was something she had vowed to herself never to do.

Cushions were piled up on the camp bed. She leaned back against them and opened Rosemary's letter. It ran on breathlessly, pages and pages about Charles and the work he had undertaken, about Jessica who had already received three proposals and refused them all, about parties and balls and summer picnics at Ravensley. For an instant in this hot airless place Laurel seemed to feel the coolness of the marsh wind and smell the scent of the meadowsweet blooming along the waterways. She wondered if she would ever take George to Westley and then knew it would be impossible. The strange haunting beauty of the Fens belonged to Jethro. There she would never escape from him. She turned back to her letter.

"Have you seen Robin yet?" she read. "He has volunteered for the Rifle Brigade. Papa was so angry about it and poor Mamma was terribly upset. You see he will be twenty-one next January and already a party was being planned. Who knows if the war will be over by then? Papa went to Uncle Harry at the

War Office and they tried to stop it, but Robin had lied about his age and had already been sent abroad so nothing could be done. He didn't tell me or Jess or anyone about it, but I think it is because of you and Jet. He admires you both so much, he just couldn't bear the thought of staying here and doing nothing when you and he are in the thick of it."

Oh God, thought Laurel, stricken with remorse, what have I done? I didn't urge him to do anything so foolish and he is the Aylshams' only son. He probably thinks it's all wonderfully heroic to come out here and it is nothing of the kind. I've found that out already. All the army is doing is sitting here and dying of terrible sickness while George is driven nearly crazy with frustration.

She sighed and picked up the closely written sheets again. "Margaret of course was shockingly upset. I think if she could have run after him, she would have done so and she did do something rather startling. She actually obtained an interview with that Miss Nightingale and asked to be accepted as one of her nurses! And the funny thing was, she was refused. I must admit that Jess and I had a laugh over it. I know it was unkind but she was so cocksure, so high and mighty about it, and she was given such a set-down!"

Laurel spared a moment of pity for Margaret guessing at her bitter humiliation. She wiped the sweat from her face and went on reading.

"And now, dearest Laurel, a piece of information that came to my ears and is so strange that I felt I must tell you because it concerns you so closely, and Jet too of course. It was a week or so ago when Charles came to spend a few days at Ravensley and I was telling him our family history. I thought he ought to know the worst since he's soon to become one of us so I told him about wicked Uncle Justin and your mother and all the horrid scandal that came out of it and he looked at me very oddly and said, 'I think you had better speak to my father about that.' Well, of course I was terribly curious and badgered him about it and at last he told me. Apparently years and years ago before your grandfather took your mother to Italy, he went to Dr Townsend and asked a favour from him. He informed him that he had obtained permission to have the body of a young woman called Alyne Leigh removed from where she had been buried in unconsecrated ground and carried into the church at Westley to be reinterred in the Leighs' family vault. As a special request he

229

asked the doctor to be present when the coffin was opened. This he did and found the remains of a young woman with a baby in her arms. It was all done very quietly and the body was reburied. I asked Charles why so little had been known about the reburial and he said that his father told him that it was Sir Joshua's wish that it should be carried out as secretly as possible. You know how remote Westley is, how cut off from the rest of the fens. The Leighs had all gone from the manor and the great house was shut up. If any of the villagers had wondered about it, they would certainly not have known that the coffin had been opened and would probably only have felt that justice had been done at last to a tragic young woman who had taken her own life. But you understand what this means, don't you? Your mother was not Justin Aylsham's daughter after all. The baby must have drowned with her poor mother so all that vicious scandal and the wretchedness it caused were suffered for nothing."

The paper shook in Laurel's hand and the writing blurred for a moment, then she resolutely went on reading.

"I used to think that you and Jet were specially fond of one another and then of course this would have been very important but when you married Captain Grafton I realized that I must have been mistaken. But all the same I thought you would like to know, and Jet too. If you see him, perhaps you would tell him? I've not yet spoken to Dr Townsend about it because I think I should tell Papa first but Charles was absolutely sure about it."

The letter dropped from Laurel's shaking fingers. So that was why she had searched the ground around the church in vain last Christmas. The irony of it struck her so forcibly that she didn't know whether to laugh or cry. Why had Dr Townsend said nothing about it? Why? And yet of course why should he realize its importance except to Sir Joshua? He scarcely knew the Aylshams at that time and in any case would not have wished to rake up old slanders best left forgotten. Nobody had ever been aware of what it meant to her and Jethro and now it was too late. She was married to George. She owed him loyalty and affection, now more than ever. Why had she let frustration and wretchedness rush her into something so final? Why? Why? Looking back it seemed like a madness and now she was being punished for it. She folded the letter carefully and put it away. The air in the tent was so heavy and still, it was difficult to breathe. She felt the sweat running down her back under the

230

thin cotton blouse. With Polly's help she had stitched up skirts of grey holland. How shocked they would have been in London to know she had discarded most of her petticoats and wore little beneath but a flimsy shift and linen drawers.

She picked up the small package that had come from Jethro. Would she tell him this extraordinary news if she saw him – yes or no – she could not make up her mind, afraid of what it might do to them. Her fingers shook as she fumbled with the seal and fastenings. The box contained medicines, tincture of opium, calomel, other drugs that had been used to try and combat the cholera and dysentery that racked the army. The short letter gave practical instructions as to their use and she was touched that he should have thought of her and George at a time like this. There was news too, more recent than any that had reached them in this remote place cut off from where decisions were being made.

"I sometimes think that the powers-that-be are suffering from softening of the brain," he wrote, "and I truly believe that Lord Raglan is under the impression that he is still fighting the French with Wellington as he did forty years ago! Now that the Russians have withdrawn from Turkey, we could all pack up and go home but that's too easy. I am reliably informed that at the Council a decision was taken to invade the Crimea, destroy Sebastopol and smash Russian naval power in the Mediterranean for ever and this, God help us all, with an army ravaged by sickness and with morale at its lowest ebb. I'd like to force some of these stuffed prigs to walk through the cholera wards at Scutari . . . it might teach them a lesson! My regards to you and to your husband."

Despite the formal words she felt the passion and the anger behind them and she was reading the letter for a second time when George came into the tent looking utterly exhausted, his uniform grey with dust from head to foot. He unbuckled his sword belt and began to unhook the high collar of his tunic. She jumped off the bed putting aside the letter and hurrying to help him off with his heavy braided coat.

"If Cardigan wants to kill us off, then he's going the right way about it," he said wearily. "Endless drills, endless marches, useless parades in blazing sunshine, severe punishments for the slightest lapse, a button left unfastened, boots not polished to the requisite perfection – two of my men collapsed today during inspection and had to be carried off."

"Cholera?" she asked fearfully.

"God knows. Could be only heat stroke. I was damned near to it myself I might tell you! At this rate the battalion will be dead and buried before we strike a single blow at the Russians."

"Perhaps it won't be so long as you think. It appears that a decision has been reached to invade the Crimea."

He looked up from the bowl of water in which he was dipping his face. "How do you know that?"

"I had a letter."

"Who from, for God's sake?" and when she hesitated, he turned on her, heat and exhaustion making him unusually irritable and out of temper. "Your surgeon lover, I suppose. How many times has he written to you since we've been up here?"

"As it happens this is the first," she said with dignity. "He sent us medicine which he thought we might need and any news he had been able to pick up. You can read it if you wish," and she held out the letter.

He brushed it aside. "I've no wish to pry into your correspondence. Tell me what he says."

"Simply that at the Council a decision has been taken to attack Sebastopol at last."

"Thank God for that. We need action badly."

"Jethro says he thinks it unwise with the army so demoralized by sickness."

"That's the opinion of a civilian. The men will be overjoyed, I can tell you that, and so will I. The sooner the better. I pray God that he is not mistaken. Anything that will take us out of this hell hole would be a relief."

But Jethro was proved right. Within a few days orders came through that the brigade should move back to Varna. It was a long, hot and uncomfortable journey and Laurel, riding Lucifer, thought ruefully that by now she was becoming as sunburned and hardened as any of George's troopers. They arrived back in Varna after an eleven hour ride, tired and very hungry, to be greeted with the distressing news that no wives were to be permitted to accompany their husbands to the Crimea. This time not even Lord Cardigan could do anything to help and for the first time Laurel lost her courage and burst into tears. Varna had become a place of sickness and death. The thought of being abandoned there was more than she could endure.

232

George was sympathetic but dubious about flouting army regulations and it was Polly Cobb who came up with a solution.

"It's the officers' ladies, ma'am, it don't apply to us. If you don't mind wearin' one of my gowns and puttin' an old shawl over your head and shoulders like one of them Turkish females, you could come with us in the cart. No one'll be any the wiser. We can smuggle you on board and once the ship's at sea, what can they do? They'll never turn back."

George was strongly against it when she told him. "My wife going aboard with a lot of raggle-taggle women half of them no better than whores – it can't be done, Laurel. What would they think of me? I'm not permitting it. Maybe you can follow after in another ship."

He wouldn't listen to her protests and Polly said wisely, "Don't tell him about it, ma'am. I know men. He don't want to get the blame, see, but he'll be pleased as Punch when you bob up in his cabin. You get that Seth of yours to put your baggage on board secret-like and we'll do the rest."

She watched George embark with his men. Then with some trepidation she bunched Polly's best gown around her, smudged dirt on her face, draped an old black shawl over her head and climbed into the cart with the other women. There was one awkward moment when they reached the dock and the embarkation officer began to check through passes but Polly rose to the occasion. At the crucial moment she began an argument with the woman behind her, the others joined in and with the strong possibility of a gaggle of wretched females screeching and fighting one another like wild cats, the harassed officer let them crowd into the boats and resigned them to the responsibility of the unfortunate Captain. The sailors rowed them out to the ship. Negotiating the swaying ladder up the side took some doing but then she was safely on board.

For a day and a night while the ship remained in harbour, she had to endure being shut below decks in a confined space, hot, airless and smelling disgusting, with a bunch of women, some of whom resented her and showed it. She didn't know how she could have borne it if it hadn't been for Polly's sturdy company. Then the ship sailed and once out in the Black Sea, she ventured up on deck. It was dark already, only the ship's lanterns giving a glimmering light. The sailors eyed her curiously since the women were expected to keep together down below, but she put a bold face on it and they grinned slyly as they directed her to

233

George's cabin. He was lying on the bunk when she cautiously opened the door. He saw the tousled untidy figure sliding its way in. There were always women willing to sell themselves to the officers for a few shillings.

"Get out, damn you," he said impatiently. "I'm not in the market for your charms."

"I'm very glad to hear it," she said and pushed back the black shawl.

He stared at her. "Laurel, by God! How the hell did you get here?"

"Aren't you pleased to see me?"

"Am I pleased?" He was on his feet by now pulling her into the cabin and shutting the door. "You little devil! How did you manage it?"

"I came with the other women."

"What the deuce am I to say to Cardigan?"

"Will he throw me overboard?"

"I'd like to see him try! By God, what a wife I've got!" and he began to laugh.

He drew her into his arms and kissed her still laughing and that night in the warm companionship forged by hardships suffered and survived, there was peace between them and a measure of happiness she had never thought to feel again.

16

On September 14th the ships anchored in Calamita Bay and officers and men crowded on to the decks to catch their first glimpse of the Crimea. The little town of Eupatoria shone white and pretty in the brilliant sunshine and the countryside stretched, a green grassy steppe rolling away to the distant hills and to the River Alma which they must cross to capture Sebastopol. The ten-day voyage had been pleasant, sunlit days and cool scented nights when the lights of the transports passing and repassing made a moving pathway of coloured stars – a romantic interlude with a touch of macabre. They sat down to dinner one night with the grim knowledge that on the other side of the screened-off saloon one of George's brother officers was dying of cholera. The champagne was brought out, corks popped but a chill hung over them and Laurel found it difficult to eat.

She remained on board during the muddle and confusion of disembarkation and a sudden freakish rainstorm when the troops caught without tents or any kind of shelter were forced to sleep in their sodden greatcoats huddled beneath carts or gun carriages. A week later the army was at last on the move.

Laurel, taut with excitement, her throat choked with pride, watched as the men, wave after wave of them, marched by to the stirring martial music of the regimental bands, the neighing of the horses and the rumble of the gun carriages. Earlier that morning she had kissed George goodbye and seen him ride at the head of his men magnificent in cherry colour and scarlet and blue, his furred pelisse laced with gold. The Guards marched in bearskins, enormously tall in scarlet uniforms slashed with the dazzling whiteness of the swordbelts. The sun glittered on epaulettes and buttons, on brass helmets and bayonets and lances. Everywhere colour and brilliance, a shimmer of gold and polished steel.

The order had gone out that no women were to ride with the cavalry but Laurel was determined not to be left behind. Seth waited with Lucifer and the new spare horse, saddlebags

235

thoughtfully filled with provisions, rugs and canvas strapped to the saddles. With the utmost misgiving about his mistress's safety, he helped her to mount and they trotted after the marching army followed by the carts where Polly Cobb rode with some of the bolder amongst the other women.

Jethro bringing up the rear of the army with the rest of the doctors and surgeons was torn between thankfulness that at last they were going into action and a sharp awareness that the splendid show was little better than a sham. With Dr Alexander, Staff Surgeon to the cavalry division, he had been horrified at the lack of equipment. The ships from Varna had proved hopelessly inadequate to carry all the men with their horses so that hospital marquees, medicine chests, bedding, tents, cooking stoves and stores had been left behind. Thirty thousand troops were going into battle without litters, carts or any kind of transport for the wounded. Already after the first hour men were falling out of the ranks, stricken with sickness, prostrated by heat and exhaustion. The sunlight, the larks singing in the cloudlessly blue sky, the thyme-scented turf springy beneath their feet seemed to mock at their plight. The bands no longer played and there was an uncanny silence as the men plodded on soundlessly over the soft ground. Once when he looked up he saw with a horrible foreboding the vultures that soared and hovered above their heads. No enemy was in sight. Occasionally on the distant heights a solitary Cossack could be glimpsed looking around at the advancing army and then disappearing again. That night when they camped they could see the watch fires of the Russians glimmering on the heights beyond the Alma. A long breastwork on one of the ridges bristled with guns and beyond it lay a smaller rampart – the Great and the Lesser Redoubt commanding the path the British must take to cross the river.

It was one o'clock on the following day when the bugles sounded the "Advance" and the infantry commenced their shoulder-to-shoulder march into the mouths of the Russian guns. Laurel was too far back to see anything clearly. She had shared a little canvas shelter with Polly Cobb during the night and was up early too excited and tense to eat. The smoke coiled and eddied blotting out much of the action and she clambered up on to a little ridge not far from where Lord Raglan sat motionless on his horse, his staff around him. One of the officers, a Major Fraser whom she had met on the ship from Varna, recognized her. He pointed to where the line of red-coated infantry could just be glimpsed marching forward with an exact precision only halted by death.

"Look well," he said with rising excitement, "look well, Mrs Grafton. The Queen of England would give her eyes to see that!"

Laurel caught her breath. Toy soldiers marching to war – it was difficult to believe that they were real, that guns were actually firing cutting down great swathes through them, and yet it was happening. She was overwhelmed with wonder that she should be there and part of it, still too far away to have any idea of the agonizing price that would have to be paid. All day the tide of battle surged backwards and forwards and what news came to her was hopelessly confused. Messengers galloped to and fro between Raglan and the commanders on the field. She shouted to one of them as he rode by.

"Can you tell me? The cavalry, the Light Brigade, are they in the action yet?"

The man shook his head. "They're being held in reserve, ma'am."

"Thank God for his mercy," muttered Polly fervently.

When the news was to reach London a few weeks later, the British public was to thrill with pride at the ferocious courage of the troops who had stormed the heights of the Alma marching under the withering fire of the enemy as if they were parading in Hyde Park. Storm after storm of bullets, grape, shrapnel, round-shot, tore through them, man after man fell, but the pace never altered. Driven back a step, they rallied and pressed on again. Grenadiers, Highlanders, the Rifle Brigade smashed their way forward. The sun was sinking over the hills when the relentless charge, implacable, never faltering, slowly won through. The Great Redoubt was taken and then the Lesser before the Russians broke. They turned and fled with a strange unearthly wailing cry that tore the nerves to shreds. The tension snapped. Victory was won and after the first choking relief, they began to count the cost.

That night the army bivouacked on the slopes above the river among the dead and the dying. Many of them dropped where they were, too exhausted to move, too weary to eat the salt pork and hard barley bread in their pouches, tormented by thirst on these waterless heights, wounds beginning to stiffen as night fell and a chill wind crept across the battlefield.

*   *   *

It was still dark when Jethro left the makeshift field station that had been set up. Hour after hour he had been working in impossible conditions, amputating smashed limbs, swabbing and bandaging hideous wounds of men whose courage was beyond words and most of whom would be dead by morning. He reeled with fatigue but the pitiful rows waiting for treatment never seemed to grow less. Their stock of bandages ran out and they were using anything they could lay their hands on, rags, towels, spare shirts. There were no splints left, no morphia, no ether, no chloroform.

It was very late when Dr Alexander said, "Get some rest, man. No one can carry on for ever," and it was a relief to breathe the cool night air, get away from the smell of blood, the reek of death. He stood for a moment breathing deeply, but the agonized cries of the wounded and dying still lying out on the hill slopes were more than he could endure. He could not rest though there was little he could do for them except carry water to ease the torment of their thirst. He took the lantern and slung the refilled water bottles over his shoulder. The moon had risen lighting the men's faces to a ghastly greenish pallor. He moved from one to the other giving what small comfort he could and promising stretcher bearers to carry those with some hope of recovery back to the field station.

Other figures were groping their way across the grass, men who like himself had been unable to sleep and had fetched water from the river valley for their wounded comrades. Dead Russians lay among the British, sprawled on their faces, on their knees in an attitude of prayer, limbs twisted, bodies horribly contorted. One hardly more than a boy lay on his back staring up at the sky. Moved by pity he closed the lifeless eyes and a little white dog crouched beside him growled softly. He whined when Jethro tried to tempt him away and huddled closer to his dead master.

By dawn stumbling with exhaustion he had turned back towards the camp when a voice stopped him.

"Here, if you're a doctor, I don't think this fellow is too far gone."

Wearily he turned aside and fell on his knees. The young man's hand and arm were thick with blood and he looked up at Jethro with huge terrified eyes.

"Hallo, Jet."

"Robin!" He stared at him in utter astonishment. "What in God's name are you doing here?"

238

"Didn't Rosemary write to you?"

"I've been moving about. I've missed my letters."

"I'll not lose it, Jet, will I, not my right hand, not now you are here?"

"Not if I can stop this infernal bleeding."

"Here, use this."

The soldier kneeling on the other side of Robin held out a strip of silk, a woman's scarf. Jethro looked at it dully before he met the other's eyes.

"I know this. It belonged to Laurel."

"Yes, it did," said George curtly. "Use it if it will help the bleeding."

He took it and bound up the arm tightly and then as if by mutual consent they hoisted Robin to his feet between them and began to assist him back to the dressing station. The wounded lay in heart-breaking rows without shelter, some of them dead already, many of them shivering with fever and the cold night air.

"We've not enough blankets, no drugs and God knows where the carts are coming from to carry them back to Eupatoria," said Jethro savagely, "and even if we do get there, I doubt if there'll be the ships to take them down to Scutari."

George said nothing but helped him to make Robin as comfortable as possible. Jethro covered him with his own greatcoat and the boy clutched at his hand as he bent over him.

"I had to come," he whispered. "You and Laurel were here. I couldn't stay at home acting the coward."

"You great fool!" said Jethro gently. "Whatever made you do such a crazy thing? What did your father say?"

"He was furious of course, but he'd have done the same, you know, if he had been me."

"Yes, he probably would." Jethro sighed. "Try to rest a little."

When he came away, George was still there leaning against one of the posts that supported the rough awning.

"I used to think that boy in there was something of a milksop mooning after Laurel but it takes guts to volunteer, come out here and serve in the ranks."

"Oh the Aylshams have never lacked guts, no doubt about that," said Jethro dryly.

They eyed one another warily. The experience of war was new to both of them and a thread of sympathy ran between

239

them. Then by the flickering light of the lantern Jethro saw that George's sleeve was dark with blood.

"You're wounded yourself. Better let me take a look at it."

"It's nothing. Damned funny really. A Russian I was trying to help took a pot-shot at me." He moved restlessly as Jethro eased off his tunic. "God Almighty, the idiocy of this war! If the cavalry had been allowed to pursue, we'd have driven the Cossacks back. We might even have reached Sebastopol. But Raglan forbade it. I thought Cardigan would have gone off his head with frustration. We sat there on our horses watching a beaten army on the run, guns, standards, colours. We were within ten minutes gallop of them. We could have won a resounding victory, taught them a lesson they'd never have forgotten and we let them escape so that all is to do again. It is the most infamous outrage!"

"I'm committed to save life, not destroy it, but I'd have given five years of my time to have charged with you," said Jethro feelingly. He had slit up George's shirt sleeve by now and was examining the wound. "You're lucky. It's not touched the bone but I'll have to extract the bullet or there could be infection and there's not a damned thing I can give you, not even brandy."

"Carry on. Others have suffered worse than this pinprick."

"You'd better sit down."

George dropped on to one of the wooden boxes that had been serving as tables and gritted his teeth while Jethro probed and swabbed. He tossed away the spent bullet.

"That's done it. It should heal cleanly enough now. Have you such a thing as a handkerchief? All mine have been used already." He tore the cambric into strips and bound up the wound. "Have it looked at again as soon as you can."

George had picked up his coat and slung it around his shoulders. "Do you return to Eupatoria with the wounded?"

"If I can. Somehow we've got to organize some medical supplies to help these poor devils."

"If by chance you should see my wife, will you tell her I'm still all in one piece and Fred Cobb too. Polly Cobb has been acting as unofficial maid to Laurel. She'll be glad to know her husband is not wounded."

"I'll do my best."

"What will happen to young Aylsham?"

"The lightly wounded will move on with the army. He'll have a better chance of surviving that way than sent down to Scutari."

240

The sun was coming up in the eastern sky with streaks of gold and crimson. Bugles were sounding rousing the exhausted men.

"Breakfast," said George, "if we're lucky." He saluted Jethro and strolled away to where the cavalry were camped.

Someone had begun to brew coffee. Presently one of the orderlies brought it to him and Jethro accepted it gratefully. Hot, strong and black, it drove away some of the weariness of the night and helped him to face what still had to be done. He took a cup to Robin. An hour's rest had already restored him a little. Loss of blood coupled with shock and exhaustion had caused his collapse. Now with the resilience of youth he was eager to rejoin his unit.

"I'm lucky to have been accepted into the Rifle Brigade. It would never have happened if the battalion had not been under strength. They're wonderful chaps, brave as lions."

Jethro put an arm around his shoulders. "Look after yourself, boy."

Robin fiddled for a moment with the improvised sling Jethro had fixed for him. "Will you be seeing Laurel?"

"Now why the devil should I?"

"Well, if you do – give her my love."

"She's married, Robin, and far out of your reach."

He looked up at Jethro. "That's bad luck – for both of us, isn't it?"

"Go on with you, impudent brat. You're too young to be fretting after Laurel. There's plenty more fish in the sea."

"But not like her."

"Nonsense."

Jethro watched Robin swing away in his green uniform, a spring in his step despite the night's misery. How extraordinary that the accident of war should have brought the three of them together and then separated them again within a few hours. If Robin survived, this could make a man of him – *if he survived* – that was the question. He refused to let his mind dwell on it. There was too much else to be done.

It was a long and painful task getting the wounded on to the farm wagons that had been commandeered and the morning had gone before they could begin their slow journey back to Eupatoria. His orderly had already brought his horse when he saw the little white dog. Someone must have brought it into the camp. It ran distractedly from one to the other, then stopped at his feet looking up at him and whining pitifully. It was ridiculous in the midst of so much carnage and suffering but he could not resist the appeal. He picked up the little creature and it nestled confidingly against his shoulder.

"Shall I knock it on the head, sir?" asked his orderly.

"No, by God. Find a basket. Go on – do as I say," he said sharply to the staring man. When the basket came, he put the little dog in it and slung it from his saddle.

They could only travel with frequent stops when Jethro and his assistants went from cart to cart with water to assuage the men's raging thirst. They lay close together half fainting from the pain of the jolting over the rough ground and he swore under his breath because there was so little he could do to help them, not even an awning to shield them from the glaring sun.

It was at one of these stops that he saw Laurel. She was with a bunch of women who ran eagerly to the carts fearfully scanning the faces of the men who lay there. She had pulled Lucifer to the side of the road to allow them to pass by. She had lost her hat and he noticed how the sun had bleached the red gold hair. He rode up to her.

"Not a pleasant sight, is it?"

"It's terrible." She was shaking and he saw how white she was under the light golden tan. "I never thought . . . I never imagined . . ."

"I told you that war was not a pretty affair."

"Oh, Jethro, it's worse . . . far far worse . . ."

He realized then that she was very close to tears and put a hand on hers, clasping it tightly, trying to give her reassurance. "What are you doing here anyway? I understood from George you were remaining in the town."

"He is not dead then . . . ?"

"Of course he is not dead," he said bracingly. "He is very well, a slight wound that's all. He asked me to tell you that and also that Fred Cobb is unhurt."

"Thank God for that – Polly will be so happy."

"The army are pushing forward but in what direction we don't know yet. Nothing is decided. The best thing you can do is to return to the town and wait for news."

"May I ride with you?" He hesitated and she looked up at him pleadingly. "Please, Jethro. I won't be any trouble. I'm not afraid, not any longer. I might even be able to help."

"There's not much any of us can do but there is one thing. You can take this little creature off my hands." He held out the

242

basket with the white dog. "His Russian master is dead. I think he'd appreciate some kindness. Will you care for him?"

"Of course I will." Her face brightened. The first appalling shock at the sight of the wounded, the first stunned realization of the horrors of war was passing. By giving her something to worry over, even if it was only a little dog, he had already helped to steady her.

They rode side by side and when they stopped again, she insisted on going with him carrying water from man to man, lifting the heads of those who could drink, moistening the cracked lips of those too weak to sit up. It was little enough but he saw how their eyes lit up, saw one of them reach out to touch her hand, saw how they tried to smile in the midst of their pain and his heart warmed towards her.

A great many of the inhabitants had fled out of Eupatoria when the British landed and it was Seth who found the little white house and bargained with the terrified owner. There was only one bare room with whitewashed walls, two tiny bedrooms upstairs and a stone lean-to which served as a primitive kitchen. Polly Cobb declared it paradise after Varna and Yeni-Bazaar. With her usual thoroughness she scrubbed every inch of it and then went hunting for provisions in the tiny market. It was there that Jethro left Laurel and spent a day and a night of frustration battling for food and shelter for the wounded who died like flies as more and more carts came lumbering into the town and down to the harbour. He fought lethargic authorities for blankets, for medicines, for ships that could carry the men down to the hospital at Scutari. Everyone was far too busy to listen to him but he would not give up convinced that if he could only cause enough trouble, in the end something would be done if only to get rid of him.

It was evening when he found his way back to the little house. Polly had managed to get hold of a chicken and was cooking it with what vegetables she could lay her hands on.

"That smells appetizing," he said bowing his head to enter under the low doorway.

"You look half dead. When did you last eat?" asked Laurel.

"God knows. It's been a hell of a day." He looked around him. "You're lucky to have found this place. The town is swarming with visitors come out from England to see the sights."

"I know. I've met some of them already."

"I met a fellow from *The Times*, an Irishman called Russell, and gave him all the information I could. If he can make the government at home understand one half of the shambles it is out here, maybe they'll wake up. The War Office needs a bomb under it to make it realize this is 1854 and not 1815!"

"I'm sure you've done your best. Will you stay and eat with us?"

"May I? I'm not really fit for decent society. I only came to make sure you were all right."

"You don't need to worry about me, I'm fine and this is much more comfortable than a tent. There is plenty of food for all of us."

He looked at her appreciatively as they sat down to eat. Despite the heat, the problems of laundry and clothes being perpetually packed and unpacked, her white blouse and grey linen skirt were clean and fresh. Her hair was newly washed and tied simply with a ribbon transforming her into the schoolgirl he had met first in Rome. Was it barely two years ago? It felt like a lifetime. While they ate he told her about Robin.

"Did you know that he was coming out here?"

"Not until Rosemary wrote and told me. If I'd had any idea of such a thing, I would have tried to stop him."

"The boy loves you, Laurel."

"Is that my fault? I know his mother hates me for it."

"Clarissa doesn't hate anyone but he *is* her only son."

"I know," she said miserably. "It makes me feel guilty. He will be all right, won't he?"

"He is a good lad and he is learning to stand on his own feet."

When Polly had taken away the dishes, they sat by the crackling fire of olive branches. After the intense heat of the day, the nights could be cold. It was very peaceful, the turmoil of the day with its problems receded a little and he fell asleep over the wine that had survived from George's stock. Laurel took the glass from his hand and stood for a moment looking down at him. He had grown thinner in the last three months and the days and nights without sleep had deepened the shadows under his eyes. She touched the thick dark hair that fell across his forehead and then went back to her chair. The little white dog leaped into her lap. He had attached himself to her and would look at no one else.

It was late when Jethro woke, sitting up suddenly, looking dazed, and rubbing a hand over his face.

"I'm sorry — I must have nodded off. What time is it?"

244

"Almost eleven o'clock."

"Good God! You should have woken me up."

"You needed to sleep. You were exhausted."

"All the same . . ." he got to his feet. "I must go."

"Have you found a place to stay?"

"I haven't thought of it," he confessed. "There was too much else to be done. Don't worry. There will be somewhere. Thank Polly for me. That was a wonderful meal."

"Why not sleep here?"

"My dear girl, how can I do that?"

"Why not? We're in the middle of a war. Who cares about propriety? Besides, Polly and Seth are both here."

He smiled at her, shaking his head. It was so like Laurel, the girl he had brought back from Italy who cared nothing for what people might think, the girl he loved and who could never be his.

He refused to remain that night but day after day while they were held there waiting for ships, waiting for news of the army, he came to eat with her in the evening and twice it was so late by the time they had finished that he stayed on sleeping for a few hours in the chair by the fire and going off again at dawn.

It was strange, thought Laurel, how happy she was. For this short time they were at peace with one another. It was like the days they had worked together at the settlement. She wanted to go down to the docks with him, to the rough hospital shelters that had been set up but he would not allow it though she believed it helped him a little to have a ready listener to the problems that beset him. It worried her because she knew his outspoken criticism angered the army die-hards who resented the civilian interference but he would not be deterred from fighting for better conditions for his patients.

One day he took a few hours off and they rode out together visiting a little Greek church and an ancient tower where roses climbed over grey walls and there was a gnarled twisted vine with bunches of huge muscatel grapes hanging in clusters. As they walked in the quiet sunlit garden it was easy to believe in an illusion of peace. Once or twice she longed to tell him of what Rosemary had written and then drew back. What would happen if the barrier between them was swept away? She was George's wife but she was not sure whether that would be sufficient to hold back a tide of passion if once it broke through so she said nothing and at the end of the week news trickled through that the army had skirted Sebastopol and was moving down to the port of Balaclava.

That evening Jethro said, "The transports have come in at last. The sick are being moved on board. There's a ship sailing down to Balaclava. It will be easier for you to travel by sea than by land."

"And you? Will you be coming on the same ship?"

"I must go with the wounded."

The thought of parting with him so soon suddenly seemed more than she could bear. She had to steel herself against it.

"I shall be going on board tonight so I will say goodbye," he went on. "With any luck George should be in Balaclava by the time your ship docks."

"Yes, I expect so."

He had taken her hand and then against all his resolutions he drew her to him and kissed her. For an instant she clung to him, then pulled herself free and ran away up the narrow staircase and into the tiny bedroom. She dropped on the bed, her hand pressed to the mouth he had kissed, horrified at her response, at the swift tumultuous delight and longing.

Polly Cobb watched Jethro ride away and shook her head doubtfully. She approved of Dr Aylsham. He had been courteous, complimenting her on her cooking and finding a salve for her that was curing a tiresome skin infection, but she also had a great respect for the Captain and it worried her. Not that she would have mentioned it to anyone. She was the soul of discretion and it wasn't for her to judge her betters. But there were some who did. Other officers' wives had arrived in Eupatoria by now and they resented the way Laurel kept herself aloof. She had always had a contempt for gossip and politely refused all invitations to tittle-tattle over coffee or tea. A man's woman, they said disparagingly. Who was she after all with her airs and graces? Money wasn't everything and that doctor with his dark good looks, courteous enough but so reserved, and yet going every day to the little white house and riding off again in the early hours of the morning.

"Didn't you know, my dear? It's quite true. My maid saw him. Six o'clock it was and poor Captain Grafton fighting out there, dying perhaps. It isn't decent."

If that same maidservant had hinted a word to Polly, she would have received a stinging retort but she didn't because Polly's tongue was well known. So Laurel went on board the ship the following evening quite unaware of what was being said about her, not that she would have cared very much if she had. She had a disdain of such stupidities. She stood on the deck watching the harbour of Calamita Bay fade into the distance and worrying about Jethro on board the transport. Twelve hundred cholera cases and battle casualties had been crammed into the *Kangaroo* equipped to hold no more than two hundred and fifty. She had caught a glimpse of it as they overtook the heavily laden vessel. The men lying in rows on the open deck were flung helplessly against one another as it pitched and rolled, some of them crying out in agony as their wounds were torn open.

The sky darkened and a sharp wind scudded across the surface of the water. She shivered in her thin gown and pulled her shawl closer about her shoulders. Sudden squalls were frequent in the Black Sea. She went below to make sure that the horses were safe in their canvas slings and paused to lay her cheek for a moment along Lucifer's neck. He whinnied softly. He had grown thin during the last weeks and his coat had lost its gloss but he was still in fair condition. It seemed a long way from England, from morning canters in the park, from sweet autumn days with the scent of burning leaves instead of heat, vermin and the ever present shadow of death, and yet she was glad she had come, glad that she was sharing the glory and the horror with George and Robin and Jethro.

17

Seen from a distance the port of Balaclava looked extraordinarily beautiful. The harbour almost landlocked had the appearance of an inland lake, a silver mirror reflecting the surrounding cliffs. Roses, clematis, luxuriant vines climbed over white villas roofed with green tiles. There were orchards stretching up the slopes and vegetable gardens laid out with rows of tomatoes, pumpkins and lettuce, but by the time Laurel's ship sailed slowly into the harbour much of the quaint charm had vanished. The water was choked with refuse, rotting food, dead animals, even the bloated corpses of cholera victims, insufficiently weighted, had come floating to the surface. A sickening smell of corruption hung on the evening breeze. Laurel shuddered and quickly averted her eyes from the hideously distorted faces that bobbed against the ship's side.

A picturesque summer resort had been invaded by an army of twenty-five thousand men and when she went ashore on the following morning it was to find flower gardens trampled, fences broken down, roses and vines torn away and the inhabitants who had come out with welcoming flowers and fruit bewildered and shocked by what had happened to them. Accommodation seemed impossible to obtain and after repeated enquiries Laurel discovered that the cavalry were encamped at Kadikoi three miles above the town on the slopes below Sebastopol. Gunfire had been heard sporadically all that morning and though she was warned against it, she left Seth and Polly in charge of baggage and resolutely rode out of Balaclava and along the narrow mountain road that followed a steep ridge between the two valleys.

A detachment of Hussars returning from picket duty and a sharp skirmish with a raiding band of Russian cavalry were astonished to see a woman galloping wildly across the plain towards their camp, her full riding skirt blowing in the wind. Then George gave an exclamation and put spurs to his horse. He caught her up and grabbed at her bridle.

248

"Laurel, what the devil are you doing up here? You could have been shot at – don't you realize that?"

She turned to him not in the least frightened but laughing and exhilarated. "I wondered if they were Russians. Now I can truly say that I've been under fire!"

"My dear girl, you could have been killed," but he couldn't resist laughing with her, filled with a mingling of exasperation and pride.

The rest of the men had come galloping up. They clustered around as he lifted her from her horse, asking questions, eager for news. A beautiful woman was a rarity and they fussed over her, unwilling to let her go, until George put an arm round her waist and firmly drew her aside.

"Clear off, you fellows. I think it's about time I had my wife to myself."

She glanced up at him anxiously thinking that under his tan he looked drawn and haggard. "Has it been very hard?"

"More frustrating than anything else. Cardigan and Lucan are at loggerheads as usual and between contradictory orders we sit here doing nothing with the Russians coming out to jeer at us and our Commander calling us 'a damned set of old women' for not taking the law into our own hands and going in to attack."

"Poor George." She pressed his arm. "It's so unfair. Are you well? Jethro told me that you were wounded."

"So you did see him."

"Yes. He was very occupied with the sick men. Polly was so grateful because you thought of her. Has your arm healed?"

"More or less. Listen, dearest, you can't remain up here, I'm afraid. We're abominably overcrowded as it is. I'm sharing a tent with three other fellows. You'd best take a cabin on one of the ships in Balaclava and I'll come down whenever I can get away."

"I can't stay on the ship, I can't – it's unbearable." The thought of the harbour with its horrors, its filth and its stenches overwhelemed her for a moment. He saw the dismay on her face and took both her hands in his.

"What is it? Are you sorry you came with me?"

"No, of course I'm not." With an effort she pulled herself together. "Don't worry. I'll find somewhere. I did in Eupatoria and I've got Polly and Seth to help me. I'm luckier than most, but you will come, won't you, George? You won't leave me there alone."

249

"It may not be easy. They keep us on the go, drills, parades, foraging expeditions. We're desperately short of fodder for the horses."

"Do come please, darling. I miss you so much."

She reached up to kiss him trying to make amends, trying to convey the love she could not feel for him.

"I'll get down to Balaclava somehow," he promised.

"I'll be waiting for you," she whispered.

She rode back to the town to find Seth eager to give her the good news. It seemed there had been Russians living in the port who had fled after the arrival of the army. Polly had found an abandoned villa and had promptly taken possession of it. The owners could not be found and must have left in some haste as it was still partly furnished, Bokhara rugs on the tiled floors, simple cane furniture and even a battered piano in the small sitting room. Laurel felt some compunction at taking it over but was assured that this was part of the fortune of war so they settled in and within a few days it had become a meeting place for officers on duty in the town or convalescing from wounds. Food was hard to come by but Laurel and Polly contrived always to have something to offer even if it was no more than goat cheese and rough country wine and hardly an evening passed without half a dozen young men bringing little gifts, lounging in the tiny room, listening to Laurel playing the piano or to someone else singing a comic song. Apart from Fanny Duberly who held court in her cabin on the *Shooting Star*, Laurel was the only officer's wife in the place. She found she always had willing escorts when she exercised Lucifer and on several occasions was joined by Lord Cardigan himself. It worried her that the others melted away whenever he appeared. She would have infinitely preferred not to be alone with him, but mindful of George's career, she smiled ravishingly at him and took pains to thank him prettily for the case of wine he sent her.

It was to this villa that Robin came one day still holding his injured arm stiffly but seeming to have filled out and grown taller, a lovesick boy no longer, and she was so pleased to see him that she flung both arms around his neck kissing him between tears and laughter.

Afterwards when they were alone he said, "I've brought you something." He took a handkerchief from his pocket and unwrapped a small silver icon no more than five inches square.

"It was after the Alma," he said. "It was the damnedest

thing. Prince Mechnikoff must have felt so sure of himself that he invited his friends and their ladies to celebrate his victory and they had to make a run for it when we stormed in to the Russian camp, leaving food, clothes and possessions behind them. The men looted whatever they could lay their hands on as you can imagine and one of them brought me this."

He turned it over. Engraved on the back in Russian characters was the name Dmitri and a date.

"Of course it may not have belonged to Prince Malinsky but we did hear that he was there with his regiment and I thought you would like it as a souvenir."

"Is he dead?" she whispered.

"I don't know but one of the Russian prisoners told me that he had been very badly wounded."

Her eyes filled with tears as she looked at the calm sweet face of the Virgin. She had grown familiar with death and learned to accept it. It was the only way to go on living and yet this moved her deeply. How absurd to think that the young man who had given her Marik, who had been so charmingly devoted in London, should now have become an enemy and lay wounded, maybe already dead.

By now it was the middle of October and the weather had changed dramatically. The nights had an icy chill, foretaste of a severe winter. Fuel was difficult to obtain and logs were an exorbitant price. Heavy rainstorms turned the steep slopes to sticky glue-like mud and riding Lucifer became well nigh impossible. One morning Laurel was walking on the quay when she saw a faery-like yacht come sailing into the harbour, the sails like the wings of some gigantic seabird. It was Lord Cardigan's *Dryad* with his French cook and all the luxuries of home. On the plea of ill-health he was given permission to eat and sleep on board and each day one or other of his officers was forced to make the exhausting journey to and from Kadikoi carrying his orders. To make it worse, up at the camp Lord Lucan in fierce reaction against his detested brother-in-law had the wretched cavalry turning out morning after morning before it was light, struggling through icy mud, their fingers so numbed with cold they could scarcely grip the reins of their starved overworked horses.

"It's a damned outrage," said George angrily calling in at the villa for a few minutes on his way back to the camp. "The men are taking it very badly that their Commander issues a stream of

251

useless orders from his luxurious featherbed on the *Dryad* while they're living in conditions to which you wouldn't condemn a dog!"

"I don't know how he can do it," she said sympathetically putting her arm through his.

"I was promised promotion after the Alma," he went on, "but pigs will fly before the old man remembers it." He looked around at the comfort she had somehow contrived in the bare room. "You're a clever puss. How do you manage it? The lads are all talking about how much they enjoy coming here. What magic do you use?"

"No magic. They just come and I let them talk, that's all. It seems to help."

One part of him was proud of her popularity and yet naggingly he resented that she should give so much of herself to others while his duties kept him away from her. He would have liked to stay longer, easing the cold from his bones in front of the log fire and afterwards making love slowly and luxuriously, falling asleep in the comfort of a real bed instead of a hard palliasse on the dirty earth floor of a freezing tent. But it wasn't possible. He had to oversee the marine party landing the siege guns from the ships and command the detachment occupied with the endless wearying task of manhandling them through the streets and up the slippery slopes for the assault on Sebastopol. There was only time for a hurried embrace and a promise that he would come again as soon as he could.

A few days later a ship arrived loaded with tourists and sightseers. The veterans who had suffered all the hardships of a prolonged campaign looked on them with loathing as they rode through the town, well dressed and well fed, their ship amply provided with good food, the ladies' crinolines fresh and crisp making Laurel acutely conscious of her crumpled skirts and faded silks, of the unbecoming yellowish tan on face and hands. Not that she let it trouble her. She felt she was one with the men who suffered and died. She caused great offence by contemptuously turning down an invitation to one of their parties on board the *Alexander*.

On the morning of Tuesday, 17th October, Laurel was awakened by thundering explosions followed by a deafening volume of shot and shell that seemed to shake the villa to its very foundations. Alarmed she scrambled out of bed and hurriedly dressed. She was sharing a cup of tea with Polly when one of the

252

officers not yet on duty came knocking at the door telling her the assault on Sebastopol had begun at last and if she made haste she might see something of it. Mounted on Lucifer with Polly perched up behind Seth they rode up to the heights where tourists and townspeople had already gathered though very little could be glimpsed through the thick greasy smoke that eddied and billowed over the plain. During the afternoon the broadsides from both Russian and English guns intensified and Laurel was riveted to the spot, her throat tightening, shuddering at the agony and death that lay beneath the pall of black cloud. As the day wore on, it soon became sickeningly clear that the defences of the fortified city were unlikely to crumble so easily. After sunset as the smoke slowly drifted away, the onlookers could see the Russians, women as well as men, coming out to work on the defences renewing broken battlements, repairing crumbled bastions, and with them came priests singing hymns, raising crosses and icons, sprinkling holy water on the defendants as they moved about their work.

The days that followed were filled with deep depression at the thought of a long siege through the icy cold of a Russian winter. A sense of failure gripped everyone, soldiers and civilians alike. Hospital tents had been set up for the wounded and daily Laurel saw the carts go lumbering by carrying the sick down to the ships. She would be roused at night by the rumble of the hearses taking the dead to the common burial pits. The coming of winter had relaxed the grip of the cholera but it still claimed its victims. The young men who called at the villa sat glum and silent, no longer thundering out patriotic songs on the piano. George did not come and Robin was a rare visitor. In the midst of the general gloom one of Lord Cardigan's aides came one morning with a note inviting her to take supper on his yacht. She hesitated before accepting it. She was not in the mood for parties and her gowns had fallen into sad disarray. On the other hand in a roundabout way perhaps she could remind him of the promotion she knew to be near to George's heart. So at last she dashed off a note of acceptance and hoped she had not been foolish.

Her one presentable gown was a deep moss green moiré silk trimmed with velvet. Polly pressed it and she washed her hair catching it up away from her neck in a bunch of curls with a few pink roses still blooming in the tiny garden. She pulled on a heavy cloak and escorted by a young officer who had been sent to fetch her, she was led down to the harbour. The yacht lay at anchor and lit by a dozen lanterns presented an enchanting picture against the evening sky. She was a little surprised to see no bustle on board, no sign of other guests arriving, but maybe she was late and they had already gone below. The boatman was waiting to row her out and she went up the side of the yacht to be greeted by Lord Cardigan on the deck. He kissed her hand gallantly and she went with him down the stairs to the saloon. It was only then that she realized to her dismay that there were no other guests. She had been invited to a tête-à-tête supper and afterwards what . . . ? Her heart missed a beat. Had he mistaken her smiles and gay response to his gifts and gallantries for a willingness to be seduced? He took her cloak letting his hands stray caressingly across her bare shoulders. She tried to put a brave face on it and cover her panic with bright conversation. Cardigan could be an amusing and witty talker when he put his mind to it and he was obviously showing off in the company of an attractive woman. The food, exquisitely cooked, was better than anything she had tasted for months but she could not enjoy it, keeping up a show of flattering attention to her host while she desperately tried to think of a way out of what promised to be a highly embarrassing situation.

The meal finished, they moved from the table and he invited her to sit on the sofa richly upholstered in French silk. The manservant poured the coffee into porcelain cups, then Lord Cardigan waved him away and stood smiling down at her.

"I'm arranging for your husband's promotion, my dear," he said, "as soon as it can be carried out. He has done well, very well indeed, a splendid officer. I wish I had more of his stamp on my staff."

He's bribing me, she thought, what a fool he must believe me to be! Aloud she said, "George will be grateful, my lord. He thinks only of his men and his duty."

"Of course, of course, to be sure."

He came to sit beside her sliding his arm along the back of the sofa behind her. The pressure tightened as he moved closer to her.

Oh God, was her thought, what do I do now? How do I escape a man on his own yacht? Will it come to throwing myself overboard?

"George is blessed with a very lovely wife whom, I fear, he does not fully appreciate," he murmured caressingly.

"It is not his fault that I see so little of him, my lord."

"So lovely and so very brave. I like a touch of spirit in a woman." He turned her face towards him and his moustache brushed against her cheek.

It was any moment now and what on earth was she going to do? Scream? Make a run for it? She did not want to offend him for George's sake but escape she must . . . and soon. She slipped away from him and stood up.

"It's been a wonderful evening," she said, "but it must be growing late. I ought to return."

"Nonsense, it is early yet," he replied indulgently. "Surely you can spare a few hours to amuse an old man who longs for a little relaxation, a little of the pleasure to be found in a pretty woman's company."

He thinks I'm playing hard to get, she said to herself, and no doubt that will only spur him on. He had risen now and come up beside her, tall and commanding at close quarters and in his own way still possessed of a considerable masculine charm. He put an arm around her waist and she thought wildly, there's nothing for it. I must tell him flat out that Commander-in-Chief or not, I'm not for him. He drew her closer trying to reach her lips. She turned away her face pushing hard against his chest and he laughed.

"Don't be coy, my dear, it doesn't suit you."

His grip tightened, she opened her mouth to protest and then suddenly, miraculously she was saved.

There was a loud knock at the door and the manservant appeared looking agitated.

"What the devil is it?" said Lord Cardigan testily, withdrawing his arm. "I thought I told you I was not to be disturbed."

"I'm sorry, my lord, but there's a messenger from Lord Raglan."

"Can't he wait till morning?"

"He is insisting that it is urgent, my lord, very urgent indeed."

"Damnation!" He turned to Laurel. "I apologize, my dear, the exigencies of war, you know, but I shan't be long, I promise you. Give Mrs Grafton more coffee while she waits. Now where is this wretched fellow?"

"I have shown him into your day cabin, my lord."

"Oh very well. I'll see him there."

The moment the door closed behind him, Laurel said

hurriedly, "I don't want any more coffee. It's very warm in here. I think I'll go up on deck for a breath of air."

"As you wish, Madam." The man was stolidly putting together the cups on the silver tray but she knew that he guessed at her predicament and she wondered how many times it had happened before and whether the others had been more complaisant.

When she came up on to the deck, it was already very dark. The sky was studded with stars and the night air felt icy on her hot cheeks. She huddled into her cloak and looked quickly around her. None of the crew were visible except the man who had rowed her out. He crouched beside the rail half asleep. She tapped him on the shoulder.

"Can you take me ashore?"

He looked up startled. "Already, my lady."

"Yes, now, quickly."

She was in a fury of impatience to be gone and he seemed to take an age to climb over the side and hold the ladder steady for her to clamber down rewarded for his pains by the sight of long slim legs in white silk stockings as the wind blew aside her skirts. The ladder swayed horribly but at last she was in the boat and urging him to row quickly . . . quickly.

He landed her at the bottom of a flight of steps covered in green slime where the water splashed over her feet and soaked the hem of her skirts as she climbed up them. She hunted in her little bag and found a silver coin pressing it into his hand. He pocketed it with a sly grin and she felt sure that the story would be all over Balaclava by morning if it was not already spread abroad. Pray God that George didn't hear of it before she told him herself and they had laughed over it together. She pulled the hood of her cloak over her hair and ran across the dock stumbling on the cobbles and splashing through pools of dirty water. Then in her haste she fell headlong over a bale of goods and would have gone sprawling if a man coming ashore from one of the other boats had not caught her in his arms.

"Steady on," he said, "what's the hurry?" and then as the hood fell back from her head he was staring in surprise. "Laurel, what on earth are you doing here alone at this time of night?"

"Running away from Lord Cardigan," she said between a laugh and a sob. "Oh Jethro, what a relief that it is only you!" She leaned against him momentarily exhausted. "I didn't even know you were in Balaclava."

256

"I've been back from Scutari for a week. What do you mean — running away?"

"I think he had seduction in mind. Oh dear, I've been so foolish and it was all so silly." Breathlessly she told him the whole story beginning to laugh at it a little now the danger was past.

"I had no idea that he meant it to be a party for two and I thought it might help George if I flattered him and now – oh heavens, what a dreadful muddle I've made of it. His pride will be hurt and he'll take it out on George and then what shall I do?" He took her arm and they began to walk together threading their way in and out of the puddles. "Still that's my trouble, not yours." She looked up at him. "How lovely to find you here. Where have you been?"

"I was called out to the tourist ship. One of these travelling gentlemen had a belly-ache from overeating himself and thought it must be cholera. I gave him a dose of calomel that'll make him wish he hadn't been born tomorrow," he said unfeelingly.

She giggled. "Oh Jethro, how could you be so cruel?"

"It'll do him all the good in the world. If I had my way they'd all be dumped in the sea! We've enough to do caring for the men without running after people who have nothing wrong with them and shouldn't be here anyway."

She clung to his arm as they climbed up the narrow street of the town feeling suddenly secure and protected because he was with her.

"Did you get the wounded safely to Scutari?" she asked.

"Safely is hardly the word," he said ironically. "I can't begin to tell you what it is like there. That appalling barracks has been turned into a hospital if you can call it that – pesthouse would be nearer the mark. The men had endured enough hell on the ships but that was nothing to the conditions we met on arrival. No provision had been made for them. There were no beds and they were lying in rows on the filthy floor wrapped in blankets saturated with blood. There was no food and no kitchens where it could be prepared, not a cup, not a bucket to carry water around to the sick. No furniture, not even a table on which to operate. Dr Menzies, the Medical Officer, is nearly out of his mind trying to find the barest necessities and every hour men are dying in agony."

"It can't be true," she said aghast. "Surely something can be done."

257

"It's true enough," he said grimly. "I never felt closer to despair. My only hope is that someone tells them in England before it is too late and the whole army is destroyed."

"And yet you came back here."

"I'm a surgeon, Laurel. There is going to be a big push here. I thought I could be of more use on the field."

"When will it come?"

"I'm not sure. Possibly within the next day or two."

"Perhaps that was the urgent message that was brought to Lord Cardigan. Well, at least it saved me from a fate worse than death," she said trying to smile. "I wish there was something I could do to help."

"From what I've heard since I've been back, you're already doing your best. The men need cheering up, God knows."

"I try but it isn't much." She pressed his arm. "I take it very badly that you didn't come and see me before."

"There's been no time," he said evasively. "We've been working night and day to make what preparations we can. I beggared myself buying up every drug I could lay my hands on in Constantinople but it is a mere drop in the ocean and the Ambassador secure in his fine palace listened to me and did absolutely nothing. Some fool of a doctor, he probably said to himself, exaggerating as usual. Both he and his lady have taken very good care not to set foot inside the hospital. Not that I can really blame them. The stench and filth are beyond description. And that's quite enough about me and my tale of woe. Now tell me your news. How is your husband?"

"I've scarcely seen him now the cavalry are out at Kadikoi but I have an idea his wound still troubles him. Robin came one morning and brought me news of Prince Malinsky. It seems that poor Dmitri was very badly wounded when they stormed the Russian camp after the Alma."

"It's a sorry state of affairs, isn't it, when friends are on opposing sides."

As they came up to the villa they could see the yellow lamplight streaming through the window.

Laurel said uneasily, "That's strange. Polly must still be up. How late is it?"

"Not much after ten o'clock."

A figure crossed the light, then the door opened and a man appeared on the step.

"It's George," she exclaimed.

"Were you expecting him?"

"No, I wasn't. Something must have happened."

She began to run towards him and after a momentary hesitation Jethro followed more slowly.

George did not move forward to greet her. He said coolly, "I thought I'd wait for you. Polly told me you were dining with Cardigan on his yacht."

"Yes, I was. Oh darling, it was all so silly. I was going to tell you about it."

But he ignored her, looking towards Jethro and frowning. "And was Dr Aylsham also a guest at the party?"

"No, it wasn't a party. We were quite alone. That was the awful part of it. I had no idea of such a thing and you can imagine how I felt when I realized it." She was running on, saying far too much and yet unable to stop herself, frightened by the stony look on George's face. "I had to escape somehow and heaven knows what he is going to think when he knows I begged his boatman to row me to the shore. Then fortunately I met Jethro on the quay . . ."

"As fortunately, it seems, as after the Alma when he shared your lodging at Eupatoria."

"Who told you that?" she said quickly.

"Never mind who told me." He took a step towards Jethro and she went after him catching at his arm.

"But it's not true . . . George, listen to me," but he shook himself free from her.

"Be quiet, Laurel. When I asked you to convey a message to my wife, Dr Aylsham, it was not an invitation to take her to your bed."

"George!" exclaimed Laurel outraged.

"This is ridiculous," said Jethro evenly. "Whoever has been talking to you has told you a pack of lies."

"Do you deny it? Do you deny that you went to Laurel's villa daily, supping with her, sleeping there night after night?"

"No, I don't, not entirely. Food and lodging were almost impossible to find. She offered me hospitality and I was grateful for it but that was as far as it went."

George laughed contemptuously. "Do you take me for a fool? I don't believe you."

"Take it or leave it as you please. It is the truth."

"God damn it," went on George violently. "If we weren't on the eve of a battle, I'd call you out. I'd blow your blasted head off!"

259

"And a great deal of good that would do," said Jethro levelly. "If you cannot trust your wife, then I pity both of you. She is loyal to a man who is not worth her little finger. I have better things to do than argue with someone blinded by stupid prejudice. Goodnight, Laurel."

He strolled away leaving George staring after him, angry, frustrated, half inclined to call him back. Laurel with one look at him had already gone into the house. After a moment he turned and followed her.

The last week, ever since the failure of the attack on Sebastopol, had been extraordinarily exhausting. Up at Kadikoi it had been well nigh impossible to maintain discipline and keep men cheerful who felt they had been miserably cheated, their uniforms wearing out, their boots falling to pieces with nothing to look forward to but a long siege during a freezing winter. It had been desperately difficult to sustain morale in leaking tents and on a vile monotonous diet of salt pork and mouldy biscuit. George's arm had festered. It had been crudely lanced by the army surgeon and the constant pain had fretted his nerves into shreds. The last straw had been that morning in the mess. One of the damned civilians looking for sensation had come up to inspect the camp making himself unpopular by commenting scathingly on the poor condition of the horses and then standing in the mess tent drinking their rapidly diminishing stock of brandy and gossiping idly about the attractive young woman at Eupatoria and the handsome surgeon who had obviously hastened to take advantage of her husband's absence.

"The ladies were full of it over the tea tables," he went on carelessly holding out his glass to be refilled, "and it seems she is still playing her pretty games in Balaclava. Even Lord C. is not immune to her charms – morning rides, gifts of wine and cosy little suppers on board his yacht. No wonder she turned up her nose at our party on the *Alexander*."

There had been one or two embarrassed glances from his brother officers. He would willingly have crashed his fist into the fat foolish face silencing the slack mouth dripping with malice even if he were cashiered for it, except that no names had actually been mentioned though everyone knew to whom the wretched man referred. He did not believe it, he dare not believe it – he trusted Laurel, he told himself repeatedly – and yet it tore at his raw nerves.

260

It was in his mind now when he came into the sitting room. She had dropped her heavy cloak on to the chair and stood in front of the dying fire, slim and erect, her eyes blazing with indignation. She did not wait for him to speak but attacked at once.

"How could you treat Jethro in such a manner and how dare you insult me with such a detestable accusation? Do you think I enjoy Lord Cardigan's company? The sole reason I accepted his invitation was to help you to the promotion you want so much. I never dreamed that he would be alone and immediately I realized it, I left as soon as I could."

He had been almost ready to apologize longing to be at peace with her, but now suddenly he was shaken by a deep burning resentment.

"For God's sake, when have I ever asked you to prostitute yourself on my behalf? I can look after myself."

"You could at least be grateful."

He made an angry gesture. "To hell with Cardigan. I have never believed you cared a row of pins for that stuffed dummy of a soldier. That's not what troubles me."

She looked at him for a moment and then let herself drop wearily into the chair. "If it is Jethro you are worrying about, then you can put it out of your mind once and for all. What he told you was the absolute truth."

"If only I could be sure of that . . ."

"You must decide that for yourself," she said proudly. "Conditions in Eupatoria were vile. We were fortunate enough to find food so we shared it with him. He was working desperately hard and once or twice after we had eaten he fell asleep in utter exhaustion and I didn't disturb him. It never occurred to me that you would listen to silly women with nothing to do but invent slanderous gossip."

"And here in Balaclava? Does he come here day after day?"

"Tonight is the first time I've seen him since we parted at Eupatoria and it was purely by chance."

He was pacing up and down the room in an agony of indecision before he turned on her. "You were lovers once, you told me that yourself. You had time and place and opportunity."

He knew perfectly well that he was tormenting himself needlessly and yet he could not stop. He was only too well aware of Laurel's magnetic attraction. What man could have resisted it, he thought wretchedly? He crossed to her pulling her round to

261

him, one hand tilting up her chin so that her eyes met his. "Can you swear to me here and now that there is nothing between you, that he doesn't come first with you before me, before anyone?" he said urgently, hoping against hope that she would give him the answer he wanted even if it was a lie. He would accept it thankfully, longing only for the comfort she could give him.

She hesitated, still angry that he should accuse her of disloyalty, not realizing how strain and pain had drained the strength from him making him exceptionally vulnerable. She had her own innate honesty and she said slowly, "I will not swear to anything. I've never lied to you. Believe what you like but I've never betrayed you with Jethro or with anyone and I never will. Can't we forget all this?"

She reached out a hand to him but he jerked away, bitterness welling up in him. Without another word he crossed to the chair where he had thrown his riding cloak and picked it up.

Alarmed she got to her feet. "Where are you going?"

"Back to the camp. I know when I am not welcome."

"But you are, you are. When have I ever said such a thing?"

She realized suddenly what she had done and regretted it. Now at this crucial moment she should have lied, should have pretended anything to make him happy.

"I have to leave in any case. Orders to stand by can come at any time. That's what I came to tell you." He shouted to Seth to bring his horse.

She followed him to the door. "But you could stay for a little— an hour, half an hour," she pleaded. "We have been at such odds."

"No more than we have always been."

"That's not true . . ."

"Isn't it? Why in God's name did you ever marry me?"

She saw the hurt on his face and passionately wanted to make amends. She put a hand on his arm. "George, please please come back . . . don't leave like this."

He shook her off. "No time now. When it's all over, then we'll sort something out."

Seth had brought round his horse and he swung himself into the saddle.

"If you want to see something of the battle, then up on the heights is the best place."

She looked up at him, wanting desperately to keep him with

262

her, and for an instant he let his eyes devour her, the silky red hair falling around her bare shoulders, the slim white neck in the low cut gown. Faithless to him or not – but he loved her, by God how he loved her! Then abruptly he turned away from her, dug spurs into his horse and galloped into the night.

18

Disturbed and unhappy it was a long time before she slept that night and it seemed as if she had only just closed her eyes when Polly was shaking her awake.

"It's begun, ma'am, it's begun already. That Mrs Butler called out to me as she went by. If we hurry we'll see most of it. The Captain, ma'am, and my Fred, they're goin' to be in the thick of it. While you dress, I'll put some food together in a basket. We may need it."

How fantastic it is, thought Laurel, her hands shaking as she pulled on her riding dress and made a hasty toilet, we might be going on a picnic instead of preparing to watch a battle in which hundreds will be killed or wounded. She felt sick and quite unable to force down more than a cup of scalding tea before hurrying out to the horses. At the last moment the little white dog whined to go with them so she picked him up and Seth helped her into the saddle.

On the heights above the valley the tourists were already gathered in an excited chattering group, the ladies dressed more for the races than for a battlefield. Servants were unpacking hampers of food and cases of champagne. She drew away from them in disgust finding a quiet vantage point for herself with Polly and Seth. The little dog already a war veteran lay beside her, head on paws, eyes following every movement on the slopes below them.

It was seven o'clock. The thick morning mists had been sucked up by the sun and everything stood out bright and clear and highly coloured like a child's picture book. From the height of six or seven hundred feet above the plain they were watching the battle array as if from a box in a theatre. There was an extraordinary effect of unreality. The mountain ridges, the brilliantly blue sky were an operatic backcloth to the wheeling squadrons with their standards fluttering in the breeze, the artillery, the Highlanders in their kilts, the brilliant blue, scarlet and green of uniforms. They were like puppets being moved here and there by some giant masterhand and it was impossible to believe they were in deadly earnest.

The first fierce onslaught of the Russian troops had poured across the slopes in the early morning overrunning the redoubts and earthworks manned by the Turks putting the men to flight and capturing the twelve-pounder naval guns. At one moment it had seemed that they must surely sweep all before them but the steady red line of the infantry had held firm. Men fell and died but the ranks closed up and did not break. Now it was deadlock. With the aid of glasses loaned by one of the men, she could pick out faces and searched for George and the other young men she knew. There was a strange unearthly silence broken by the neigh of a horse, a chink of steel, a shouted order. The Russians came on in a great grey tide advancing remorselessly but the companies that made up the heavy brigade of cavalry still did not move. Officers rode up and down apparently more concerned with the dressing of their squadrons than with the approaching clash. Men must ride even to their death armoured in perfection. Then suddenly there was the shrill scream of the trumpets. Major Scarlett at their head raised his sword and they rode forward, slowly at first, then with quickening speed until they were riding headlong, stirrup by stirrup, up the slopes and were lost to sight engulfed in the grey Russian mass.

"They are surrounded, they must be annihilated," muttered someone close to Laurel.

"No," she said quickly, "no, it's impossible. I will not believe it."

She pressed her hands to her breast hardly daring to breathe as she watched the heaving body of men who fought so savagely, the grey and bright scarlet inextricably mingled, sword arms waving like toys, the clash of steel, the sudden wild yells as the Russians surged and heaved, swaying this way and that. It seemed hours and lasted for about ten minutes. Then there came a new sound, unbelievably wonderful, the sound of British cheers. The great Russian mass gave a gigantic heave and disintegrated, breaking into flight. A tremendous roar went up. The men and women watching from the hills fell into one another's arms laughing, crying, throwing hats in the air. Laurel sank to her knees, burying her face in her hands, whilst beside her Polly was clapping madly and the little dog barked shrilly.

But victory was still very far off. There was no pursuit. The main part of the Russian cavalry had been allowed to escape. She saw messengers galloping backwards and forwards across the plain. It was agony not knowing what was happening. Minutes passed. The sun rose high above the valley, the air was crisp and clear. Some of the tourists settled down to eat and drink waiting for the next act in the drama. It was eleven o'clock and the Light Brigade had still not gone into action. Laurel could see them sitting motionless on their horses, still magnificent though their bright uniforms were faded, their finery tarnished by sun and weather. She wondered about George, desperately worried lest their quarrel of the night before should drive him headlong into recklessness, realizing only too well his frustration as the Hussars were held back from playing their part in the day's battle.

Polly unpacked their picnic basket and brought her food but she could not eat. She accepted a glass of wine sipping it slowly. It was then that she saw an officer come racing precipitously down the slope from where Lord Raglan watched the action with his staff around him and recognized him as Captain Nolan, an outstanding horseman with a reputation for reckless courage. She wondered what orders he carried.

The Hussars with the Lancers and Dragoons who made up the Light Cavalry Brigade held in check by Lord Lucan were boiling with impatience and fury. Were they to be denied their chance to distinguish themselves as had happened at the Alma? George, sitting his horse at the head of his detachment, shifted in the saddle. When he had returned to the camp the night before he had found his absence had passed unnoticed. There had been little opportunity to rest or sleep. The regiment were turned out at four o'clock in the morning when it was still dark. They watered their horses by the yellow light of lanterns. They had been in the saddle since dawn with nothing to eat or drink and the hours of waiting seemed endless. George tried to put Laurel out of his mind but it was not possible. He bitterly regretted his precipitate action of the night before and now it was too late. He might never have the chance to say that he loved her, that he had never really doubted her and that when this damned war was over, they would build their life together on new lines.

His mouth was dry as a bone and his stomach groaned with hunger. There was only dry biscuit to eat and he swallowed a mouthful of brandy from his flask. Then he saw Nolan ride up to Lucan for the second time within the last hour and a garbled version of the order drifted back to him.

"Lord Raglan wishes the cavalry to advance rapidly to the front, follow the enemy and try to prevent the enemy carrying away the guns."

There seemed to be argument and he heard Lucan's caustic question, "Attack, sir? Attack what? What guns, sir!"

"There, my lord, there is your enemy, there are the guns – what are you waiting for?" Nolan waved his arm impatiently in a sweeping gesture towards the western end of the valley where the Russians had their batteries, horse and foot, and it passed fleetingly through George's mind that by attacking the guns, Raglan must mean retaking the twelve-pounders captured earlier that morning by the Russians, but Nolan's contemptuous taunt stung his pride and it was not his place to question. Lord Lucan had approached Cardigan at the head of his men. There was more coming and going and then once again there came that strange tense pre-battle silence when the very air seemed still and charged with menace.

Laurel could see George at the head of his troop. She saw Lord Cardigan take up his position the correct two horses' length in front of his staff. The trumpets sounded "Walk, march!" The sun glittered on gold lace and brass helmets, spurs touched horses' flanks, there was a creaking of leather, a jingle of steel and they began to move forward in parade ground order, cool, disciplined, not a head turning, hands easy on the reins. The pace increased to "trot" and seconds later to "gallop". It was then that Laurel saw a single horseman break away from the main body and ride left to right across the brigade. It was Captain Nolan turning in the saddle, shouting and waving his sword as though to change the direction of the advance. A single gun fired. He disappeared in a cloud of smoke as the shell tore into his breast and a cry broke from him so piercing, so unearthly that the onlookers gasped and Laurel shuddered. The brigade did not falter. They rode steadily forward making for the western end of the valley where the Russians stood motionless beside their guns. She could not take her eyes from them. The men were riding faster now, knee to knee, driving home spurs, more and more quickly, and the Russians recovered from their first astonishment at this splendid body of men riding to their doom loosened a hell of round shot,

267

grape and rifle balls full in the face of the charging squadrons. Saddles were emptied, riderless horses galloped crazily here and there, but discipline held, the ranks closed up and rode on without pause.

All George could see at the end of the valley was a white cloud of smoke from which flashed great tongues of flame indicating the position of the Russian guns. He chose one and deliberately rode for it. The firing grew more intense and the casualties heavier. A madness seized them. Their gallop became headlong. All around him men were cheering and yelling. He glimpsed a gap between two guns and rode wildly for it. There was a tremendous roar, the earth shook, a sheet of flame seemed to engulf them followed by so dense a smoke that they could see nothing. The Russians had fired a salvo of all twelve guns wiping out the first line of cavalry. George's horse was hurled sideways by the blast, a tongue of flame seemed to run all down his side. He swept forward blindly and suddenly he was in the battery and among his troopers. They were cutting, thrusting and hacking like demons. The force of their charge carried them beyond the first line until emerging from the smoke they were confronted by a solid mass of Russian cavalry drawn up behind the guns. With a rallying cry George hurled himself at the Cossack Commander engaging him in single combat and running him through with his sword. Blinded with fury he drove onwards but now a second body of Russians was on them. He realized dazedly that they must retreat or be hopelessly trapped. Again he rallied them fighting a rearguard action and as he dragged his horse's head round, he was conscious of a numbing blow going right through his body almost throwing him from the saddle, only long practice keeping him rigid, knees still clamped to his horse's sides. Then someone seized his bridle. Dimly he recognized Fred Cobb. Vaguely he heard him shouting, "You'll be all right, Cap'n. Hold on . . . I've got you . . . you'll be all right . . ." He was still upright in the saddle. All around him as he galloped the ground was strewn with dead and dying. Riderless horses screaming in an agony of wounds ran wildly from side to side bumping into the stumbling staggering survivors. The smoke was vanishing but it had grown strangely dark. He tried to brush away the mist that seemed to hang in front of him and then he pitched forward over his horse's neck.

*   *   *

Laurel straining her eyes saw the last of the brigade disappear into the thickening clouds of smoke at the end of the valley. There was a flash of swords rising and falling, the rumble and thunder of the guns and then nothing but the terrible wreckage of men and horses. Some of the officers who watched from the heights, men who had marched fearlessly into the hail of bullets at the Alma, were crying like children. It could not have been much more than twenty minutes after the trumpets had sounded when from out of the grey fog there came a few scattered horsemen. At first they thought they were Russians, then Polly whispered, "Merciful God, ma'am, it's the brigade, all that's left of 'em!" and Laurel realized the dreadful truth. These few pitiful survivors were all that were left of the six hundred men who had made the magnificent charge. They came slowly, staggering, crawling, limping, supporting each other, swaying helplessly in the saddle. With them horribly came the riderless horses, terrified and lost without a guiding hand, maimed and wounded, falling in the tracks of the men they had carried in their last splendid ride. Her eyes, smarting with tears and smoke, looked for George and could not find him. Without stopping to think, she clambered into Lucifer's saddle and went stumbling, slithering, skidding down the steep slopes impelled by an urgency to find him. He must be there somewhere, he must be alive. There were still random shots. Russian snipers were picking off survivors. She did not heed them. She reached the valley and slid from the saddle dragging Lucifer behind her. The ghastly sights that met her eyes, the desperately wounded men, the blood and wreckage, the torn and mangled horses, so sickened her that she almost turned back but a strong determination conquered her revulsion and carried her forward.

She moved from one to the other looking for the brilliant uniform, the cherry coloured overalls, the blue gold-laced jacket. There was blood on her skirt and on her hands as she bent over the dead and dying. Some of the men clutched at her hand feebly asking for help. A bullet from a sniper grazed along her wrist but she did not notice it. She saw one of the young officers who had come to the villa leaning forward on his horse's neck, one arm hanging useless at his side, and stopped to question him.

"I saw him once beyond the guns, ma'am, but afterwards ... God knows," he shook his head wearily.

She let him go and stumbled on. There were other women,

privates' wives, hunting for their men through the mangled heaps. She had paused in despair when suddenly she heard her name called. It was Fred Cobb, covered with blood from a sword slash down one side of his face, but alive and immensely reassuring.

She said, "The Captain . . . where is the Captain?"

"He's here, ma'am, he's here, only he's . . ."

But she had already dropped Lucifer's bridle and run past him to fall on her knees beside George. He lay on his back with no visible sign of injury, his eyes closed. She lifted his head on to her lap, frantically stroking his cheek.

"I'm here, darling," she whispered. "We'll care for you now. You'll be all right." She gently wiped a froth of blood from his lips. His eyes flickered open but there was no recognition in them.

Fred said awkwardly, "I did my best but it were his back, see. He were thinkin' of us . . . he tried to cover our retreat and they ran him through."

"We must carry him back. Dr Aylsham will know what to do."

She was aware that Seth and Polly had come up. They must have followed her. She tried to pull herself together. "We can't leave him here. You must carry him between you. Polly and I can bring the horses."

Seth and Fred exchanged a glance and then bent to their task. They lifted George between them and laid him along the back of his horse supporting him on each side while Laurel took Lucifer's bridle. All over the valley men walked or crawled. Stretcher bearers had begun to carry in the wounded. At the end of the valley a medical station had been set up with temporary hospital tents. There the doctors were working separating the wounded from the dying and already dead. One of them paused in his grisly work, took one look at George and said brusquely, "The man's done for. Put him with the rest of the dead."

"No," said Laurel, "no, he's not dead. He's only wounded."

The doctor looked at her wearily. "Madam, when you have been at this game as long as I have, you know when a man is finished. My job is to save those who still have a chance to live."

He turned back to the bloodstained table but she refused to accept it. All day she had blamed herself bitterly for the way she had let him go from her. Now in shock and grief it seemed to her

270

that she had driven George to his death. He had gone heedlessly into danger. He had made no effort to save himself and it was her fault. But Jethro would help. Jethro would know what to do. She clung to that thought.

She said to Seth, "Wait here. I'm going to find Dr Aylsham."

She picked her way through the rows of tortured men scarcely seeing them intent only on one purpose. When she found Jethro, he was treating a man whose thigh had been slashed open to the bone. She shut her eyes for a moment shuddering at the hideous sight of mangled flesh and then waited while he stitched and bandaged.

At last he straightened himself wearily. "He'll do," he said, "bring up the next."

As he turned to plunge his bloodied hands in the bowl of water beside him, his eyes fell on her.

"Laurel, in God's name why are you here?"

"It's George, Jethro, he's hurt, terribly hurt. Come, please come."

"I can't leave here. There are others waiting."

"I know . . . I know, but please . . . please . . ."

He realized then that she was on the verge of breaking down and he nodded to his orderly. "Carry on, I'll be back in a few minutes." He took her arm. "Now quickly, where is he?"

Seth and Fred had laid George on a blanket and they moved away to let Jethro kneel beside him. He knew at once that it was useless but he still examined him lifting him with Fred's help so that he saw clearly how the lance had pierced his back and then broken off. He got slowly to his feet.

"There's nothing I can do," he said gently.

"But he is still alive . . ."

"Only just. The lance has reached his lung. If I take it out, he will die at once."

"But you could try," she said frantically. "There must be something you could do . . . you can't just let him die."

"It would be far kinder. If I operate, it will cause him intense pain and it will be useless. Now he feels nothing. Let him die in peace. It will not be long."

"No, no . . . how can you be so callous?" she said wildly. "You don't care what happens to him. You want him to die."

She was beating at him with her fists and he took both her hands in his own firm grip.

"Control yourself, Laurel. You know that's not true. If I

271

could save him, I would, but there are hundreds here who need me far more than he does. George was a soldier. He would have been the first to acknowledge it." He felt the frenzy slowly die out of her and released her hands. "Be brave, my dear. Stay with him if you wish." She turned away from him silently and he nodded to Polly. "Take care of her. I must get back to my work."

"It were us he was thinkin' of, not hisself," said Fred suddenly, tears mingling with the blood on his face. "He were one o' the best, not like some others."

It was already being talked of that Lord Cardigan, miraculously unharmed, had ridden straight back through the lines and returned to his yacht with no thought or show of concern for the men who had followed him so gallantly.

"You'd better come along with me, my man," said Jethro brusquely. "I'll clean up that face of yours and get the wound stitched."

It was evening when George died, the October light already fading from the hills and valley. Lanterns had been lit and the wounded carried into the hospital tents but still the doctors and surgeons were working in the flickering yellow light. She sat beside him holding his hand, talking to him sometimes though she knew he could not hear her. There had been no opportunity to try and make amends or to tell him how sorry she was. She had meant to be so good a wife and had failed dismally, she thought in her wretchedness. He went from her so quietly that she did not realize it until Polly who had been helping with the wounded came back to her.

"He's gone, ma'am. No use sittin' there any longer."

"No, I suppose not." She got up stiffly. With the going down of the sun, it had become very cold and she shivered. "What will they do with him?" she whispered.

"He's an officer. They'll not push him into the pit with the others. He'll be buried proper, you need have no fear o' that. Now you come along o' me."

"What about Fred?"

"Fred'll be all right. The doctor has fixed him up nicely. He'll be no beauty. 'You'll have a right fine scar,' I told him, 'won't be no use ogling the girls!' Not that my Fred ever did much o' that, bless him. Don't you fret now. The doctor'll see everything is done as it should be." She went on talking cheerfully, her arm around Laurel as she led her away.

272

It was very late by the time they reached the villa and it felt icy cold. The little dog had followed at their heels all day and when Seth brought him into the room she saw that his rough white coat was blotched and stained with blood. For some reason she couldn't bear it.

"He'll have to be bathed," she said and found herself trembling.

"You leave that to me, ma'am," said Polly. "Let's get you settled first."

She set about lighting a fire and Laurel crouched in front of it feeling that she would never be warm again. She let Polly wash and bandage the bleeding furrow along her wrist but refused the food she brought to her. She drank some hot tea and sat staring into the crackling wood. She would not go to bed so Polly brought blankets, wrapped them around her and left her there. The dog, damp and clean smelling, pushed himself in beside her. In her ears was the din and roar of the guns and when she dozed her dreams were filled with blood and horror so that she woke with a start and was afraid to sleep again. When dawn came at last after that terrible night she had come to a decision.

19

Polly was shocked. "But you can't do it, ma'am. You can't go up there nursing the men like that. It wouldn't be decent, not a lady like you."

"If you and that Mrs Butler can do it, then I can."

"We're different. We've not been brought up dainty, like you," went on Polly dubiously. "Besides the surgeons mightn't be too pleased."

"They'll be glad of any help they can get. I saw a little of it after the Alma with Dr Aylsham. If I can do nothing else I can at least give food and water to those who can't help themselves. It's no use arguing, Polly, my mind is made up."

It was better to have a purpose, something to occupy her time. She remembered what Jethro had told her and sent Seth into the town to buy any supplies that might be useful. She knew as everyone did that food and clothing for the troops came off the ships and disappeared mysteriously into a black market. It was expensive but she had plenty of money. George had made sure she was kept well supplied. It might not be much that she could do, but it would be something. Late in the afternoon they set off up the sticky muddy road to Kadikoi leading a mule laden with sheets, blankets, arrowroot, preserved soup, potted ham, port wine, jellies, biscuits, a few bottles of George's brandy and a portable cooking stove, this last item being Polly's practical suggestion.

"We'll need to heat the food, ma'am. No use relying on what they've got up there."

In the aftermath of the battle the camp and the village were still in some confusion so that their arrival passed unnoticed. They discovered that many of the wounded had by now been carried from the field hospitals into the small church. It was a dank cold place but at least provided better shelter. They lay in rows on straw-filled sacks or simply on blankets covered with their greatcoats and they filled every inch of available space. As Laurel opened the door, the terrible sights, the smell of blood and sickness, was so overpowering that for a moment her spirit quailed. She wanted to shut it out, run away, go home to England. There was nothing to stop her. She was free now, not bound to anyone, and yet something stubborn within her, a courage she did not know she possessed, came to her aid and sustained her. In the long lonely hours of the night it had seemed that the only way she could salve her conscience and fulfil what she owed to George was by helping those who had suffered with him. She squared her shoulders and resolutely went in followed by Polly and Seth.

With some difficulty they found a corner in a small side chapel and set up their own little unit asking permission from no one. If the medical board had not been in such a state of chaos and quite overwhelmed by the tremendous number of casualties, they would never have been allowed to remain there, but all the next day, which afterwards Laurel thought the worst she had ever lived through, everyone was far too busy to question their presence.

Again and again she was tempted to give up and go away. The little they could do was a mere drop in the ocean of suffering. At first the sight of bleeding amputated stumps, the helpless agony of men on the point of death, the lice that crawled from the stained filthy shirts, so sickened her that nausea rose in her throat and more than once she was forced to go outside taking deep breaths of clean cold air before making herself return. What kept her there was the patience, the dumb, uncomplaining endurance of the soldiers, rough ordinary men as well as officers, lying side by side. Their gratitude for the smallest kindness was heart-breaking.

It was not until two days later that she met opposition and was very nearly thrown out. She was kneeling by a sick man feeding him from a bowl of arrowroot which Polly had prepared in pails early that morning when a voice thundered above her head.

"What the devil is this woman doing here? Get her out at once."

She looked up to see a thickset middle-aged man in a tightly buttoned military frockcoat glaring down at her from under bushy eyebrows.

"Isn't it obvious what I'm doing?" she said calmly. "The poor fellow can't feed himself so I'm making sure he takes some nourishment."

"There are orderlies to do this kind of work."

"But they don't do it," she retorted. "They leave the food beside men who are too weak to sit up or lift a spoon."

"Do you presume to criticize my methods?"

"They could certainly do with a great deal of improvement."

"Once and for all I will not have women inside my hospitals. This is the army, Madam, not a brothel."

Laurel rose slowly to her feet facing up to him boldly so that he was taken aback. "My husband, Captain George Grafton of the 11th Hussars, was killed two days ago in the cavalry charge. Not you, not anyone, is going to prevent me helping those who fought with him and survived."

She thought he was going to explode. He went purple, his eyes bulged and the two doctors accompanying him on his rounds looked frightened to death but she refused to be intimidated.

In a choked voice he said, "We'll see about that, by God we will!"

Deliberately she turned her back on him and knelt again by the sick man. Nonplussed by this slip of a girl daring to defy him on his own ground, Dr John Hall, Chief Medical Officer of the British Expeditionary Force, stalked on only too well aware of the covert smiles on the faces of his companions quickly wiped off as he glared at them.

The Sergeant of Dragoons lying beside the man Laurel was tending gave a throaty chuckle.

"You've got guts, Miss, if you'll pardon me sayin' so," he said admiringly, "but you take care. That Dr Hall can be the very devil if he feels like it. He don't stand no interference from nobody. A little tin-pot God he is with everyone on the medical staff under his thumb."

"Well, he has not got me under his thumb," said Laurel sturdily. She gently wiped her patient's mouth and made him as comfortable as she could before she passed on to the next. The young man sent to turn her and those with her out of the niche they had made for themselves conveniently forgot it when Dr Hall moved on to further inspection.

The dead were buried hastily only those of the highest rank receiving military honours and one of George's brother officers brought her the personal possessions left behind in the tent – his watch, a few books, a leather wallet. Among the papers was the flower she had laughingly plucked from her wedding bouquet and put in his buttonhole, brown and withered now but carefully preserved. It moved her inexpressibly. She felt guilty because it was as if shock had numbed her and she had not been able to weep for him as she should have done.

She did not see Jethro until one evening when she had come out of the church, leaning against the wall and looking across the darkening valley. Operating tables had been set up in one of the hospital tents. He came out wiping his hands on a rag of a towel and walked across to her.

"I was coming to look for you. One of my colleagues told me that you were here and already having a brush with Dr Hall," he said frowning.

"I didn't know who he was but I'm glad I said what I did. If the conditions here are due to him, then they are a disgrace."

"That's true enough," he said sighing. "The wretched man is not even a real doctor. He didn't get his M.D. until a few years ago. All he is concerned about is his future career, the men can go hang." And then he put a hand on her shoulder and turned her to face him. "It's not Dr Hall that worries me right now, it's you. Why are you doing this, Laurel? Is it because of George?"

"Maybe. I failed him, Jethro. The night before the battle we parted in anger," she said wretchedly. "I can't forgive myself for that."

"Isn't that being a little foolish?"

"Perhaps it is. I only know I feel it. We're both to blame."

"You think I should have done more to save him."

"I don't know . . ." She shivered and turned away from him. "I don't know."

He wanted to take her in his arms, soothe and comfort her, but knew he must not. It was too early to make her see reason. A gulf had opened between them and he was not sure how to bridge it. He said gently, "Wouldn't it be more sensible to go home to England?"

"That would be cowardly. I'm not running away."

"You can't stay here, not in conditions like these. It's madness, Laurel," he went on urgently.

"It's no use. I must go on though I know you think what I'm doing is useless."

"That's not true. If I believed that, I would give up surgery tomorrow. If only one man lives because of what you do, that

277

makes it worthwhile," he said earnestly. "But that's my job, that's what I am here for, but nursing the men is not yours."

"I've made it mine," she said stubbornly, "and nothing you can say is going to stop me."

"Very well." He sighed. "In that case there is just one thing I must say and it is very important. Go back to the villa each night. Be careful what you eat and make sure you keep yourself scrupulously clean. In that way you may escape infection. Promise me you will do that."

"Does it matter so much?"

"It matters a great deal to me."

"All right. I'll do what you say," she said wearily and turned away from him bracing herself to go back into the evil-smelling hell of the makeshift hospital.

Although at first it had seemed impossible, it was astonishing in how short a time she became accustomed to horror. She found that she could even assist Jethro in dressing a gangrenous wound without feeling she might faint or vomit. They began to work side by side as they had done at the settlement concentrating on the small section they had taken under their wing. It was the best they could do. The blankets came into use at once. The sheets were torn up for bandages and she sent Seth into Balaclava to buy more. When the supply ran out, Polly stripped them from the beds in the villa until finally they were driven to ripping up their white cambric petticoats. One or two of the other women joined them in their work and Mrs Butler, whose husband Michael was in the infantry, became ingenious in finding ways of supplementing the poor equipment. They began to collect biscuit bags for use as poultices and when the stock of surgical thread ran out and the doctors were in despair, they rendered down a mixture of fats and greased the pack thread so that it held the gaping wounds together.

It was a fortnight later on the morning of November 5th that Laurel woke to the sound of the guns. She had become accustomed to firing at all hours of the night or day but this was different, more heavy and sustained. There had been rain the evening before and when they set out on their usual ride to Kadikoi, a thick mist lay deep in the valleys curling up like smoke and covering the hills and slopes with a dense white blanket. They could see flashes blazing through the mist followed by the rumble of guns and when they reached the camp, they found it deserted. Every able-bodied man had already left.

The Russians, they were told, had launched a surprise attack on the Inkerman Ridge and aided by the mist had overrun the pickets.

All that day the women and the sick men could hear the sound of the battle and yet could see nothing. Frightening rumours reached them that the cavalry had been destroyed and thousands lay dead. It was not until the winter darkness began to close in that the first of the men came back and they heard how, greatly outnumbered and half choked with fog, they had stood at bay among the brushwood that covered the heights and fought like demons, each man for himself, clinging on to the ridge by the skin of their teeth until at last, when all seemed lost, a lightning charge sent the Russians reeling back to the shelter of Sebastopol and it was all over.

During the night the wounded were brought in. The mist had vanished and a brilliant moon flooded the slopes with silver lighting a path for the women searching for the men who had not come back. Laurel and Polly had not returned to the villa. They stayed giving what little help they could and it was about six o'clock in the morning when Robin was carried in.

Laurel had been going from man to man trying to ease them as best she could and carrying water to moisten their parched lips when she saw him. His right leg had been shattered. She looked at the hideous mangled mass of broken bone that made her shudder as she knelt beside him. Despite the pain he was conscious and even managed a feeble smile.

"I'm afraid I've had it this time, Laurel. It'll be old peg leg from now on."

"Don't say that." She gently lifted his head and held the cup to his lips.

She made sure that he was carried to where Jethro was working by the light of lanterns. When it came to his turn and the orderlies lifted Robin on to the operating table, he stretched out a wavering hand.

"If it's got to come off, I'd rather it was you, Jet."

"Take heart, boy. It may not be as bad as you think." Jethro nodded to his assistant. "Have we any chloroform left?"

"Precious little, sir."

"Bring it."

"Let me do it," said Laurel quickly.

They had no proper masks for administering the drug. The best they could do was to hold a soaked pad over the patient's nose and mouth and Laurel had already done it once or twice before when assisting Jethro.

"You'll need to hold it steady," he warned her.

He had already begun to slit up the ripped and bloodstained breeches when a rasping voice spoke behind him.

"I believe I issued orders that none of my staff was to use this damned chloroform. I've always maintained that a sharp cut of the knife acts as a stimulant. When a man bawls out in pain, at least you know he is still alive."

"The shock can also stop his heart," replied Jethro, calmly going on with his work. "I shall continue using whatever I consider best for my patients."

"Will you indeed?" said Dr Hall explosively. "I am not accustomed to being defied by my subordinates."

"I am not one of your staff. I came out here of my own free will."

"You're one of these God-damned volunteers, I presume. More trouble than they are worth. Well, sir, we don't need your interference or your criticisms. I have ways of dealing with the likes of you and of this woman here. I understood that she was to be removed from the camp."

"I am not subject to your orders nor am I afraid of your threats," said Jethro coolly. "As for Mrs Grafton, a great number of wounded men would have died but for her and those who work with her and for that you should be grateful. Now if you will forgive me, I have a patient to attend to."

Part of Laurel rejoiced at his bold defiance but she saw the baffled angry look on the older man's face and was afraid for him. Dr Hall was not only a bully but possessed unlimited power.

"You've made an enemy," she whispered as Jethro bent over Robin again.

"So much the better. Someone has got to stand up to his petty tyranny. It's clinging to outdated methods that's killing off more of the army than the Russian guns," he muttered impatiently, intent on his delicate and exacting task.

Operating conditions were crude but Jethro was an exceptionally skilful surgeon. Any other doctor would have amputated the leg without a second thought but he believed he could save it so he set the broken bone patching and stitching. Laurel watching Robin's laboured breathing did not dare to look until at last Jethro straightened himself.

"Can you save him?" she asked trembling.

"I shan't know for some days but there's a chance and better a lame leg than none at all. I think I know which Robin would prefer."

In some strange way in the days that followed Robin's recovery became vitally important to Laurel. If he died, she thought despairingly, she would go on feeling guilty for the rest of her life. She worked herself to the bone, not neglecting the other patients, but always coming back to sit beside him, persuading him to eat, nursing him through nights of feverish delirium when he clung to her hand as if she were the one anchor holding him to life and sanity. Jethro watching her knew better than anyone how strain and shock were taking toll of her strength but she would not listen when he tried to persuade her to take more rest and seeing her daily grow thin and hollow-eyed, her bright hair dull and lifeless, her radiant beauty dimmed, he knew he had never loved her so much.

The crisis came on the night of the hurricane. It had been a busy day. Orders had come through that the wounded men in the church were to be carried down to Balaclava Harbour and embarked on the ship taking them to the hospital at Scutari. Jethro went amongst them deciding who should go and who should stay. The slow tortuous journey strapped to mules jolting over the mountain road fetlock deep in mud could be fatal to men still suffering from agonizing wounds. He made up his mind that come what may he would keep Robin under his eye as long as he could. Despite the cold wretched conditions in the church, they were still better than he would have to endure on the open deck of the hospital ship.

Late that night when Laurel went to make sure that Robin was settled down, she was horrified to find him tossing and muttering in a restless fever. She turned back the blanket to see his thigh swollen and hot to the touch. She called Polly to stay beside him and went in search of Jethro. Outside the church a tremendous gust of wind flung her back violently against the wall. With her cloak pulled around her, her head down, she tried to force her way to the hospital tent that Jethro shared with the other doctors, but she could make no progress. With a shrieking howl the gale came again increasing in strength, tearing through the camp like a tornado, hurling objects of every kind in front of it. Nothing was safe. Tents were being

281

carried away, trees uprooted, bushes torn out of the earth. Horses were screaming in terror and men raced everywhere shouting to one another and trying desperately to save valuable equipment from destruction. Clinging to the wall Laurel tried to creep back into the church. She stumbled falling against the door and someone picked her up and thrust her inside. It was Fred running to find out if his wife was still safe. At Laurel's urging he went to find Jethro.

It was an hour before they returned and while outside the storm raged with great gusts of rain and icy sleet, they fought together for Robin's life. There was one moment that night when it seemed there was no hope. If the poison could not be prevented from spreading, then the leg would have to be amputated. Jethro had opened it up draining away the pus, cleansing, swabbing, in the hope and belief that Robin's youth and his sound healthy flesh would carry him through. By morning, though it was still touch and go, the worst was over for the time being. The fever had subsided and the boy lay quiet and exhausted, his forehead cool and the unhealthy flush faded from his face.

Polly brought them tea and there was a sweetness of victory as they sipped it smiling at one another, but when they went outside, it was to find a scene of devastation. One of the hospital tents had blown away completely leaving the sick exposed to the heavy showers of sleet rapidly turning to snow. The forage carefully preserved for the horses had vanished, no one knew where, the road and the camping site were a foot deep in freezing mud. Worse news reached them through the day. The ships in the harbour of Balaclava had snapped their moorings and smashed against one another. More than half of them were hopelessly wrecked and supplies of food and warm clothing intended to carry the army through the bitter winter cold were irretrievably lost.

In a few days the violent winds blew themselves out but the sleet and snow continued. It was impossible to ride back to the town or to bring up provisions. Conditions throughout the camp were appalling. So much had been lost and blown away that men dare not take off their rags of uniform no matter how sodden they were since they had nothing else to put on, the trenches were knee-deep in snow and freezing water and there were no fires anywhere, every fragment of wood even the roots of the smashed trees had already been burnt. Men who had survived the Alma and Balaclava froze to death in their tents and a wave of suicides and self-inflicted wounds swept through the encampment.

Laurel and Polly, unable to go back to the villa, slept in their tiny corner of the church living on tea and biscuit, never taking off their clothes and wrapped in every rag of blanket and rug they could spare from the wounded while Robin still hovered between life and death. Then quite suddenly one morning, almost miraculously it seemed, the sun came out. It was still bitterly cold and there was thick snow on the ground but they had survived, their spirits rose, and best of all Robin improved. The corner had been turned at last. Early one afternoon on his usual round of the sick men, Jethro unwrapped the bandages. The flesh was mending cleanly, no hint of corruption, the bone beginning to knit together. It would be a long time before it healed, he would need to use crutches for months, and he would limp for the rest of his life, but at least he would still walk on his own two legs.

"It'll be Ravensley for you, my boy, and sooner than you think." said Jethro cheerfully, tucking the worn blankets around him. "They'll be holding that coming of age party for you yet."

Robin grinned weakly looking from him to Laurel. "I know whom I have to thank."

"Yes, well, I hope you do. It's your nurse who needs my care now more than you do."

Laurel went with him as he completed his rounds. At the door of the church she said, "Did you just say what you did to cheer Robin up or is he really going to recover?"

"He's young and resilient. I am as sure as anyone can be and I shall do my best to recommend that the medical board invalid him home as soon as reasonably possible."

She felt for the first time since George's death as if a heavy stone had been lifted off her heart. Outside the sudden dazzle of brilliant sun on a carpet of fresh snow made her turn giddy. She swayed and would have fallen if Jethro's arm had not gone around her.

"You're tired out and no wonder. We can get through to Balaclava now, I'm told. I'm going to put you on Lucifer and take you straight back to the villa."

"No," she protested, "no, I can't go away. There is always so much to be done and Robin still needs me."

283

"Robin will do very well with Polly to care for him and nothing will be done at all if you fall sick, will it? For once you'll do as you're told. Doctor's orders."

The tension had eased and she was suddenly too exhausted to argue. Somehow Seth had managed to keep Lucifer alive though his ribs showed up plainly under his dull rough coat grown thick against the cold.

"Poor darling," she murmured, rubbing her face against the tangled mane. "He's like Rosinante in *Don Quixote*, a scarecrow horse, all bones," and she giggled weakly as Jethro lifted her into the saddle.

It seemed amazing after the agonies of the past weeks that the villa was still standing, the sturdy stone walls resisting the gusts of the hurricane. Even more astonishing it had not even been looted, maybe because neighbours had been too occupied in saving their own goods. It was icy cold but Jethro found wood, built a fire and then discovered that there were still a few stores left in the cupboard from Jane's last food parcel. He boiled water and made a jug of hot chocolate. There was no milk but they piled it with sugar, added a lacing of brandy, and sipped it gratefully. Then he rolled her in rugs.

"Sleep," he commanded. "You need that more than food, more than anything."

"What about you? You're not going to leave me here alone, are you?"

"Not for long. I'm going into the town. If I know anything about these rascally shopkeepers, they will have been busy in the harbour salvaging what they can. I'll try and find some food for both of us." His hand strayed gently across her hair. "You close your eyes like a good girl. I'll be back."

She had no idea how long she had slept when she opened her eyes and saw him lying back in a chair, the dull red glow of the fire lighting his face, lean and gaunt from the privation and strain of the last few months, but the face she loved above anything else on this earth. She felt marvellously happy. One of the logs fell with a small crash and he stirred from his doze and sat up. He looked across at her smiling.

"You're awake. How do you feel?"

"Wonderful. What time is it?"

"Two o'clock in the morning. Hungry?"

"Ravenous."

284

"There wasn't much to be had but I've some eggs, a loaf of bread and a bottle of wine."

"It's a feast. Shall we cook it?"

"I had to break up a chair to keep the fire going," he admitted ruefully, "but I think we can manage it."

He lit the lamp and raked the embers to a fiery glow. He brought a pan and they stirred the eggs over the fire and ate them spread on slices of toasted bread. He poured the rough country wine and she was reminded of that other night almost a year ago now when they had gone to Westley after Moggy's accident. She felt as if they were isolated in a world of their own. Outside was the misery of George's death, the blood and suffering of the war, the filth and horror of their daily tasks, but here for a little while they were warm and safe and alone with one another. She sat up.

"Jethro, I have something to tell you."

He put down his glass and turned to poking the fire to a brighter glow. "What is it?"

"It is something Rosemary wrote to tell me, something important she had learned from Charles Townsend."

"I wondered if she had told you."

She stared at him. "You know?"

"Yes, I know about the baby in the coffin."

"So it is all quite certain."

"Yes, quite certain. Oliver wrote me that he has gone into it further with Charles's father. It seems that your mother was not Justin Aylsham's daughter after all but some other abandoned waif plucked out of the Fens."

"But why was nothing said about it? Why – when it had caused so much pain?"

"I think I know," he said slowly. "You must realize, Laurel, that when Justin died and there was a great deal of scandal, all Oliver wanted to do was to hush it up, make as little of it as possible. Your grandfather was taking your mother to Italy and that was the end of it so far as he was concerned. He was glad to put it behind him."

"But why didn't Grandfather say anything when he found out about the baby?"

"It's difficult to know exactly how he felt but you must realize he had lost the son he adored and all he had to look forward to was his son's child . . . and that was you." He leaned over and took her hand. "I believe that all he wanted was to remove the girl who would have been your grandmother from her lonely grave in the unconsecrated field and place her among the family to whom she belonged. The discovery of the baby must have been unexpected and, I imagine, a great relief to him. At last all doubt was removed. But by that time he had severed his connection with the Aylshams and possibly saw no need to rake up what had been so damnably painful." He smiled ruefully. "I don't suppose he thought of me for a single moment, a boy away at school. How could he know what I felt about it and after a time it had no importance – not until you came to Ravensley."

"What a lot of trouble I caused. You should never have brought me from Rome."

"Would you rather I'd left you there?" he said banteringly.

The shadow between them had lifted but they were still a little unsure of one another. After a moment she said, "When did you know?"

"Not until after the Alma when I went to Scutari and my letters caught up with me."

"But you said nothing about it when I saw you on the quay that night."

He smiled. "Neither did you."

"I was afraid of what it might do to us."

"So was I."

With the relief of tension after so long, they began to laugh, then suddenly she was serious again.

"If George hadn't died, would you still have been silent?"

"Who knows what one will do?"

"George was so jealous of you."

"Not nearly so jealous as I was of him. I grudged every minute he spent with you."

"You needn't have done. Poor George, I was so unfair to him." She shivered suddenly. "I'm cold."

"The fire is going down. I'll forage for some more wood."

He stood up and she caught at his hand. "Don't go."

"Don't be afraid. I'm only going into the yard."

"Don't go. Stay with me." An unreasoning panic had seized her. She could not bear him to go out of her sight. She pulled him down to sit beside her reaching out a hand to caress his face.

"I love you," she murmured.

He knew he should resist temptation. George had been dead scarcely more than a month, but they had been through too

286

much, yearned for each other too long and now there was nothing to hold them back. The moment her lips touched his, he knew it was useless. The torments of the past had vanished. He felt liberated in body and spirit. He gathered her into his arms. She had grown so thin, he felt her bones, light and fragile as those of a bird. Then they were lost in one another, the outside world blotted out, coming together in a rage of passion and tenderness.

20

"We must be married," said Jethro, "as soon as possible. We'll go to Scutari. Lord Stratford's Chaplain will arrange it for us."

"It's too soon after George's death," said Laurel doubtfully, "people will talk."

"They are talking already," he replied wryly. "I want to call myself your husband. I want the right to protect you."

"I know I ought to feel guilty and I don't, not now," she murmured ruefully. "Is it very wicked of me?"

"Very wicked," he said gently. Her complete lack of inhibition, her defiance of ordinary convention had always been part of her enchantment for him.

It was a week since that night at the villa, a week of unexpected happiness when they had both been seized with a kind of madness. It was as if the gruelling work of nursing the sick had repaid the debt she owed to George and she was released from the burden. Every day they still laboured at the hospital enduring stoically the miseries, the stenches, the many revolting tasks that had to be carried out, but afterwards they escaped to Balaclava spending the few hours of the night in each other's arms, not always making love – they were often far too exhausted – but finding a marvellous joy in simply being together. At any other time conventional restraints might have kept them apart but living in the constant shadow of death, every hour was precious so that the bonds of ordinary social behaviour no longer had any meaning for them. Polly knew and so did Seth, while the doctors who shared the tent with Jethro guessed at the reason for his frequent absences and said nothing. He worked as hard as any of them and they did not grudge him his pleasure with a pretty widow.

Winter had set in now in grim earnest. Snow lay thick on the ground but the sun shone and the air was dry and sparkling. The plight of the army was still atrocious and growing worse every day. At the beginning of December Fred Cobb came to

Jethro one afternoon with information that he could scarcely believe. The *Avon*, the hospital ship bound for Scutari, was still at anchor in the bay. Several hundred sick and wounded men had been lying out on the open decks for a full fortnight with nothing to cover them but a greatcoat or thin blanket and with only one overworked assistant surgeon to care for them. Their frightful condition filled Jethro with a helpless rage. He sought out one of the regimental officers and dragged him unwillingly on to the ship. Equally appalled at the sight that met his horrified eyes, the Colonel galloped off to Lord Raglan's headquarters. Though it was close to midnight the Commander sent at once for Dr Hall, censuring him severely and demanding immediate action.

"There's going to be the very devil of a rumpus but at least there will be an enquiry and something will be done," Jethro told Laurel the next day. "Thank God, I didn't permit Robin to be taken down to that infamous ship."

Laurel looked at him anxiously. Jethro had never hesitated to speak his mind freely criticising the conditions under which the doctors worked and consistently ignoring orders that he considered harmful to his patients.

"Will Dr Hall realize it was you who supplied the information about the ship?" she asked.

"God knows. I don't care if he does. The important thing is to get the frightful muddle cleared up as soon as possible and make sure it never happens again."

"But he doesn't like you. He'll do everything in his power to destroy you."

"What can he do? I have never been subject to his authority, not like some of the other poor devils in the medical service." She still looked worried and he took both her hands in his. "To hell with Dr Hall and his machinations. They're not important. Listen to me, my darling. I've been thinking. Robin is stronger now. In a few days he'll be walking with the help of crutches. As soon as a passage can be arranged for him, he will go to Scutari to convalesce and you must go with him."

"No," she said at once. "I'm not going to leave you."

"It will only be for a short time and it will help him to have you with him. I will come to Scutari as soon as I can. There's a stalemate in the siege for the moment and there are not so many casualties. I can be spared for a while. Besides I heard a wonderful piece of news this morning. Believe it or not but the

289

government have woken up at last. Sidney Herbert has sent out Miss Nightingale with a band of nurses. Just think what that is going to mean. I'm told she arrived at the beginning of November."

"So that is the reason you want to go to Scutari," she said teasingly. "I know how greatly you admire her."

"Jealous?" he tweaked her nose. "It's only one of the reasons. You didn't see her in action as I did when she was in Harley Street. I'd back Miss Nightingale against Dr Hall any day in the week."

She did not want to go. Their happiness was too new, too fragile. She feared to lose it and it was only because Robin still needed so much watchful care that she gave in at last.

Polly came down to the harbour to see her go on board. "Now you look after yourself, ma'am, and don't worry about the doctor. Fred and me — we'll see he don't lack for nothing."

"Bless you." Impulsively Laurel leaned forward and kissed her cheek.

Jethro was making sure that Robin was as comfortably installed as possible in the crowded sick quarters. "Now you be careful of that leg of yours, my boy. Don't try to run before you can walk," he said warningly. Up on the deck he took Laurel's hand in both his and kissed it. They dare not show their feelings too openly. "I will be with you by the New Year at latest," he promised.

It was hard to part from him. Huddled in her thick cloak she stood in the freezing wind gazing over the rail while the ship nosed its way slowly out of the harbour.

Two days later Dr Hall, boiling with rage at the slight put upon him, took his revenge. Chance made it easy for him. The Russians had made one of their marauding sorties and overrun an advance picket close under the walls of Sebastopol. The one survivor who had made his painful way back to Kadikoi reported as many as thirty wounded left there to be either bayoneted by the brutal Cossacks or frozen to death if they were not brought in very soon.

"An ambulance wagon must go out immediately," Dr Hall said in his rasping voice, "or there will be more unjust criticism of neglect on the part of the medical staff and we have all suffered sufficiently from that during the last weeks." His eyes roved over the assembled surgeons and orderlies coming to rest pointedly on Jethro. "Perhaps one of our gallant volunteers might find it an opportunity of distinguishing himself," he went on sarcastically. "It is always so easy to criticise when not called upon to take part in any action."

He had judged his man to a nicety. Jethro flushed and stepped forward.

"I will go willingly but I may need assistants."

Half a dozen of the men including Fred Cobb volunteered immediately to accompany him as an armed escort. The little band with the cumbersome wagon rocking beside them rode out through the snow and ice on its dangerous errand of mercy.

Constantinople and the Hotel d'Angleterre despite its shabbiness, strange cooking smells and nightly invasion of cockroaches, seemed the very acme of comfort after the last few months and a stormy winter voyage from Balaclava. Laurel had goaded the Turkish servants into providing a bath and luxuriated in steaming water lavishly scented with rare perfume bought in the market. They had arrived just ten days before the end of December and while she brushed her newly washed hair into shining ringlets and examined her face critically in the mirror, she thought about the invitation to Lord Stratford de Redcliffe's Christmas ball which had arrived by special messenger that morning. Maybe it was frivolous to be concerned over what she should wear but all her gowns had suffered severely from being packed into trunks for months and subjected to heat, damp and the ravages of vermin. In any case she ought to be in mourning but where to find a suitable black evening dress in a couple of days seemed well nigh impossible. It would have to be white, limp and creased though it was. She was shaking out the satin and lace and wondering if the hotel chambermaid possessed such a thing as a smoothing iron when there was a knock at the door and Robin came limping into the room.

The same Medical Board that had declared Lord Cardigan unfit for further duty had also bowed to pressure from Lord Aylsham and his brother-in-law at the War Office and summarily dismissed Rifleman R. Aylsham from the service. Robin found his discharge ignominious but accepted it with a shrug of the shoulders. The months he had spent in the ranks rubbing shoulders with men of every type and condition had changed him. At first he had found it utterly appalling. He had scarcely known how to endure the dirt, the discomfort, the

291

bullying, the bawdy talk, but you can't fight alongside men in three bloody battles and not discover other qualities, generosity of spirit, a rough kindness, a stubborn courage and endurance.

"I'm privileged," he said wryly when Laurel protested about it. "I'm here with you at the Hotel d'Angleterre and I still have my leg even if it does hurt like hell, not like the other poor devils packed off home to a country that accepts their sacrifice and doesn't care a damn what happens to them. No medal, no pension for them, not even decent hospitals if they are still sick. If I ever get a chance to open my mouth about it, I swear I'll do it."

Whenever he could he discarded his crutches, gritted his teeth and walked with the aid of a stick, and that morning when the invitation arrived, he limped along the passage, knocked on Laurel's door and entered waving the piece of gilt-edged pasteboard in the air.

"What the devil do I do about this?" he said humorously waving the piece of gilt-edge pasteboard in the air.

"If it's an invitation to the Palace, then you accept and come as my escort," said Laurel.

"There are a dozen war veterans with stars and ribbons all over them who will only be too pleased to dance all night with you," objected Robin. "Private Rifleman Aysham with his crippled leg will be sadly out of place."

"You also happen to be the Honourable Robert Aylsham or the Ambassador, high-powered snob that he is, would never have invited you and if you don't go, then neither will I," was Laurel's firm reply.

Robin collapsed on to the bed with a little sigh of relief. After the weeks of nursing and the voyage on the ship, these two were on very companionable terms. He grinned at her.

"You've become very masterful lately, my girl. What does Jet have to say about it?"

"Why should he say anything?"

"Oh come now, you're going to marry him, aren't you, Laurel? I've kept my mouth shut – not my business really – but I have eyes in my head."

She got up and moved across to him. "I'm sorry, Robin."

"Don't be. I suppose I shall go on loving you till the day I die, but I never really had any hope and it never prevented me from realizing in my heart that it was always you and Jet from the very beginning, wasn't it?"

"From the very beginning," she repeated, "even when it was utterly impossible and now . . ." she took a few dancing steps and laughed deliciously, "and now I'm so wonderfully, marvellously happy that it makes me feel afraid. Dear Robin," she leaned towards him and kissed his cheek, "I'm so glad you're here. You are such a comfort to me."

Laurel went to the ball on the arm of the Honourable Robert Aylsham still obstinately wearing his rifleman's uniform and they caused a minor sensation in that rich and glittering throng. In the crowded ballroom, she thought sadly, there were a great many faces missing, their places taken by newcomers from England magnificent in gold laced jackets, their ladies elegant in fresh silks and wide spreading crinolines. They gazed with astonishment and some envy at Laurel, hand in hand with Robin in his stained green tunic, and wearing her faded satin and lace like a badge of honour proud to belong alongside the battle veterans with their scarred faces, some limping, some with empty sleeves pinned across their breasts, a great many with wine-coloured patches still to be seen on their worn uniforms.

But it was not all sadness. The band of the Rifle Brigade played enchanting waltzes, the young officers came crowding around Laurel, many of them men who had attended the parties at the villa or been patients in the church at Kadikoi. Quadrilles and Cotillions were followed by games, Pig-in-the-middle and Blindman's Buff, with the midshipmen from the Navy blindfolding their old Admiral and shrieking with laughter like children as he blundered around the ballroom. The celebrations ended at midnight with the company gathered in a darkened room where a great dish of plums in brandy had been set on fire. The young men competed with each other in reaching for the fiery fruit, Robin limping forward with the others to snatch one out of the flames and pop it into Laurel's mouth.

There was a hush for a moment when Lady Stratford came in with another lady who smiled a little grimly at their antics. One of the young men, a doctor who had been working side by side with Jethro, seized Laurel's hand.

"Come with me," he said leading her across the room before she could protest.

The strange bluish light from the burning spirit fell upon a

293

pale face with fine grey eyes framed by soft brown hair under a cream lace bonnet. The severe black dress was only relieved by a touch of white at neck and cuffs.

"Miss Nightingale," said the young man with a charming deference, "I want you to meet a lady to whom we all owe a large debt. If we had our way we would award her a medal and bar for what she did for us after Balaclava and Inkerman."

Laurel blushed as those searching eyes examined her. "You shouldn't say such things," she murmured. "I did very little."

"I have heard otherwise," said Florence Nightingale. "The men talk, you know, sick as they are. We have met before, I think, in London."

"Yes, very briefly, at Lord Palmerston's house. Miss Nightingale," went on Laurel earnestly, "I shall be staying here for some time. May I come and help in your hospital at Scutari?"

Florence studied the charming face for an instant, noting the fragile bones, the pallor beneath the light dusting of rice powder. This girl had already worn herself to the end of her strength. She smiled a little. "You will scarcely believe it, my dear, but my battle is as much with the outdated rules and regulations of the medical board as with caring for the sick and wounded. We are still living in the midst of the utmost filth and squalor but my nurses have at last been accepted and permitted to work in the wards. Every day I am feeling my way forward inch by inch and I dare not take one wrong step or I am under fire from Dr Hall."

"I understand completely but Jethro said he would back you to win any day," exclaimed Laurel impulsively.

"Jethro?"

"Jethro Aylsham. He's a surgeon working at the front line."

"I remember him. He came to my assistance more than once when I was in Harley Street. Is he a friend of yours?"

"A very dear friend. He will be here soon."

"Well, my dear Mrs Grafton," said Florence thoughtfully, "I can't afford to turn away any offer of assistance. If you really mean what you say there is one thing you could do for me. We have a great number of women to care for, wives of serving soldiers, who have been shamefully neglected by the authorities. They do not care whether these poor creatures and their children live or die. A Dr Blackett and his wife have been doing what they can for them but they're always in need of more help." She smiled suddenly and charmingly. "With that pretty face of yours, come and show them how to trim a bonnet. Give them something that will bring back their self respect."

The cool hand pressed hers for a moment and then she had moved quietly out of the room.

Jethro did not come at the New Year as he had promised and by the middle of January there had still been no word from him. Severe storms had held up shipping in the Black Sea and Laurel tried to tell herself that his delay must be due to the weather though no one knew better than she how cholera or what had begun to be called 'Crimean fever' could kill a man in a day. She endeavoured to still her anxiety by taking Lucifer for long morning rides. He was growing sleek again under Seth's watchful care. The little white dog had been left behind with Polly and sometimes she regretted it. The pleasures indulged in by the other ladies living in the hotel, the little winter picnics, the gossips over morning coffee or afternoon tea taken with the Ambassador's wife at the Palace seemed to her unbearably trivial. She knew they were shocked because she had refused to turn herself into a weeping widow heavily veiled in black and they disapproved of the tales told about her working in the hospital alongside the wives of the men forgetful of rank and privilege. They thought she was crazy because every afternoon she took a caique across the Bosphorous and went to give what help she could in the cellars of the Barracks Hospital.

"How can you bear to mix with such abandoned creatures, harlots and sluts most of them," murmured a Major's wife one morning in disgust meeting Laurel on her way out of the hotel.

"Would we be any different if we had to live in conditions like theirs?" she retorted.

"Well, really!" I trust you speak for yourself!" said the other lady indignantly.

Laurel, her pity stirred, had found that the women forced by the bitter winter cold to crowd together in appalling squalor were very far from abandoned sluts. The army had given them transport to accompany their men but once landed in Turkey disclaimed all responsibility. Some of the more enterprising like Polly Cobb had battled their way to the front in the Crimea but others, ignorant and penniless, hampered by babies and in many cases sick or pregnant, had no one to whom they could turn. The authorities obstinately shut their eyes to the problem and thrust into the stinking stone cellars, was it any wonder that they squabbled among themselves? If they were filthy, their rags lice-ridden, their children starving and running wild as animals, it was because it was nobody's business to give a helping hand or make sure they received their due from the money, the gifts of food and clothing beginning to pour in from Britain. Shown a little kindness they responded with a touching gratitude.

One afternoon at the end of January Laurel had brought with her a collection of cheap straw bonnets that she had purchased in the market. With Seth's help and under Robin's direction they were piled into the slender gondola-like boat and rowed across the water. The women went crazy over them. They were vying with each other in front of the fly blown mirror hung on the wall, jostling for position, fighting over the flowers and ribbons, until Laurel intervened and began to show each one the best way of trimming it. It was a merry laughing scene in that gaunt cold place with its dirt-stained walls and stone floor running with black slime. The women were watching with envy as Laurel with skilful fingers pinned a rose to the crown and twisted a knot of ribbon around the brim. She planted it on the head of a young girl and was standing back to admire it when one of the hospital orderlies made his way towards them.

"Miss Nightingale would like a word with you, ma'am," he said.

"With me?"

"Yes, ma'am. Up in one of the wards."

"Very well. I'll come at once."

She gave the bonnets and their trimmings to one of the other helpers and followed the old man out of the cellar and up the stairs. After a moment's hesitation Robin limped after her.

Already in the two months that she had been there, Miss Nightingale had worked miracles in cleansing the wards and providing blankets, food and medical care mostly out of her own pocket, but more and more men flooded in from the Crimea and the death toll was still high. The stench as Laurel entered the ward was worse even than it had been in the church at Kadikoi. She took out a handkerchief but went bravely forward. Around her on each side, crowded together, lay men suffering not only from wounds and fever, but from frostbite, malnutrition and scurvy. The supplies lost in the hurricane had not yet been replaced and in the last week alone a thousand more cases had come in from Balaclava.

"I wondered if you would come," said Miss Nightingale. "This is a man from your husband's regiment, Mrs Grafton, and he has been asking for you ever since he was brought in last night."

Laurel looked at the gaunt face beneath the blood-stained bandage. "Fred," she exclaimed, "Fred Cobb!" and went down on her knees beside the pallet bed. "How are you feeling, Fred?"

"Nicely, ma'am, thank you." He tried to smile. "It's a deal warmer here than it was up at the camp."

"Fred, I'm so sorry to see you wounded. Is Polly with you?"

"Nay. They wouldn't let her come with us on the transport, but if I know my Poll, she'll get herself here somehow."

"You wanted to see me, Fred," she said gently.

"Aye, ma'am, I did that. I thought the news mightn't have reached you . . . and you and him being so friendly like, and he being so good to me an' all . . ."

"Do you mean Dr Aylsham? He's not come with you . . ."

"No, ma'am, I wish he had, that I do. It's just that I was with him, see, when it happened . . ."

Robin had by now come up behind Laurel. He bent down to the sick man. "What happened? Speak plainly, man, for God's sake."

"What is it you have to tell me, Fred?" went on Laurel quietly taking the big rough hand in her own. "Are you trying to tell me that he is dead?"

"Nay, ma'am, leastways I hope it en't come to that. It were like this, see . . . that Dr Hall, he more or less forced him to take out the ambulance wagon to bring in some of the wounded, miles away from the camp it were, right under the ramparts of Sebastopol. A few of us volunteered to go with him, but we met up with a band of Cossacks, brutes they were huntin' us down and tryin' to stop us gettin' anywhere near. Two of us were shot down and the rest ran like rabbits – couldn't blame 'em really – but Dr Aylsham, he were carryin' one of the wounded and he wouldn't give up. They fired at him and we saw him fall. I wanted to go back but they had caught him up, took him prisoner, yellin' they were like loonies, and there weren't a thing we could do . . ." He fell silent panting for breath and Miss Nightingale picked up the cup of water and held it to his lips. He swallowed a few mouthfuls and then went on. "We got back to the camp somehow though it weren't easy 'cos it

297

had come on to snow . . . then afterwards we heard what had happened."

He paused and Robin said brusquely, "Go on, man, what did happen?"

"We heard that them Russkies were accusin' him of bein' a spy."

"But that's ridiculous," exclaimed Laurel. "He is a doctor. He has treated some of the Russian prisoners as well as our men."

"Aye, we all know that," said Fred unhappily, "but you see when the news comes through, Dr Hall denied that he was ever part of his medical team and so he weren't goin' to take any responsibility for what he was doin' that day so near their naval dockyard."

"But that's infamous," said Robin. "He can't do that."

"I'm afraid he can," said Miss Nightingale. "So far as medical matters are concerned, Dr Hall is all powerful. I know . . . I've suffered from his pig-headed obstinacy already."

"What does it mean?" Laurel slowly got to her feet. She felt as if a cold hand had suddenly gripped her heart.

Fred turned away his face and Robin said slowly, "It's impossible to be certain but spies have been shot before now."

"Oh no, no . . ." the cold seemed to invade her whole body, she began to shake and unaccountably the ward had begun to swim around her. She put out a groping hand and felt it taken firmly. Miss Nightingale's arm had gone around her steadying her. She took a deep breath and tried to pull herself together.

"I'm sorry. I'm all right now. It was stupid of me."

"Not stupid at all. Very natural in the circumstances. You'd better come to my room for a few minutes and rest, then your friend can take you back to your hotel."

Still giddy, Laurel let herself be led away leaving Robin with Fred Cobb. It was a bare plain room she was taken to with nothing but a narrow pallet bed and a desk piled high with papers. It was icy cold.

Miss Nightingale put her in the one chair. "Now, my dear," she said gently. "Tell me . . . are you pregnant?"

Started Laurel said, "Why should you say that?"

"It's a look some women have. I grew familiar with it when I was working in London and so many young women came to me for help. You needn't answer if you don't wish to."

"I'm not sure . . . perhaps."

"If you are, go home to England. You have lost your husband, don't lose his son as well." Laurel shivered and Florence put a hand on her shoulder. "This is no place for a woman to bear a child. Those poor creatures you have been helping have no choice but you have. Go home and if you still want to do something for us, then tell them in London what you've seen with your own eyes. That is what we need. Public opinion that will put to shame all these petty tyrants who think only of lining their own pockets. You know, my dear, what I'm doing here is not just going around the wards, smoothing brows and giving food and medical care though that's an important part of the work, but more than that it's fighting a battle to see these wretched men receive what is their right and to make sure that it can never happen again and to achieve that end I would sacrifice anybody and anything. Oh I know quite well that there is not one of these officials who would not burn me like Joan of Arc if he could but if the country is with me, then I'll win through."

"Jethro said that is what you would do," then the realization of what had happened to him swept over her and she turned her face quickly away. "I'm sorry to have wasted your time, Miss Nightingale, and thank you for your kindness. I will go now."

"You will take my advice?"

"Yes . . . I don't know. I'll think about it."

"Don't hesitate too long."

Even before she left the room she saw that Florence had turned again to her desk bent over the endless paperwork and realized the implacable strength of will that was driving this slender frail woman slowly step by step nearer her goal.

Robin was waiting outside on the stairs looking anxious and he tried hard to reassure her as they were rowed back across the Bosphorus.

"I am sure that fellow was exaggerating the danger," he said. "He means well but how can he be so sure? It could be all a mistake. It may take time but the Russians must release Jethro."

She hardly heard him. All she wanted was to be alone. When they reached the hotel and he would have gone up with her, she gently pushed him back.

"No, Robin, I'm all right. I just want to lie down for a while, that's all. Don't worry about me."

Alone in her bedroom she stared at the pale shadowy face

reflected in the mirror. Did she look any different? Miss Nightingale had put into words what she had suspected already and tried to dismiss as impossible. If it was true, then it was not George's child, she was quite sure of that. Circumstances had kept them apart since before the battle of the Alma. The father of her baby was in the hands of the Russians, wounded, condemned as a spy, already perhaps brought up before the firing squad. It was nearly two months since he had been captured and they had done nothing, nothing to secure his release. She trembled and could not remain sitting still. She paced up and down the room, all kinds of crazy ideas racing through her mind – she would go back to Balaclava, appeal to Lord Raglan, go on her knees to Dr Hall, ride out to the Russian camp and implore Prince Mechnikoff to have mercy – all utterly ridiculous. She could hear their laughter – a frantic woman begging for the lover she had taken only a month after her husband's death. She stood shivering in the cold room. That's why it has happened to me, she thought distractedly. I'm being punished. I'm a slut just as my mother was. I wanted Jethro so much I couldn't live without him and now I'm suffering from it just as she did. I thought I was so different, I thought I was myself, strong and self reliant, and I'm like her after all.

She sank on the bed obsessed with the conviction that she and Jethro had never been meant to be happy. It was like a curse, a legacy from the old guilt-ridden past that still clung about them and there was no one to talk to, no one in whom she could confide. She had never felt so desperately alone.

She sat for a long time chilled to the bone until at last the sturdy streak of common sense that had been temporarily lost stirred within her. Slowly she recovered from the shock. She was still not certain. She need not despair about Jethro yet. There could be a mistake as Robin had said. Only one thing was clear. She could not go quietly home to England and wait in this dreadful uncertainty. Miss Nightingale's advice was good but she did not know the circumstances. She made up her mind there and then to go back to Balaclava. It would be easy enough. A party was leaving in a few days – she had heard them talking about it. She was the widow of a man who had died in the charge which had already become famous, a byword for heroism. It should not be too difficult to obtain permission to return.

She was calmer now. She had faced the situation and

conquered it. She was able to meet Robin and reassure him but she told him nothing of her intentions. Her resolution hardened when she went back to the hospital the next day only to be told that Fred Cobb had died during the night. She wept for him then as she had not been able to weep for George, the big inarticulate soldier who had possessed so much gentleness and true kindness and her heart bled for Polly.

She made all her arrangements secretly and slipped away early one morning with Seth and Lucifer leaving most of her luggage behind and a note for Robin knowing full well that he would try to prevent her going or insist on accompanying her when he was still only barely convalescent.

During the week of the voyage the plans that had seemed at first so wildly improbable became more practical. She remained withdrawn from the other passengers letting them believe her wrapped in grief and since the crossing was rough and most of the ladies vanished into their cabins, it was not difficult for her.

Frustration began immediately she reached Balaclava. Lord Raglan was a kindly man and treated her with consideration though regretting that he could hold out little hope. In one way she understood. He was a tired elderly man faced with the problem of keeping the army intact through one of the worst winters on record and the possible loss of one man among thousands must seem very unimportant. How should he know that that one life was all the world to her? She refused to give up. She was certain that Jethro was not dead and didn't know whether it was the new life growing within her that made her so sure. She had consulted no doctor but there were times when a sick nausea threatened to overcome her and she thought she could not go on but something stronger than herself drove her forward.

She tried to reach Dr Hall but he refused pointblank to see her and the doctor in charge at the hospital was equally discouraging. There was only one thing left and it posed a problem. How could she reach the Russian camp? The Crimea was still in the grip of intense cold but for the time being it was dry and the pot-holed muddy road to Kadikoi had frozen into hard ruts. The army might be suffering agonies from starvation and frostbite but there was still a flourishing black market in Balaclava. In one of the shops she bought a sheepskin-lined hooded cloak that must have once belonged to some captured Russian officer and adapted it to fit herself. Much against his will she left Seth on the ship without telling him what she intended to do. Then very early one morning just after it was light she saddled Lucifer and set out up the familiar mountain road. Once she had to draw to one side as a long procession of mules carrying the sick and wounded strapped to their sides came jolting slowly down from the heights. She caught her breath at the pitiful sight, the haunted white faces, the pain-filled eyes and open mouths, the distorted limbs. Then they had passed and she could go on.

It was strange coming back to a place so packed with memories. Some of the men came running to greet her, scarecrow figures in tattered uniforms, their faces gaunt with hunger, their feet bound in rags. She had bought up an entire stock of illegal chocolate and brought it out of her saddlebags, a futile gesture but all she could think of doing and her eyes filled with tears as she watched their pathetic gratitude. Was this to what the magnificent British army had been reduced, these tragic figures, hollow-eyed and starving? She asked one of them for Mrs Cobb and he pointed to a little brown tent set up in the lee of the church. She tethered Lucifer and as she crossed to it, Polly herself pushed back the flap. She stared for a moment and then came running, half laughing, half crying.

"Oh ma'am, Mrs Grafton dear, I'm right glad to see you but you shouldn't have come back here – not like it is now."

There was an instant's hesitation, then they flung their arms around one another forgetful of rank and class, just two women who had both suffered loss. They moved into the shelter of the tent and Polly looked at her fearfully.

"It's Fred, en't it, ma'am?"

"Yes, I'm afraid it is."

"He's gone, en't he?"

For answer Laurel put her arm around the other's shaking body and drew her close. "I saw him," she whispered. "They were taking good care of him in the hospital."

"But it weren't no good?"

"No."

"I think I knew all along though I tried to go on hopin'. I just wish they'd have let me go with him. I'd like to have been there when he . . ." she choked on the words and turned her face away before she went on in a stifled voice. "He were right upset about Dr Aylsham. He felt he ought to have done more to help him."

"I know. He told me, Polly. That's why I'm here. No one will listen to me or make any effort to find out what has happened to him so I'm going myself into the Russian camp."

"But you can't, 'tisn't possible, ma'am, not a lady like you."

"That's why. They wouldn't listen to a man but they might to a woman. It's worth trying."

"But those devils – they've no heart – they could do anything to you."

"I know but I still have to go. You see, I love him, Polly," she said simply.

"But the Captain . . ."

"He was my husband and I was fond of him but Jethro is my whole life. I can't let him go without trying to save him." Polly still looked unhappy and she put a hand on her arm. "Try to understand. It's a long story. Perhaps one day I'll tell you about it but there's no time now. I must go soon before someone finds out and stops me."

Laurel had brought a few provisions with her, some tea, sugar and biscuits. The little white dog desperately thin climbed on to her lap. They talked about ways and means while Polly boiled a kettle and poured the hot milkless tea into two chipped cups.

"The relief parties for the pickets go out at midday," she said doubtfully. "You could join them a mile or so beyond the camp. Nobody could blame them if you follow in their tracks and they would guide you."

She still did her best to dissuade her from such a foolhardy venture but Laurel was stubborn. In some queer way the very fact that she was frightened strengthened her resolution. She knew she could be molested, humiliated, even imprisoned. Russian soldiers had a reputation for callous brutality and she would have to pass through their hands before she reached the officer in charge, and yet she still would not give up. It had become a kind of test, a payment for her sense of guilt.

She followed out exactly the plan they had made. The little company of horsemen warned by Polly knew very well that she was riding behind them, but they went on, eyes straight ahead, taking no notice until late afternoon when they halted and the young Lieutenant at their head came back towards her. He was intensely curious. There was something strange about this undoubtedly beautiful woman in the heavy cloak, her face shadowed by the fur-lined hood, venturing into the enemy camp for the sake of a man whom many of them believed to be already dead.

He pointed ahead. "If you take the track to the left there is an entrance into the city heavily guarded. You will have to take your chance there. If you meet with any trouble – "

"I must get out of it as best I can," she said quickly. "I don't want any of you to be in danger because of me."

"No British soldier worth his salt would stand by and see a lady suffer at enemy hands," the young man said stiffly. "We shall be watching."

"Thank you."

She gave him her hand and he surprised himself by taking it and kissing it.

"Good luck," he said huskily.

She rode forward shaking inwardly now that the moment had come. High up in front of her she could see the guns that had wreaked such havoc amongst the attacking British army. They were silent now and all was quiet in the frosty air. The light was fading fast when she reached the gates and braced herself to meet the astonished guard who stepped out to challenge her. She spoke to them in French demanding to see their Commander and they stared at her with their flat peasant faces. Even in her anxiety she could not help noticing how much better equipped they were than the British in their long grey overcoats and fur hats. One of them tried to thrust her back pointing to the way she had come but she shook her head and spoke to them again. They jabbered together in Russian, then one of them went inside and came back with an older man, a Sergeant, she supposed. He spoke a heavily accented French and was obviously puzzled by this well dressed young woman riding a fine horse who insisted over and over again that she must speak with Prince Mechnikoff himself. It was an unprecedented situation. They had occasionally had deserters and camp whores clamouring for admittance but never anyone like this. Finally he nodded. The gate was opened and she was permitted to enter. She dismounted, saw Lucifer led away with some misgiving and was hustled inside what looked like a guardroom where half a dozen men sprawled at their ease round a littered table.

"Wait here," said the Sergeant and disappeared.

She sat down by the heavily barred window as far away as possible from the soldiers drawing her cloak closely around her. With every minute that passed she became more and more aware of the folly of what she had done. The impetus that had driven her forward began to ebb away into flat despair. Polly was right. Why should they listen to her? What would Jethro himself think if he knew that she was jeopardising the life of their child by this mad venture? It grew dark. She had eaten very little all day and began to feel sick and faint. One of the men got up, lighted a lamp and then strolled across the room. He stood in front of her, a little unsteady on his feet, and she thought with a stab of apprehension that he was probably drunk.

"What is it you're after?" he said in barbarous French. "Food eh? That's what most of them want, food and drink. Are the English all starving over there? Food . . . and perhaps kisses too eh? Let's take a look at you."

He leaned towards her pushing back her hood. "Pretty too. If you've an eye to the Prince, then you'll be unlucky. His excellency has his own whores. You'll have to make do with the likes of us."

He reached out and pulled her to her feet. She could smell the spirits on his breath and tried to draw away but he gripped her hard. One of the other men said something in Russian and her tormentor laughed. In a rough bold way he was good-looking with a mop of curly hair and an impudent grin.

"Fight me, would you? That's not the way to get what you want, my girl."

He swung her against him and his mouth came down on hers with a bruising force. Panic swept through her. She brought up her arm, hitting him as hard as she could. He swore but did not release her.

"A wild cat, eh? I've hunted that sort before now."

The other men were laughing and she knew it was useless to appeal to them. She opened her mouth to scream and a dirty hand was clapped over it. What a fool she had been – what a crazy fool! She was struggling now and she brought her knee up kicking hard against him when suddenly a cold incisive voice cut across the room. What it said she had no idea but the effect was instantaneous. She was freed so abruptly that she almost fell and the men were on their feet, straightening their uniforms, standing to attention, eyes lowered as the young impeccably dressed officer in the doorway rated them.

Then he turned to Laurel. "My apologies, Madame, for the behaviour of my men. It is many months since they have been shut up in this place. Will you come with me please?"

She tried to pull herself together and with the cloak once

305

more drawn closely around her followed the young man out of the guardroom and along the street. He stopped outside a tall dark building where again they were challenged by a sentry. Then they went in, up the stairs and along a corridor. He opened a door, motioned her to enter, said, "The young lady, your excellency," and went out closing the door behind him.

It was a sparsely furnished room but with a certain look of comfort and warmed by a fire on a stone hearth. A man stood in the window with his back to her. After her experience in the guardroom she was suddenly terrified. How far did the chivalry of a Russian officer extend? Had she put herself at the mercy of a man who wouldn't scruple to amuse himself at her expense? She stood motionless hardly daring to breathe, then with a sigh the man turned round. He wore a plain dark blue uniform with a jewelled cross at the collar. His right sleeve was empty and pinned across his breast but the fair hair, the face lined and bearing traces of recent sickness, was that of Dmitri Malinsky.

Their surprise was mutual. For a few moments they simply stared at one another. Then Laurel took a step forward.

She said impulsively, "I thought you were dead."

He smiled. "I almost was but not quite." Then he came to meet her. "Laurel, I can't believe that it is you. It seems impossible. What on earth are you doing here?" He had taken her hand and pressed it to his lips. "You are cold. Come to the fire." He led her across the room. "When Laski told me a young woman was asking to see the Commander, I could not imagine who it could be." The relief and the sudden change from cold to heat made her feel temporarily faint. She swayed a little and he guided her to a chair. "You are exhausted. We have little to offer but would you care for brandy?"

She shook her head. "No, I'm all right."

"I will order some tea. That will refresh you."

"Not now, later perhaps." She sat up pushing back the disordered hair. "Oh Dmitri, I'm so thankful it is you."

He saw then how dishevelled she was. "Did the men treat you badly? Damn them! I'll have them punished."

"No, don't please. It was nothing."

He stood looking down at her, puzzled but courteous. In England he had believed himself in love. It seemed like a century ago. "Tell me," he said gently, "what you are doing here in the Crimea and what it is that I can do for you?"

306

"I came with my husband – George Grafton."

"The gallant Captain – so you married him after all."

"Yes. He was killed in the cavalry charge at Balaclava."

"I am sorry. I was in hospital when I heard of it. It was magnificent but such things are not war."

"It was heroic and terrible but that is not why I am here." She leaned forward. "Dmitri, two months ago at the beginning of December a party of men who had come out to pick up wounded were attacked outside Sebastopol. One of them, Jethro Aylsham, was captured and accused of spying which was absurd. He is a doctor, a surgeon. You met him when you were in London. You must remember."

Malinsky frowned. "If he is a doctor, then he will have been released. That has been our agreement with the enemy up to the present."

"It did not happen. You see he is a volunteer, not part of the regular medical team. Since then there has been no word about him, absolutely none. That is why I have come. I must know. I must make you understand about him. He is not a spy but a brilliant surgeon. Not even the Russians would wish to shoot a man like him."

"And he is also a man who happens to be very dear to you," said Malinsky dryly.

"Yes, it is true." She cast caution to the winds. "He is dearer to me than anyone else on earth."

"I see." He was silent for a moment. "To be frank I don't know how I can help you. Unhappily I was not here at that time. I have in fact only returned to duty recently." He indicated his empty sleeve. "This took longer to heal than anyone expected. I can make enquiries for you but it may take a little time and meanwhile I will have my orderly bring you some tea. Yes?"

"Please. I should be grateful."

"Very well. I will go now and see what I can find out. Stay here and rest."

He touched her hand for a moment and then went out closing the door after him.

Now it was done, the tension began to ease and a feeling of relief, almost of relaxation stole over her. Presently an orderly knocked and came in with a tray placing it on a small table beside her. There was tea and sugar, a tall glass, even a slice of lemon, no shortages here it seemed. She sipped it gratefully and

307

nibbled one of the almond biscuits he had brought from a special box in a drawer of the desk.

It was more than an hour before Malinsky came back and she had closed her eyes for a few minutes, soothed by the warmth from the burning logs.

"I see they have brought you tea," he said, "and some of my mother's biscuits. Poor dear, she insists on sending me food parcels. I think she believes I am still at school."

Laurel smiled at the homely touch. "They are delicious. Can I pour tea for you?"

"No, thank you." He stood with his back to the hearth looking at her noting how clearly the fragile bones showed up in the pale face lit now by the rosy glow from the fire. She must love that fellow very much to risk all this for him, he thought, and knew a sharp spasm of envy. "I'm afraid my information is not very encouraging," he went on.

She sat up clasping her hands tightly together. "You don't mean that he is dead?"

"No. He was wounded apparently but it was not serious. The fact is that with others he has been sent back into Russia for further interrogation. I don't know exactly why this should be but that is all I can find out at present. There is one thing to remember, Laurel. If he is a surgeon as you say, then his services may well be used in the prison hospital and elsewhere. We have suffered from the cholera as well as the British and we have a great many wounded. Many of our best men have died."

"Will that be until the end of the war?" The thought of it seemed to stretch to eternity.

"Who can tell? I have some small influence perhaps. An uncle of mine is concerned with prisoners. If I can do anything to hasten his release, then I will."

"Bless you. I'm so grateful, so deeply grateful. I wish I had some way of showing it."

She had dropped the heavy cloak into the chair and stood up, slim and vibrant and lovely in the black riding skirt and tightly fitting jacket, her eyes bright, her red hair tumbled. He stretched out his sound arm and drew her towards him.

"If I were one of my ancestors, I would demand a price," he murmured huskily. "A night with me as payment for your lover's life."

"It sounds like bad melodrama," she said with a little laugh but he had seen the momentary terror leap into her eyes.

"Don't be afraid. I'm not as ruthless as they were and a one-armed man is at a certain disadvantage as a ravisher of beautiful women." He bent his head and kissed her cheek and impulsively she turned her head so that she met his lips. It was a light caress but it stirred them both and he released her at once. "Now we must decide what best to do with you. To remain here with me would be impossible both for your reputation and for mine. On the other hand it would be better if the Prince did not know of your coming here."

"I'll go," she said quickly. "I'm not afraid of the dark. Our picket camp is not too far away. They will make sure that I return safely."

"I don't like it," he said. "It is too dangerous for a woman alone. I will send two men to escort you to within sight of the camp."

"I don't want to cause any trouble to you or to them."

"The men who will go with you are trustworthy. You needn't be afraid."

Half an hour later it was all arranged and he came down with her to the gate of the city. Laski and the elegant young officer who appeared to be his second-in-command were there, already mounted, and holding Lucifer's bridle. Malinsky helped her into the saddle and patted the horse's neck.

"I see he has survived even the rigours of the Crimea."

"Yes. It wasn't easy." She bent down to touch his cheek caressingly. "You won't forget your promise, Dmitri."

"I'll not forget. God go with you."

The young Lieutenant in the British camp saw the approaching Russians and stiffened to the alert. Then he noticed Laurel with them and relaxed. They halted some distance away and she came on alone. The two men stood watching until she was within a few yards of him, then turned their horses' heads and trotted back to the citadel.

"Were you successful in your mission?" he asked.

"Yes. I found a friend. Wasn't I fortunate?"

He would have liked to ask questions but something in her face forbade it. Instead he said, "We ride back in an hour. Is that too much for you?"

She was so tired that she could scarcely remain upright in the saddle but she nodded. "I'll be ready to go with you."

When they set out, she rode in a dream. Her anxiety was still there and yet in some way it was appeased. She had done all she could, all that had been demanded of her. She had stilled George's restless ghost and expiated her sense of guilt. When she reached Kadikoi she found Polly watching for her and was glad to go with her into the little tent. They slept that night side by side on the hard straw palliasse under the sheepskin cloak. There was nothing left to do now but go back to England and wait for the coming of Jethro's child.

The next morning she rode down to Balaclava and set about obtaining a passage back to Scutari. Ironically the first night at sea the ship passed within a mile of another vessel carrying a party of ladies led by Mary Stanley, sister of the Dean of Westminster, who to their chagrin had been utterly rejected by Miss Nightingale as untrained and unfit for work in her hospital. Among them was Margaret proud to have achieved her aim at last and intent on proving to Robin that she could be as brave and determined as ever Laurel had been.

21

"If I have to listen to any more young women just out of the nursery reciting Tennyson's patriotic verses, I shall stand up and scream," said Laurel coming into the drawing room in Arlington Street one warm afternoon in June, dropping the silk shawl from her shoulders and sinking wearily into an armchair. "The concert in Carlton Gardens in aid of the Nightingale Fund was the most tedious affair imaginable and Robin made it worse by falling into a fit of the giggles. I had great difficulty in keeping a straight face."

"It is high time you gave up attending all these concerts and committee meetings," said Jane. "You're wearing yourself out. The Nightingale Fund can go on very well without you."

"It's not the money so much, though heaven knows it's needed badly enough out there, it's trying to make people realize what it is really like in the Crimea."

"Did Lady Emily ask you to speak?"

"Yes, she did, and now old Pam is Prime Minister, I didn't dare refuse. Robin, the traitor, shirked it by saying his leg was giving him trouble." She sat up. "You know, Jane, you just can't make them understand –

> 'Storm'd at with shot and shell,
> Boldly they rode and well
> Into the jaws of Death
> Into the mouth of Hell.'

That's what they love. It all sounds so marvellously heroic. They clapped and clapped with tears in their eyes and I wonder if any one of them there had the remotest idea of how ghastly it really was – how cruel and hideous and utterly *useless* – that was the terrible part of it."

"I know how you feel, my dear," said Jane gently, "but a year ago you would have thrilled to it yourself just as they do."

"Yes, I suppose I would," sighed Laurel. "Heavens, what a difference a little experience can make! But I did promise Miss

Nightingale that I'd do my very best to make the public know something of the grim reality and that's what in my own small way I shall go on trying to do. I owe it to George."

"But not for too long, dearest. You must think of yourself and the baby."

"Yes, I know," she got up and moved restlessly across the room. "I'd like to get away for a while. Perhaps in a few weeks we could go down to Westley."

"Would that be wise? Ought you to be travelling just now?"

"Oh we can take it in easy stages."

"What if the baby comes when you are down there. It's very remote and Dr Townsend is here in London."

"It won't. There's plenty of time still," she said impatiently. "And I need to go away. The city streets are stifling in this heat."

Jane looked at her a little anxiously. "Aren't you feeling well? Shall I ring for some tea?"

"No, thank you. I think I'll go up and change into something cooler." She paused at the door to look back with a hint of mischief. "Rosemary told me something amusing today. Margaret has been sent home. You know she went out to the Crimea with Mary Stanley's party. Well, it has proved too much for their delicate stomachs. Quite a number of them have come back and Margaret with them."

"Laurel, you are being deliberately unkind."

"Am I? Oh well, it is a little funny, don't you think? They were so top-lofty about it, they deserved a set-down."

Her laughter died as she went slowly up the stairs, Marik padding after her. Ever since she had returned the big dog had scarcely left her side. She patted him absently and thought of Dmitri Malinsky. No word had come out of Russia. She did not know whether Jethro was alive or dead and sometimes the sheer agony of it became almost unbearable. She had told no one, not even Jane, that he was the father of her child. If he never came back, the baby would bear George's name until the right moment came to tell the truth. No child of hers was going to be left to grow up in ignorance and suffer the shock of discovery as she had done.

The great British public had woken up at last to the enormity of suffering endured by the army in the Crimea. William Russell's dramatic despatches in *The Times* together with the stories told by men invalided home had done their work. Public indignation had stirred the government to action. Societies sprang up overnight collecting funds to supply clothes, food, medicines, equipment. The Poet Laureate's heroic verses inspired by the charge of the light brigade had been published in December. Thousands of copies had been distributed throughout the troops and who better to be asked to speak in halls and drawing rooms than Laurel Grafton, the young and lovely widow of a dead hero, who had herself witnessed the famous charge and knelt on the battlefield beside her dying husband. From the very first moment of her return she had been invited everywhere and Robin with her, the gallant young man who had volunteered to serve in the ranks, still limping badly and looking older than his twenty-one years. The young girls were ready to swoon at sight of him and were madly jealous of Laurel because he had eyes for none of them. Sometimes she giggled over it with him and at other times she thought they might have been talking into the air for all the good they were doing.

"You'll never believe it," Robin had said to her that very afternoon, "but some enterprising rogue has started tourist jaunts, five pounds a head for a trip to Constantinople and the battlefields, and we're still fighting a war! I wonder what Jethro would have had to say about that."

"He'd have had them all drowned at sea, and don't speak of him as if he were already dead."

"I didn't mean that." Robin pressed her hand. "Don't despair, Laurel. Even the Russians won't find it easy to get rid of old Jet."

"Oh Jethro, Jethro," she murmured to herself despairingly stepping out of her flowered silk gown and muslin petticoats. She slid a hand over her rounded figure before she reached for her dressing-gown. "How am I to live out the rest of my life without you?"

George had never shared this room with her. There was nothing in it to remind her of him and yet sometimes he seemed to be there. One of the first things she had done when she returned to England at the end of March was to write to Barton and Alice Grafton telling them how gallantly he had died and asking if there was anything among his possessions which they would like to have. There had been no reply. They ignored her letter as they had ignored her wedding so she shrugged her shoulders and tried to put them out of her mind. She was therefore totally unprepared for what happened the next afternoon.

A group of ladies had gathered in her drawing room to discuss the distribution of money and gifts to the men who had been invalided home – crippled, maimed and blinded, they were crammed into hospitals or begged in the streets, penniless and uncared for. It was a task Laurel was sure she and Jane could have carried out far more efficiently alone but the ladies of the Committee enjoyed feeling useful and involved. Tea had been served and they were just preparing to leave when Franklin came in asking if Laurel would receive a certain Mrs Grafton who was urgently requiring to see her. Before she had time to reply, Alice Grafton had thrust the butler aside and come storming into the room. She was dressed in black from head to foot and threw back the heavy veil, piercing grey eyes in a grey pinched face taking in Laurel's lilac muslin and the pretty flower-decked room.

"So this is the way you mourn my son," she said in bitter accusation.

Laurel rose slowly to her feet. "George died eight months ago, Mrs Grafton," she said quietly. "There are other ways of expressing regret than by wearing mourning and shutting oneself up."

"Such as flaunting yourself in public, I presume. Oh I know what you have been doing and it disgusts me. I suppose it is only what can be expected from the young woman who drove him to his death."

Some of the ladies looked shocked as Jane gently shepherded them from the room. They were a little sorry to miss such an interesting dramatic interruption and listened avidly as they adjusted bonnets and shawls in the hall.

"There was never any question of George being driven against his will," went on Laurel steadily. "He was a soldier. He obeyed orders and as his wife I was glad to go with him wherever possible."

"Did you? Was that the only reason?" Alice took a step forward, her face ugly with dislike. "Barton told me about you. You married him so as to have an excuse to run after your fancy man who had deserted you."

"No," said Laurel faintly. "No, you're wrong."

"Do you deny it?"

"Yes, I do. I was always deeply fond of George."

314

"Fond, fond! Is that all you can say? And whose child are you carrying? Answer me that. George wrote to me, you know. He would have told me if the baby was his."

"When he died, I didn't know, neither did he."

The front door closed behind the last of the guests and Jane came quickly back into the room looking anxiously at Laurel who had gone very white. One hand clutched at the table as if for support but she kept her voice calm.

"What else did George write to you?"

"You'd like to know, wouldn't you? Oh he was in love with you all right, fool that he was. The best wife in the world, he wrote, over and over again." Then suddenly she crumpled, her face twisted into grief. "It tortures me to think of him dying out there alone in that dreadful place."

"He was not alone. I was with him," said Laurel gently, "and he was buried with honour as far as it could be done. That is why I have been flaunting myself as you call it. I wanted people to know. I didn't want others to die uselessly as he did." She stretched out a hand. "If there is anything I can do for you, anything at all you need . . ."

Alice Grafton's head jerked up. "I want nothing from you, nothing. From the first moment you entered this house, you brought trouble with you. I knew it then and I was right. You bewitched my uncle as you bewitched George. You're like your mother. There's no good in any of your kind."

"If your only purpose in coming here is to abuse Laurel," said Jane angrily, "then I'm afraid I must ask you to leave."

"Oh I'm going, you needn't concern yourself," said Mrs Grafton contemptuously, her eyes still on Laurel. "I just wanted you to know. You can deceive the whole world but you can't deceive me and one day they will find out what you are and you'll get what you deserve."

She turned and went out of the room letting the door slam behind her. Jane would have followed but Laurel stopped her.

"Let her go," she said wearily. "Franklin will see her out."

Then her courage suddenly broke. She dropped into the chair trembling, burying her face in her hands. Jane came and knelt beside her.

"Don't upset yourself. She's jealous, that's all it is, jealous because George loved you. He was her son after all."

Laurel was staring in front of her, her eyes haunted. "It isn't

315

true what she said. I didn't love him but I tried to make him happy, I did try."

"Of course you did." Jane put her arms around the shaking body and held her close. Laurel had told her nothing but she had guessed a great deal and was aware of the fretting anxiety that tormented her.

Presently Laurel whispered, "Let's go away from here – soon – tomorrow. I don't want to stay in London any longer."

Jane stroked her hair soothingly, "Whenever you wish, dearest."

She had longed to escape and for a little while during that beautiful summer the days passed peacefully at Westley. She lived in a dream some instinct helping her to keep worry about Jethro at bay until after the child was born. They were very quiet. Rosemary came sometimes with Charles bubbling over with plans for their marriage next year. Jessica rode over always with a new young man in tow making Laurel laugh and then there was Robin. There were not many days when he did not look in, bringing a basket of strawberries from Ravensley or a gift of fresh fish from Moggy. Now and again he took her out in the punt gliding through the waterways alive with birds and fragrant with meadowsweet, bog myrtle and water mint. Once alone she went to the ancient church and saw the small brass plate discreetly placed in the Leigh chapel by Lord Aylsham, a plate commemorating Alyne Leigh and an infant child both unhappily drowned. For some reason she shivered as if an icy finger from the guilty past had stretched out to touch her before she could shrug it away, as if even now they were not entirely released from it. In this wild lonely countryside she felt very close to Jethro and she ignored Jane's gentle reminders that they ought to be returning to London for the birth of the baby.

In August a garden party was held at Ravensley in aid of the Nightingale Fund and though she would rather not have gone, Laurel felt obliged to be present. She was sitting on the terrace watching the children from the school go through their country dances on the lawn. There were stalls of all kinds and Tom was giving the little ones pony rides. Jessica flitted here and there among the guests and Rosemary with Charles hovering in attendance was presiding over bowls of fruit and ice cream. Robin was lounging at Laurel's feet using his lameness as an excuse for opting out of anything strenuous much to the disgust of his sisters. They had been laughing together when Laurel had a curious sensation of being watched and looked up to see Margaret a few yards away. She was wearing a severe dark blue dress and the lustrous black hair was swept back in two wings framing the pale face. It was the first time they had met since her return from the Crimea and for a brief moment Laurel felt icy cold which was so absurd on this summer day that she was angry with herself. Then Margaret moved away and Jessica came across the grass with a tray of tea.

"Did I see Margaret a moment ago?" said Laurel casually, accepting a cup.

"Oh yes, she's here somewhere casting a blight on everyone as usual."

"Oh Jess, what a horrid thing to say!"

"It's true. She's been very odd lately. She goes about like a thundercloud. Aunt Cherry says it all comes from the dreadful things she saw out in the Crimea but it doesn't seem to have had that effect on you or Robin. I guess she's just jealous."

"Jealous?" repeated Robin. "Jealous of what, for God's sake?"

Jessica grinned at her brother. "As if you didn't know!" She struck a dramatic attitude. "'Oh beware, my lord, of jealousy. It is the green-eyed monster which doth mock the meat it feeds on.' That's in *Othello*. Papa was reading it to us the other evening." She giggled. "I must go. I'm helping Mamma to serve the teas."

"It's only one of Jess's madcap notions," said Robin a little uneasily. "Take no notice of it."

But he was wrong. Jessica had judged her cousin more exactly than she realized. Margaret had become possessed with a deep rooted jealousy, a corroding bitter envy that over the past year had become close to obsession. It seemed to her that wherever she went, whatever she did, Laurel had been there before her stealing the limelight to herself. Her own miserable failure to overcome her horror and sick disgust in the Crimea, Robin's utter indifference, his brusque impatience whenever she tried to approach him, were all Laurel's fault. A burning sense of injustice nagged at her. It was not fair. Why should all the men be so ready to adore her? Other women who were pregnant hid themselves away, but not Laurel – oh no, she sat there in her delicate muslins, lovely still, and even the family were deceived admiring her courage, grateful for what she had done to save Robin's life. She had brooded over it until anger welled up in

317

her like a hot burning tide and early that evening when most of
the guests had left and the family with a few close friends were
gathered in the drawing room, the windows wide open to the
sweet summer air, it suddenly erupted into an explosion. It was
so small a thing that sparked it off.

Jessica and Tom had been counting the money from the stalls
and gleefully announced the result.

"They can do with every penny," remarked Lord Aylsham.
"The siege drags on and on. Sometimes I wonder if our army
will ever capture Sebastopol."

"Has there been any fresh news?" asked Laurel suddenly.
"Have there been any letters today?"

Mail was brought to Ravensley every morning but sometimes
if anything important was expected, one of the stable boys
would take the pony and collect a delivery from the afternoon
train.

Robin stood up. "I'll ride in and find out, shall I?"

He knew how hungrily she waited for the letters that never
came. She looked up at him.

"Should you go? How about your leg?"

"To hell with that!"

The smile she gave him, the easy familiarity between them, so
galled Margaret that something snapped inside her.

"Go on, Robin. Run and do as she asks. She has you dancing
on the end of a string, hasn't she? Laurel's little lap dog. What
else does she teach you? Do you sit up and beg for a biscuit?"

Robin frowned. "What the devil are you talking about?"

"I think you know very well," and suddenly the need to hurt,
to destroy, became too much for her. The words poured out
scaldingly. "You all think she's so wonderful, don't you,
kneeling by her dying husband, nursing the sick, acting the
angel of mercy, but in Balaclava there are people who know
different. I met them. I heard what they said about her, and
here in London too since I've been back." Her voice rose shrilly.
"Ask her who gave her the child she carries, the baby that is so
unaccountably late in arriving. Go on – ask her about the men
she entertained at her villa night after night when George was
away at the front . . ."

"Stop it! Stop repeating those stupid lies!" Robin was white
with anger.

"You would say that because you're besotted with her, but
they are not lies."

318

"Be silent, both of you," said Lord Aylsham sternly. "I will not tolerate such behaviour in my house."

Margaret turned on him, two spots of colour burning in her cheeks, her eyes blazing. "Oh we all know about you, Uncle Oliver. You were crazy about her mother and now you feel the same about her."

"This is ridiculous," exclaimed Clarissa. "Have you taken leave of your senses, Margaret? Apologise to Laurel and to your uncle at once."

"There's no need for apologies, Lady Aylsham." Laurel had risen to her feet. She was very pale but quite steady and suddenly she was weary of evasions and pretence. "Margaret is perfectly right. You may as well know now as later. The father of my child is not George, it is Jethro."

There was an uncomfortable silence. The family instinctively drew together while the others, guests and neighbours, shifted awkwardly and wished they were not there.

Then Lord Aylsham said slowly, "If this is true, Laurel, then what in God's name was Jethro thinking about to do such a thing to you."

Laurel smiled faintly. "It is quite true and I am just as much to blame as Jethro." She faltered for an instant and then went on quietly. "I don't expect you to understand – how could you? – but it was when we were working at the hospital after George was killed, after Robin was wounded – and I'm not ashamed, not in the very least. We intended to marry out there at New Year but he did not come to Scutari . . ." her breath caught in a sob.

"Oh my dear – to be married – so soon after . . ."

"I know it must sound shocking to you, Lady Aylsham. I never meant to be disloyal to my husband, but Jethro and I – it had been so long and we had both been so wretched – every hour we were living in the midst of death – it was like stealing a few minutes of happiness on the edge of an abyss – but I realize what you must think of me and so now I think it better that I should go."

"No, you mustn't feel that. This house has always been Jethro's home. Where else should his child be born?"

"Thank you, Lord Aylsham. That is kind of you but I still think it would be best if I went back to Westley."

Jane made a move towards her and she went on quickly, "I'm quite all right. Don't worry about me. I'll go up and fetch our

319

wraps. Perhaps you would ask for the carriage to be brought round."

She had an overpowering need to escape. Outside in the hall she took a deep breath feeling a little giddy and yet released as if a burden had been lifted from her. She went slowly up the stairs to the bedroom. She had picked up the silk shawls when she heard the clatter of hooves outside and saw from the window that the postboy was coming up the drive. There must be a special delivery. She felt a stir of excitement and turned to go when the door opened and Margaret stood there, letting it swing shut behind her and leaning back against it.

"I suppose you hate me for what I said just now."

"No, why should I? You can't help being what you are."

"It was the truth," she said defensively.

"I don't deny it."

"Don't you mind that everyone will know about you because they will. Those people downstairs will talk."

"Let them. I love Jethro. I'm glad I shall have his child."

The very fact that she showed no shame, no distress, drove Margaret beyond all reason. She wanted to strike, to smash that calm acceptance and could find no way.

Laurel said, "Would you let me pass please?"

"Not unless you promise to give Robin up."

"I don't know what you mean. Robin can do as he wishes. I have no hold over him."

"Of course you have and you glory in it," said Margaret wildly. "You want to keep him dangling just in case Jethro never comes back."

"Don't be absurd. I would never marry Robin, never. He knows that perfectly well." Outside someone was calling and she tried to push Margaret aside. "Now I must go. Jane will be waiting."

"You're not leaving until you give me your promise."

"This is ridiculous. What can I do? Bolt my door against him?"

"You could make him feel he is not welcome."

"I shall do no such thing."

"If it were not for you, I could win him back to me."

"Never!" Abruptly Laurel lost all patience. "Never. Robin cares nothing for you. He never has."

"You're lying. He did once, I know he did."

320

Margaret had seized hold of her. She was shaking her in a kind of frenzy and for the first time Laurel was afraid.

"Are you crazy? Let me go."

"No."

They were struggling together. Outside Robin was shouting something and suddenly Margaret released her. She flung open the door.

"Damn you! Go to him then!" and she gave her a violent push.

Robin was halfway up the stairs, a letter in his hand. "Laurel, are you there? Wonderful glorious news. Jethro is coming home."

Whether she slipped or whether it was Margaret's rough handling that caused her to lose her balance on the polished floor, no one afterwards knew for certain, but she pitched head first down the stairs. Robin tried desperately to break her fall but was hampered by his lame leg and she rolled bumping and crashing to the bottom.

They heard the noise and came running out of the drawing room. She was only dazed at first. She knew that Lord Aylsham was kneeling beside her, Charles was there and Jessica looking frightened with Rosemary's arm around her and the others staring as she struggled to sit up.

"I'm all right," she murmured and then remembered. She turned to Robin. "Is it true, is it really true?"

"Yes, it's true. He's been released. He's coming home."

She closed her eyes, the joy so exquisite it drowned the giddiness, the queer breathlessness. "Thank God. I can go now."

"No, my dear," said Clarissa, "you're not going back to Westley, not after a fall like that. You'll stay here with us." She looked around her helplessly. "How did it happen?"

"I must have tripped. So silly of me," then she remembered Margaret and was silent.

"Tripped be damned! I saw what she did." Robin's face was stormy and he went limping purposefully up the stairs. She wanted to stop him but he was gone already.

They fussed over her then. Lord Aylsham carried her upstairs. Jane and Clarissa helped to undress her and put her to bed. Despite her protests that she was not hurt, only bruised, she found that she was glad to lie quietly between the cool lavender-scented sheets. It was not until late evening that the first pain struck her coming so swiftly and unexpectedly that she cried out and alarmed Jane who was sitting with her. She fetched Clarissa. Then Charles came and was calmly reassuring.

"No need to worry. The baby will take its time of course, that's only to be expected. You must be patient."

How like a man! she thought wryly and was angry that it should come now in this house where nothing was prepared. She braced herself to go through with it.

Only it did not follow the usual course. In the morning after a wearying night of intermittent pain Charles began to look anxious though he took care to betray nothing of it to Laurel. Between the bouts of numbing agony she tried to buoy herself up by thinking of Jethro but the day wore on and she began to weaken. Jane sat beside her, wiping the sweat from her forehead with a cool towel. The August heat hung heavy in the room and the windows had been opened to catch every breath of air. Towards evening she seemed to be living in a world of pain. Again and again she bit her lip hard to stop herself screaming. She saw them moving around her bed in a kind of mist, Jane, Clarissa, Charles, Patty Starling who had been sent for from Copthorne and had helped more than one baby into the world. They were talking above her head but she could not understand what they were saying. Then it was dusk. The lamps were lit and carefully shaded. The pain went on and on so that she wondered vaguely if she were dying and knew she couldn't die – she must not die – not before Jethro came. Much later still she heard dimly the sound of horses outside, footsteps running, voices hushed but excited, then someone else was in the room with her. She saw him outlined against the yellow lamplight, tall and very thin, someone who bent over her.

"Hold on, my love, I'm here – I'm with you."

"Jethro," she murmured incredulously, "Jethro," and was sure she was dreaming except that strong capable hands were touching her, hands she knew and loved.

The voices went on, low but urgent.

"You can't do it – it's dangerous."

"She's exhausted. Leave it any longer and it could be too late."

"It's too great a risk to the child."

"Pray God that I can save them both. Don't argue with me, Charles. Do as I say. It's my responsibility."

Jethro was leaning over her again. "Breathe deeply, my

322

darling. Don't be frightened. It's going to be all right. I will be with you – all the way."

The heavy familiar smell of chloroform sweeping her back to the Crimea, the horror of the hospital, the blood and the men who died – then a merciful easing of pain. It was receding far away into the distance. She was floating – floating into a warm darkness.

It was during the evening of that same day that Margaret walked out of the house, Robin's bitter accusing words still rankling inside her.

He had come pounding up the stairs to where she stood on the landing stunned by Laurel's fall, horrified at her own part in it. He had thrust his face close to hers.

"You might have killed her," he had said in a harsh whisper. "Is that what you wanted, what you were hoping for? You hate her because she is beautiful, loving, kind, all the things you are not and could never be. If any harm comes to Laurel or her child, I swear I'll make sure that everyone knows, everyone d'you hear? And I'll never forgive you for it, never so long as I live!"

She denied it, she pleaded with him, and he pushed her aside as if he could not endure her even to touch him. And worse than that, far worse, was the frightening realization that for an instant she *had* wanted to kill. It had been like a red mist sweeping across her eyes, blinding her to reason, and then was gone leaving her cold and shaking. But in that second of time what had she done?

All that night and the following day the whole household had revolved round Laurel, her own mother, Aunt Clarissa, Rosemary, Charles, going about with anxious concerned faces.

"Oh God," she thought, "if Laurel dies or the child is harmed, then I shall be to blame and I never meant it, I swear I didn't!"

By late evening it had become unbearable. It drove her out of the house and across the lawns to the river and no one saw her go or even noticed her absence. The punt was moored near the boathouse and she stepped into it and took up the paddles. It was very warm still. The reed beds along the banks, the sedge and grasses were motionless under the heavy sky. Even the birds were silent and the fens she had loved since childhood had become sullen and menacing.

She paddled slowly letting the punt drift in and out of the

323

narrow creeks until looking up suddenly she saw that she had reached Spinney Mill. The catwalk had been taken down and it stood gaunt and black and derelict. She let the boat float into the bank and stared down at the still water where Ram Lall had drowned and Justin Aylsham had gone horribly to his death with his enemy's hands clasped around his throat. She felt as if the evil he had done so long ago now clung to her and she had a morbid desire to let herself slip into the pond, down, down, into its dark weed-infested depths. Then perhaps they would be sorry – then Robin would realize that his rejection had driven her to a cruel death. She tied the mooring rope to the wooden post at the foot of the mill and stepped out on the bank. The green scum-covered water lapped at her feet. Then while she stood poised, uncertain, the stillness around her broke. With the fading of the light, the night creatures stirred. The reeds and sedge were filled with stealthy movement. All about her life was going on, uncaring, indifferent, making her troubles seem small and of no acount, and in that instant she knew that she couldn't do it. She hadn't the courage.

The hand on her shoulder made her shudder violently as if the ghosts of those who had drowned there had glided out of the slimy water to claim another victim. But it was no spectral figure behind her but Robin, alive, warm, reassuring, whose arm around her waist was drawing her back from the brink and shivering she collapsed against him.

"Jess missed you when she went to call you to supper," he said, "so I came to look for you."

She stared up at him. "How did you know where I'd gone?"

"I didn't, not at first. Moggy told me that he'd seen the boat."

"And Laurel?"

"We don't know yet but Jethro has come."

In helpless reaction she began to cry and he stood quite still gently stroking her hair with a deeper understanding than she had ever glimpsed in him. During the night and day of anxiety his furious rage had faded and when she could not be found, he remembered the small pointed face, white and desperate after his brutal attack. He had searched the fens with a growing fear of what he might find. The relief brought kindness with it.

Her face still hidden from him she whispered, "Why did you come? I thought you didn't care – "

"For God's sake, Margaret, we're not deadly enemies, are

324

we? We're both in the same boat – the trouble with us is that we fell in love with the wrong person, I with Laurel, you with me. We can't alter that, we have to accept and live with it. There are worse things. I learned that out in the Crimea."

He spread his coat on the damp turf and drew her to sit beside him. In the warm darkness of the summer night he went on talking quietly until the trembling stopped, the tension slowly drained away and she began to relax. Then he pulled her to her feet.

"Now, I'm going to take you home."

The first glimpses of the dawn were streaking the sky when they reached Ravensley and he moored the punt. A light shower had begun to fall but she would not go in with him.

"You'll get wet," he said with concern.

"I'm all right. I want to walk a little. I'll come soon."

He put his coat around her shoulders. "Better not stay out too long."

She watched him go up towards the house, shaken still but a little comforted.

Laurel swam slowly up through mists and bouts of nausea until at last they faded and she was fully awake. Amazingly it was early morning. There had been rain but sun streaked through the half drawn curtains and outside birds were singing, sleepy threads of song running from tree to tree. She turned her head and knew it was not a dream. Jethro leaned back in an armchair close beside the bed. She stretched out a hand to touch him and he was instantly alert clasping it in his own.

"How do you feel?"

"Light as air. Where is everyone?"

"I sent them to bed and stayed with you myself."

She was still a little dazed. "I can't believe you're here. I thought I was dreaming."

He gripped her hand tightly. "I'm no dream and it's all over. You have a baby girl."

"May I see her?"

She saw the wooden cradle they had brought down from the old nursery, the cradle that had held Ravensley children for generations. Jethro gently lifted the sleeping baby and put her into her mother's arms.

She looked down at the tiny face, the straight little nose, the tuft of dark hair and then up at the man smiling down at her. The sheer wonder of it took her breath away so that for a moment she could not speak. The opening of the door took them both by surprise. Margaret stood there, her long dark hair hanging in ratstails over Robin's coat, the skirt of her summer gown streaked with mud.

"Good God," said Jethro, "What on earth have you been doing to yourself?"

"I've been out on the fens," but Margaret's eyes were fixed on Laurel. "I thought – they told me that you were . . ."

"Hallo, Margaret." Laurel smiled and stretched out a hand. "I have a daughter and she's beautiful. Come and look."

Margaret moved slowly to the foot of the bed. "I wanted to say I'm sorry," she whispered, "sorry for what I said . . ."

"It doesn't matter. Nothing matters now that Jethro has come home."

"I'm glad . . . oh God, you don't know how glad!" Margaret choked and caught her breath in a sob. Then she turned and ran out of the room.

"What the devil does all that mean?" said Jethro, "and what does she think she's doing running about the fens at this hour and getting soaked to the skin?"

"I think I know." Laurel looked up at him suddenly shy, uncertain of his reaction. "Didn't Clarissa tell you?"

"Tell me what?" He sat on the edge of the bed. "What is all this mystery and what has Margaret to do with it?"

"Nothing really, nothing important. It concerns us." She paused before she said, "What name shall we give to our daughter?"

He frowned. "*Our* daughter?"

"I thought you might have guessed."

"*Our daughter?*" Then as realization struck him, he got slowly to his feet. "You mean . . ."

"Yes. She is yours, Jethro."

"But I thought – I believed – oh my God, my child and she will bear George's name!"

"She'll never know any other father than you."

"Of all the damnable things!"

She smiled at his dismay. "It's the Ravensley touch. It seems we can't escape it after all. My mother and then me and I believed myself so different. Only I'm more fortunate than she ever was – I have you."

326

"Oh Laurel," he was overwhelmed by what she had told him. "All these months you have been alone and I knew nothing about it. Oh my darling, what can I say to you?"

"It's over now and the past too."

"I did try to get letters through to you but it wasn't possible. We were miles away from civilisation and God knows what happened to them. It was Malinsky who tracked me down and obtained my release. His uncle told me how you had gone to him in the Russian camp, you crazy beloved idiot. You could have been killed or worse and no one any the wiser."

"But I wasn't, was I? and he did help."

"He did it for you," he said wryly, "not for me."

"You look so thin, darling. Was it very bad?"

"Not much worse than the camp at Kadikoi and when they discovered that I could patch people up, they put me to work in the hospital. As a matter of fact though conditions were crude, I learned a great deal. Perhaps that's the only good thing to come out of a war."

"You'll not go back there, you'll not leave me?" she said quickly.

"No. Things are better out there now. The need is not so great."

She leaned back suddenly weary and he took the baby from her. "Besides you've had a hard time, I want to keep my eye on you."

She saw the pride and tenderness on his face as he held the child against him for a moment before tucking her back into the cradle.

"Am I one of your guinea-pigs?" she said, smiling up at him.

"Guinea-pigs?" he repeated puzzled.

"I remember something you told me on the boat when you brought me from Italy. One day, you said, you would be using this new chloroform to help women in childbirth. I thought you were very wonderful and very brave. Am I the first?"

"No. I would never have dared to experiment with you, but it will come. We'll overcome prejudice in the end. There's so much to be done, Laurel. One lifetime is not long enough."

"We'll make it long enough." She reached up a hand to caress his cheek and he caught it in his. The gold wedding ring had grown loose. He slipped it off her finger and then put it on again.

327

"But first, before anything, I have to replace this."

"Not replace it, add to it. I was fond of George. You don't mind that, do you?"

"Why should I when I am so fortunate? I'm alive and I have you *and* a ready-made daughter. What more can a man ask for?"